VIOLATION

The stairs were empty, and yet the noise continued. Step after step, slowly and deliberately, someone was climbing towards her. *Someone she couldn't see!*

She was stunned for a moment. A chill started at the base of her skull and notched its way down her spine. She wasn't crazy . . . someone was there, she'd heard him.

A foul, acrid odor stung her nostrils and turned her stomach. There were harsh whisperings assaulting her ears, but she couldn't hear what they were saying.

Hands were touching her, lots of them; cold, monstrous hands; they violated her sanity, aroused her in an erotic manner. Someone whispered. No! Someone screamed her name. Then she was falling . . . into an endless void in time . . . just falling.

Also by Dana Reed:

SISTER SATAN
DEATHBRINGER

DANA REED

The Gatekeeper

LEISURE BOOKS ∞ NEW YORK CITY

To
Lauren Reed,
who contributed a great deal of time to the
research for, and editing of, this book, and
without whom it might not have been possible.

A LEISURE BOOK

Published by

Dorchester Publishing Co., Inc.
6 East 39th Street
New York, NY 10016

Printed in the United States of America

PROLOGUE
Father, Son, and Holy Beast

"Amelio Rodriguez lay in bed and tried to remember when it was that things had gone sour. It was close to impossible though; the room was noisy, full of sounds that didn't belong. After all, here he was, in the privacy of his own home, with the cold, motionless body of his wife beside him. It should've been quiet!

"Night had fallen hours before, bringing a terrible amount of activity, the house was alive with madness. Furniture moved . . . No! It *slammed* across the altar room with fury. But no one was present in that room. And there were noises, all sorts of noises. The low throated groans of an enraged beast had filled him with dread at first until something far worse assaulted his senses.

"It started with heartbeats, several of them, letting Amelio know they were there. And the whisperings . . . a chorus of creatures with harsh, gravelly voices told him about death, promised him pain, and took the breath from his wife!

"He shuddered spasmodically when the door to his bedroom opened—locked and bolted though it was—and a black, swirling mass of raging hatred drifted in to greet him.

"Julio! This was his father, Julio's, fault. Julio,

7

master of the Black Arts, turning his only son into a prodigy. But Julio, in all fairness, had seen the error of his ways. He became enlightened when daemons from the lower order of Acheron gouged an inverted crucifix an inch deep into his chest, leaving a raw, painful wound. Then they wrote the name of their master, Mephisto, over the altar with Julio's blood.

"And to think, the altar, placed in a room with blue walls and blue carpeting, had been meant to pay homage to the beast because blue is the color of evil. But the Beast turned, the Beast demanded payment for past favors, and Julio ran back to Puerto Rico.

"The black, swirling mass floated in a dizzying pattern until it reached the foot of Amelio's bed. He was frightened beyond belief; these were his friends, but they were turning . . . turning on *him*. Then perhaps, he thought, it was only fitting and fair if he did the same. But where to begin, the words were stuck in his throat. He had never used them before.

" 'Dear Lord,' he moaned—

"An arm reached for him from the core of the black mass; an arm rippled with muscles and edged with claws that glistened like steel in the dark. His heart went into spasms as his life passed before him in tiny vignettes muddled with confusion. These creatures had once catered to him, had sung whispers of praise in his ears. Now, those same whispers were angry with intentions of destruction.

"They told him plainly, in an open display of defiance, that despite their former allegiance, he had been created in the image of a God they hated above all else. And what was created in that image must not be allowed to survive! Then they filled his head with frighteningly sadistic descriptions of revenge.

" 'Oh, Jesus, Lord,' he choked. 'Help me!'

" 'FUCK HIM!' came the whispered answer. 'SATAN IS SAVIOR!'

"Amelio felt himself rising, being sucked into the swirling mass in front of him as though it were a deadly cyclone. He grabbed the frame of his bed and tried to hold on, but it was useless, the force was stronger than he. This was it! Payback was a bitch! He screamed, but the sound died in his throat and fear knotted the base of his skull. The arm was in motion, its claws tearing his clothes, slicing through the tender flesh of his body, shredding his face . . .

"Why hadn't he stopped when Julio begged him to? Why had he allowed stupidity and conceit to dominate his senses? 'You're old,' he'd said to his father, Julio. 'When you cannot control the Beast or its emissaries, it's time to pack it in.' So fucking *cool* he was, standing there surveying the angry, bleeding ridges of his father's body and acting so fucking *cool!* Well, he wasn't *cool* now. Hell no! Now it was his turn to pay the price, and he was terrified.

" 'Oh, God, Jesus, help me!' he raged as the razor-sharp claws sliced through his body in layers, shredding his flesh, searing his skull with agony. And the heartbeats increased in rhythm, and the whispers turned to mocking laughter in the face of his helplessness.

" 'JULIO THE FATHER; AMELIO THE SON, AND MEPHISTO THE HOLY BEAST.' They chastised him with their words, and declared that no form of aid could be expected from a God he had forsaken years before. Then they reveled in the thought that victory was theirs, this *house* was theirs, along with any future inhabitants.

" 'Jesus, Lord,' Amelio pleaded, his vision gone, a steady stream of blood running from two empty sockets in his face. He was blind, and half-mad with pain. Half-mad with the knowledge of his own destruction. His ears were ringing with blasphemies; vile, filthy, frightening blasphemies.

" 'FUCK JESUS AND HIS MOTHER MARY! WHORE BITCH! AND FUCK YOU TOO,

AMELIO!' ''

Henry Wittaker reread the last few pages of the novel and shuddered. The story, especially the ending, ran on a plain parallel to what he had recently experienced.

Particularly the part about the house being *theirs*—

1

Erica Walsh felt a warm shaft of sun on her bare back. The weather forecaster had promised clear skies. At least there was no mention of snow in his predictions. She rolled on her side, stared through her bedroom window, and saw that it was a real spring day for a change, a house-hunting day!

She reached for her cigarettes and listened to the usual sounds of morning around her; the children down the hall, Kayle by her side, all snoring softly. She rolled onto her back and threw off her covers, exposing her nakedness. She felt wonderful, wonderful and warm and sexy. Her dream was coming true—a house, her own house.

She puffed on her cigarette, then exhaled while the sun wedging in through the window caressed her body. But deep inside of her there was an uneasiness casting a pall over her positive emotions, otherwise she wouldn't have been smoking so early in the day. Would her dream really come true? Knowing Kayle . . . She felt a sense of urgency at this point, a need to confirm a promise.

She shook Kayle, whispered to him, "You awake?"

Kayle mumbled and started to snore again.

She shook him harder this time. "Kayle, are we

still looking at houses today?"

"Don't be so friggin' insecure," he mumbled.

But it wasn't her fault that she was insecure. Kayle wasn't always a man of his word, he'd broken promises before. After a minute she heard his shallow breathing. No use asking any more questions, she thought, and watched him while he slept. There was something about this man that stirred her to a pitch at times, and she had to wonder why. He was far from being handsome, and he wasn't rich. In fact, he was downright cruel when he wanted to be, which was often enough. So why did she stay?

For more reasons than she cared to dwell on at present.

She stared down at the slight scar on his face, running along one cheek; then at the rise and fall of his chest; her gaze scanning the length of his long, sinewy body, thick with black, curly hair, her attention finally coming to rest on the mound of his briefs where his manhood lay hidden. She quickly ditched her cigarette and wondered if there was time to show Kayle how much she loved him. The children were still sleeping . . .

She rolled towards him and laid her leg gently across his while her hand made small, circular motions on his chest before moving downwards with determination. Yes, there was time, she'd make time.

Kayle opened his eyes, glared at her dazedly at first, then smiled when he felt her hand connect with his groin. He flipped on his side to face her. "You're so beautiful, baby."

Her platinum hair, caught by darts of sunlight at her back, had an almost halo-like effect. Her deep blue eyes still had a natural innocence. He sucked in his breath while her fingers wove their magic on his body, moving in gentle swirls, yet with an urgency for fulfillment.

"This is the only way to wake up," he husked, especially when his dreams had been overtaken with painful flashbacks, tiny vignettes of an ugly childhood. And Mother was in it, as usual.

He was drawn then to the curving allure of Erica's mouth and slipped his tongue between her lips to taste the sweetness of her flesh. He kissed her softly at first, but his lust soon became rough and cruel, the way he imagined Erica liked it. Erica never wanted to be pampered, in his opinion, setting her apart from the other women he'd known over the years. Besides, Erica drove him crazy when they made love. Her body was so soft and so yielding that she deserved his acts of bestiality.

He stopped kissing her and slid his tongue hungrily across her neck, her shoulders, working his way down until he connected with the rigid nipple of one breast. He toyed with it gently at first, but soon became bored. Opening his mouth, he took in a good portion of her breast and clamped down hard with his teeth.

Erica moaned and tried to push him away. Kayle felt she was ready, that she wanted it now! He released her breast, then shed his briefs and mounted her.

Erica was relieved, he hadn't really hurt her this time. But still, she found herself wondering again why she stayed with him, and why she insisted on making love with a man who had absolutely no idea of the meaning of the word *love*.

Erica was sitting at the table in the kitchen when Kayle stormed in, naked except for a towel around his waist. By the way his lips were drawn into a tight grimace, she knew he was angry. She stared straight ahead to avoid looking directly into his eyes, her gaze focused on the hair on his chest, all glistening wet and curly from the shower. Whatever his problem was, she didn't want to face it now. Not today when they were supposed to be hunting for a house. Why spoil the mood? But Kayle didn't share her enthusiasm.

"Tell them boys to straighten up," he ordered. "Get them pillows and blankets and the rest of the shit off the couch!"

"That's where they sleep. If they had their own bedroom like the girls do—"

"Don't start *your* shit again! In other words, 'Buy me a house, Kayle.' " The mocking tone in his voice matched his twisted expression.

She knew there was more.

"Why ain't you fixing breakfast?"

Erica shot a weary look at the stove, then back at Kayle. Her silence said it all.

"The friggin' stove's not working again?" His voice rose to an angry pitch in the stillnesss around her, shattering her nerves. She stifled the urge to scream.

"We gotta get outta here," he bellowed. "This fucking place's driving me nuts!"

"Tell me about it!" she shot back. "What the hell do you think it's doing to me?"

But Kayle never heard a word she said. He was already halfway through the door, dismissing her opinion as though she had none worth hearing.

Kayle treated her like her mother did at times, which was ironic because she'd left home to escape this same sort of treatment. Hell, she wasn't a child. She sighed and lit a cigarette and fought the urge to follow Kayle and really tell him off. If she did, that would surely turn his anger to rage. Then she could just as well forget about buying a house. And Erica had to get out of this dump before she went crazy.

The kitchen alone threw her into helpless fits of despair; the torn and faded linoleum, the heavily marred cabinets over the sink with the new handles she'd bought at the hardware store. And hell, if she hadn't bought those handles herself, there was no way the landlord was about to. He did shit around here. She and Kayle were always putting their hands into their pockets for repair money.

Like the day they moved in, it was a nightmare. There were cavernous holes in every wall in the house, the roof leaked and water puddled the floor. But, like it or not, they had no choice other than to take this place.

Up until then she'd been renting an apartment near her mother. It was small and cramped, but it was a palace compared to this. Then there was a fire, a bad one, and they needed a roof over their heads. It was either take this place or move in with Mama.

Both she and Kayle had chosen to move in here!

Erica was startled when a small, moist hand touched her. She looked down and saw Sam, her youngest son, still in pajamas, a shock of blond hair almost covering his eyes. She lifted him to her lap and brushed her lips against his forehead.

"The stove's not working, honey. You'll have to eat cold cereal. No eggs."

"It's okay, Mommy. It's not yer fault."

Sam became quiet at that point and followed Erica's gaze. There was a pan under the sink to catch the leak. The water in it was rust colored and coated with scum.

"Did hippies wreck this place?" Sam had the biggest eyes when he was curious.

"You've been listening to the landlord again." Erica nearly smiled despite her anxiety.

"Well, he had to call the police to put 'em out, didn't he?"

"That's what he said." She did smile this time.

"And he hadda hire a *terminator* to kill the roaches and mice." Sam had faith in the wrong people.

"It's called an exterminator, Sam. And I figure the landlord wasted his money. The roaches and mice still have the run of the place."

She put him down and started to plug in the

electric coffee pot, but Sam stopped her.

"Mom, ya gotta pull the plug on the fridge first. Ya wanna lose the 'lectricity?"

"Oh, Christ. I almost blew the circuit breakers again." She wiped her face with her hands. "Mommy forgets sometimes. Or maybe she wants to forget what a dump we're living in."

"It's okay. Daddy's buying us a house, right?"

"Right."

Thinking about a new house made her feel good inside. "And, Sam . . . the house we're looking at . . . it has three bedrooms." Her words sounded apologetic.

"Ya mean we don't hafta sleep on the coach anymore? Yippee!" Sam jumped in the air and skipped around the table in wide circles.

"And it has new kitchen appliances."

She suddenly wanted to skip along beside Sam but for one fleeting second she stopped to reflect on how they had moved in here because of a deep sense of urgency. Then she found herself hoping she wasn't making the same mistake twice. They were buying a new house for the same reason—a sense of urgency!

Henry Wittaker was in the kitchen when the lid on the mailbox out front clapped shut. It was a horrible sound and it caused the blood in his veins to congeal into knots. They never missed a day, them lawyers, with their son-of-a-bitch letters that just as well called him a deadbeat. *Pay up or else*, the bastards said in them letters as if he had piles of money hidden away somewhere and was saving it for better things. *Send a check for this amount within ten days or we'll see you in court*, they said, as if they'd get the money with their threats alone.

Well, the way Henry saw it, he'd damned well be spending every single day of the next two years in court if they *all* kept their word. The most absurd thing about those letters was that the bastards never gave a thought to reality. Like each one must have imagined his letter was the first and only. But whenever Henry called them and told them the full story, then it was different, then their attitudes changed, only not a whole lot.

It was always, "We're sorry to hear about your situation, Mr. Wittaker, but Dr. So and So wants his money *now*!" And Henry invariably wound up telling them to stand in line and wait their turn. And now, as if he wasn't depressed enough, his son, Buddy, was selling his Corvette to help out. Jesus, what a blow to the balls that was.

Buddy was barely eighteen and already he was learning the cold facts of life. It wasn't fair, especially since Henry had vowed years ago that things would be different for his kids. Henry, himself, had grown up holes-in-the-shoes-poor, and had sworn an oath on his mother's grave when he was Buddy's age that life wouldn't repeat itself. In other words, he would make it where his own father had failed. He was going to be the best damned provider the world had ever seen, and he almost had been.

But he was fired—

From his dream job—

Through no fault of his own—

And now he was earning shit—

And the burner on the stove was flickering . . .

Henry felt sweat running between his legs and wondered if he'd peed himself. Maybe he had. His nerves were shot lately, ever since he'd run into that listing in Monroe, the one he was showing today. Strange house. He knew that for a fact.

Henry was an occult buff, and prided himself on his knowledge as well as his senses. He had the ability to *feel* unseen presences when nobody else could. Hell, he could *feel* a spook in a house big as a mansion with his eyes closed and blindfolded and

his hands tied behind his back. What's more, he *felt*
something in that house, and it made his nerves do
the Dance of the Seven Veils. It happened as soon as
he crossed over the threshold and entered the living
room. Zingo, his senses went wild, picking up one
here and one there, one on the staircase, one in the
kitchen, a few in the bedrooms upstairs . . . Cor-
rection, a few in the *closets* in those bedrooms.

Then the strangest thing occurred. He had the
sensation of being followed when he left the house.
The feeling was strong enough to cause him to turn
and glance over his shoulder, which was silly
because you only saw them when *they* wanted you
to, so he saw nothing. But he sensed plenty, *felt* it
following him, right out to his car. He *felt* it sitting in
the back seat when he drove home too. At one point,
he went so far as to look in the rear view mirror, half
expecting to see a face staring back at him. But
again, that was silly shit; you only saw them when
they wanted you to. And, obviously, this *thing* wasn't
ready to be seen yet.

But it was here, in this house. And now the stove
burner was flickering.

Henry rose and poured fresh coffee into a silver
server, then placed the server gently onto a silver
tray; leftovers from his better days. Still, his mind
wasn't on the task at hand; it was on that flickering
burner . . . and the sudden chill in the kitchen even
though he had the heat running on high to keep the
house warm for Bess.

That fucking thing was energizing itself!

Henry knew from studying these matters that
invisible entities sucked energy from different
sources whenever they wanted to materialize. They
stole wattage from lights, drew the heat from a
room, and filled their devilified veins to the over-
flowing with stolen energy so that you could *see*
them and *hear* them. Energy heightened their
powers.

Well now, Henry thought to himself, fuck this bastard. He hadn't time for this nonsense, and he was scared besides. He took the tray and left the kitchen.

Bess Wittaker ran until she thought her lungs would burst. The ground was soft and warm beneath her bare feet, wild crocus and snow-on-the-mount caressed her ankles. She was laughing. Henry was behind her, running in the slow motion of her dream.

They were young again, both of them. She glanced back at Henry with his muscled chest and virile body and felt proud that she hadn't let herself go. Henry was a man's man, envied by most of the men in town, and desired by most of the women. But it was her supple breasts and slim-waisted figure that had him on the hook and kept him there.

She turned to look ahead and at that point, as always, Henry caught her from behind. She felt his strong, muscle-knotted arms encircle her waist, his hands reach up to fondle her breasts. She stopped running and swung around to press her body against his, to feel the heat of his manhood as it rose with desire.

"Henry," she whispered hoarsely, "take me now."

But Henry was a tease, he wanted it to last. He started with the buttons on her blouse, then her underclothing until she was naked from the waist up. He played maddening games with his tongue and the nipples of her breasts, while his hands traveled down her body, drawing her lower torso together with his.

It lasted a long while as Henry had wanted, and by the time he was finally ready for penetration, she was screaming with desire. Those screams woke her and she found herself alone in bed as usual, and as usual, she cried.

Bess Wittaker listened to Henry coming up the
steps and prayed for death. She knew it was him by
the slight hesitation of his footsteps every third step.
Bess had been confined to bed for so many years
that she'd developed a finely honed sense of
hearing; a gift from God, she imagined, to compen-
sate for her illness. Big deal, she thought, she
would've traded it in at any time for a month's
worth of good health.

At any rate, she could damn well recognize the
footsteps of nearly everyone who came to see her.
Mainly it was her doctors who came up those stairs,
her friends had stopped coming a while back. Long
illnesses scared most people, especially when you
stayed sick longer than they expected you to. It kind
of made them think about death and their own lack
of immortality.

So, other than Henry and her children, Buddy and
Patricia, only the doctors came. And not so many of
them came anymore.

She heard Henry struggling with the knob
moments before he came in carrying her breakfast
tray. "Poor, Henry," she mumbled. Then she
inhaled deeply several times and fought the urge to
cry. She was no longer useful to him. She was no
longer a wife, or a mother. She was a frail, dying
thing; an albatross around his neck.

She forced a smile and lied when he spoke to her.
"How do you feel?" he'd asked.

"Oh, much better," was her answer, the lie rolling
off her tongue with ease while pain throbbed in her
kidneys. The truth was that the pain was excruciat-
ing and she wanted to die.

Henry laid the tray on her lap, then bent over and
kissed her. But the kiss was too quickly over and
done with to suit her. She longed for the days when
there had been more, before those damned renal
scans proved she was finished!

"Where to today?" she asked, wanting so desperately to remain a part of his active life.

"I'm showing a couple of houses this morning. Won't be in the office at least until noon."

Henry wiped his palms on his shirt, a grease stain darkened the pocket. He glanced down at it absently and took a tie from the closet. He was trying desperately not to think about showing those houses, especially the one in Monroe. It had him bothered to hell and back.

Bess sipped her coffee, never taking her eyes off Henry. The healthy, virile body had long given way to middleage. His feet shuffled heavily when he walked. She watched him putting on a wrinkled tie and slipping into a soiled jacket like a man in a trance. This wasn't Henry; normally he was very meticulous about his appearance.

"What is it?" she asked. "What's eating you?"

"Nothing much. I'm just tired."

He turned his back before she could look at his face. Bess was good at reading faces. She was equally good at seeing what was written in your eyes. Eyes told the truth, and his said that he was beaten, stomped into the ground.

Henry had gotten the mail from the box on his way upstairs. Today's mail had contained the usual collection notices. One was from her urologist, along with a note telling Henry to find another doctor. The others remained unopened. What the hell was the use, he reasoned, his insurance coverage was gone, and now they were starting to pick his pockets. Only the pockets were empty as the cupboard was bare.

And he had to show that damned house today because they needed the money from his commissions so badly.

"Henry? Are you sure there's nothing else bothering you?"

Bess was smart. She was waiting for an answer, one he could not truthfully provide without hurting her deeply. She had no idea just how tight the money situation was.

He forced a smile and turned. "I just realized, I'm walking out of here looking like a bum. There's stains all over my jacket. Tie's wrinkled—"

"Well, it's nothing to brood over," she joked.

And, I have to show that *Goddamn* house, he wanted to scream, but he swallowed and took a deep breath instead. No use taking it out on her.

"Come on, baby," he said in a silly way. "How's about a big, juicy kiss before I leave."

2

The house in Monroe looked different in the light of day; there was no threat. It was a white two-story dwelling, nothing more, nothing less. Of course it was in dire need of a paint job, and could have used some grass seed out front. Otherwise, everything was cool.

Henry Wittaker laughed at his choice of words. At the moment, his children seemed to be dominating his deepest thoughts. Their crude diction had become the norm for him. But then, they were part of his reason for existing, part of the reason he was here today, trying to make a buck selling this . . . house to an unsuspecting couple.

Buddy had that damned FOR SALE sign on his Corvette. Buddy wanted to help out because of the doctors' bills. Henry had to sell this house, whether he wanted to or not. But it was haunted!

He was tempted momentarily to call the Walshs' and confess all. And yet, somewhere in his mind he was telling himself to grow up! The house was perfectly normal. Hell, here he was in the yard and nothing had happened yet. He'd gotten this far without *feeling* anything. And he was able to stare up at the windows on the second floor with no one glaring back.

Nothing wrong with this house, he reiterated to

himself, and glanced at his watch. It was 9:45, the
Walshs' were due at 10:00. He had fifteen minutes to
air the place out. He approached the front door with
determination, but hesitated when the stench hit him
full force. This time it smelled like acid poured over
rotted meat. What a hell of a way to make a living, he
thought bitterly, because it hadn't always been this
way.

Henry could remember the good old days when he
lived in Nassau County and worked for a prestigious
insurance firm in Valley Stream. He really had the
world by the short hairs then; a big office, a private
secretary, a company car. He was a hot shot insurance
executive on his way to the top.

Money was no object. Hell, he threw the stuff
around as if it grew in the dust under his bed. Bought
both his kids brand new cars; Corvettes, nothing
cheap. Bought a house on a large estate for Bess.

Then a positive reading on a renal scan shattered his
world beyond repair.

Time off, that's what killed him, time off; for
doctors' visits, in-hospital tests, dialysis sessions. He
literally committed occupational suicide. But, other
than his kids, there was no one else to see that Bess
had proper care. Then too, he had to be honest with
himself. It was his responsibility. Hadn't he taken her
hand in marriage for better or worse?

He could still recall the day he was terminated!
He'd missed a meeting, one that had taken months to
set up. It was for a group package on a large corporation; life insurance, health, disability; thousands of
small commissions on each and every corporate soul,
all adding up to a very comfortable sum. Not to
mention the referrals he would've gotten. And he
missed it. And the corporation, whose business he so
desperately desired, bought elsewhere.

But it wasn't his fault. Still, he was fired by his own
company for not caring. But he did care.

He cared about Bess! She was bad that day,

spasmodic pain racking her kidneys, her sweat-drenched body huddled into a ball, scaring hell out of his kids when she screamed. He had to stay with her . . . and at what a cost.

Now, here he was in Suffolk County, where it was cheaper to live, working for a real estate firm, on a commission only basis, forced to hustle to make ends meet, forced to sell *haunted houses* for those doctors' bills.

Henry forced himself to smile at the last part. He had to be able to effectively deal with what he was doing, he had to forget those hundreds of books he'd read on occult phenomena. Besides, everyone knew there was no such thing as a haunted house, right? Some were a bit stranger than others, which meant they had character.

Keeping that thought in mind, he was able to turn the key in the lock and open the front door.

But the house was ready for him . . .

It was cold inside; a cryptic, paralyzing, silent cold. *They* were drawing energy from the room, had sucked heat from the air. Oh God, he wanted to run. He felt his body shiver, his joints ached.

And the walls were still blue. . .

How many coats of paint would it take to cover it? The blue was a dominant force, meant to pay homage?

Henry made himself move, made his feet carry him to the nearest window, made his hands undo the lock. The place had to be aired. There was an imprint of a hand pressed against the glass, but he ignored it because it was too large to be . . . human. And the fingernails . . . No, he cursed inwardly, no beasts, no demons here. He would not allow himself to think or *feel* or sense anything this time around, especially since he was here to make money and nothing else.

But there were movements upstairs, doors were closing. Slowly. Deliberately. The hairs on his neck bristled. Character, he thought. But it was cold in here, *they* were energized.

The first window offered resistance as though it had a mind of its own and could tell him *no, don't open me!* But Henry knew that the window was not human, so he blamed his inability to open it on fear, forced himself to think this way. Fear hampered his movements. Right! The window was just that, a window; wood, metal, glass—no mind to think with.

Henry tugged at the damn thing until he swore he was ruptured. It finally gave way, then he walked to the next. What a hell of a way to make a living, he thought again, his nerves rumbling beneath his skin when the first window slammed shut behind his back.

He ignored it, *had* to ignore it.

He opened the second and the third and stood mutely by and watched them close themselves in rapid succession. He wanted to run, but running wasn't cool, as Buddy would've put it. Besides, these were just windows, nothing else; no brain to think with, to be purposely defiant. He opened the windows again, and saw them slam shut in front of him. Sweat beaded his forhead as the banging and slamming echoed in his ears.

And someone approached the landing at the top of the steps. He heard him, *felt* him. He wanted to turn and look, and at the same time he felt it would be safer for him to ignore the noises in this house and to forget those books he'd read as well. Ignore it and it will surely go away, he told himself. And yet, would it?

He crossed to the kitchen thinking perhaps he'd open the windows in there. He put his hand to the door to push it open and saw a streak of white, something that maybe wasn't really there, flash in the corner of his eye. It was upstairs, and it had substance. It was a solid form. He shuddered, closed his eyes and reminded himself that the house had character. Isn't that what he thought outside? It had character. No ghosts! No spirits!

Well, keep on thinking like that and ignore the goddamn thing, he screamed inside!

He turned the knob on the kitchen door and pushed at it. The door swung halfway open before he felt a resistance, like something was leaning against it from the other side, using weight as leverage to keep it halfway closed. Henry couldn't see what it was and didn't want to see. He knew it was a large, immovable object and the knowledge suited him fine, scant though it was. Any more and he would've been forced to leave the house for sure.

He was still holding the knob when it spun between his fingers, but Henry wasn't the one doing the spinning. And a click, he heard the tumbler click just before the door slammed shut in his face. He didn't try the knob again because the door was locked, no doubt about it.

He turned and scanned the interior of the house. It was dim and eerie. He could *feel* a blanket of death creeping across the floor like mist on a moor, and there were things creeping along with it, only he couldn't see them, but he *felt* their presence just the same. Ancient beasts. Henry wondered if they craved his flesh or were they just curious? Oh, God, he wanted to run, but where to?

He was trapped; the doors, windows, everything, all shut tight and bolted. He was a prisoner in a two-story tomb, in a great Sphinx, in a breathing entity. Sand had dribbled from its pores, setting off a chain reaction, and huge granite blocks, each weighing several tons, had been released and slid into place. Now the tomb was sealed! With him inside.

And someone was watching him from the top of the steps. Henry was trapped in a place full of character with a beast who had been energized and now was materialized so that Henry could see him. And he was perhaps the most dangerous of them all, this one who had solid form.

"They reveled in the thought that victory was theirs, this *house* was theirs, along with any future inhabitants."

When Henry had first read those words, he knew it was so. The house in that cursed book was real, ran on a plain parallel to this one. The book could've been written here for all he knew. Even the walls were the same.

The walls were still blue out of a hateful defiance, they refused to be painted over, because blue was the color of evil and had been purposely chosen to pay homage to the beast; to honor the beast. The beast! King of all kings. He who reigns over a throne in the strange outer world of the occult. He who hides in the farthest recesses of the human mind, who rises in the night to torment our dreams, who lurks in the shadows of darkness on stormy nights.

Henry swore he saw him once . . . hiding in the blackest corner of his basement. Henry was in the basement checking out the boiler, and something had moved in a corner near the stairs. Something had knocked over a mop and had caught his attention, and it had *red eyes*. A rat maybe? Of course, Henry smiled, his lips a thin line of fear. A rat had been foraging for food and had knocked over a mop. Simple. And as long as he was in this house, he wouldn't allow himself to think otherwise.

But truth is a funny thing. One can only hide it and distort it until it yearns to be free, like a bird in a cage, because eventually it struggles to spread its wings, to take flight out in the open, to escape the entrapment of lies.

Henry could no longer lie to himself about the incident in his basement. The truth was, it couldn't have been a rat. Henry remembered that he'd been scared enough to run for his life when he heard heavy footsteps coming after him out of the darkness. And they were much too loud for a small animal like a rat.

No, that thing was big and it moved with determination.

Big as a beast should be?

He suddenly felt his heart thumping wildly in his chest. This was no time to dwell on his past, especially when it scared the hell out of him, especially when he already had a good start in that direction to begin with. Don't let your mind wander, he thought. But it was too late. He choked on his fear, gagged actually. Out! He had to get out. And away. Eyes were watching him, voices were whispering.

A solid form was coming down the stairs!

He ran to the front door, the blanket of death, the fog, hugging his ankles, invisible ancient beasts brushing against his body, whispering threats. He twisted the knob on the door, but it wouldn't turn; it was frozen, atrophied, cemented by unseen hands. *They wouldn't allow him to open the door!* He pounded against it with his fists and cringed when laughter assaulted his senses.

Out! He had to get out. The voices were telling him to GET OUT! And yet, they were holding him prisoner, entombing his body, threatening his sanity. He felt a wetness and touched his face—tears, he was crying. "Men don't cry," he raged and crumpled to the floor, his eyes roaming to the figure on the stairs.

Someone was coming . . . for him . . .

Kayle Walsh pulled onto Sunrise Highway near Patchogue and headed east. Monroe was about ten miles from this point. He felt his stomach sour with anticipation. This was a big move for him, a firm commitment. Was he ready? He wasn't sure.

And suddenly, even with Erica next to him and the kids in the back seat, Kayle felt lonely and miserable. Everything was resting on his decision.

"You're happy about the house, aren't you?" Erica was studying him closely. "We can afford it, can't we?'' Her words were clipped, her voice riddled with uncertainty.

Kayle pulled into the left lane to pass a slower moving vehicle ahead of them before answering. His tone was nasty when he spoke. ''Yes, Erica. For the last time . . . . We got the money.''

He reached up involuntarily and rubbed the scar on his face. He'd gone over the mortgage payments again that morning, they were affordable, especially with the second job he'd taken, the one Erica didn't approve of.

''You're positive now?''

She was ready for anything. Kayle had broken promises in the past. She concentrated on the road in front of her and waited for an answer. But Kayle was driving much too close to the car ahead and that made her even more nervous.

''Don't be so friggin' insecure. Grow up! We're looking at the goddamn house. What more do you want?''

He slid up until he was almost bumper to bumper with the car in front. Money wasn't the issue here. The issue here was freedom; what he was sacrificing for Erica and those kids. He glanced at them in the rear view mirror. They were quiet, and sitting up straight in their seats, both boys and both girls. Kayle had them well trained.

A commitment meant buckling down in his mind, no more chicks on the side, and the idea of becoming a one-woman man frightened him. He might even grow mellow enough to ask Erica to marry him, to give those kids a legal right to call him ''Daddy.''

Then again, it might not be such a bad idea, he thought to himself. Erica had been his screwing partner for a long time, at least ten years. She even used his last name; and the kids *were* his. No doubt about it. Erica was the most faithful bitch he knew, even after catching him with other women.

For the first time since climbing behind the wheel

that morning, he noticed how tense she was. He'd been so involved with his own feelings that hers seemed of little importance until now.

"Come on, loosen up." He poked her playfully and tried to get her to smile. It made him nervous whenever Erica turned serious. He never knew what was running through her mind, especially about him.

"Loosen up," he repeated.

But Erica was so hyper she could do nothing except stare at the road ahead, her mouth drawn into a tight line. She was wearing blue jeans and a heavy wool sweater that accentuated her breasts. He ran his hand down the front of her sweater and she half-smiled and slapped him away. She wasn't entirely amused.

"Both hands on the wheel, Kayle. And watch where you're going."

"Yes, ma'am!" Kayle slipped his hand along the seat and pinched her bottom. She slapped at him again.

"I'd like to get there in one piece. Will you watch the road!"

There was a tightness in her voice until she heard muffled laughing coming from the back seat. If the kids were thrilled with Kayle's behavior and excited about the house, then why spoil the mood? Why give Kayle an excuse to lose his temper? He was just dying to turn the car around and head back to that dump they called home anyway. She smiled broadly at him, her mouth drawn back to the point where dimples formed on her cheeks.

He was pleased, she wasn't thinking anything bad about him. "You know, kid," he said, his tone on an upswing. "Maybe it's time we settled down. Made a commitment."

Erica hoped he was sincere. For the first time in years she wanted to believe him.

Henry Wittaker rushed out of the house and slammed the door behind him, his face contorted with fear, his body sweaty and limp. He couldn't sell this house, no siree! He'd talk to the Walshs', make them take the one over on Evergreen. And to hell with the doctors' bills and the medical collection agencies if the Walshs' decided to buy from another broker. His conscience was involved here!

Of course, he wasn't absolutely sure of what he'd seen. It might have been an illusion. A pair of legs, that was it. A pair of legs coming down the steps, with no body attached to it. He heard noises too, clicking noises, like heartbeats, lots of them. And the whispered threats telling him to "GET OUT!", those were the worst of all.

No! The worst part was his forced entrapment. It was a warning. "DON'T COME BACK," the voices said, "OR DEATH WILL BE IN YOUR FUTURE."

So he GOT OUT, and what's more, he was STAYING OUT!

He glanced at his watch and noticed that his hands were still trembling. It was after 10:00, the Walshs' were late. Maybe they weren't coming, and that was fine with him. He wouldn't have to come up with an excuse for showing them another house.

He'd wait ten minutes longer, and if they didn't arrive by then, he was leaving.

But the windows in the house were open. Henry looked at the windows and his skin crawled. Everything was done in defiance. Now he wanted the windows to be closed, and they were open. *Defiance!* Henry took out a handkerchief and mopped his face. Someone had to close those windows. This town was crawling with punk, bastard junkies. Those sneaky, little assholes would drive by here, spot the open windows, and it would be goodbye copper plumbing and anything else they could nail. Henry would lose his job.

But he made no move to re-enter the house. Instead, he allowed his gaze to wander up to the second floor, his breath catching in his throat when he saw HER there, standing in front of one of the bedroom windows, in broad daylight, waving at him. A little girl with long, black hair hanging in ringlets; a sweet-faced girl, with large, black innocent eyes. And to think she was one of *them!*

There was a sudden hardness in his chest that hampered his breathing. It felt like he'd been slammed with a mallet. He staggered to the curb and climbed into his car. Screw the open windows, screw his job, and screw this house! He was leaving!

Carol Anderson watched Henry through the spaces in her rose bushes out back. The man was visibly upset and she felt sorry for him.

There was a time, not long ago, when the house was a showplace and realtors tripped over themselves trying to sell it. But the house had other ideas and refused to cooperate. It became vengeful and monstrous and threw temper tantrums like a spoiled child wanting its own way and not getting it. Doors fell off their hinges, the exterior paint bubbled and peeled, the grass on the front lawn went to rot.

Now Henry Wittaker was the only realtor who persisted.

"You know, Burt," she began, but Burt wasn't listening. He was setting up the timing on the engine of her old Chevy. "That house deteriorated so fast. Just a few short months. It wants everyone to stay away."

Burt picked up the last part of her sentence and scowled. "Yeah. Like it has a brain and thinks for itself."

"Not a brain, a soul. All houses have souls, in a way. Almost living, breathing entities. Only this house is evil."

Burt acted as though he hadn't understood what she'd said. Then again, his mind didn't travel that deep. She clutched the rose bushes tensely when Henry ran to his car.

"Would you get the hell over here and help? Screw that fucking place."

There were large sweat stains under the arms of his shirt, but a chill swept over his body. It happened every time his wife mentioned that house.

"Over here, love." He watched her walk towards him, her face lined in thought. "Whenever you're ready."

"We cannot turn our backs on that house." She wiped a wisp of brown hair from her face. "What if the taint spreads here?"

"Oh, for shit sakes! Hold the timing gun. I gotta get another screw driver."

She watched his short, stubby legs hurry out of sight, her attention then drifting to the discarded items in the yard next door; the black leather sofa and chairs, the fairly new bedroom set, the kitchen utensils. "Why would anyone in their right minds leave such expensive furnishings behind?"

"They would if they were one step ahead of their bill collectors." Burt was back, wielding a smaller screw driver.

Carol stiffened. He never looked beyond the obvious and mocked her because she did. "Not everyone lives as we do."

Burt smiled, his words laced with anger. "We *all* got bills, honey. We're all in the same fix." But then the smile faded and his voice rose. "Now, hold the damn timer still, will ya?"

She watched him lean over and concentrate on the car, ignoring her fears about the house and the people who once lived there. But Carol couldn't let go. She knew that Burt was wrong. Those people were driven away, and it had more to do with the house itself than with bill collectors. She was even willing to sink to Burt's level and bet real money on that.

She still recalled, with a great deal of anguish, the night she stood in the living room next door and . . .

It was about a year ago. Burt wanted tea, light and

sweet. Carol was out of sugar. So, at Burt's insistence, she went over there to borrow some.

Carol now wished she'd defied the son-of-a-bitch and refused to go. But Burt had an edge over her, he knew how eager she was to please him, to be the closest thing to the perfect wife as she could possibly be. He often used this to his advantage. That night was one of those times.

She could still remember the man who'd answered the door; a light-skinned Spanish man with coal black hair and teeth that were even and white when he smiled. But his eyes . . . The expression in his eyes was different, no eager to please politeness there. Rather she saw a mixture of fear and caution and didn't know why, not at first anyway.

He let her in and told her to wait while he got the sugar. After he'd gone, she looked around with an inane curiosity. To her knowledge, none of the other neighbors had ever gotten this far, she was the first to be allowed inside.

She found herself standing in a large living room with cathedral ceilings and expensive black leather furniture and walls that had been painted a hideous shade of blue. There was a staircase near the kitchen that disappeared beyond her line of vision. And there was something else. She'd tried to suppress it because it left an emotional scar.

Carol heard footsteps on those stairs. Thinking it was his wife, she glanced up and smiled politely . . . at nothing. Then she jammed her hands into her jeans and giggled because she felt foolish.

The kitchen door, separating her from the Spanish man, was closed. She stared at it impatiently and waited for him to return, finally praying for his return when the footsteps continued to descend the stairs. Heavy boots. She recognized the sound because Burt had a pair, and when he walked Burt's footsteps were similar to . . . to what?

But the staircase was empty! Down one step, down

another, still the sound of those heavy boots.

There was a cut across the top of one of the cushions on the sofa, she fixed her attention on that. When the man returned with her sugar, she'd tell him where to get a repair kit.

A knot started at the base of her skull and caused her to tremble. Someone had reached the bottom of the stairs by this time. Someone she was unable to see. And the heavy boots were crossing the living room, right over to where she was standing.

She forced her attention to the sofa again. The slit in the cushion was even, she noticed, no jagged edges. And leather was easy to fix.

Carol tried to keep a tight rein on her emotions, but her hands were sweating, and her mouth had begun to quiver. She sensed a face close to hers, and felt hot breath on her neck that was so foul and stale she winced. A voice whispered obscenities, called her a "CUNT" and a "BITCH." She crossed herself with the sign of the crucifix and refused to listen when the voice boomed with laughter, and she pretended not to notice when two firm hands, laced with the coldness of death, fondled her below the waist.

The Spanish man returned and she hastily thanked him, took the sugar, and ran. She ran until she reached the safety of her own front door, and never looked back, and never returned to that house. More importantly, she never told Burt what happened. Why give him more ammunition to throw her way?

Carol knew it had been real, more real than she cared to remember, and more real than she could ever forget.

3

"You don't really want this house," Henry Wittaker was leading the Walshs' through the living room to the kitchen. Henry had not been able to make his escape in time, they drove up as he was pulling away from the curb. Henry was in one hell of a fix.

"There's a strange odor in here . . . and we're having trouble getting rid of it," he stressed.

"In other words, it stinks in here. We know." Kayle was disappointed, everything else about the house seemed perfect. Erica's face flushed red and she glared at Kayle, silently admonishing him for his crudeness. He gave her a sharp look in return. So he was crude in his mannerisms. So what? At least he wasn't putting on airs, at least he was being honest.

Erica went at once to the kitchen, letting out an audible sigh of relief when she opened the door. It was something out of the pages of a magazine, everything new as promised. She ran her hand over the smooth formica on the counters, and across the soft wood-grained cabinets. She bent to feel the pile of the lavish carpet beneath her feet, her gaze coming to rest on the screen door leading to the back yard, and finally on a clutter of discarded furniture. Kayle saw it too.

"What about that junk outside?" He crossed to the

door and glared back at Henry while he waited for an answer.

"I'll have it removed." Henry was sick inside, it sounded as though they were seriously thinking of buying this house. He mopped his face with a handkerchief and shuddered when a chill iced his spine. He felt hot and cold at the same time. The smell inside hadn't been enough to discourage these people; he'd failed.

And what would *they* do to him because he'd come back, because he'd defied their authority, ignored their warning to STAY OUT!

"We'd like to see the bedrooms, please." Erica had large dressers, and Kayle had promised to buy her a king-sized water bed. It all had to fit. It just had to.

Henry Wittaker was nervous and almost crumpled in front of her. She pretended not to notice this when he led them up the staircase directly outside of the kitchen. The man must've had personal problems, and it was his business, not hers.

She squeezed Kayle's hand excitedly as they climbed the stairs, but Kayle pulled away from her. He was sulking because of the odor; he didn't want the house. Then why did he give Henry Wittaker a hard time about the discarded furniture? The only answer she could think of was that Kayle was a small person with an inflated ego, and this was his style.

"I'll use a pine cleaner," she whispered tensely behind Henry's back. "It'll kill the smell." But Kayle continued to sulk.

As she climbed the steps, Erica noticed that the medium blue color on the living room walls extended to the walls adjoining the staircase. This wouldn't do; she pictured it a different color, white maybe, to emphasize the majestic charm of the cathedral ceilings.

She was startled when she bumped into Henry who was poised on the top landing, his eyes nervously scanning the upper floor.

"Something wrong, Henry?" Kayle was abrupt. He was picking now, looking for any little thing he could find, any flaw to discourage Erica from wanting the house. She ignored him for the second time. After seeing this house, nothing could force her to accept life as they lived it in that dump they called home.

"We can see the bedrooms, can't we? I mean, there ain't nothing wrong with 'em?" Kayle was persistent, still looking for flaws.

Henry couldn't answer at first, his heart was pounding heavily in his chest. Although he hadn't seen or heard anything, he knew they were here, scowling at him, repeating their threat, "DEATH WILL BE IN YOUR FUTURE." He wanted to run, but controlled himself.

"The bedrooms are this way," he managed, not looking at Kayle.

There was nothing wrong with the bedrooms, all three of them were large and full of sunshine and a cheery atmosphere. Nothing wrong with the bedrooms, he wanted to tell Kayle. It was just that there were problems with the *closets* in those bedrooms.

Sam Walsh was five by the time he was able to assert himself and speak up in his own defense. Sam was the next to the last in a line of four children. There was Todd, age seven, Didi, six; Sam, and Katie, four. All born a year apart, they were often referred to as "steps and stairs" by their maternal grandmother, Mary Rogers.

Sam was a hyper child, always climbing and jumping and otherwise getting himself into one awful mess after another.

Today was different though. He was much too excited over the idea of a house of their own to cause problems. Besides, if he misbehaved, Kayle might use this as an excuse for not taking the house. And Sam wanted to be blamed for as little as possible this time. So he sat on the front lawn with his legs crossed, silently ignoring his brothers and sisters, although they were teasing him quite a bit about being such a Goody Two Shoes.

The other kids were racing around him in wide circles and throwing grass and crumpled leaves in his hair. Sam reacted by ignoring them and turning his full attention to the house. It fascinated him. White, with large shutters on the windows, it was, except for the peeling paint, the best looking house he'd ever seen. He prayed with everything in him that his parents would like it as much as he did, and maybe buy it.

"Come on, Sam. Don't just sit there," Todd shouted. Todd was standing over him, his face sweaty and flushed from running.

"Yeah, Sam," Didi chimed in. "Let's go look at the back yard. I seen lotsa good junk back there."

But Sam refused to budge. He was content to sit where he was and dream about having his own room, to be shared with Todd, of course. It sure beat sleeping on a sofa in the living room.

Katie plopped down next to him at one point to envision her own dreams of living there. She allowed her eyes to roam freely, to take in everything at once, finally coming to rest on an upstairs window. She saw a small girl, probably around her own age, standing there; a sweet-faced child, with long, black hair hanging in ringlets, who wore a white dress edged with lace.

The little girl gazed down at Katie intently and smiled, then waved. Katie waved back.

Sam observed Katie's behavior with rigid silence, at first. He didn't want to challenge her and upset his parents, Kayle especially. But when Katie continued to wave at an empty window and otherwise act like a fool, it was too much for him to bear.

"What the hell ya wavin' at?" he wanted to know.

Katie turned to face him, a smug grin creasing the corners of her mouth. She had him now. "That little girl upstairs," she replied haughtily, pointing at the window, her gaze riveted on Sam.

Sam followed her direction and concentrated as hard as he could. And yet, there was no one standing in front of the window Katie was pointing to. "Yer nuts! I can't see 'er."

"She's right there!" Sam could damn well see her, Katie imagined. He was just acting stubborn and trying to make an ass out of her. In her frustration, Katie took hold of his head and forced him to look at the window again. The little girl was still there, waving down at them. "See, smarty?"

Sam snapped at this point. Not only was she making a fool of him, she was hurting his neck as well. He tried to pull her hands away, and when he failed, he balled up his fist and punched her.

Katie howled in pain and gave Sam a you're-gonna-get-it-now kind of look before concentrating on the little girl in the window upstairs once again.

Erica wanted to see the master bedroom first. She followed Henry down the hall, but hesitated when a commotion started outside. The children were fighting.

"*Your* kids again," Kayle snapped and ran downstairs. They were always hers whenever they were bad.

"Don't hit them," she pleaded as he disappeared out of sight. Henry was watching her. She wondered if he'd heard what Kayle'd said to her. Henry might misunderstand the relationship.

In her opinion, Kayle always referred to them as *her* children so he'd be free to leave whenever the mood struck him without looking back. But Erica was no fool, she had a strong hold on Kayle. Even with the scores of women he'd dated on the side, he was still her man.

To her amazement, Henry seemed more concerned with her words than Kayle's. "Does he hit the children often?" It was more of a statement than a question. She sensed confusion in his voice. "I can't imagine anyone beating a child."

"He doesn't beat his children. Or me." Her answer was quick, almost too quick. "He doesn't drink either." That sounded contrived, she thought.

Kayle had made a terrible impression on Henry. He'd come off as sounding gruff and crude. How could she expect this man to believe her? At that point, she was embarrassed by Henry's opinion of her, not by his opinion of Kayle. It was degrading to think she'd allow Kayle to beat her children and then lie to protect him.

And especially since Kayle was, in essence, a man who never used his hands to enforce punishment, not when the tone of his voice and the expression on his face had always been enough.

She was disturbed by Henry's silence, and the way he kept his head lowered so he wouldn't have to look at her. But she decided to let the matter drop.

"Would you show me the bedrooms, please?"

The stench of decayed animal flesh, as she perceived it, so overwhelming throughout the rest of the house, wasn't evident in the master bedroom. It did smell bad though, sweet and sickening. The heady aroma of several types of cheap perfume mixed together caused her head to reel. She felt her stomach tighten with nausea.

Henry walked into the room ahead of her, then wheeled to face her, his expression somber, almost depressed looking. "Erica," he began, then thought better of it. "May I call you *Erica?*"

She nodded silently.

"I wanted to speak to you alone. Mr. Walsh doesn't like this house. And frankly, I agree."

She'd been expecting this. Over the years she'd learned never to trust realtors, or lawyers, or public officials . . .

"In fact," he continued, "there's a house over on Evergreen that's more suited to your needs." He tried to be nonchalant, but his words sounded choked and strained. He wiped his palms with a handkerchief.

"The house on Evergreen . . . it just happens to cost more. Am I right?"

Henry diverted his gaze and remained silent.

"Look. You gave us a big buildup about this place. Raised our hopes. Now you don't want us to buy it. You think we're stupid or something?"

It was hot up there. Her jeans were glued to her body with sweat and she felt very uncomfortable.

And who the hell used that awful perfume, she wondered? The son-of-a-bitch must've taken a bath in it. Good Christ, her head was reeling.

"You do think we're stupid! Otherwise you'd have something to say in defense of yourself."

Henry stared down at his feet while Erica waited for an answer. His voice sounded even more strained than before. "I'm not promising you anything . . . but maybe I can get you the other house for the same price."

"I want this one!" She brushed her hair away from her face, wishing she had some pins to put it back with. It was so hot in that room. "I want this house," she repeated firmly.

Then she turned her back on Henry and concentrated on the room. It was perfect, except for the color, the same hideous blue covering the walls throughout the entire house. Well, it can be painted over, she thought, admiring the room for its size. There would be plenty of space for that king-sized water bed and . . .

She heard footsteps on the staircase down the hall and knew it had to be Kayle. She rushed out, full of childish excitement, to tell him about their new bedroom. Kayle would have to buy this house now. It was everything they hoped it would be, and more.

But when she reached the top of the landing and looked down, the stairs were empty. And yet, the noise continued. Step after step, slowly and deliberately, someone was climbing towards her. *Someone she couldn't see!*

She was stunned for a moment. A chill started at the base of her skull and notched its way down her spine. She wasn't crazy . . . someone was *there*, she'd heard him.

The footsteps grew louder, the footfalls sharper, as they drew closer to the landing, closer to where she stood. And although her mind was clouded with confusion and she was unable to reason this out, her senses sharpened with the tenacity of a radar scan.

A foul, acrid odor stung her nostrils with the force of a punch and turned her stomach. There were harsh whisperings assualting her ears, but she couldn't hear what *they* were saying. And laughter, she detected its mocking laughter; several voices, but only one set of footsteps. She felt overwhelmed by the riddle.

The voice of a child, a girl, rang out from behind, calling her "Mommy!"

And someone stepped onto the landing, giving Erica the courage to back up. Henry was still in the master bedroom. If she were at least able to reach the door. . . and yet, her senses told her that it would be useless to try. The force behind the footsteps was an ancient evil, well acqainted with pursuit and afraid of nothing. It could move with great swiftness, surround her completely, and choke the life from her body before she even took another step, if it so desired.

Sweat beaded her forehead. She brushed it away with trembling hands as her mind began to cooperate with the invisible entity in front of her. Only seconds had passed since she'd rushed to the top of the steps, but it seemed longer. She felt trapped in a time warp. It was as though everything around her continued on in normal sync, except for her own movements. Her body dragged at a maddening half-pace and she longed to be free to run from the danger she felt.

Hands were touching her, lots of them; cold, monstrous, hands; they violated her sanity, aroused her in an erotically sexual manner, played games with her clitoris. Someone whispered. No! Someone screamed her name. But the voice was unfamiliar. Kayle? Kayle was standing at the top of the stairs only a few feet away.

But Erica had trouble seeing him, could barely hear him. Kayle hadn't screamed her name. She reached out for him, for the strength of his hands to protect her. She reached through the invisible mass separating her from Kayle and felt blackness clamping down hard on her brain. Then she was falling . . . into an endless void in time . . . just falling.

Henry Wittaker pulled up in front of his house and sat in the car for a few minutes, his hands clutching the wheel so tightly that it caused the veins in his neck to protrude.

He was no closer now to knowing whether the house had been sold than he'd been this morning. The Walsh' had left right after Mrs. Walsh, Erica, had recovered. And Mr. Walsh had refused to listen when Henry shouted after him. Henry wanted to explain about the house on Evergreen.

The entire commission could've been lost to him at this point, and all because of . . .

"Those fucking bastards wouldn't stop playing their games!"

Henry was startled when he realized he'd been shouting at the top of his voice. He scanned the street ahead of him and checked the rear view mirror; no one in sight. Good, he told himself, and stepped from the car.

Buddy's Corvette was parked in the driveway with the FOR SALE sign in the back window. Tears misted Henry's eyes. "Goddamn *them*," he cursed, and raised his fist to an invisible enemy.

Henry's plan had been to sell a house! Maybe not the one the Walsh's wanted at first, but a house nevertheless. Then he could come home and rip that son-of-a-bitch sign off the kid's car and tear it to shreds. Then, perhaps he'd regain the respect he felt he'd lost in the eyes of his son, his daughter, and his wife, too, if the truth were known.

But it wasn't meant to be. And Henry would have to live with that sign in the back window of the Corvette for a while longer. God, he thought suddenly alarmed, the kid might even have to sell his car if the Walsh' bought nothing!

"That you, dear?" Bess called down as soon as he got in the door. Then again, she didn't have to ask, she already knew it was him.

"Yes, love. Are you okay?" He wished to hell *he* was.

"I'm fine." But her voice was choked with pain.

"I'll be right up. I'm getting a cup of coffee. Can I bring you some?" Thankfully, she said no. He needed time to talk to Buddy alone, to reassure his son, and himself, that the car wouldn't be sold.

Buddy was doing this unselfishly, but Henry knew it had to hurt. The car was three years old and still looked brand new. A boy and his toy, he thought, an expensive toy, one that aroused the right set of chicks and made Buddy a king of the hill.

Of course, Buddy would never admit to using the car as bait. His face would always flush whenever Henry taunted him about girls, and Buddy would then swear the car was only used for "dependable transportation, Dad." It became a running gag between them.

Plus, the car was impressive at the right times. Buddy had gotten himself a pretty good after-school job because old Rick DeSota, the owner of the one and only newpaper in town, had seen the kid pulling up in that car. Rick told Buddy that anyone smart enough to acquire a Corvette at his age, whether or not he bought it himself, deserved a job with his paper. Then he hired the kid for five bucks an hour, way above minimum wage.

Now Buddy was throwing it all away because he wanted to help. "Goddamn them," Henry cursed again.

Buddy was in the kitchen reading a paper when he got there. Henry surveyed the brown hair, the knotted muscles, and thought about himself and about how old he'd gotten; the gray streaks on his temples, the paunch over the belt of his trousers. It was hard to believe he'd ever looked like Buddy.

The boy watched him with anxious eyes, searching Henry's face for a sign of victory. Whenever Henry sold a house his cheeks were puffed red with excitement. At the moment, the boy saw only the grayness of defeat and turned back to his newspaper.

Henry had to say something, even if it was a lie. He just couldn't admit to failure in front of his son. "I have to show another house to the Walshs' tomorrow. They're gonna buy. It's just a matter of which one."

Buddy looked up at him, forced a smile, and tried to believe what he'd said.

"Well," Henry began, rubbing his hands together. "Let's see the insurance ads. Maybe with a bit of luck I'll find something good." Buddy smiled again and handed him the employment section. "After all," Henry continued in a falsely jubilant tone of voice, "I still have my licenses."

To Buddy, this was further proof of Henry's failure. Whenever Henry struck out in real estate and his future looked bleak, he tried to go back to insurance. However, Henry had been fired by a large insurance company, leaving him with no references. A fifty-year-old man didn't walk into a swell job with no references. There would be no company cars, no secretaries, and most of all, no weekly salary.

Henry had but one choice; a commission only sales job in the insurance field, working his ass off from morning 'till night, the same as he had in real estate.

Henry knew this, and Buddy knew it, too. But Buddy also knew that pretension played a large part

in his father's life at this point. And damned if he was
going to be the one to burst the old man's bubble.

Henry hadn't heard the front door open and close
with a strange rigidity after he walked to the kitchen.
But Bess did. And Henry hadn't heard someone
climbing the steps to the second floor. But Bess did.

And Bess damned well knew the identity of
everyone who entered by their footsteps alone. This
one had her stumped though. It wasn't a familiar gait.

And it frightened her as well.

She felt that footsteps, like body movements, were
an extension of an inner personality. People had a
tendency to shuffle their feet and take smaller steps
when they were depressed. But when they were
happy and didn't have a care at all, they took long,
vigorous, confident steps. These footsteps didn't
match either category.

This stranger wasn't happy or depressed. He was
angry. His footfalls were slow, true, but they were
also deliberate, as if he knew where he was headed
and why. It was one step after another, with a kiss-
my-butt attitude, yet hardly with confidence. She
sensed defiance more than anything else; he was after
trouble and getting caught was the least of his
worries.

Oh, yeah! His footsteps told her a lot; they told her
she should probably be screaming for help at this
point. But Henry and Buddy were in the kitchen.
Would they hear her cries? Would they reach her in
time? Or would she just be telling this person her
exact location in the house by screaming?

With a great deal of physical pain and effort, she
rose into a sitting position and allowed her legs to
drop weakly to the floor.

The stranger was on the upper landing now.

Bess tried to stand, but a hot bolt of pain shot into
both kidneys and she fell back in anguish. She'd seen
this same thing happen once in a Barbara Stanwyck

movie. Stanwyck was killed by her intruder.

The boots were coming down the hall with grim determination, headed in her direction.

"Henry," she yelled, her voice weak, his name sounding as though it had been forced through a prism and had come out muffled and distorted. "Henry," she tried again with the same result. A weapon, she needed a weapon to defend herself with. Her breakfast tray was still at the foot of her bed, along with a plate and cup that Buddy had used for her lunch. She searched for a weapon . . .

He was outside of the door now.

. . . her eyes coming to rest on a knife. It was only a butter knife . . .

He was turning the knob.

. . . but it did have serrated edges . . . This bastard was going to have a run for his money . . .

The door opened.

. . . Bess wasn't about to make it easy . . .

A black, swirling mass rose in front of her, scaring her half to death. It was a mass of pure rage, she sensed, blackened by hatred. She looked into it, and through it, and saw misery and death and knew she couldn't fight this thing. It wasn't solid; it was ethereal, untouchable, not really there.

But it was there, and it was real. It was torture and destruction and violence, and it was after her!

"REVENGE," it hissed in her ear, "FOR HENRY'S INTERFERENCE." It spat in her face. It clutched at her with almost human hands, numbing her senses until she was blind with terror and could hear nothing but its vile profanities.

"CUNT," it called her and, "COCK-SUCKING BITCH!" It choked the life from her body until her face was purple and bloated. "EAT ME!" it screamed and her mouth was filled with venomous fluid. Then it squeezed her lips together until she swallowed the poison and began to hallucinate.

She could see herself running through a field of

flowers. She was naked and hideous, her body sagging and swollen like an old hag's. Henry was behind her, only it wasn't Henry. It was nothing. No! This black, ethereal mass was chasing her.

There were eyes watching her as she ran: they were hot and icy, red and ravenously insane, and they glared at her, daring her to look back. Her kidneys were outside of her body, mounted on her hips like pistols, and they stank, reeked of urine and ammonia.

Bess ran as fast as she could, but the raging mass caught her anyway, and it squeezed her kidneys with those not quite human hands, and sliced them apart with its claws. The pain was ungodly. The *mass* was ungodly.

It threw her on the ground and forced her legs open, penetrating her very being with its hateful lust. It slammed her body against the earth with such fury that her exposed kidneys exploded, splattering her blood on the purple and white crocus growing wild in the field.

Then the mass of raging fury flipped her like a rag doll and penetrated her rectum, driving itself up into her bowels, then her intestines, and it hissed in her ear that it was, "RIDING A HORSEY." And it rode her through the flowers, and over the fields, and into the valley below, until Bess screamed . . . and the air around her was shattered by a final agonizing plea for death to release her.

According to the offical autopsy report that Henry would later receive, Bess died because her bowels had exploded; a condition symptomatic of the following; cirrhosis of the liver, due to an extreme case of alcoholism that eventually led to kidney failure, etc., etc. Although, curiously enough, there was *no* evidence of the kind of excessive formation of connective tissue in the liver generally found to be associated with cirrhosis.

Carol Anderson read of Bess' death and angrily discounted the article in the newspaper. There was an insinuation, in a round about way, that Bess was a drunk who died by her own hand. In other words, she drank herself into hell. Only Carol knew the truth; Bess was murdered. Any fool, with any sense at all, knew the house would rebel.

The house had closed itself to the outside world, period! It had physically destroyed its own exterior to discourage any would-be buyers. And Henry Wittaker had chosen to ignore the obvious. He'd violated its privacy by traipsing strangers through its rooms, and had angered its occupants by endeavoring to place a family inside.

Henry was an idiot, and Bess had suffered for it.

She showed the article to Burt who sneered, "Most drunks get what they deserve." Then he finished his beer and asked for another.

Carol rose wearily and stood by the refrigerator near the window. Storm clouds were hovering over the house next door like a river of blackness, as if they too were part of the conspiracy to insure its privacy.

"Damn you all," she whispered hotly, her soul enraged by the senseless killing of a sick, tired, defenseless woman. Bess was dying anyway.

Lightning flashed across the sky, accentuating her anger and illuminating the house with all its ghastly splendor. And in that flash of light, Carol saw the outline of a form in one of the upstairs windows; someone tall, with broad shoulders, dressed in black, a small child at his side.

Carol felt the blood drain from her upper torso and swore she would faint. Then she closed the curtains and put Burt's cold beer to her forehead to revive herself.

4

Erica sat quietly at her kitchen table sipping a beer, waiting for Kayle to speak. A whole day had passed and still Kayle had said nothing about the house, or about how she'd fainted.

The children were in bed, disappointed because the house wasn't theirs yet, and from the looks of things, it might never be.

Sam took it the worst. He'd begun to believe that if Kayle and Erica had said yes to Mr. Wittaker, they could've moved in the next day. And, as he later told Erica, he blamed himself for being a jerk and letting Katie trap him into a fight again. After he'd punched Katie, his mother had fainted and they had to leave. Sam apologized to Erica for making her faint because it had to be *his* fault, and for spoiling things with Kayle.

Erica told him he had a lot to learn.

"What do we do?" Erica asked, taking the initiative. "Mr. Wittaker's waiting for an answer."

"I don't like that place. It stinks inside." Kayle wasn't giving her a solid excuse for not buying the house. He was harping on the only reason that, given his limited intelligence, made sense and afforded him a weighty argument. He knew it too, and didn't care.

"You keep telling me that a little pine would kill the

52

smell. But it won't work 'cause the smell ain't from dirt. The place was clean.''

And the place was also strange. Kayle couldn't grasp with his mind or put into words what he was really feeling inside.

''Then what do you think it was from?'' Erica tried to nail him down, a lesson she'd learned from past mistakes. She'd let the elusive Kayle escape with his silly excuses too many times before and regretted it later. But now it was different; there was a house at stake here.

Kayle didn't answer. The scum coated water in the pan under the sink reminded him of the house in Monroe. It could be scrubbed clean, but it would always be tainted. Maybe she didn't notice anything weird about that place yesterday, but he sure did.

''Well, Kayle?'' She wasn't letting go.

''What made you faint?'' he quickly asked, changing the subject. Erica wasn't the fainting type and it bothered him a lot. Either it had something to do with the house or . . . ''You ain't pregnant again?'' She was kind of sickly when she carried the other four.

Christ! This was all he needed, another kid. He narrowed his eyes and looked at her abdomen, but it was hard to tell in those tight jeans he was so fond of.

''I had my tubes tied, right after Katie, don't you remember? You wanted it done, Kayle. In fact, you insisted! But then you do have a knack for remembering only what you want to—nothing else.''

Her fainting spell had nothing to do with pregnancy, she thought, but she wished it had. Then it would've been easier to understand. She closed her eyes and shuddered as if the truth was more than she could bear. There was an open window over the sink where cool night breezes were lifting the curtains upright. She rose slowly to her feet and closed it.

''I'm waiting for an answer. What made you faint?'' Now he was the one holding on, pressing for the

truth, pretending he really cared why she fainted.
Bastard, she cursed to herself, her back still to him.
He was searching for an excuse to put her on the spot
for a change, to be the one doing the interrogating.
Anything to call attention away from himself and how
he was breaking his promise.

"It was hot upstairs," she lied, turning to face him.
But she'd lied for a good reason. How could she
explain it to Kayle when she barely understood
herself. Everyone knew there was no such thing as an
invisible spirit who climbed stairs, and wore heavy
boots so you could hear them. "I remember . . . my
jeans were sticking to my body, my hair was
wringing—"

"We ain't taking that house then if it's so fucking
hot you faint."

Erica saw the house slipping away. She had
substituted a lie for the truth and lost. But either way,
the result would've been the same.

"We could install ceiling fans upstairs."

"Yeah, sure. Make plans to spend my dough before
we even move in."

"Mr. Wittaker has another house on Evergreen—"

"I told you, if we didn't take this one, I wasn't
fucking running all over the goddamn Island looking
at others!"

This bullshit was getting to him. First it was the
house on Longacre Drive in Monroe, then another
house on Evergreen Drive in Monroe. Next she'd
probably be dragging him thirty or so miles down to
Farmingdale to look at a *cream puff!*

And just maybe . . . each house was as spooky as the
last . . .

"It was this house or nothing, remember?"

Kayle's statement cemented her suspicions; he was
ready to back out no matter how much she argued or
how good her arguments were. The idea of a firm
commitment was beyond him. She saw her dreams
shattered, the childrens'. But it wouldn't happen

without her giving it one last try.

"I'll call Mr. Wittaker in the morning." She was still standing by the sink. Her nerves at a pitch.

"And tell him what?" Kayle wanted to know.

"That if he can get rid of the odor, and do something about the ventilation upstairs, we'll take the house."

She shuddered again and tried not to think about what took place on the top landing of the house yesterday. How it walked through her, and around her, and enjoyed her body immensely, because basically she knew the entire incident never could've happened.

Kayle narrowed his dark eyes threateningly, but said nothing. He didn't care if she called Wittaker or not, or what the terms were. He was afraid to go back there.

"Look at how we're living," she continued as if there had been no break in her line of thought. It was a desperate bid to make Kayle understand her point. "This place's collapsing on our heads. There's mice and roaches. The plumbing doesn't work half the time. *Or* the electricity."

Then, as if to strike at his conscience, she added, "The boys are sleeping in the living room. It's not right."

"At least they got a bed," Kayle didn't care. He lit a cigarette and made a hissing sound when he exhaled. "At least they know where they're gonna sleep nights."

Erica was expecting this, she could've said the words along with him, verbatim. The elusive Kayle often brought up his past. However, he only told her as much as he wanted her to know, which was very little. Then he'd stop cold, leaving a veil of secrecy over the rest. But she was ready for him.

"Sure. We'll stay here. In this palace. If it's good enough for you, and the mice and roaches, then Heaven knows, it's certainly good enough for the children and me." She pounded the table with her fist in a fit of frustration.

"You know what you are, Kayle? You're a selfish bastard, that's what. You only think of yourself and I'm sick of it, and damn sick of you!"

Kayle was tempted to hit her, except he wasn't that kind of a man. He's seen his old man do it to his mother a hundred times or more and swore he'd be different. Now he was fighting with everything in him to keep his vow.

He grabbed his cigarettes and got up, knocking over his chair, and went on down the hall to his bedroom. For spite, he slammed the door behind him, not caring at this point if he woke the kids. Erica was a bitch, always starting with him, telling him how selfish he was. And the worst part of all was that she'd been right. He *was* a selfish bastard, grabbing what he could and holding on. But Erica never had to fight and scrounge for a damn thing when she was growing up. She couldn't possibly know what it was like.

And besides, this time he wasn't acting selfish and he wasn't afraid of a commitment. This time—"Admit it, asshole," he cursed in an angry whisper. "You're backing out because you're afraid!"

He shivered then because it was cold and damp in his bedroom. There were heavy winds blowing outside, and the walls were paper thin. The place was a real shithouse. Still, he had to accept what he had and stay here, in this dump. It was too awful to even think about buying that house.

That house was weird.

Weird? Yes, weird was a good word for what happened on those steps yesterday.

But, no! Nothing happened.

Ohhh yes!

Someone passed him on the steps when he went down to break up the fight between Katie and Sam. Someone! He felt the sensation of a body brushing up against his, then he was pushed by two angry hands because he was probably in the way, pushing him hard too, slammed him against the railing. He damn near fell down the stairs.

Flushed with indignation, Kayle was tempted to ball up his fist and give it to them good, or shove them back, or something . . .

But it was impossible, he didn't see anyone. There was no one to shove back. No one! Now how could he explain this to Erica? Erica was sensible and intelligent compared to him, she'd never believe his story. She'd swear he was just copping out, that he just didn't want to buy her a house. In fact, she felt that way now. But it wasn't so.

He was pushed! And now he was afraid to go back there, and afraid to admit to his fears.

Kayle laid across his bed and lit another cigarette, the glow of the match casting eerie shadows in the dark. He exhaled and imagined the smoke rising in a thick, white column over his head. But there was an awful taste in his mouth, his tongue felt thick and dry. He snubbed out his cigarette.

Being pushed was nothing new, he reflected, and huddled into a fetal position. He'd been pushed all his life; shoved, thrown into a corner, discarded like excess trash. There was never enough food to eat, and he'd slept on the floor because he was afraid to go to bed.

His mother!

Kayle buried his face in a pillow and tried to hold back, but there was so many scars; some barely visible, like the one on his cheek; others that went deeper; rejection, neglect, despair. He felt tears coming, heard himself cry out and knew then he'd have to bow to Erica's wishes.

Rejection was a scary thing; it was like some huge, tentacled monster that ate at your insides and left you feeling weak and spent. It was with him constantly, had control of his manhood, and gave him migraines.

Kayle couldn't take any more.

Erica was all he had left, all he cared about. She was the only one who had stood by him this far. It was better to live in fear in that house than to have her turn her back on him.

Erica had to be led down a different trail. Beautiful, sweet, wonderful Erica had to be manipulated into loving him forever.

Erica took a rag and wiped off the table. There were tears in her eyes, but not from happiness or despair. She was angry, more so than she'd been in a long time. Kayle *was* a selfish bastard, just as she'd said. Now he was leaving it up to her to break the news to the kids. He was always sticking her with the rotten jobs he lacked the balls to do himself.

She emptied the pan under the sink, the rust colored water forming a whirlpool when it ran down the drain. That was her life with Kayle, she thought: a whirlpool of empty promises, always being suckered into believing his fantasies, and everything eventually wound up going down the drain. And all she had left was the scum coating on top.

Now it was her job to tell the kids.

She considered bringing them into the kitchen here, and telling them one at a time. Then she decided it would be better if she told all four at once. Why prolong the agony for herself? Why say it over and over when once was bad enough? They couldn't have the house; it was simple.

But was it really that simple? She was so tired of living with a fraud.

Erica wondered if she'd ever get used to it. Before she had left home to live with Kayle, she had everything she wanted and more. Mommy and Daddy gave her the universe on a string, while Kayle gave her nothing but empty promises. So why had she stayed with him for ten years?

Her anger began to subside at that point and she

was able to think without disgust obliterating her point of view. She stayed because she owed him a lot. It was a hard thing to admit, but it was the truth.

Before Kayle, Erica had been a whimpering idiot, an emotional cripple, afraid of people. Her parents had stumped her intellectual growth simply by loving her too much and pampering her beyond reason. They told her she was a delicate, sensitive child, then they literally wrapped her in cellophane. As a result, Erica spent most of her time cooped up in her bedroom listening to records because, somewhere along the way, she'd lost the courage to go out and mingle.

Thus, she had no friends her own age to do the things with that kids usually did when they were together, such as, sharing secrets, copying homework. Birthday and holidays were the worst of all. Her parents managed to turn those events into a *menage a trois* of sorts. It was always the same three-some; Mommy, Daddy and Erica. And since both of them shared the same possessive love for Erica, she often compared their relationship to a *menage a trois.*

Then she met Kayle, and it was instant love. Kayle was strong and forceful; he guided her, manipulated her, and in less than a month, helped her to sever the umbilical cord. She never forgot. Kayle removed the protective plastic coating and restored her freedom. He turned her into an independent free-spirited woman. No monetary value could be placed on what Kayle had given her in terms of dignity.

She got herself another beer and popped the tab while her thoughts drifted back to the children. She'd tell them about the house right after breakfast tomorrow morning, when their stomachs were full and they were bound to be more receptive. She did, however, expect a bad scene; tears, bitterness, the whole bit. And Sam, of course, was sure to take it the hardest. He already blamed himself as it was.

But those kids had to be made to understand!

Maybe Kayle was unable to afford the house; maybe he had only pretended he could to save face. After all, he was the man in charge around here, the main provider. And if there wasn't enough money coming in, then it had to be his fault. Given Kayle's egocentric personality, he would be sure to use pretense to salvage his faltering pride.

Poor Kayle, she thought, the economy was so bad, times so hard, it wasn't his fault they constantly ran short of money. She decided to mention this to him over coffee in the morning, and perhaps make him feel better about not being able to afford the house. She sat down at the table to finish her beer.

Henry Wittaker was forced to delay the funeral for several days; at least until the County Coronor's office was ready to release Bess' body, or what was left of it after the sons-of-bitches got through peeling back her flesh and slicing her every which way but sideways. They were looking for clues as to what killed her, they said at the Coroner's office.

Well, then the stupid morons should've asked Henry. Henry knew. It was them demon bastards at that house in Monroe who killed Bess, or one of them at least. The materialized one, most likely, for he was the most dangerous of them all.

Henry was in the den making funeral arrangements over the phone when a horrible thought stabbed at his already pounding skull. Suppose Bess' dying wasn't enough to satiate the deadly, vengeful appetites of those . . . fiends? Suppose they wanted more? His kids perhaps, just to watch Henry suffer through this agony again? Well, they'd better not try, he thought, they'd just better not try.

Henry's thinking had been far from realistic the past few days. He'd been grieving for Bess with little or no thought left for Buddy and Patricia. However, this morning he rose from his self-imposed trance and noticed that the children were also grieving. And yet, they had hardly any tears for Bess because she was dead and beyond help; whereas Henry was alive, and his dark melancholia had become their main concern.

Well, now he had to think of them also and forget Bess for the time being. At least until the wake and subsequent funeral when there would be no choice. But, for the moment, the children had to be considered. They had to be told the truth. They had to be forwarned in the event of his own untimely death. Henry would tell them that the ageless entities in the house in Monroe were responsible for killing Bess and might kill him too. Those murdering bastards!

And his children had to be told now. Hell, he'd spent the entire day on the phone and there was little time to waste.

Henry heard footsteps that sounded as though they were coming from the hall just outside of the den and he smiled. The kids were checking on him; at least they were concerned. He started to cross to the door, to tell them he was fine, but he stopped dead when he realized the footsteps were coming from below, down in the basement. Another rat, perhaps?

He was confused and thought about it for a moment. Buddy and Patricia never went down there . . . never! It couldn't be them.

Henry had warned them years ago, after he and Bess bought this house and moved in, that he basement was off-limits. He kept sharp tools down there, and the boiler room was next to his workshop; too many things to hurt them.

Besides, what if they were in the basement and a mop fell over and a creature with red eyes chased them? His legs were wobbly, he needed a drink. He found some scotch in the liquor cabinet and poured himself a shot. He took it all in one swallow. It wasn't Buddy and Patricia who were strolling around in the basement, that was for damn sure. Then who? Oh, God!

The answer was clear; it was the creature who'd

followed him home the first time he visited the house in Monroe. Oh, God! Henry had nearly forgotten, it lived here now. Henry had no choice at this point but to sell his house immediately, to take his children as far away as he could, to China if that would keep them safe. And himself as well. Any one of them could be next.

The *rat* was walking around in circles just below his feet.

He poured himself another scotch and swallowed it as fast as the first. The idea of selling this house and running was a bizarre joke, and Henry knew it. He'd studied enough about these matters to realize there was no sense in him even attempting to try and outrun those bastards. Once they had their hooks in your flesh, that was it! They would follow Henry for the rest of his life, but maybe not his kids!

Buddy and Patricia had to be warned, had to be forced to move without Henry. But how? They'd protest! He crossed to the door—something followed his movements below—then he headed for the kitchen. He wanted to speak to his kids without delay, to tell them about his knowledge of the occult world and how those creatures might be after him now. He especially wanted to tell them to get out and forget they even had a father.

Buddy and Patricia were in the kitchen eating dinner; their whispered conversation came to an abrupt end when Henry walked in. Henry's face had a bit more color, but there was a craziness in his eyes that disturbed them.

Patricia rose and took him by the arm, and all he could do was stare at her. She was so like Bess it unnerved him at times. She led him to a seat and set a cup of coffee in front of him. She looked worried. "You okay, Daddy?"

"It's cool," Henry rasped. "I got it together now."

"All right!" Buddy shouted, hugging him across the

table while tears rimmed his eyes. "Geez, you had us scared."

And those bastards back at that house, along with the one who lived here, had *him* scared, he thought.

"Look, kids. We have to talk. There's something you should be aware of." Stay cool and do this right, he told himself. There's no need to enhance their fears.

But Patricia's mind was traveling in another direction. "You haven't eaten since yesterday, Daddy. I'll fix you some dinner first. Then we can chat." She moved in the same slow, sensual way as Bess had, before Bess became ill. He watched the sway of her hips, her erect posture. She even had Bess' hair; long, auburn tresses that rode in waves across her back when she walked. And like Bess, she was about to become a part of the vengeance of the beast.

"Uh . . . Don't bother, coffee's fine. I'd rather we talked and got it over with."

Patricia shot a look at Buddy. There was no mistaking the concern that passed between them. Well, he thought, if they think I'm crazy now, what will they think when I'm finished? He closed his eyes and prayed for the courage to go on.

Something walked beneath his feet in the basement below.

Nobody seemed to notice it but him.

Was he crazy?

Was it all a dream?

No, no no!

It wasn't a dream and it wasn't caused by a psychotic state of mind. His children were unaware because Henry hadn't enlightened them yet, hadn't taught them to listen for those sort of noises. And he hadn't told them about his first visit to the house in Monroe, when one of those bastards followed him home.

"Before I get to the point, let me give you a bit of

background." Henry was trying to keep this on an impersonal, highly educational level. Crazy people never made sense. This was going to be a testament to his sanity.

"And please, bear with me. This isn't easy to explain. Now, how much do you know about ghosts . . . specters?"

Henry could've answered that one himself, they knew about as much as the average person did. Ghosts were pale, shadowy apparitions that only appeared in movies, never in real life. They almost always lived in old haunted mansions and they wore sheets that flapped in the wind, while they flew around yelling BOO and dragged chains behind them. Ghosts were a joke.

"Are you serious?" Buddy half-smiled for the first time in days. "Dad . . . Ghosts?"

"Yes, ghosts." Henry *was* cool, had to be cool. He wasn't nuts, not yet anyway.

Patricia nudged Buddy under the table. She still had that worried look about her. "What do you think we should know?"

"Uh . . . Yeah, Dad. Tell us all about it." Buddy had stopped smiling. Now they were patronizing him as if he were ready to be committed. But Henry paid it no mind. If they learned from him, then nothing else mattered.

"Okay. Now that I have your full attention, there are two types of *spirits* in this world. The first is your average ghost . . . the *disembodied* spirit of a dead person, their *soul*, so to speak. Ghosts were once living, intelligent organisms who died, mostly quite violently and quite unexpectedly.

"In other words, it isn't as though they'd suffered from a long illness and were waiting for the end to come. No. These people were taken by surprise. So, sometimes they don't realize they're dead. Therefore, by not knowing they're dead, they tend to become confused. They roam in surroundings that are familiar to them. You often hear stories about a home being haunted by someone who was killed there—''

"How do you know all this?" Buddy sounded skeptical.

But Henry remained cool. "From reading books."

"And what if they find out they're dead?"

"Then they go away. In fact, it's the best way to get rid of a ghost. Let him, or her, know they're dead."

"You two are having a conversation about ghosts. . . Christ, and my mother just died. Why are we talking about this?" For a moment, Patricia *was* Bess, her large, brown eyes so filled with concern.

"Honey," Henry began, "I'm sorry this's such a bleak reminder of your mother's death. But I'm trying to say something . . . and I must start with a background." He had to be objective and concerned with realities rather than with his own thoughts and feelings.

"Now, for the second part. The other type of spirit never was alive to begin with. And, unlike a ghost, they can be, and are, dangerous!"

Patricia shuddered visibly. "No more, Dad! That's it! I've heard enough." She got to her feet and started to leave.

Bess might not have listened either, but Patricia's actions still took Henry by surprise. Her rejection was like a slap in the face. "PATRICIA, SIT DOWN!"

But Patricia defiantly remained standing. He looked to Buddy for help, but Buddy's face was glazed over with shock. Henry had never yelled at them before. Henry's shoulders slumped forward and he almost crumpled in front of them. "Even if you think I'm crazy, listen to me. For Christ's sake . . ." He was almost pleading now, pleading with two people who were like strangers to him since their mother died. No, incorrect, he thought, since their mother was *killed*.

Patricia's face softened. She sat down and rubbed his arm, her hands trembling against his flesh. "All right, Daddy. We owe you this much at least." She was patronizing him again.

Henry sighed and continued, and managed to ignore the footsteps in the basement. "The spirits that never were alive are your demons. They've been around since time began, and they exist for nothing more than the total destruction of a human soul. They know more about you than you know about yourself, and they use this knowledge to their advantage. I'll explain this as I go on.

"These spirits are usually not seen or heard like ghosts are. They're invisible charges of static electricity floating in the air. And their voices are on the same decibel level as a dog whistle. Animals can hear them, as we cannot. For that reason, demonologists, who spend a lifetime studying these particular spirits, use cassette tapes. They *can* be heard on tape. If the spirits, or demons, as you will, choose to become visible or to be heard, they will draw power from an energy source such as heat or light."

"You mean . . . when the lights in my room flicker on and off for no reason, it could be one of them drawing power?"

Buddy was full of interest now. He even sounded as if he almost believed Henry. Or was he just pretending, was it part of an act? Henry remained undaunted, he had to.

"Exactly. Lights are powered by energy and they need this energy to materialize. Then too, you know how it feels when a room is hot in the winter, then it suddenly goes cold for no reason at all? Well, it might be one of them drawing power from a heat source. Without this energy they can't touch you or hurt you."

"Daddy. What's the point?" Patricia was growing impatient with his babblings. This was where she differed from Bess.

"The point is, this house I'm trying to sell . . . it's loaded with these . . . these sons-of-bitches. And *they* control the house and all who enter. *They control me!"*

Henry had to get up, to keep moving, so he wouldn't have to think about what he was saying. His children were lost to him at this point. He could tell by the expression on their faces. But they had to be made to understand, to be *forced* to realize their lives were in danger.

"The house is full of minor demons. Your noise makers, they slam doors and move objects." He waved his hands for emphasis. "They just try to scare you, but they're harmless." He stopped and poured himself another cup of coffee.

"There is one though who's not so harmless. I think it may be the Gate Keeper. From what I've read about him, he's the most logical one. Anyway, he's a head honcho. I wondered why he was there? He's really quite important in occult circles."

He turned to face them. "Well . . . and this is only theory, mind you, I believe he's there because the last occupant was involved in Satanism, and fooled with things he had no control over. He conjured up the Gate Keeper, then couldn't get rid of him."

"What happened to this last occupant?"

Henry detected a bit of hidden sarcasm in Buddy's tone.

"There were two couples, both Spanish, both related. The older couple, husband and wife, were scared off and ran back to Puerto Rico, leaving the house in the care of their son and his wife. Then the son ran—"

"What happened to the son's wife?"

Henry shrugged. "Who knows? She just disappeared."

But Henry did know, the truth was evident as was written in that *book*, the story ran on a parallel plane.

"They took the breath from his wife."

The book said it all. "And they took the breath from

mine too, those bastards!'' Henry was shouting, and it
brought him back to reality and away from that book.

Buddy and Patricia were looking at each other, but
not as though they were concerned. It was pity that he
detected in their brief exchange this time. They
imagined he'd gone over the edge, that his mind had
caved in under the pressure of losing Bess. Be cool, he
told himself, get it together, be nonchalant. But he
could not continue, not now, not when his children
were totally lost to him and wouldn't respond, not
even if he forced them.

"Look, kids . . . why don't we finish this up later,
when our minds are clear.''

And not on my insanity or your mother's funeral,
he thought. There was a crack in his voice, but he
went on as though they'd been discussing the weather
and not a subject as cumbersome as demons. "I'm
going to lie down. Meanwhile, please remember what
I've told you, no matter how strange it may sound,
because it's important.''

Henry left the kitchen and leaned against the door
outside for support. He heard them whispering again,
Buddy and Patricia probably talking about how crazy
he was, and how he ought to be committed. And he
heard something else as well. The footsteps were
coming closer, up the back steps to the main portion
of the house.

Henry had talked about *them*, had angered *them*,
and by revealing the truth, he had forced their hand.
He imagined he'd given the spirits no choice now but
to retaliate in the form of another warning; like the
warning he'd received when they killed Bess.

Sweat laced his forehead. Buddy and Patricia surely
had to be told the full story now. What's more, he had
to get his kids out of this house! Then he thought
about the farcical scene he'd starred in just a few
minutes ago, and wondered how he was supposed to
convince them he was telling the truth? Maybe they
would be more receptive after Bess' funeral.

5

Erica was still sitting in the kitchen, engrossed in thought, when the phone rang, wedging a crack in the stillness around her. She stared at it and heard the wind pick up outside. She shuddered as though a prowler had just broken into the house. It was an intrusion, and she couldn't bring herself to answer it. But the phone rang again, louder this time. She was afraid it would wake Kayle, and the man had to get up early for work. He needed his sleep.

"Hello," she began, and looped the cord around her fingers in a nervous gesture when she heard the voice on the other end. It was Aaron Pace.

Erica imagined him standing in a phone booth, leaning against the frame of the door, one leg crossed kind of casually in front of the other, a smile turning up the corners of his mouth in a way that she found arrogant . . . and appealing.

"Kayle's asleep," she heard herself say and wondered why. After all, the call was for her. She placed the phone under her chin and took a swallow of beer. "What do you want?" She wanted to hang up because this wasn't right. It couldn't continue, but she held on and listened instead.

"Oh, this's new. Now I need an excuse to call."

She knew he was smiling again, his pale blue eyes

full of mischief, a shock of blond hair hanging in his face.

"Kayle buy you that house? Or is it up to me?"

You can't even afford a phone, she thought, but kept it to herself because it was too cruel a thing to say to him. "We're thinking about it."

"Really. Bet he doesn't buy it." There was a pause, then, "You sound kind of strange. Like you don't seem so hot to talk to me right now."

No, she wasn't, not at this point anyway. It had been different, though, in the beginning, at the start of their friendship. At the time, Erica couldn't go a day without hearing his voice, or wanting the feel of his hands touching her, caressing her body.

But, over the past few months, she'd begun to think with her head and not her heart. This was not love, it was cheap and dirty. And what if Kayle found out? What if he told the children their mother was a whore? Kayle would've felt that way about her, that she was a whore. Then Erica would have to face those kids every single day for the rest of her life and know what they thought of her.

Still, something stirred inside of her whenever Aaron Pace called, like now.

"Say something," he prodded. "What's up?"

"I never want to see you again." After it was said, she refused to believe those words had come from her. Oh, God, she wanted to meet him someplace, to have his body on hers; dominating her, rattling her senses, making her achieve the ultimate orgasm as Kayle never had. But then, poor Kayle, she thought, she hadn't been honest with him. His affairs had been open. Kayle had seemed at times to challenge her to end them. But her affair was different, hers had been behind closed doors, sneaky. She felt sick.

"Do you hear me? I never want to see you again." Harsh words spoken to the man she once thought she loved.

Aaron said nothing at first, but when he did speak,

his voice was tinged with bitterness. "I told you, Erica. If you ever tried to break it off, I'd give Kayle a lesson in biology, remember?"

She listened to the wind outside rustling through the trees. This was awful, it was ugly, and she longed to be anywhere but on the other end of this phone. Good Christ, did she have the courage to follow through? And yet, she kept telling herself that it was over!

"You can tell Kayle anything you want. But he'll never believe you."

Aaron laughed. "Oh yeah. I keep forgetting. It's an insult to his manhood. And Kayle's too much of a man—"

"He's more of a man than you'll ever be," she blurted. But it was a lie; she knew it and Aaron did, too.

"Then tell Kayle to ball you and see what you get out of it. Maybe next time you won't have to pretend it's good."

"I don't pretend all of the time."

Like yesterday morning, before they looked at the house, she'd had sex with Kayle and enjoyed it, once the cruelty stopped.

"Bullshit!" He paused then and she heard him sigh with disgust. "Listen, I'll call you tomorrow."

"No. Never again."

But he ignored her. "Think this over . . . carefully. We'll talk about it some more, after you've had a good night's sleep." There was something solemn, almost threatening, in his voice.

She stared at the phone and cursed herself for not being more aggressive, for being such a wimp when it came to Aaron. She should have called his bluff and dared him to tell Kayle about their affair. As a matter of fact, she should've told him to drop dead!

But there had been rumors once, circulating around town . . . about Aaron and his first wife: Lorraine went to California with him and nobody heard from her since. Did he kill her? Where was she?

She shuddered and took another sip of beer. Water was dripping steadily into the pan under the sink; it suddenly sounded so loud she wanted to scream. She braced herself and poured the rest of her beer down the drain. She wasn't afraid of Aaron. Besides, most rumors were gross exaggerations of the truth, like fairy tales. Only, this was right out of Grimm's!

Aaron would not hurt her!

Still, he had her by the short hairs and she knew it. And now he was mad enough to use this to his advantage. He might even try and force her to see him more often, or force her to do things Erica had refused to before. She closed her eyes and shuddered again.

Aaron was inventive, always wanting her to try daring, new, and exotic positions when they had sex. But some of them hurt. Then, there was the time he wanted her to put her mouth between his legs and kiss him. She tried, she honestly did, but it was so repulsive she gagged. And Aaron never asked again, mainly because he claimed he loved her.

But that was then, and this was now. She tried to dump him, she put a crack in his massive ego, she'd have to pay. The wind outside howled through the eaves in the house and it sounded like a dying animal. There was a draft on her back and she felt cold.

Oh, God, it was blackmail time. Aaron wanted to give Kayle a lesson in biology. And when Kayle found out the truth, he'd kill Erica and himself as well. There was so much more to her relationship with Aaron; it was more than just an affair. She felt sorry for Kayle, and ashamed inside. Kayle was a rotten bastard at times, true, but he never minced his words or hid behind deceit.

Like the afternoon several months ago when she quarreled with Kayle and took the kids to her mother's, vowing never to come back. But something happened after she got there. For the first time in her life she had regrets about running out on a fight. She realized it would've been much better to have stayed with Kayle, and to have patched things up, than to have left when there was this enormous amount of hostility between them.

Erica went home, alone. Thank God she'd had the common sense to leave the children with her mother.

The house was quiet when she walked in, and it made her feel uneasy. Kayle was usually home; he seldom went out by himself. But no . . . It wasn't absolutely quiet. There were sounds drifting in the air, strange sounds for *one* person to be making, especially when he was alone. She traced those sounds to her bedroom, the door was open a crack. Kayle was in bed with some woman, their bodies locked in heat. Kayle was laughing and whispering, the woman was groaning.

Erica's soul raged with his arrogance. He'd actually brought a woman there, into her home, and he didn't care if he was caught or not. But, at least he was being honest!

She remembered screaming at him and telling him what an uncaring pig he was, and that she was leaving, for good this time. But Kayle wouldn't have it that way. He begged her not to go, and said he loved her, she was the best thing that had ever happened to him . . .

The best thing? "Oh, Kayle! I'm not. I'm really not." She put her hands to her face and cried. "I called you a pig!" Well, what the hell was she, something pure and wonderful? Only Kayle *thought* she was, and that was the part that hurt!

Henry Wittaker stood in the front yard in the dark and stared at the small, single bulb over the front door, vainly trying to throw more light than it was capable of. Henry's eyes were glazed over with pain. Not a pain you could see or feel, but it was there, an old familiar hurt.

He recalled suffering a similar pain when his
mother died, leaving his father with a slew of kids.
But the feeling faded after a year or so.

Then his father passed away and the pain struck
again, a feeling of irreplaceable loss, of confusion
about death, of the finality of the grave. He saw
strangers in satin-lined coffins; their eyes closed, their
mouths sewn shut, their faces obliterated by
mortician's makeup. And there was always a nameplate saying that Henry had known them.

Impossible!

They were corpses, hideous shells reeking of
embalming fluid, and Henry couldn't imagine they'd
ever lived in the same town, let alone the same house,
as he, or that he'd once loved them. No, not those
corpses, those lifeless, three-dimensional, cardboard
figures!

It was the same with Bess.

He couldn't recall the sound of her voice when she
laughed. Like the time he'd stood in the hall outside
of the bathroom and howled like a mad dog to lure
Buddy out. It was late at night; the boy had been in
there for such a long time. Henry had to pee real bad,
and this had been his plan to painlessly extract the
boy from the bathroom, and to have a little fun while
he was doing it. And it worked; but it backfired, too.

Buddy had been scared half out of his wits by
Henry's mad dog impersonation. He ran out of the
bathroom and threw the door open with such force it
slammed into Henry's mid-section. Henry went down
on his knees, damn near peed on the floor. Bess was
there, and she laughed.

But the sound of her laughter was beyond him at
the moment, as was the feel of her in the night, before
she'd taken ill; her breath sweet and hot on his face,
her body soft and supple. Those things were forgotten, dismissed by pain, had happened centuries ago it
seemed.

And yet, he was able to recall, with vivid accuracy,

the corpse in the coffin with the nameplate that lied and swore she had once been Bess Wittaker. Her thin face, with the skin so tight it was almost skeletal, had been dabbed with too much rouge. Her mouth, stretched into a frozen smile by a mortician's hands, had been painted a whore's red! Bess hated the color and never wanted to be caught *dead* in it. There was too much gray in her hair.

Henry pulled his collar up around his neck to protect it from the wind. A tree on the side of the house was swaying heavily, its branches, resembling twisted fingers, scratched against the windows on the second floor. He didn't even know why he was standing in front of this wretched house!

He remembered the deafening quiet at home; Buddy and Patricia, sullen and brooding, the empty bedroom upstairs, the hollow pain that kept screaming at him and telling him Bess was gone! He'd gotten into his car and had driven in circles for hours and had finally wound up here.

Dead leaves and sand were swirling in the front yard; somewhere in the distance a dog barked. Henry shuddered and listened to the wind assaulting trees, and the gate near the garage that groaned hideously when it opened, driven by the wind perhaps? Of course!

The light over the door flickered.

He knew he should've been afraid because of the significance of that flickering light, one of them was energizing itself. But Henry wasn't afraid, not this time. He was perfectly calm, no shaking hands, no palpitations in his heart.

He crossed the yard to close the gate, his feet sinking into a soft mire of ground where there used to be grass, before the house destroyed itself. Something small and gray brushed against his leg, then hurried out of sight. A wild rabbit perhaps? Henry stopped walking. The branches on the tree were moving faster now, its fingers shrieking over glass like chalk on a

blackboard. Small droplets of moisture fell on his face
and they were warm on his flesh, too warm to be
water. Blood was warm . . .

But Henry still wasn't afraid, not even when the
gate slammed shut by itself, not even when the
clicking noise it made seemed louder than it should
have, not even when the light bulb continued to
flicker in a staccato-like rhythm.

Henry ignored the theatrical tricks, the special
effects being provided by the occupants of the house
solely for his entertainment. He didn't have the time
to dwell on nonsense. There were questions to be
answered, so much to ask. Still, he found himself
thinking about that horrid book again.

"A chorus of creatures with harsh, gravelly
voices told him about death, promised him pain,
and took the breath from his wife."

They kept their promise, they took the breath from
his wife. Then they delivered their pain by destroying
the section of his brain that controlled his emotions. It
was like having a frontal lobotomy: he felt no grief, no
fear, only pain. *They promised him pain!* And that
wasn't an emotion; it was an after-effect, although not
drug induced, from having spent three days viewing
the body of a white-faced, hand-painted corpse; a
gruesome looking thing in a white, satin-lined coffin.

The nameplate said it was Bess Wittaker.

Henry turned and was able, for the first time, to
stare back at the multitudes fighting for space at the
side window, without wanting to run. A myriad
number of ancient faces, each was more hideous than
the next. *Bastards*, he wanted to scream, *you don't
belong here.* And yet, Henry was the enemy, the one
who didn't belong in this yard, in front of a house
they controlled. He was the enemy!

"Created in the image of a God they hated

above all else. And what was created in that
image must not be allowed to survive!"

But why Bess? It was a thought running through his
mind.

"WHY NOT!" was the reply.

A countless number of misshapen forms crowded
the living room, waiting their turn to get near the
window to look at Henry, their eyes insanely red,
brimming with an insatiable hatred for this craven
image of a God they hated.

"BESS WAS GOOD. SHE CAME LIKE AN OLD
WHORE!"

A trick, Henry thought, strike where it hurts the
most. But he felt no anger and could not be stirred to
foolish action, and he ignored the sound of the front
door when it opened and closed behind him. These
were fagot demons, devils of the lowest order, foul
smelling lumps of shit! They were incapable of
murder, not having been sanctified by their Lord and
Master. These were the usual house haunters, the
things that went bump in the night; they flung objects
and whispered obscenties. *Fuck them*, he thought.

Henry was after bigger game, the one who killed
Bess. And for one second he stopped to wonder why
the heavy artillery had been employed. Why had an
ancient evil one, with powers so great it boggled the
imagination, been sent to take possession of an
average home?

There were footsteps behind him. What was the big
deal here, he wondered and turned, his lips drawn
into a frozen smile when he faced the Gate Keeper.

Kayle's dream had been tormentingly confusing
since he'd first visited the house in Monroe.
However, tonight was different. Tonight he dreamed
of his past, of one horrible event, clearer now than
when it had actually taken place.

He dreamed of being a young boy again, back in the

living room of the old house they owned in Huntington. It was summer time, but the windows in the house were closed. His father and mother were arguing, and they always closed the windows, and the shutters too, so the neighbors wouldn't hear what was being said.

He could almost feel the air in that house on his face. It was hot and stifling and thick with hatred, especially behind the sofa where he lay hidden, his body curled into a fetal position. Kayle hid there a lot because it frightened him when they fought, yelling and slamming things. Then too, his father would soon tire of the argument, usually around the time he felt he was losing, and he'd use his fists to settle it.

Of course his mother deserved to be hit now and then, in Kayle's opinion. Hell, she started most of the fights and she had some sharp mouth on her. And yet, she was still his mother; he couldn't stand to hear her cry.

On this particular afternoon they were in full swing, shouting at each other, using the same old insults, honed to a fine cutting edge. It was as if their words had been memorized from a script that had been indelibly etched in their minds. Only, this time something was different. His father made a statement Kayle had never heard before. It threw his mother off and she missed her cue. His father had said—he could barely remember exactly how it went—but it sounded like, "Are you forgetting the truth? I *had* to marry you?"

His mother cried then, and without being slapped, and his father stormed from the house. Kayle stayed behind the sofa, he knew what was coming next. The cupboard in the kitchen creaked, she was searching for the bottle she kept hidden there. She meant to get drunk; nasty drunk and mean. Then, soon after, one of those men, whose names he had trouble remembering, would drop by for a drink.

Mother usually took the man upstairs to her bedroom, but not before warning Kayle to, "Keep your mouth shut about this!"

Sometimes he laid behind the sofa for what seemed like hours, crying because he was hungry and there was nothing to eat in the house; plenty of booze, but no food. At those times he found himself wondering how much more he could take. His life was a living nightmare.

Then he woke up.

The bedroom was dark; it must've been somewhere around midnight. He lit a cigarette and gave silent thanks for having awakened when he did; the worst part of his dream was yet to come. Somehow he'd been spared years ago from reliving the pain of it in his sleep. He was, of course, able to recall in vivid detail what happened next, but it wasn't so bad when he was awake.

The man who shared his mother's bed that night had been drunk and abusive. Nick was his name, the only one Kayle could remember as if this happened yesterday. Nick was the tough bastard with the pencil-thin moustache and the brass knuckles. Nick was loud, and talked nasty to Kayle, drunk or sober. Nick was the psychopath who loved to deliver pain.

Nick had hit his mother. Kayle heard the sound of flesh striking flesh, heard her cry and quickly ran upstairs to protect her. His father hit her, that was enough. This guy had no right.

Kayle shuddered then and rolled on his side to stare at Erica as she slept. He'd never told her the truth about the scar on his face and wondered if she even cared.

This Nick obviously had heard Kayle coming up the stairs and he was ready for him. He hid behind the bedroom door with his brass knuckles in place, and as soon as Kayle stepped over the threshold, Nick delivered one hard, dizzying punch to the side of his face.

Kayle hit the floor and grabbed his cheek. There

was a long flap of skin hanging almost to his chin, his
jaw was slack. He knew it must've been broken. His
head buzzed with pain. He laid where he was,
huddled into a ball, and watched his mother step over
his body, her face a veil of indifference. Nick
extended his arm, she took it and they left.

Kayle laid where he was until his father came
home, stumbling drunk, and took him to a hospital.

Kayle's philosophy on women changed at that
point. He'd never abuse one, he'd always make sure
she had plenty to eat, and he'd never get nasty drunk
and frighten a woman. It was just that he saw no
reason to marry one just because she'd gotten
knocked up. Why marry a cow when you can get the
milk for nothing? His father had made the mistake of
obligating himself to a woman he could've screwed
anytime he wanted to, a mistake Kayle wouldn't
repeat if possible.

"Like not obligating myself to you, Erica," he whispered, reaching for the warmth of her body in the
night.

Kirsten Larsen was asleep in a hotel room in
Denver, Colorado, when she dreamed of Henry and
the Gate Keeper. Kirsten was well acquainted with
the Gate Keeper. He was an old enemy who had
sought many many times in the past to stop her
intrusions, her constant interference in matters that
didn't concern her, such as the total possession of a
human soul, a most worthy prize to a demonic being.

The two were engulfed in darkness, standing near
the front of a house. She found the darkness disturbing; things lurked in that darkness, unspeakable
horrors, creatures who snapped at your heels and
sucked the breath from your pores, and who feasted
on the thin slivers of your nerves. The man was
ignoring their presence, his attention focused on the
moving, heaving, dangerous semi-mass in front of
him.

Then, for one instant, Kirsten stopped watching them and concentrated on the house because it played an important role in this scenario. The house was an entity; a thing that had real existence, had the power to think for itself, and the house was filled with a number of enemies. *Her* enemies.

She scanned the interior, heard the heartbeats in the walls, saw a staircase leading to—

"No!" Her voice was shrill in the near silence of her dream. "Mustn't go up there . . . never!" But it was just as dangerous to stay downstairs. There was a room off to one side of the kitchen, a den. Yes, it had once been a den. Then it had been converted to a chapel. Kirsten saw the blue walls, the black onyx altar, the Satanic Bible.

And there was something else . . .

Kirsten moaned. That room contained the black hole, the pulse of the house, an entrance way to . . . Oh, sweet Jesus!

And the Gate Keeper was in charge.

The man in her dreams was screaming now, shouting words that meant nothing to her, words laced with challenge. The fool!

"No," she moaned. "No challenges, no dares, back off. They thrive on challenges." But the man was unable to hear her and he persisted. She sensed his angry pain, saw the empty void in his heart, felt the recent loss he'd suffered.

The Gate Keeper was amused; the muscles in his heavy jaw were frozen into a grin. Large and partly formed into shape, there was something psychotic in the eyes; a madness long out of control, the look of a thousand eons of silent battle, of the unsuccessful use of trickery and deceit turned inward.

And Kirsten knew why he was so very angry and dangerous.

As was foretold in the Book of Revelations, the Master Beast and his followers had been cast from the Heavens without being stripped of their powers. But those powers were useless unless the almighty human welcomed them with open arms and said, ''Come to me. I accept your ways.'' That was our protection from God.

The Gate Keeper was a timeworn soldier, his id badly scarred by the adhesions of defeat and human rejection. However, this time he swore it would be different, this time he would win. Still, it wasn't the man he was after. No! A bigger prize. A woman, for with the woman, came her children . . .

Kirsten woke up. But it wasn't fair. She wanted to see more, *had* to see more. Where was this taking place? Her vision drifted so far at times it was difficult to narrow it down. Was in New York? Detroit? Where?

She slung her legs over the side of the bed and reached for a cigarette. Her hands ached from the strain. It would come to her eventually, the location of the house, but would she see it in time to stop the worst from happening? She felt a sense of urgency. There were strong powers present in that house.

She moaned with frustration and clutched at the nape of her nightgown. Sweat ran into the area between her breasts. She took a drag from her cigarette and noticed the old familiar tremors in her hand, always the same reaction when those bastards showed up in her dreams.

She got up and went to the bathroom and had to lean on the sink for support. The faucets in *that house* turned on and off by themselves, and the toilet flushed as though triggered by invisible hands. All part of the game, her old friends were showing their stuff. She turned on the tap and splashed cold water on her face, but it wasn't enough. Her head still ached from the pain of her visions.

Somewhere out there, someone needed her help. But where, damnit, where?

She glanced at her reflection in the mirror over the sink and winced. There were lines in her face, bags under her eyes, her pupils were dilated. Those rotten pills had left their mark, she thought, their residue. She considered taking another one to quell the throbbing in her leg and in her temples, then quickly left the bathroom without it.

The limp was barely noticeable now. The leg, thought it hurt, pained her less than it had in the past. It had been six years now since it happened, since she's screamed in the night, six years since her voice had been riddled with unbearable agony—the blood on her face, her skull.

At the time, her voice had sounded foreign to her when she screamed, as if she had been outside of her own body laying witness to a tragedy. It did happen to someone else, didn't it? And yet, she couldn't keep up the lie, she was the one who had screamed.

Sometimes those screams came back to her, although she'd long forgotten how intense the pain was, the burning agony of her open flesh against concrete. Whatever she was going through now, it was nothing compared to what she'd suffered in the beginning.

She sat on the side of the bed with her shoulders slumped forward and stared at a worn spot in the rug. How far away was it this time? Would her body hold up? She had to make the trip by herself, there was no one else . . .

The bed went down on the other side and the springs creaked as if someone had just climbed into it. But that was impossible, she was alone. Still, she was used to this, it had happened before, so many times. She heard labored breathing and felt the vibrations of someone moving across the bed to reach her, and it caused the hairs on her neck to bristle.

This was just a trick, another illusion, a *gift* from the Gate Keeper. For surely he knew she'd been a witness to the drama outside of that house. He knew she'd seen and felt his thoughts and was as compelled to interfere this time as she'd been in the past. And, as always, he was trying to forewarn her.

"STAY AWAY!"

His words, his voice drifted to her from behind as something huge and heavy crawled across the bed. She placed her hands over her face to stifle her screams. Musn't let him know you're afraid, she told herself. But he knows. He's already taken a grand tour of your mind and he knows!

It can't hurt me! Not if I don't let it!

This was no different from before when objects levitated and flew across the room to strike her, objects flung by invisible forces. And not by the usual poltergeists, mind you. Not harmless, bedeviled, little creatures whose sole existence was to cause mischief. Oh, no. Those unseen terrors doing the throwing were trying to hurt her.

This was no different from before when a sudden indentation in a sofa told her that *someone* had sat down beside her at night, when she was alone, to rest their weary feet perhaps? She giggled at the idea, but there was a sharp edge to her laughter.

She felt hot breath on her neck; and hissing, growling noises assaulted her senses. The curtains on the windows blew straight up, although she heard no sound of the type of wind needed to trigger them into action. The bathroom door slammed, slicing her nerves like a razor.

"KIRSTEN!"

She covered her ears to block it out, and closed her eyes to make it disappear. This was nothing more than a dream she told herself, only it usually happened when she was *awake*. The bed rumbled and shook, and the springs squealed again in protest as something climbed over the side of the bed and settled down next to her.

"KIRSTEN!"

She should've taken that pill and gone off to sleep. She should've spared herself from the inevitable. And yet, the pill rendered her helpless—but no more so than she was now!

"KIRSTEN LARSEN!"

It touched her! She felt nothing but pain from the feel of its cold, death-like embrace. "Oh, Jesus Lord," she prayed, "Be with me as always."

"FUCK YOU, CUNT! AND YOUR JESUS AS WELL!"

Kirsten opened her eyes in rage, removed her hands from her ears and turned to rebuke the profanities. But her words died in her throat, could not be spoken. Nothing came out; not even a gasp of breath. Ice seared the base of her skull causing her nerves to dance under her skin.

This wasn't ethereal, not the usual sulphurous, foul smelling, puff of smoke she'd seen so many times before. This was real, had form, and was badly decayed bacause it had been dead for such a long time now.

This was her warning.

"STAY AWAY!"

6

Monroe was an old town, full of historical significance; battles had been fought there during the Revolutionary War, several signers of the Declaration of Independence had lived there, and had owned homes now considered to be landmarks. Mainly though, it was small and sparsely populated, full of just the sort of down-home, plain type of folk Erica yearned to spend the rest of her life with.

No more big shot, city types for her. No more fast talking, wheeler-dealers looking to screw the eye teeth out of your head, and teaching your kids the wrong way to go. Erica wanted to return to basics. She wanted to live in a place where back yard gardens were a source of pride; where the home canning of vegetables and jams were discussed at PTA meetings, where everyone knew their neighbors on a first name basis, a place where contracts were sealed by a handshake.

Monroe was her kind of town.

Erica left Sunrise Highway at the exit marked MONROE; her heart was beating with excitement because Kayle had said yes, they were buying the house. He'd been silent about it for days now, broodingly silent, although a couple of times he acted as if he were ready to say yes, then he'd change his

mind and say nothing. But then, after last night . . .
She shoved it out of her head. He said yes, and that
was it.

Now it was time to scour the area and discover
where the shopping centers were, as well as a school
for the children. She lowered the visor over the
window to obliterate the glare of the sun and slowed
for the stop sign on the road ahead.

It was another beautiful day, warm, but not too
warm, gentle breezes blowing, the greenery of spring
just blooming. Erica felt wonderful; so alive, so
fulfilled, the house was hers!

She shifted in her seat and tried to ignore the
soreness in her body. It ached all over, especially her
breasts and the area between her legs. Kayle had been
unusually brutal the night before. First he'd cried out
in his sleep, as she recalled, then he rolled over to her
and made love, or what was his equivalent for the act
of sex.

Why was he so rough at times, as if he enjoyed
being abusive? He swore that he loved her. Had his
temper flared because he had a nightmare about his
mother again? He called to her in his sleep. What did
Mother do that was so terrible Erica was paying for it
now? Maybe someday the truth would come out.

Meanwhile, his behavior towards her was
ridiculous, and Kayle knew it. He saw how angry she
was last night, how sexually unfulfilled, and so he
promised her the house. When Erica heard those
words, she quickly forgave him, for the sake of her
children. The house was being bought for their
benefit, so she sacrificed part of her dignity for them.

It was really ironic when she thought about her
situation. Kayle had helped to restore her dignity,
only to remove a portion of it every time he touched
her, like a mason chopping away at a stone block.
And what would he promise her the next time?
Nothing could ever outweigh a gift like this, a home of
her own.

There was no traffic on the main road, so she drove past the stop sign, turned onto Moriches Parkway and headed south.

Her mother, Mary Rogers, was in the car with her. Erica had first wanted to do this alone, then thought better of it. The most wonderful moments in life were meant to be shared with someone you loved. Her mother had been present when she graduated from high school, and had sat in the waiting room of a hospital for hours on end when Todd, her first child, was born. Now it was only fitting for Mary to share in the joy of her first home.

Erica had driven barely two blocks when a large shopping center came into view and it surprised her because it was so modern. She had expected to find small, general stores with pot belly stoves and barrels of dry goods and homey atmospheres. Still, she was far from being disappointed. A billboard out front listed the stores inside. There was a supermarket, a shoe store, several clothing shops, even a post office. That much discovered, she drove on by.

"Aren't we stopping here?" Mary's tone was anxious, but her voice was sweet and complacent. She stared at the passing shopping center with the expression of a child being driven away from an amusement park, watching until it disappeared from sight. Mary loved to browse in malls, although she rarely purchases an item unless it fell in the category of a bare necessity. She was retired and living on a widow's pension; money was tight.

"We'll stop on the way back. I promise."

Erica drove over a set of railroad tracks and several smaller shopping centers came into view. But they had little to offer in the way of variety. She knew that Mary wouldn't be interested in stopping there.

Still, Mary's attention was everywhere at once. She seemed quite satisfied with Monroe, giving it a sort of silent approval. Erica was able to unwind a bit because Mary's opinion was important to her. At least it was now, although it hadn't always been this way. Erica never thought twice about it when she left home to live with Kayle.

She paused for a red light and studied her mother for a moment. It was hard to believe that this woman, with the heavy thighs, sagging breasts and silver hair was her mother. Mary had been extremely attractive in her prime, but the passing years had been cruel to her. Erica had been cruel to her.

Erica drove along Moriches Parkway until she saw a sign near the bridge crossing leading to the beach. She was in a mostly residential area, with small, frame houses topped with pitched roofs covered in shingles; a large part of them converted bungalows. The sign ahead signalled the road's end, the bridge and the beach were next. She made a U turn and headed north, back in the direction of the first mall they'd passed on the road.

"We can't stay long," she said. "I want you to see the house while we're here, and you know how impatient Kayle can be." Kayle was watching the children.

Mary's mood changed with the mention of his name. She became sullen and bitter. "Yes. We all know patience isn't one of his better virtues."

Erica tightened her grip on the steering wheel, and she gave Mary a sidelong glance, but she continued to drive as though nothing had been said.

Carol Anderson was in the supermarket pushing a cart when Erica walked in with Mary. Erica was the young woman she'd seen looking at the house next door with her husband and children.

Carol's first instinct was to run up to Erica and forewarn her about the dreadful place. Carol thought it was a sinful waste of money to buy a home that wanted no one to live there. The house would surely reject Erica and her family. And the house had already killed once to keep people OUT!

She really should warn Erica, she thought, but her nerve ran out. The woman probably would find her story hard to believe. Christ, if someone came up to her in a store and began telling what sounded like fabricated fantasies about a home she was interested in buying, Carol would've thought she was crazy. Then she probably would've laughed her ass off.

But this wasn't funny, it was tragic. Besides, there was enough ridicule thrown her way without purposely putting herself in that position.

She scanned the prices on several boxes of cake mix and thought about Burt and being laughed at. Carol really enjoyed baking from scratch, the old-fashioned way, but Burt hated it. Or maybe he just hated her, and used her baking as an excuse to criticize her in front of the children. The cake was never light enough for him; the icing was always too sweet. Well now, the hell with him, he was getting whatever she had time to slap together out of a box.

She wound up taking the most expensive one because she wasn't really paying attention. Her hands were trembling. She had deliberately avoided telling Erica about the house. And why? Because she was a coward, that was her answer. She caught her dress on a loose wire on the cart and snagged the hem. Her conscience was destroying what little was left of her concentration.

Carol was, or at least had been, a devout Christian; not one to deliberately perpetuate a fraud by hiding the truth. So why was she doing it now, allowing a real estate agent to cheat these people out of money? And why was she dreaming up excuses, such as her fear of being laughed at, to let herself off the hook?

Her body stiffened with righteousness and determination. That woman had a right to know the truth about the house, even if she thought Carol was demented for telling tales about its being haunted. Besides, it was more than just a haunted house; it lived, it breathed, had destroyed its own exterior—

It sheltered a nest of murdering horrors.

Suddenly overcome by a sense of urgency, Carol went back to the front of the store searching for Erica and the elderly woman she'd walked in with. Carol imagined it was her mother, still, the woman was so much older.

Erica and Mary were just leaving; the automatic door at the main entrance closed behind them with a terrible finality that made her shudder. But they couldn't leave, she thought, not before she had a chance to warn them. Oh, God! She left her cart and chased after them.

This was the story of her life, always a bit late with everything she ever attempted, or thought of attempting, to do. She recalled the time she'd already been married for five years or so, and the burning desire for a career struck her full force. But it was an impossible dream to pursue. By then she had four kids to care for and another was on the way. Always a bit late.

Carol burst through the front door and stood helplessly by as she watched Erica drive out of the mall and onto the main road.

It was quite a drive from Moriches Parkway and the mall to the house on Longacre Drive. They passed a grammer school on the way and, at Mary's insistence, drove through the grounds. It was a beautiful place with the usual well kept lawns. There were stone benches for visitors to sit on and an American flag flew straight out in the wind by the main entrance.

A small, one-story building, the windows of the school were filled with hand-drawn, childish pictures of bunnies—it was close to Easter—and an assortment of multi-colored eggs in brown, heavily scribbled baskets.

After they left the school grounds, they hit an area where the streets were narrow and lined with homes similar to those by the beach. They were mostly converted summer bungalows; some with sand-encrusted lawns, some with boats on trailers ready to be towed into the water, others with wash on clotheslines blowing in the wind. Mary had good vibes about this town. Vibes were important to her and had just about governed her every move over a lifetime.

Everything on God's earth held memories of the past, like a residue that remained when all else was forgotten, and gave off vibrations that could be picked up if one had the required sensitivity. And although she'd learned years ago to heed those inner warnings, Mary was still unable to explain the scientific mechanics behind it, or how it really worked.

Sometimes she experienced a physical reaction to an object, like knots in the pit of her stomach, or butterflies as some people called them. Other times she experienced an emotional sensation such as tranquility or sadness depending on the object and what had taken place around it.

She remembered that as a kid growing up, there had been an old abandoned place in her neighborhood, a run-down mansion on a hill, and everyone said it was haunted. Her friends used to get together at night and dream up stories about what had probably gone on there to make it haunted, or what was probably living there now; spooks, ghosts, demons . . .

Some folks even swore they saw things moving around at night in the old mansion, like lights in the windows, and creatures stalking the grounds. As Mary grew older and matured, she began to realize that the haunted mansion on her block was not an oddity. Most neighborhoods had legendary abandoned homes in their midst with equally strange mysteries surrounding them. She also began to realize that abandonment didn't necessarily mean haunted.

She felt no strange or scary vibes emanating from the old mansion. But she did, however, feel something frightening about the home she lived in!

There was a sadness, a rage, and once she swore she saw someone begging for money, and heard cries in the night, a pitiful wailing. She was afraid to be alone in the house.

Years later she found the courage to go to the offices of the local newspaper and search in their morgue for something to validate her feelings. And it didn't take long to discover the truth. She found an article dealing with a triple murder and a subsequent suicide that took place in the home she grew up in some twenty years before. Mary didn't have to read the whole article to know she'd been right in her assumption. She'd run quite a gamut of emotions when it came to her own home. It did, however, make her feel better to learn the degree of accuracy surrounding her sense of vibes.

And those vibes had governed her entire life since. She avoided people—like Kayle—and places that gave off bad ones. She settled in towns, moved into homes, and made friends based on what she felt. And thus far, she had been fortunate enough to have chosen well.

7

Henry Wittaker was in bed, a wedge of sun across his face, when he heard the whispering. This was no cause for alarm though, because this time the source was human. Buddy and Patricia kept checking on him every half hour or so. The kids were worried. Henry had scared them half to death a few nights ago when he'd stumbled through the door, dirty and haggard looking, and wouldn't talk to them.

Instead, he went to the den and had been there ever since, on a sofa bed, in a forced state of trance.

The den had been his bedroom since Bess' kidney disease progressed from serious to critical. He felt, then as now, that it had been an unselfish choice on his part. How could you sleep with a desirable woman like Bess, and want her so badly when she was dying? A few times his lust got the better of him and he took her, as sick as she was. And she cried afterwards because she was unable to respond to his passion.

Henry began to feel like an animal, like a dumb thing in heat, so he made the decision to move to the den. Bess was very upset at the time, as he now recalled; her body went slack and she crumpled in front of him. And tears, he remembered those, too. They'd been sleeping together for twenty-five years—

and now she felt so useless. But he did it for her benefit.

Or did he?

Henry still had wants and needs, even if her sexuality had diminished because of her illness and the medicine she took. So, Henry came down here to dream in the night and fondle himself. It was no real substitute, but it was better than nothing.

Buddy and Patricia were moving away from the door. He heard their footsteps, the whisper of their voices growing fainter. Poor kids, he thought, cursing himself for being such a self-centered ass. He hadn't really considered them when he went to that house a few nights ago seeking revenge. Their mother was gone, what if he hadn't returned home?

He ran a hand over the stubble on his face and thought about a hot shower and a shave. His mouth was dry, as if he'd swallowed a pound of sand, and acrid from the horrible taste of brimstone emanating from the creature. The fumes had passed between his lips, seared his nostrils.

He got up and looked at himself in a mirror over the mantle and winced. No wonder his kids had been frightened when he staggered through the front door that night. If the way he looked now was any indication . . . He didn't even look human. His face was distorted, both of his cheeks were pale and swollen, his eyes were nothing more than two blue dots sunken back in his skull.

He needed that shower and some clean clothes. He'd been sleeping in the same pants and shirt he'd worn to that house, to his own mock execution.

Henry heard footsteps again, and this time there was cause for alarm. They were coming from the basement. His *rat*, he imagined, was keeping an eye on him. And Henry had been warned about this.

"WE'LL BE WATCHING YOU, HENRY!" the Gate Keeper had bellowed. And the bastard was true to his word, as he had been when he took the breath from his wife!

Only now they wanted to take the breath from his children as well; to kill them unless Henry cooperated. If he did, well then, hell's bells, the threat was off. It was like paying protection money to the syndicate.

And the funniest part of it was, if any humor could be found in this strange drama, this time the threat was in direct contradiction of itself. *They* killed Bess as a warning to Henry to stop showing the house. *They* wanted no intruders. Now, they were going to kill his children if he tried to keep Erica Walsh from buying the house. Some shit, man, he thought.

The Gate Keeper wanted Erica. And Henry knew why, but he couldn't think about that now.

Now was the time to continue his discussion with Buddy and Patricia, to warn them that their lives were in danger. After all, what if those demonic bastards decided to contradict themselves again? What if they suddenly wanted Erica KEPT OUT? Hell, they were nuts, psychotic in fact. One day it was one story, then the next day they did a complete about face.

But, the Gate Keeper wanted Erica, for reasons too insane to dwell on at this time. So, maybe they wouldn't change their minds.

But, just in case they did, Henry would warn Buddy and Patricia. He'd tell them again about the difference between ghosts and demons, then he'd tell them what he learned a few nights ago at that dreadful house to sort of reinforce his warnings. Still, they'd never listen to him as he was, a crazy looking bastard with wild eyes, wearing filthy, rancid smelling clothes, who'd taken on an emissary of the beast and lost!

Henry went upstairs to change.

Mary Rogers waited in the car for Erica to unlock the front door. The house was nice from a distance, a bit run-down, but nothing that a few nails, some paint and some grass seed wouldn't cure. It was two stories high. Erica hadn't mentioned that part of it.

Erica was inside and calling to her before Mary even realized the front door was open. Erica looked so young and juvenile standing in the frame of the door in her dungarees and sweat shirt, with white sneakers on her feet. For a moment, the older woman had a glimpse of the past; of Erica holding the door while Mary unloaded groceries from the car, and of Fred, her late husband, coming to help.

But Erica was in her own home now, and Fred was gone. He'd died several years ago. And this was now, the present.

Mary was nervous about going in there. She had knots in the pit of her stomach, butterflies. Was it bad vibes, or the realization that Erica was no longer a child and hadn't been for a long time now? It was difficult to decipher her emotions.

Erica was in the kitchen pouring water into a bucket when Mary reached the front door. The living room was large, had cathedral ceilings, was painted a hideous blue. Mary stepped over the threshold and felt the knots in her stomach tighten as if they were doing a little dance and it was dipsy-do time. There were palpitations in her chest, around the heart. Was it excitement? Was it happiness, for Erica's sake? Or was it bad vibes?

No! She wouldn't allow herself to think that way, to spoil it for Erica. The feelings that had governed her life might not be suitable for someone else. Still, she was disturbed by the awful, familiar odor of the place. She hurried to the kitchen.

"Here, Mom. Have a seat." Erica pointed to a straight-backed, expensive-looking cane chair. "I found it in the yard. There's a lot of stuff outside."

Mary glanced through the open screen door beyond Erica and saw that it was true. The yard was piled high with a collection of household articles, things

Mary would never have left behind. The former owners must've cleared out in a hurry.

"Thought we weren't staying long. You said you just wanted to show me the house." She sat on the edge of the cane chair and felt anxious about leaving.

Erica brushed a shock of hair away from her face with the back of her hand, a nervous habit carried over from her childhood. Erica was upset because Mary wanted to leave and now she was trying to choose her words carefully, without showing anger. "Well, I figured since we were already here . . . It's easier to mop the floors when the house is empty."

The house is far from being empty, the older woman wanted to say, without knowing why. But she stuck to the obvious instead. "It smells bad in here. Like something died in this house and is still lying around someplace. What is it?"

"I don't know." Erica stuck a mop in the pail; water splashed over the sides. "Mr. Wittaker was supposed to take care of the odor. But, poor man, his wife just died. I hate to bother him." She crossed to the door, then hesitated. "Are you coming upstairs to see the bedrooms?"

Mary felt vibrations drifting down from those bedrooms, awful vibrations. "No! I'll stay down here!" she insisted, a stitch of alarm in her voice. She followed Erica to the living room and felt uneasy about watching her daughter climb those stairs alone. "Maybe we should leave. Kayle's watching the kids, remember?"

Erica paused on the steps and turned to face her. This time she didn't bother to brush her hair back in that nervous gesture. This time she showed her annoyance. "The hell with him! If someone doesn't clean up, then he'll have more to bitch about! Why're you in such a hurry to leave anyway?"

Mary had left the front door open. A gust of wind swirled around her legs and she shivered, but she made no move to close it. Erica ran past her and slammed it shut, then went back up the steps. Mary remained silent, her attention focused on the now semi-darkened living room. She knew she was safer with the door open.

Erica felt awkward because of the silence between them. She owed Mary an explanation. "Mom," she began, using a milder tone, "Kayle's promise to buy this house is hanging on a loose thread." And *guilt*, she thought to herself, her body still throbbing with pain from his love-making the night before. "It has to be perfect when we move in or he'll change his mind. When I think of the way we're living now, in a dump. This's good for the kids. You know everything I do is for them."

Mary didn't have to be told. Erica loved those children to the extent that it was almost unnatural at times. Why it was just about the same as her love for Erica. "Then go clean, honey. But please, hurry."

Mary sat on the steps and waited. The vibes were hitting her from all directions at once, but she chose to ignore them. She could be wrong this time and hoped to God she was. Erica had her heart set on this place; Mary couldn't shatter her dreams over something so insignificant as bad vibes now, could she? The answer was no, Erica deserved the best.

Mary had given birth to Erica when she was approaching the ripe old age of forty, much too old, in her opinion, to be starting a family. She had considered having an abortion. But Fred would not hear of it. Fred, her late husband, was ecstatically happy. He'd long since given up on the idea of having children, and he was ready to play the role of 'papa' to the hilt.

Mary relented and had the baby, and what a glorious decision it turned out to be. Erica was born normal, with none of the change-of-lifer traits she feared, such as mongolism or dwarfism. She was just perfect in every sense, from the tip of her white-blonde head right on down to her stubby, little toes.

Gorgeous, actually. And pampered, oh hell, yes.

Mary felt a sharpness across her back. Damned
sciatica, she thought, and wondered how long it
would take Erica to wash the floors. And not because
she was worried about Kayle being stuck with the
children. If the selfish bastard didn't like it, that was
his problem.

The son-of-a-bitch!

He was nothing but trouble since he came into their
lives and stole Erica away. And only because he
didn't approve of the way she and Fred were raising
Erica. Kayle felt they were stifling her emotional
growth. Bullshit! The girl had everything she wanted,
and more. She was well taken care of, protected from
the normal pitfalls of life. She hadn't a care in the
world. After all, she was their only child!

And Kayle ruined their lives by changing Erica, by
turning her into what he felt she should be; *his*
woman. Mary shuddered. Now Kayle was buying this
house to shove it in Mary's face. But he still had no
intention of ever marrying her daughter, or of giving
those children his name.

Her head hurt; it ached so bad she was afraid her
skull was going to explode. Was it from her hatred of
Kayle and her memories of the past? Or was it from
bad vibes . . . and the feeling that she wasn't alone
down here? She gazed over at the front door. By
closing it, Erica had stimulated a growth of darkness
that was fastly spreading as though it were alive and
about to consume her.

Think of something else . . . Anything!

Her attention was caught then by a room off to one
side of the kitchen. The door was closed and she was
unable to see the interior, but she imagined it as a
sewing room where Erica could make clothing for the
children, or a den if Kayle had his way. Kayle was
already making plans for the house and with damned
little money to back him. All he did was brag about
his second job this and his second job that as if a few

extra dollars make a big difference. But the man had no head for money. They'd be just as broke here as anyplace else.

It was a struggle to get to her feet. She leaned back a bit and rubbed her spine where her old arthritic sacroiliac was supposed to be located. Her legs were stiff, but she made it to the door of the sewing room. Now what, she thought? Had she really intended to go in there alone? The uneasiness she'd been feeling right along hit her full force. She sensed something, and it was moving about inside.

This place is far from being empty! The very same statement that struck her before was burning in the back of her mind. And yet, what was it that she sensed here? Ghosts? Goblins? Or perhaps it was much worse than the usual story book hauntings.

The knob of the door was cool and sweaty to the touch and she wanted nothing more than to just casually turn the damn thing and go on in. But there was a gnawing sensation in the pit of her stomach and voices in her head telling her to STAY OUT! A hand pushed against her back. Erica? She turned and was alone, alone in the consuming darkness. It was broad daylight outside, but no light came in through the windows. She felt entombed, in a dungeon, with a cold, hateful hand caressing her spine.

She was on the stairs and climbing before she realized what she was doing. Erica was upstairs alone, and had been for the past half hour. It was so quiet up there. What was she doing? Oh, God, was she all right? Mary would never forgive herself for ignoring those bad vibes if anything were to happen to Erica.

The landing at the top of the steps was within view when she stopped and stared mutely at the wall running the length of the staircase as if it had called to her, as if it had spoken her name. Anger emanated from that wall, like black, steamy vibrations, anger pointed directly at her. She felt an intense rage, and leaned back against the railing, her face clouded by a vision. She *saw* misery and despair, *heard* screams, pleas for mercy, *heard* the cold laughter of death; all part of the hateful residue of a past life in this house.

Without knowing why, she raised her hand and ran it over the wall until she felt a thumping sensation against her flesh—beat upon beat, beat upon beat, like a pulse. The *pulse* in the wall was as rapid as her own, and kept perfect time; it had synchoronized its movements, the rhythm reminding her of a heartbeat. A heartbeat! Yes, that's what it was. A heartbeat! She removed her hand as quickly as if it had been thrust into an open inferno.

This awful place was alive and breathing. It possessed a heart and a mind, but no soul! No *sooulll!* The soul had been lost years before and in its place she sensed an empty blackness, a void, an abyss of hatred. It had the ability to hate. But who? Then again, the answer was clear, it flashed across her mind with such force that it almost took the breath from her body. It hated her and Kayle! But not Erica. It *desired* Erica and wanted her with the same amount of passion as a man craving a voluptuous woman.

Mary fell back against the railing, her breath coming in short spurts, her heart pounding heavily in her chest. Erica must not buy this house. *Must not!* Her gaze drifted upwards and she was afraid. Erica was up there, but she sensed that Erica was not alone!

Kirsten Larsen was in her car driving fast, very fast. In two days of heavy traveling she'd managed to leave the hotel room in Denver about a thousand miles behind her. Kirsten had run like hell to escape the clutches of that zombie sitting on her bed and had been running ever since.

But it ran with you!

She would not allow herself to dwell on the truth. It was too awful to wonder where it was hiding in the car and when it would show itself again, especially when she was alone. There were dark stretches of road at night; miles of highway with no traffic in either direction for hours at a time.

And there were the motels she stopped at when it was impossible to go on; when she'd pushed her body to the limit. Spooky joints, those motels were, cold and damp and dark. She almost never slept. Most of the time she laid in the dark and wondered when the creature would materialize again.

Oh, God, she wasn't stopping tonight. She had to keep going until she got home—home was in New York—and home meant being *safe* to her.

"Christ, help me," she mumbled and passed a sign announcing the last motel before an endless stretch of road. However, praying to the Lord Jesus Christ for physical strength was useless at this point since her stamina had been greatly reduced by an accident. She was able to drive only so far and that was it! He'd saved her life and had given back the use of her leg *and* her mind, now she had to do for herself.

God helps those who help themselves. A quote from the Bible came to her. Maybe not verbatim, but it was close enough. She had to do for herself before asking for His protection. And it was His protection that had saved her from the dead thing in her bed a few nights ago.

She remembered feeling the Lord's presence in the sense that she experienced a strong sensation of warmth and of jubilation. It started inside of her and grew until it radiated an outer glow, like a coat of armor, or a casing of heavy steel that nothing could penetrate.

It made her realize that this evil bastard in her room had overstepped his authority by threatening her life. There was no power in him strong enough to counteract the Lord's. Kirsten knew this, but in truth, she had been afraid until the hand of the Lord was laid upon her and she found the courage to leave the hotel.

Kirsten remembered rising from the bed and going

directly to the closet for her clothing. But the dead
thing followed her, and clung to her body like a
second skin while she dressed. The vile son-of-a-bitch
played head games with her; it mocked her
plumpness, it fingered the fatty pockets in her thighs,
it even left teeth marks on her stomach.

But it didn't kill her, not while the Lord was
present.

Then why was she running? Why was she fleeing
for her life? Because, in truth, she was afraid of the
vengeance of the Lord and falling from grace. She was
afraid of the terms of His punishment for past sins she
had committed. And if the Lord wanted to call in the
cards at any time, and punish her, he could do so by
refusing to help her. Then she would surely be open
prey for some terrible fate at the hands of her
enemies, the ancient masters.

So, she was running for her life.

And now she was a thousand miles closer to home,
and her house in Huntington. And somehow, the
closer she got to New York, the closer she felt she was
getting to the dreadful house in her dreams. If that
were so, then she'd have to face the beast again! And
yet, this was all part of her deal with the Lord. Kirsten
had a mission in life, she had to be strong to continue
playing the role of emissary, at least until the Lord
decided to punish her for past sins.

Sometimes she wished the accident had killed
her . . .

Henry Wittaker was in the shower, hot water
steaming his flesh when one of his previous acts of
stupidity came back to haunt him. He'd gone to the
house a few nights ago seeking revenge for Bess'
death!

What a fool he'd been, allowing anger to control his
sensibilities until he'd gone into a rage. What had he
sought to accomplish? He wasn't a demonologist, one
who had spent years perfecting the technique of

hunting down these entities and making them talk; making them tell where they came from, and for what purpose. And he wasn't an exorcist either, that had the power to force the bastards to return home.

He was nothing threatening to the dark outer world of the occult. He was just a simple man seeking to avenge the death of his wife, and he'd lost! In fact, those bastards told him to get lost.

Henry rubbed his face with soap and tried to forget his trial by fire at the hands of the—He could not say its name, not even in his mind, not now, not when he was alone, and a *rat* was strolling the hall outside of the bathroom. Not now, when the physical pain of it still lingered on his flesh. It was too awful to dwell on, but so awful he couldn't shove it to the back of his mind either.

There were marks on his body, down by his penis, a she-bitch, a sucubus, a substitute for Bess. Oh, God! But the she-bitch had four heads and four sets of lust-filled eyes that craved his attention, and four tongues that licked his body at the same time, driving him as no female had before or since.

After Henry had achieved orgasm, he saw the truth —the many faces of the Gate Keeper! A man! Henry had done it with a man. But no, not with a man, with a murderous, heathen bastard who could be anything at will, and who could read your thoughts and feel your emotions and use them against you. Therefore, he came to Henry as a lusty wench of a bitch because Henry had the hots. And Henry screwed him, four heads and all.

Still, there was more to that night, so much more that Henry was storing it in the blackest part of his brain. And now those memories were playing games, as if they too were living entities like the house was. And they were lying now, waiting for the proper time to come forth. And then what? Drive him insane?

His hands were trembling, he knew it wouldn't take much.

The strangest thing was, the night he'd gone to the house seeking the Gate Keeper, he seemed to feel no fear at all. He was bold and brave and determined to exact his revenge. Then, he met the Old One in person, the head honcho himself, and the meaning of fear returned in the form of terror. The Gate Keeper taught him fear again.

Shit! Why was that thing walking the hall? To scare him? Well, it was doing one helluva fine job if that was its intention.

"WE'LL BE WATCHING YOU, HENRY!"

You son-of-a-bitch, he thought, watching me and listening to every word I say and think. And think? Oh yeah! He'd just about forgotten. It wasn't too bright of him to have been thinking of warning his children. That's why the bastard was up here scaring the hell out of Henry. It had read his mind, toured his brain . . .

It was knocking on the wall—three raps, pause, three more. Everything bad came in threes, Henry thought, a sign of the master beast. Oh, Lord, he couldn't talk to his children here, not in this house. Three more raps, pause, three more. Keep your mind blank, he thought angrily, don't give it any further information. The time and the place to speak to Buddy and Patricia will come, and soon.

8

Erica hadn't wanted to go up there alone, but did because she felt foolish about her fears. The incident on the staircase had been an illusion, nothing more. It was hot the day she first looked at the house, and hotter still in the bedroom. After all, Henry Wittaker was there, and he was sweating as much as she was.

Then too, the house had been closed up tight for a while and the air was so stagnant it smelled like a funeral pyre; except for the master bedroom. There the air had been laced with the heady aroma of cheap perfume. And all of those gases: the heat, the stagnant air, the volatile oil in the perfume, all of those gases had mixed together and expanded, and had robbed her brain of precious oxygen. It was no wonder she'd hallucinated, and, *felt* someone touching her, *heard* them whisper.

Mary was downstairs if Erica needed her. Erica was very confused at this point.

Again it was like the inside of a sauna when she walked into the master bedroom. The air was so hot and heavy with perfume that it staggered her senses. She opened a window and took a deep breath, then she sat on the sill and thought about how easy it would be to hallucinate again, to relive the nightmare on the stairs, to hear those footsteps climbing towards her.

Don't do this, she shouted inwardly, don't frighten yourself. You're buying this house for the kids, and it's everything you ever wanted, and more.

Like the room she was in, for instance. It was much larger than she first pictured it to be. There was plenty of room for the king-sized water bed Kayle had promised to buy.

Kayle! She thought of him and her mood swung further down on the pendulum of depression. Everything was perfect now except that Kayle would be living here too, and there was a sickness in him she could no longer deal with. The torment he'd put her through the night before kept coming back to her; how he hurt her, misused her body and derived pleasure from it. He called it love-making; she thought he was sadistic, wielding his sexual organ like a conqueror with a weapon in his hand.

Afterwards, he'd cried, wept in her arms and begged her to forgive him. If he hadn't been brutal to start with, there would have been little to forgive. If he'd only thought before he acted and said to himself, *This is Erica. Why am I hurting her?* But Kayle was impulsive, he never used his head. He just went right on and did as he pleased, and Erica was sick of it and sick of him.

And sick of Aaron Pace as well, the way that jerk spoke to her on the phone a few nights ago, the way he threatened her. And yet, Aaron wasn't brutal, and never had been. When Aaron took her in his arms, it was like a page out of a romance novel; his gentle touch, his soothing voice, and the slow, easy rhythm of his body on hers. Aaron was ten times the man Kayle was.

In a way, Kayle's sickness had driven her to Aaron and kept her going back for more. And the time she spent with Aaron was time well-spent. There were no pressures, no pretense, and most of all, no pain.

The walls in the bedroom were sweating, she noticed. There were small droplets of moisture running from the ceiling to the floor, and she found this odd. She thought back to the winter before last, when the temperature had fallen below zero and the radiators in her apartment were going full blast. Her kids took the valve off of the one in her bedroom and steam escaped. The walls became damp and sweaty.

The same thing was happening here. But this was spring, not winter. There was no heat running. Besides, there were no radiators in this house. There was baseboard heating, no radiators. She touched the wall next to her to feel the moisture, to convince herself that she wasn't crazy. But then she quickly withdrew her hand and tried not to wonder what was going on here. She had enough mysteries in her life as it was without adding one more.

Kayle was a mystery; always hiding his past and making her pay for the worst part of it, something a woman had done to him. Aaron was a mystery also. Why wouldn't he let go? There were other women around, single women, more suited to his needs. Why the hell was he so damned adamant about hanging onto her? And what, she wondered, would be her reaction if he did leave her? She loved him in a way, and had from the first moment they met.

But Aaron Pace wasn't buying her this house! Kayle was! And, like it or not, she had to stay with Kayle for the sake of her children. She had to kiss his ass and make him happy. And she had to keep Aaron Pace on the side to make herself happy, providing of course, that Aaron had wisely chosen to ignore her recent rejection of him.

She sat still for a moment longer, a heavily salt-soaked breeze washing over her body, making her feel as if she were dreaming, and not, as in reality, facing such heady decisions. She might have sat there all day and done nothing but fantasize about Aaron if she had her way. But Mary was waiting downstairs. And Kayle, he had the kids.

She told Kayle before she left this morning that she

wouldn't be long, just long enough to show the house to Mary.

Reluctantly she left her spot at the window and dipped the mop into the pail, swishing it around until the odor of pine overwhelmed her. It was odd, she thought, to have discovered the pine mixed in with the rest of the discarded items in the back yard. Most women preferred a more exotic, more expensive brand of cleanser. But not Erica. Pine was cheap and just as effective.

She felt she had something in common with the former owner, they thought alike. Either that or the woman was on the same financial level as Erica. Maybe she also had to be frugal with her money, and not always blow it on a more expensive product. Especially those that were constantly being touted as superior by the ad execs on Madison Avenue.

Sure, there was her answer: the woman was frugal, she told herself. *Then why the hell did she leave everything behind;* the furniture, the pots and pans, things no sane person would abandon? Unless— Unless she and her husband had left in a hurry.

Did they suffer from hallucinations also?

Erica was mopping faster now, anxious to get this thing over and done with. There were so many floors to be washed, and the walls were still sweating. But it wasn't hot in there, not since she opened the window. Besides, there were no valveless radiators, so the walls should not be sweating.

And the former owners had left in a hurry.

Erica didn't want to continue on like this, to wonder what forces had driven them out. But her mind had no intention of letting go; it continued to search for answers. Why did they move? Was it money problems? Was it social pressures?

Did they suffer from hallucinations also?

Her back was to the closet when it opened. Erica was unable to see a mass of white, ethereal smoke float out and cross the room to hover over her body, unable to feel the touch of its cold, maniacal embrace. Her mind was on other matters.

Did they suffer from hallucinations also, she wondered again? But, oh, God, she had to stop this, she was up here alone. And someone had touched her when she was up here before, and they whispered in her ear as well. Because her imagination had run rampant. It was all those gases mixed together, she scolded herself, that's why you hallucinated. And maybe those people did, too. Maybe the same gases deprived their brains of oxygen. So stop this, now!

She shuddered. It was getting cold in there, and the walls were still sweating. And someone had just whispered her name. Didn't they? Or was it that wind? She laid the mop down and wanted to run, but she closed the window instead. The floors *had* to be washed; Kayle was sure to cancel the whole deal if everything wasn't just right.

She stood by the window for a moment and stared at the yard below and the bare spots in the lawn. Kayle had been disturbed by the shabby, unkempt appearance of that lawn, and he wanted Erica to call Henry Wittaker and see if grass seed had been planted yet. But Mr. Wittaker's wife had picked this time to die; if such a thing were possible. Erica could not bring herself to call him while he was still in mourning.

And she couldn't call him to inquire about the cleaning crew he promised her, so the painstaking task of washing the floors was now hers. "Wishy-washy bitch," she said aloud, then froze when a wisp of cold air, a draft maybe, brushed against her legs. It felt heavy and it had form. She glanced down, not knowing what to expect, and was relieved to find she was still alone in the room.

She crossed over to her pail and started to mop again, while the recent experience on the landing outside came back to haunt her. Whatever had passed her by at the window just now, it felt the same as . . .

But no, she wouldn't allow herself to go back to thinking about *that* again. She shook her head to free it from the cobwebs of fear that had begun to gather in her mind, and would surely make her hallucinate if given half the chance. She dipped the mop and rinsed it while spasms of uncertainty overtook her despite her attempts to prevent them.

There was something wrong with this house. But what? Did she sense some of those bad vibrations her mother was forever harping about? Was the residue of a tragic past life hovering over this house, like the residue of scum floating in the pan under her sink? Ridiculous, she thought, inanimate objects didn't hold memories.

Or did they?

And why did she think that something awfully tragic must've happened here in the past? What sort of tales would be told if this place were capable of speech? What kind of people lived here? Did they leave a residue of themselves behind?

Erica felt it again, the same wisp of air. Only this time it did more than just brush against her legs. This time it lingered, wrapping itself around her body until cold blades of fear struck the base of her skull.

But then she became aware of still another sensation, one she would soon forget. She stood very still as a strange dizziness overtook her. The room was spinning and she along with it. It made her head reel. Bile rose in her throat. Hot, white lights floated in front of her, doing a crazy little dance, and Erica swayed with them, her body moving in the same hypnotic rhythm as the lights. Her eyes grew wide, her gaze frozen. This was a dream, she told herself. I came to wash the floors and fell asleep.

She felt a *presence;* not human, but a presence just the same. She felt the solidity of a body pressed against hers, its heavily muscled torso as hard and as cold as stone. A strong, solid form, it was unyielding, unmerciful, defiant. But she wasn't afraid because it whispered to her, told her it wanted her and that it would take care of her.

"STAY WITH ME, ERICA," it husked in her ear and touched her with such tenderness she was reminded of Aaron Pace. Erica closed her eyes and leaned back against it. A pair of deathly cold arms embraced her and the form came alive. It whispered hotly this time. It promised her protection from Kayle if that was her wish, it promised her the same lusty affection she received from Aaron Pace, and it promised it would never leave her as well.

Words raced inside of her head, but they weren't her words. There were thoughts, phrases and sentences, all edged with a terrible hatred. But still she wasn't afraid because the hatred was not directed at her. *Someone* was trying to malign her feelings, trying to make her hate the very same people she had always sought to please; Kayle, her mother, the children. But that was impossible. No one could make you do anything that went against your basic nature.

"I LOVE YOU, ERICA," it husked again. "STAY WITH ME."

I love you, she thought. Someone had spoken those words to her, had said, "I love you." Nobody had told her that in years. Rather, it was the other way around. Erica was the one who constantly poured out her heart and received shit in return! When was the last time Kayle had said he loved her, or her mother, or those ungrateful, bastard kids of hers? She couldn't remember.

And did they appreciate anything she did, any effort on her part to make their lives a bit easier? Bullshit! Here she was, breaking her ass, trying to make the house look halfway decent before they moved in, and who cared? Kayle? Shit no! The bastard. He didn't even think enough of her to marry her. Jerking her in two directions at the same time about buying this house.

There was a hand on her breast, soft and tender and

cold, its manhood, hard and firm, caressed her back. Did her kids appreciate what she was doing for them? Shit again! She'd be in here five minutes, setting their beds up, trying to make it real nice, and there they'd be, she could see it now, fucking up the joint with their garbage toys.

She was the only one who cared, and that wasn't enough, not for her. "Fuck them all, big and small," she yelled, then she hurled the mop across the room in a raging fury. It struck the wall by the closet and snapped in two. The closet door slammed shut and the *presence* was gone. There were no hands caressing her body, no voice whispering that it loved her. She came to abruptly and found herself standing in the middle of the room, her thoughts muddled by confusion. She remembered washing the floors, and she remembered feeling cold, but that was all she remembered until now.

"Erica!"

It was Mary's voice, coming from outside of the bedroom. Mary sounded alarmed, probably because they had stayed so long and good old Kayle was watching the kids. "Coming, Mom. I'm ready to leave now." Hell, she was tired anyway.

She glanced around the room once more and felt uneasy when her gaze settled on the broken mop. She gave it some serious thought for a moment or two, but there was no explanation to clear her confusion. It was broken. She didn't know how or why or even who did it. She sure as well didn't smash the damn thing to pieces.

"Erica!"

There was more alarm in her mother's voice this time and it seemed she was worried about something other than Kayle and the kids. Erica knew this by the nervous inflection in her tone. Did Mary sense something awful about this place? Was it bad vibes? Erica shuddered and wondered why the walls were no longer sweating. They appeared to be as dry as though they never had been wringing with moisture to begin with. There were too many mysteries here for her to deal with at present.

"The hell with the cleaning," she mumbled and left.

"I'll have the spaghetti with clam sauce," Henry Wittaker told the waitress, a short elderly woman with dark hair and heavy thighs. Buddy and Patricia ordered two slices of pizza each. She grunted and left.

They were sitting at a table near the front, by a window. The glass was rattling incessantly from the force of the wind outside. But was it the wind, he wondered? Or was something trying to get in? Henry shuddered, then folded his hands across the table and stared out into the night. There were very few street lights in this part of town, and even less traffic. He'd chosen this restaurant for that reason, they'd have their privacy.

After all, he had to finish his story: his lecture on demons. He couldn't talk at home, not with *someone* walking in the basement, and climbing the stairs near the den, and coming into the bathroom when Henry was taking a pee. No, *they* were watching everything he did, and listening to everything he said or thought. And Henry had said and thought enough in front of *them* as it was. Now they were angry. If he continued, or rather, revealed the rest in their presence, there was no telling what would happen.

For this reason alone, he'd brought his kids here, to a deserted pizza joint on the far side of town. But now the words he wanted to speak were lost to him, he was afraid. Buddy and Patricia thought he was crazy. He fumbled with his napkin and watched them exchanging those looks again. A car drove by, its headlights nothing more than two brilliant shafts of white heat in the night. Henry cleared his throat to get their attention.

"Remember what we were discussing . . . uh . . .

just before the funeral?" He'd thrown the ball into their lane; now it was up to them.

"Yeah," Buddy quipped. "But we're not gonna talk about it here . . . ?" He scanned the restaurant. It was empty except for them and the waitress who'd disappeared through a door in the back.

"Why not?" Henry wanted to know. "We're alone."

He heard the wind rustling through the street outside, upsetting garbage cans, their lids clattering on the ground, and he tried to be objective, to be concerned with reality. They were alone, what better place to talk? *No demons here!*

"What if the old lady hears us? It's embarrassing!" It was Patricia's turn to take a shot at him. But Henry ignored her statement, especially the part about being embarrassed. It was better to feel like a fool and to gain insight, than to die a horrible, uninformed death, because that was exactly where they were headed.

"This's important to you, right?" If Buddy understood that much, it was a start. "Then please, Dad . . . don't start yelling stuff at the top of your voice like you did a few days ago. Let's just do this real quiet like."

"You're on, kid. I'll be real cool. Now, what did we learn the last time we talked?" This was beginning to sound like *Sesame Street*. Henry wanted to keep this on a higher level, but it was too late.

Buddy and Patricia gazed at each other across the table, and all Henry could hear was the vibration of the window next to them and the engine of a car that was parked across the street. It was the one whose bright headlights had entranced him moments before, but those headlights were off now, and the car was turned around.

It had been traveling north before and he saw the front of it. Now it was turned in a southerly direction, the driver's side facing Henry. Was someone watching them?

He turned his attention back to his children as Patricia was in the middle of directing Buddy to ''go first.'' Buddy stared down at the checkered tablecloth that seemed so prevalent in these types of restaurants, and started to speak in a low, nervous tone of voice.

''You were talking about two kinds of spirits. The dead ones, and the ones who never lived. And you were talking about some house—''

''The one I just sold in Monroe.''

''Yeah, that one. You said it was . . . haunted. Dad . . . I can't do this.''

''You can and you must. You'll understand why by the time I'm finished.''

Henry heard a door squealing on its hinges and his mind drifted back to the gate on the side of that awful house as the waitress showed up with their food.

''You want anything else, I'll be in back,'' she snarled.

But Henry paid no attention to her, he was listening to the engine running softly in the car across the street. He wondered why it had been there for so long. Then he tried to be reasonable in his thinking. Maybe it was a fellow picking up his date. Women took their own sweet ass time when they wanted to.

Besides, demons didn't drive.

He smiled, but it was a strain.

''Dad.'' Patricia was nudging his arm. ''Are you all right?''

''I'm fine.'' He felt a sense of urgency to get this over and done with. ''Before the food came, we were discussing a house in Monroe. I told you earlier that the place was crawling with lesser entities who were being controlled by a minor devil.''

''Before you said he was a *head honcho*.''

Was Buddy accusing him of contradicting himself? The sarcastic little bastard. ''To the others, who are present in that house, he's a leader. Otherwise, he's a minor devil." Henry sipped his wine. "There are levels of importance in Hell as on Earth. Remember that, boy. There's a caste system there, too. You have your spooks and haunts on one level, those are the ones who mainly try to scare you, but they're harmless. Then you have your devils on another, much greater level. The Gate Keeper is a minor devil.

"Houses are generally haunted by spooks. When a devil is present, it becomes a different story altogether. *Now* we're talking dangerous. Devils have powers. They can maim and kill. And they have no emotions or feelings. They're like *murdering machines,* robots who're programmed for one thing and one thing only, *to kill!"*

The Gate Keeper killed your mother, Henry wanted to scream, but didn't for fear of frightening them.

"Why did the former owner conjure him up if he's so dangerous?" Buddy was trying to sound cool and calm, but there was a crack in his voice.

"I guess because he didn't know what the hell he was doing. Let me explain. People are getting away from formal religions. They're screaming for something more exciting, like Witchcraft and Satanism—"

"Your food's getting cold." Patricia's voice was devoid of emotion when she interrupted him.

Henry heard the car's engine across the street and gazed out into the night. The window on the driver's side was rolled down, but it was too dark to see the driver. Henry knew they were being watched. He turned back to his children and tried to stay calm.

"The son-of-a-bitch who used to own the house was involved in Satanism—for kicks. And he conjured up an evil, vile, demonic bastard just to prove he could do it. But he couldn't get rid of what he conjured up and he couldn't control it either!

"The Gate Keeper is a four-headed beast with a reptilian body who has the power to be anything he wants to be . . . to come to you in any form he desires. The Gate Keeper controls that house."

He came to Henry as a she-bitch and Henry fucked him!

"When those Spanish people ran, some of those entities ran with them. There's no escaping those bastards. Once they have a hold on you, they'll follow you until the day you die."

"But you said they're still in the house," Buddy quipped.

"Most of them are. The house is their headquarters. It *belongs* to them. Only a dozen or so were sent after those Spanish people—"

"Why?"

"To lure them back. To regain control of their minds and bodies. And in doing so, they can use these *possessed* humans to gain control of others. One person might beget hundreds. And if they're in command of enough houses and enough people . . . Well, it's too frightening to think of the consequences."

"And the Spanish man never came back?"

"No, he didn't. But those evil bastards were still trying to keep me from selling the house just in case he decided to return. That is . . . until I brought Erica Walsh there. In Erica, they found a choice victim to replace the one they lost."

His mind drifted back to the night he challenged the Gate Keeper and what he said about Erica Walsh.

"A HOT BITCH," the Gate Keeper had said. "SHE LIKES HER LAY."

"Mrs. Walsh is weak and vulnerable and will succumb to the demons with no fight at all."

"Dad, this is incredible!" It was Patricia's turn to be sarcastic. "How do these creatures know whom to pick? By the color of your hair or the way you walk—"

"No, damnit! They read minds, they know your every thought. They've been around since the beginning of time and know all about us and how to deal with it. They take your hopes and desires and use them against you."

"ERICA DOESN'T WANT KAYLE BECAUSE HE POUNDS HER TOO HARD. AARON DOES IT BETTER. SHE WANTS A MAN TO FUCK HER LIKE AARON." The Gate Keeper's words, and Henry had to believe it was the truth.

"They're using Erica's thoughts to their advantage, to control her!"

"Then tell her *not* to buy the house if you know what's going on!" Patricia was incensed.

"I can't! They threatened to kill you kids if I interferred. You and—"

A pair of blinding headlights flashed in his face and he heard the roar of an engine being revved in anger. The front of the car was facing him now, and Henry felt sick with the knowledge of what was coming next. He opened his mouth to warn them, to scream, but it was too late. The next sound he heard was the shattering noise of plate glass when the car careened through the wall of the restaurant.

9

Sam Walsh figured he had it all; a new house, his own bedroom, to be shared with Todd, of course, and new bunk beds. And those beds were some heck of an improvement over the lumpy old sofa he used to sleep on. The mattresses were soft and firm, the bed frame was real wood, with hand-carved wagon wheels on the head and foot boards. They were *some* beds.

Today was moving-in day. Only it wasn't as exciting as he dreamed it would be. There was so much damned unpacking to do, and Erica told them they were responsible for their own. Imagine that! Here he was, all of five, and already burdened with the awfully tirin' job of puttin' his own stuff away, when he should've been outside makin' plans.

Hell, with their own house, he'd have the freedom to do the things he was not allowed to before. Now Sam would be able to build a tree house in that big, old sucker near the back; the one with the long, pointy branches that scared him the first time he saw it. 'Course he still felt uneasy about climbin' the damn thing, but it was his own tree at this point, or the family's, whichever way you cared to look at it. And he could learn to love it and not be afraid now. He had the time to become buddies with the tree.

Yeah, he'd make friends with it first thing in the morning. But for now, he had to unpack. Otherwise,

Erica was sure to come up here, to his bedroom, and start her ragin' again. Jeez, the way she yelled at him a while back sure gave him nervous jitters.

His Mom wasn't the yellin' type. She always talked and explained things; like *why* they were gettin' punished—the four of them—and *why* she thought they was actin' bad, and *why* she wanted them to do somethin'.

Kayle was the same, only Kayle was a half-yeller or a loud talker dependin' on your own opinion. No one knew the extent of their wrath better than Sam. Sam was hyper; and a jumper and a noisy player who was always gettin' himself into one mess after another. Still, Erica had patience with him, and the other kids as well. Punishment meant spending a day in your room, no *spankin'*, *no screamin'*, and no *dangerous rages*.

But she changed somehow. Soon as Erica stepped over the threshold of this house and walked in the front door—BOOM! All hell broke out. And Sam couldn't understand why. He didn't do anything wrong. He didn't slap Katie, or pull Didi's hair, or punch Todd. He did nothing. And he still got into trouble. Shit, that wasn't fair, nohow.

The threatened punishment was different too. Sam wouldn't spend a day in his room, or the girl's room, like he did in the old house. Hell no. Now he'd spend a day locked in his closet! Jeez! That was scary to even think about. Them closets were huge compared to what he was used to. In the old house they'd been smaller, but well-lit. These were big, dark, old walk-in closets. Sam looked at his and shuddered, then turned his head to the side in puzzlement when he realized it was open.

The door had been closed when he came into the bedroom, and hell, he hadn't unpacked so much as a thing yet. So, why was it open? And yet, there was only one real answer—Katie! Katie was hidin' in his closet. She'd come in when he was thinkin' and his mind was elsewhere and he hadn't seen her.

His next question was, why was Katie doin' this? Why was she startin' with him when he was sure to be blamed for any trouble between them? She was a bitch! She wanted him to get into trouble. As if he didn't do enough of that on his own. The bitch! He could see it now, he'd go over to the closet, find her there and whack her for bein' so sneaky. Then he'd get punished. It was always the same and he was sick of it.

But now, if he used his head, sort of found her there and made her look like a fool, that would be his revenge. There would be no reason to punch her one. And too, if he did this right, Katie might get *a beatin'* this time.

Sam was smiling broadly when he approached the opened door to the closet, mainly 'cause he was growing up. He was learnin' how to handle a situation without wantin' to lose his temper. Geez, it was hot in there, in his bedroom, and it smelled bad. It reminded him of the raccoon.

Sam had found a dead raccoon once, lyin' out back of the house by the garbage pails. He remembered, him and the other kids discovered it when they left for school in the morning; all except for Katie. She was too young for school. And that old raccoon was so dead it was stiff and cold. Sam had touched it, on a dare from Todd of course, and later wished he hadn't.

It was full of maggots inside. Sam hadn't noticed them until he touched the rotted carcass and these little white worms crawled out of its mouth. And damn, did it stink! This room had the same kind of an odor; like somethin' dead and wormy was layin' around somewhere waitin' to be found. He shuddered again, his tiny body suddenly cold and clammy, despite the intense heat in the room. His shirt was stuck to his back.

He stopped halfway across from the closet, after having second thoughts about Katie being in there.

Supposen it was a dead thing? The place did smell pretty bad. Then what? Sam wasn't as brave as he often pretended to be. The idea of finding somethin' as hideous as that raccoon scared the ass off him. After all, he was alone, in his room. Todd was helpin' Kayle set up the girls' bunks.

Sam decided to use his head for the second time in less than hour hour. He'd leave the closet alone until he was finished unpackin'. There was a baseball bat in the bottom of one of those boxes. Once he had a weapon in hand, he'd gladly search the inside of that closet, and see if Katie was there or if it was somethin' dead. 'Course he realized he maybe didn't need a bat to handle a dead thing. Then again, if it was only half-dead, and could jump or attack or somethin' like that, he'd probably need the bat to protect himself.

Sam backed over to his pile of boxes, never taking his eyes off the closet door. He figured he'd stand a better chance of seein' somethin' come *out* of there, and of runnin' like hell, *if* he watched it while he was backin' up. The only trouble was, he couldn't see behind himself. And somethin' . . . sure as hell . . . was breathin' . . . over by his boxes . . .

And it was callin' his name . . .

Sam figured he was in one helluva fix!

Katie was pissed as usual. Erica, her Mommy, had yelled when they came here and told them, in a loud voice, ''To unpack your damn stuff and put it away, neatly!'' But, Katie was only four. It wasn't fair. She never learned how to do things neatly. She'd tried, so many times, and it never worked. Somehow or other, she just couldn't fold her own clothes like Mommy did, or put her dresses on hangers so they wouldn't fall off again.

Now, as if that wasn't enough, her Daddy and her brother, Todd, were puttin' up bunk beds so she had no room to unpack!

In desperation, Katie had decided to explore her

closet. And oh, what a wonderful place it was; big and roomy and bright. The boys' closet wasn't bright, she thought, smiling with sadistic satisfaction 'cause hers was better. She even dragged some of her dollies inside to play house with. She was haunched back on her legs, with a doll spread across her knees, feeding it a bottle, when it struck her that something was not quite right here.

She was playin' house, just her and the doll, but somethin' was missing. Then it dawned on her. It was all wrong because Sam wasn't here to play the Daddy. Sam usually took the role after a lot of threatening and temper tantrums on her part.

Once she even had to promise she wouldn't tell Erica about how he'd peed in the bushes around back of the old house. Sam got mad, said she was pullin' blackmail on him. But he gave in and played dolls with her. And the way she figured it, it was more than he deserved for whippin' out his . . . thing . . . and peein' in front of her. Erica would've done worse. Erica would've killed him if she'd found out.

"Eat, dollie, eat," Katie said and shuddered because it was so cold in the closet. Still, it was nicer in here than it was in her bedroom, which was as hot as an old furnace. Then again, Mommy had promised to hang ceilin' fans so it would be more comfortable up here, where the bedrooms were.

But then Mommy also promised to lock them in the closets if they were bad. So, what good would the fans do? She'd smother. And too, the closet was sure to be dark with the doors closed.

She shuddered again because the thought of being locked in a big, dark closet was more than she could bare. She'd never been punished that way before. Mommy sure was actin' strange. And Daddy Kayle said to "ignore her", whatever that meant, because Mommy was just nervous about movin' into this house.

"I love you, dollie," Katie said.

"AND I LOVE YOU BACK," the doll said, its lips moving in a hideous manner when it spoke.

Katie wasn't a bit startled at first. She often imagined hearing her dolls speaking to her when she played with them. Only, this time its lips had moved, and that bothered her. Still, her dolls were real to her. Why they were just as real as any baby was to its mother.

Weren't they?

Maybe she just imagined it . . .

She decided not to speak to it again . . .

Not just yet anyway . . .

She'd wait until Sam was here . . .

"I LOVE YOU, KATIE."

The doll had spoken again. But this time its lips didn't move. This time the sound came from behind her. Katie sat very still and tried to think this over, her tiny dress stuck to her body with a dampening chill. The doll had spoken again, but those wooden lips had held fast—no movement! The sound came from behind her—and now there were other noises coming from behind her. Shuffling noises, like someone was crawlin' her way. She felt hot breath on her back.

And the closet was growin' dark inside. But why? The door was still open. It should've been bright in there; as bright as it was when she first came in.

Something brushed against her back.

She glanced in the direction of the bunk beds and couldn't see Todd or Daddy Kayle. They must've left the room without tellin' her. Hell. Here she was, only four, and alone in a dark closet . . . No . . . *Not really alone.* But there was no one outside to help. Katie closed her eyes and began to cry just before a hand, a small, deathly cold hand, touched her shoulder in a comforting manner. The frail voice of a child echoed in her ears.

"I LOVE YOU, KATIE," the voice said.

Erica was in her room unpacking when the children

screamed. She recognized two voices: Sam's and Katie's.

Erica had been there for a half hour or more, unpacking and checking out the water bed. Kayle had bought her one as promised, and had it delivered the day before as a surprise. It was a king sized one, also as promised.

Seven foot wide and six foot long, the frame had been upholstered in chocolate brown leather. Erica loved it. As soon as she saw the bed, she laid across it and felt her body go limp with the slight rocking motion of the water. God, it was wonderful and everything she ever wanted besides.

She laid in the bed for a while, disregarding the boxes of clothing stacked in a pile by the door, and gave silent thanks for the house. Weird though the house was, it'd been purchased for the children. She felt they would all adjust to the idiosyncrasies of the place in time. After all, compared to the dump they used to live in, this was heaven. Strange, but still heaven.

At that point, she tried to recapture her first thoughts when she came in the front door a while back. Surely they'd been different from the thoughts she'd had when she'd been here a few times before. She'd walked in here this morning knowing the house was hers, and that she'd never have to leave. This was it!

So, what had she been thinking at the time? Odd, but she couldn't remember. Kayle had unlocked the front door, after which the kids went storming in behind him. Then it was her turn. Her mind was a bit clouded by excitement, so she wasn't really thinking about anything specific at that point. But what about afterwards? Before the smoke?

She remembered seeing a white, smoky-like substance hanging in the air when she closed the front door. She recalled staring at it and thinking it was cigarette smoke, probably from the workers who'd delivered the water bed. But it wouldn't have lasted all night long, and that was the last thing she could remember with vivid accuracy.

Then, suddenly, as if she'd awakened from a dream, she was up here, in her bedroom, unpacking and checking out the water bed. There was nothing in between. Was she losing her mind? Erica had never suffered from memory lapses before. Unless . . . Maybe the exhilaration she felt from just owning the house and knowing it was theirs had temporarily affected her this way?

Yes, she decided, that was it. The excitement from finally owning a dream house had affected her. It surely had nothing to do with the *voices* emanating from the smoke when it floated down . . . and engulfed her body . . .

She quickly scolded herself and tried to force something sensible into her head. Smoke was a gaseous substance with no brain. Period! It didn't have the ability to talk. Besides, what if she'd continued thinking along those lines? What if her mind really let go and went back to the first time she came here, to this house?

Someone had touched her then . . . and had spoken to her . . . like the smoke did . . .

Bullshit! She'd hallucinated then from the gases mixing together: the stagnant air in the house, the volatile oil in the perfume she smelled in the master bedroom. And the smoke in the foyer this morning had affected her the same way. End of flashbacks, she thought to herself, enough for one day! She was alone now, in this room. This wasn't the time to let her imagination run wild.

In fact, she was alone in the house except for Sam and Katie. Kayle had run out to the store for soda and cold cuts, and had taken Todd and Didi with him. So, if Erica became frightened and fainted at his point, she was on her own!

Erica forced herself to move, to leave the warmth

and comfort of the water bed to finish unpacking. The box she'd been working on last, to her, was one of the most important. It contained a long, plastic, cartridge case full of irreplaceable treasures, cassette tapes of her childrens' voices, recorded during the most wonderful times in their lives—birthdays, holidays, just any day that was special. There were short, childish speeches on those tapes, and songs, all sorts of songs; most with fairy tale limericks.

Those tapes were like a progress report of her childrens' emotional growth. Tape after tape, year after year, she could hear them maturing, their voices changing, their choice of words becoming more defined, more intelligent in use. It was hard to tell on a daily basis, but when she played those tapes, the truth became evident. The kids were growing up.

She placed the case of cassettes on her dresser: Kayle could put them on the top shelf of the closet when he came back. Then she searched until she found a box labeled "personal." This was her own special vanity box, full of her makeup and perfume. Erica had quite a few bottles of perfume and used them according to her mood swings. *Empress* was one of her favorites. *Empress* made her feel sexy.

Aaron Pace loved *Empress!*

The thought amazed her. She had actually allowed herself to dwell on Aaron when her mind should've been on other things. She removed the *Empress* and opened the bottle, sniffing its delicate aroma until it brought back memories. She imagined herself in Aaron's embrace. But no! She couldn't do this, want and need him so badly when there was so much to be done. She didn't have the time to stand there like a fool smelling a bottle of perfume. Hell no.

Especially when the room already reeked from the stuff as it was. How, she wondered, would she be able to stand the scent of her own blended with the rest?

Erica stuck her hands into the back pockets of her jeans and studied the room with an eye towards decorating it. The water bed was chocolate brown; her dresser's brown mink. If she painted the walls white or egg shell, she could use the dark brown ceiling fan she planned on buying. Provided, of course, that the color she chose would cover the hideous blue the walls were painted now.

She could also picture a large, dark brown, wall fan, made of cane, hanging on the wall behind the water bed. That would add just the right touch. She really didn't want so much dark brown in here unless it complemented the lighter colors. Hell, then she'd only wind up throwing things away—

The former owners had discarded a black leather living room set. Why had they left in such a hurry?

No! She wasn't starting that again, allowing herself to wonder why they'd left, or if they'd hallucinated as she had. She dug down once again into the box marked "personal" and froze, her blood curdling in her veins when Sam and Katie screamed.

Kayle wasn't about to admit the truth; why he really went to the store for soda. He'd just about convinced himself that he had an overwhelming thirst and they needed some cold drinks in the house. So he gathered up the two oldest kids, with Erica's sanity in mind, and headed for the store.

Todd and Didi were in the back seat, chattering with excitement over the new town, when his thoughts on the subject of thirst were interrupted by reality. The truth was, he was running. Just for ten minutes or so, or however long it took to get to the store and back, but running just the same.

That house . . . That fucking house. Weird, spooky. Like the first time he'd gone there; someone pushed him on the steps, nearly knocking him headfirst over the side of the railing. Jesus! But, he'd promised the house to Erica, so, with that in mind, he had to forget his own personal feelings towards the place. He'd made every effort to convince himself that the incident on the staircase was just a fluke. It never happened. It was just his imagination.

He rubbed the scar on his face and followed Erica's directions to the store. It was a bit confusing, but he'd learn the way in time. They were going to be living there for how long? Probably for the rest of their lives. Learning the proper roads to take and where the stores were would become second nature—

One thought stayed with him: they were going to be living in that house for the rest of their lives. Kayle paused for a stop sign, then turned left onto Main Street, not knowing if he could hack living there forever. Jesus! Here he was, running now, after a short hour or so of exposure to the craziness he sensed inside. And if he ever slipped to Erica, about how he really felt, he could damn well kiss his life good-bye. She'd call him a nutty bastard and dump him for sure.

But there *was* something wrong, only he couldn't quite grasp what he was trying to formulate in his mind. He never was good at putting things together, not like Erica was, and he found himself searching for sensible answers. What exactly was it that scared him so? What had he felt when he was inside; in the living room, in the bedrooms, the kitchen? Damn, it was beyond him!

He felt what . . . A presence? Several presences? Nothing he was able to see of course, but he felt he was never alone, even when he was. That was it! Kayle would be alone in a room, Erica and the kids somewhere else in the house, and he'd sense someone watching him. And sometimes . . . Sometimes, there were *voices* whispering to him, telling him things he either couldn't or wouldn't understand.

But, that was ridiculous!

Kayle didn't believe in ghosts. Jesus! The living always worried him more than the dead. Like his mother, for instance. She was dangerous when he was younger and she'd been among the living. However, once she died, the threat was gone. Therefore, he concluded, the dead were harmless, and didn't walk once they were buried. No ghosts, baby!

He pulled up in front of a small convenience store and ushered the kids inside. Todd grabbed a six-pack of soda while Didi searched for cold cuts and bread. Kayle got the beer, for himself this time, not Erica. That amazed even him. Kayle had never been a drinking man, had never even tasted liquor, and had sworn he never would, because of his alcoholic parents.

But now he was looking at the idea in an entirely different light. Liquor numbed your senses. If he was going to exist in that house, he needed a crutch, even if the crutch was only a temporary one. At least until he learned to live in harmony in the house with whatever had lived there first!

And, if it wasn't ghosts, then what?

Anyway, a few beers wouldn't hurt. Not if he didn't succumb to the violence and nastiness associated with alcohol. Then, once his nerves were settled, he'd give it up.

Todd and Didi spotted the beer and smiled. Kayle smiled back. The kids probably figured it was for Erica. Not so. Old Daddy Kayle was about to knock off his first case. And not on the sly either. No, sir! He planned on drinking it, casual like, so as not to draw attention, right there in the kitchen at home.

When he got outside, he was struck by what seemed like another sound idea. There was safety in numbers, and he needed that safety, or at least a feeling of being safe now. One of the guys he usually hung out with at work had moved to Monroe months ago. Kayle toyed with the idea of stopping by his place to maybe invite him over for a few beers, or maybe to help unpack. He searched his wallet until he found the address.

"Come on, kids," he said to them when they climbed into the back seat of the car. "Let's stop at a gas station for directions. There's someone I wanna pick up. You don't know him, but his name's Aaron Pace.''

Erica found Sam standing in the middle of the floor in his bedroom crying. Katie was in her closet. It was odd to discover they had both been frightened for similar reasons, considering they'd been in separate bedrooms. *Something* or *someone* had called them by name, and had touched them or grabbed them or whatever. But, they were *alone* when she found them.

They also complained of feeling hot breath on their necks.

Erica wouldn't admit it in front of the children, but their experiences had been the same as hers. The day she fainted, hadn't someone spoken her name and touched her, someone she wasn't able to see? And, of course, rather than imagine she was crazy, she charged it up to hallucinations. Well, then, the children must've been suffering from the same thing, flights of fantasy brought on by the various gases in the house mixing together!

No! That wasn't true and she knew it!

There was something wrong here. But what? And whom could she turn to for answers? Kayle? Hell no! He'd swear she was nuts. Then he'd rage for days because Erica had forced him into buying a house that frightened her. And then to tell him she'd been aware of it for a long time now and wouldn't admit it, not even to herself. Shit! The bastard would kill her for sure. It would be all over with!

Then who else could she turn to? Henry Wittaker? Sure! Run up and tell a man who's just lost his wife that your house is haunted with ghosts! Right good sense that made.

Then who else was there? Her mother? Oh, Lord! Mary would give her a load of bull about bad vibes again.

She was frustrated. There was an answer to all of this and in all probability, the answer was an easy one. Wait a minute, she thought. Just because their experiences—Katie's and Sam's—had been the same as hers didn't prove a thing! They were in a new house, maybe they felt strange. After all, it was the biggest house they'd ever owned: two stories, three bedrooms, three baths, not to mention the dining room, the den . . .

Maybe the kids found it a bit overwhelming. Maybe all those spooky movies on T.V.—the ones where the houses were always large, and had a lot of rooms— were finally getting to them. And maybe, just maybe, she, herself, had hallucinated.

"Honey," she told Katie, "This is your home. We're going to be here for a long time. There's absolutely nothing to be afraid of."

"But there was a little girl in my closet," Katie protested. "I *saw* her."

Sam stood silently by and just listened. To Sam, Katie was a girl; she was supposed to talk like an idiot. Sam was not about to admit there might be some truth behind what she was telling Erica.

"She said she loved me, Mommy."

"Katie, listen," Erica began, thinking back on her own childhood and an answer that made better sense. "It's not unusual for little girls—and—little boys, to conjure up imaginary playmates in their minds."

The last part was directed at Sam also, and he sensed it. But he remained silent, although he was mad as hell inside. Playmate indeed! The voice he heard wasn't full of love. Far from it! They were standing in the hallway, near the opened bedroom doors. Katie, he noticed, kept her back purposely turned as though she couldn't bear to look inside of hers. Sam tried to be fearless as he quickly scanned the interior of his own. But he shuddered, his body quaking with fear.

Erica noticed this and closed the doors before going on.

"You see, I was lonely as a child . . . And I had playmates. But . . . I was the only one who could see them. They talked to me, played dolls . . . Told me they liked me . . . And I didn't look for this. They just sort of came out of nowhere—"

"But, Mommy. I've not lonely. I got Sam and Didi—"

"You may not think you are. But you are." She put her arms around Katie and held her close. "When the other children go to school, there's no one to play with. You're alone for at least six hours a day. So, out of frustration, your mind takes over and . . . *invents* little friends for you to play with."

"Then . . . what happened to me?" Sam protested. He couldn't stand any more of this. "I ain't lonely. I go to school."

"But you do not interact very well with other children," Erica insisted. "You constantly fight with your friends. Maybe you were looking for someone who would stay with you no matter how you treated them." Erica was proud of herself. Her explanations made better sense than she'd originally thought.

"Look, kids. We have a bit of unpacking to do. And you're both nervous . . . Sam, you stay with Katie—"

"Oh, Mommm!" Sam rolled his eyes in despair.

"Listen to me!" Erica was losing her temper, yet tried not to give in. Her children needed support, not anger. "It would be nice if you could help each other. This way, neither of you will be lonely. And you won't start *imagining* things again." She let go of Katie and rose wearily, backing away, in the direction of her own room. "I have to finish before Daddy gets back. He promised to help me unpack the stuff in the kitchen. I don't have all this time . . ."

Sam watched her disappear down the hall and turned to Katie. There was something he had to say, only saying it wasn't easy. Katie tended to side with the grownups and to develop their points of view; while he was an individual and stuck by his own beliefs. At the moment, he believed that Erica's answers were wrong. But saying this to Katie could turn out to be a mistake., The snitching little creep!

Katie, however, surprised him when she spoke up, relieving him of some of the pressure. ''Mom's wrong. There's a little girl in my closet . . . An' she's like me . . . Not made up . . . An' there's lots of other funny people livin' there, too.''

Sam listened quietly and wondered if she really felt this way, or if she was baiting a trap for him. He was further relieved when the downstairs door opened and slammed shut. He heard Todd and Didi talking. This was the excuse he needed to get away from Katie without discussing what took place in their rooms. And he wouldn't have to stay and help her unpack, as he'd promised Erica he would. Didi could damn well stay with her now!

He looked at Katie and started to walk away, speaking over his shoulder as he did. ''Didi's home. She can come up here with ya . . . Nobody'll bother ya with *her* around.'' Then he ran downstairs without another word, leaving Katie alone in the hallway.

Katie held onto her dollie and watched him go. Surprisingly, she felt no anger at him for going back on his promise to stay in her room. After all, Didi was older than Sam, so it was better to have Didi with her. Besides, her sister was smarter about a lot of things, since she'd lived longer than any of them—except for Todd, he was the oldest. And anything living in that closet had to know they weren't facing a helpless little girl this time. Didi would fix them!

Katie stood in the middle of the hall, where it was safe, away from her bedroom door, and waited for her sister to come upstairs. But, after a minute or so, she impatiently realized Didi wasn't coming. Probably because Daddy Kayle had her doing something else. She looked at her bedroom door in despair. She hated going in there alone. Still, Mommy had told her to put her clothes away. Facing a make believe playmate was maybe safer than facing a raging Erica.

Her bedroom door was open. She looked inside; at the new bunks she'd be sleeping on tonight, at the endless pile of cardboard boxes waiting to be unpacked, and at the closet. Then she thought about going in there alone. But something cropped up in her mind, and all else was forgotten. She was able to see inside of her bedroom because . . . *the door was open!*

Mommy closed the door when Katie was crying and insisting she'd heard voices in her closet, didn't she? Yes! Mommy closed the door and told her to calm down. So . . . *who opened it?*

Maybe Sam did just to tease her and scare her.

Yeah, that was it, she reasoned. Rotten Sam opened the door. He had to be the one because there was nobody inside. Not even her make believe playmate. Sam sure was mean when he wanted to be. He knew she was lonely, and her mind was making things up and he did this to scare her.

Katie wouldn't allow herself to even think about what she'd told Sam before; about how Erica was wrong and her playmate had been real! Little girls couldn't afford to dwell on reality when they had to be brave and face things on their own.

Katie went back into her bedroom alone, slowly, one tiny step after another, her eyes scanning the room for signs of movement. Her doll, still in her arms, was held fast, under the neck, close to her chest for comfort. *Nothing moved.* She was safe.

Her dresses were in a box on the floor, the cardboard lid slashed open. Wearily she clutched a dress without even thinking about it, and laid the doll on the bottom bunk. That was easy, she told herself. The hard part was putting the darn dress in the closet, on a hanger. Damn! If Mommy wasn't always buying her dresses, she wouldn't be faced with this danger right now.

Then again, the danger was all in her head, as Mommy had said it was. If she didn't think about being lonely, nothing would happen. Katie approached the door to the closet using the same slow pace she'd used to enter the room. It was a large closet, and now it loomed larger than usual. Why, the door alone went almost clear up to the ceiling! And the sides of it stretched almost the entire length of the wall. Lots of funny people could be hiding in there, as big as that closet was.

But, not if she kept her mind from thinking about it.

The handle on the door was in her hand before she knew it and she was turning it slowly and deliberately. All she had to do was to hang up this one dress without anything happening and the rest would come easy. She could hang up the others in no—

"I LOVE YOU, KATIE."

It was a small voice, coming from the mouth of a small child. Katie felt chills racking her body, but she couldn't move. And this time she couldn't even scream. Her vocal cords were constricted with fear. And yet, what was she afraid of? Why had she been so frightened before?

The child she faced was no older than herself, and didn't look dangerous. A sweet-faced child, with long, black hair hanging in ringlets, and large black eyes. She wore a frilly dress that captured Katie's attention. It was trimmed with real fluffy lace. No one who was about to hurt her would wear a dress like that.

"SPEAK TO ME, KATIE. I'M YOUR FRIEND."

Her smile wasn't too friendly, and that upset Katie. But still, the little girl said nice things. Besides, if she got nasty with Katie, Katie would punch her with the same ferocity she used on Sam. Having settled that much in her mind, Katie began to feel at ease. She even began to imagine that made-up playmates weren't such a bad idea after all. At least it was a girl. It could've been worse. She might've wound up with someone like Sam. She shuddered.

"What's yer name?" she asked her playmate.

"ANGELICA."

"You like to play with dolls?" Katie hoped she did.

''YES, LET'S PLAY WITH DOLLS, KATIE. THEN I'LL SHOW YOU SOME NEW GAMES. ONES YOU'RE SURE TO ENJOY!''

''Okay, Angelica,'' Katie said, entering the closet, oblivious to fear when the door closed behind her, also unaware of Didi's presence. Didi had come in when she was conversing with her playmate, Angelica. And now Didi stood quite still, staring at the closed door, listening to Katie having a one-sided conversation with someone she, herself, couldn't see or hear.

10

Although she was exhausted from her almost non-stop trip from Colorado, Kirsten Larsen pulled into the driveway of her Huntington home and felt a happy sort of euphoria. She rolled down the window of her car and inhaled the wonderfully fresh scent of honeysuckle, and watched robins dance across the lawn.

Oh, Lord, she thought, it was so good to be home she couldn't move from the car. Being here after such a long absence made her want to just sit and stare at the house and reflect.

The house was situated quite a distance from the main road; set back about eighty feet in the woods. The location was ideal, because it gave her the privacy she needed; privacy that was so important after the tremendous amount of notoriety with the police, and all . . .

And yet, at times she paid dearly for that privacy; times when her *friends,* the ancient masters, went out of their way to torment her.

Then she would've given her soul . . . No! Never her soul. Rather, she would've paid any price to be able to run to a neighbor and ask for help. But, that wouldn't have been right and she knew it. There never was a reason valid enough to involve innocent people in her predicament. What if her *friends* decided to stay and visit the neighbors? Then someone would be knocking at her door asking for help.

Besides, she was under the protection of the Lord; she was his emissary. She had to do this alone.

The house looked so forlorn. The boards on the windows and the padlock on the door had an air of permanence. Probably from being closed up for so long, she imagined, a year to be exact. However, she knew she'd return someday, *and so did her friends;* once the hate mail stopped and the nuts went back into the woodwork. It took all kinds, she thought, but somehow she attracted mostly psychotics. And Satanists. Some said they belonged to the Religious Order of Satan. Indeed!

She got out of the car and leaned against it after smoothing the wrinkles from her dress. The house really hadn't changed much. Not that she'd expected it to. Still, a year was a long time; so many bad things could've happened. A storm might've wrecked the house, or prowlers might've vandalized it. Kirsten had been lucky.

Something moved in one of the front windows. The curtains were still rustling. Impossible! Nothing moved, she told herself. Besides, if someone were there, she couldn't have seen them; the windows were boarded up. She stared at the boards and wondered what was happening. Why was it starting this soon? Were *they* inside waiting for her, making her see things that weren't really there? Yes, *they* knew she'd come back, and *they* were ready.

The padlock was partly rusty and didn't give easily, but she got it open. She twisted the knob of the door with her fingers and was almost inside when a car door closed behind her. She didn't have to look to see who it was since hers was the only car in the driveway. Curiosity made her turn and look anyway. The dead thing, the one who followed her from that motel room in Colorado, had just gotten out of the back seat.

She couldn't see him, but she sensed him there, near the car. She hoped it wouldn't follow her into the house. They didn't always come inside. Most of them were content to hover on the grounds and make noises to scare her.

It was too bad she couldn't *see* the damn thing and where it was headed. Christ, what if this bastard decided to be in the minority and he followed her inside? What if he wound up in her bed late at night, or in the bathroom when she was taking a shower?

Don't think about this, she raged inwardly. Ignore the bastard . . . and he might go away.

She sighed and went on in carefully closing the door behind her. If anyone opened that door, she'd hear them. She stiffened and looked around. The house was full of cobwebs and there was a musty odor to it. It was dark too because of the boards covering the windows. But once it was cleaned and those boards removed, Kirsten would feel a bit better. She smiled, but it was a strain. Feeling a whole lot better was beyond her reach, and always had been.

The nightly visits from her *friends* had to stop first, then she'd be living like everyone else. . . like everyone else . . .

Wearily she sat down on a sheet-draped chair and tried to recall the last time she'd been allowed to live like everyone else. Had it been six years already? Six years since the accident?

She closed her eyes and tried not to think beyond this point. And yet, the memories were there, like scars that never went away. She saw the truck again, the tractor trailer, coming down the road in the opposite direction. It was raining and the roads were slippery. Why was the driver going so fast? Too fast! Oh, God, he'll never make the curve in the road ahead. And the car she was riding in would be rounding the curve at the same time. Thank God she wasn't driving, she might have a chance—

The nerve shattering sound of metal striking metal echoed in her ears, and lingered, with the shocking revelation that her fears had become reality. The driver of the truck didn't make the curve. She remembered seeing the body of the truck when it jackknifed and slid sideways across the road, just before it hit them.

She'd been holding onto the passenger door, and wouldn't let go, not even when the door separated from its hinges and careened through the air. Then she was flying, with the door, in slow motion, through a horrible black void in space. Just flying.

But the door loosened from her grip and flew away, just as something hard and solid struck her body. Or, rather, just as her body struck it. She landed on the pavement, by the side of the road, her skull splitting, melonlike from the force of the impact; one of her legs shattering when it twisted itself beneath her body and she landed on it.

Odd, though, she could not recall having any pain in her head. The doctors at the hospital told her, much later, that severe head injuries never hurt much after the initial impact. She laughed again, and again it was a strain. Those same doctors very professionally omitted the rest. They never warned her about the headaches and the throbbing jolts that would strike her skull, days later, with the force of a clap of thunder.

Sometimes she felt like beating her head against a wall just to stop the incessant pain. But she couldn't walk. Her leg.

Oh that hurt, within minutes after the accident, when she'd been lying on the ground, praying that it all had been a nightmare. She could almost feel the sensation, even now, after six years, of her bare flesh, those delicate inner layers that had always been protected by skin, lying exposed against the pavement. Cold, unyielding concrete. And the rain beating down on her body. At the time, she wondered if she were dead.

But no, if she'd died, there would've been no pain, only a feeling of total peace and serenity. Unlike most people who saw death as a final state of rest, she thought of death as a beginning. Her soul would've lived for an eternity, and she would finally have met her Lord.

But something so wonderful wasn't meant to be. Not for her; not yet anyway. She was alive. She was taken to a hospital, to suffer through the agony of recuperation. And the only thing that made it bearable was the relationship she developed with her roomie, a kind, sympathetic, good natured woman by the name of Bess Wittaker.

Bess was someone special all right. She had two bum kidneys, and no chance of recovery, and she knew it. But she still managed to keep her chin up. During the nine months they roomed together, she inspired Kirsten to get better, to fight for life despite the endless struggle. And . . . she supported Kirsten when the visions manifested themselves, when everyone else thought Kirsten was crazy, her mind gone from the accident. Bess was a good person all right.

Kirsten opened her eyes, stared into the semidarkness around her, and had the sudden urge to turn on the lights. But the electricity was off. Had been for a year. Then she scolded herself for dropping her guard by allowing the past to crop up in her mind as it had. They wanted her to drop her guard and be helpless.

It was dark in there because of the boards covering the windows; they thrived in darkness. She could feel them, could sense them, could see one in an open doorway ducking back out of view.

No! Don't do this, she shouted inwardly. Don't let them spook you. Remember the protection of the Lord! Get your mind on something else, like Bess. Think of Bess Wittaker. Now!

Bess was a true, practicing Christian, in every sense

of the word. That was the best she could manage. A door slammed somewhere in the house. Kirsten had to get out of there, if only for a while, to build herself up to face them again after such a long absence. And yet, where would she go? Think, she said to herself inside. Where will you go? You have no friends. *They* wouldn't allow it. Where will you go, she repeated in despair?

But the answer was simple. She would bring her suitcases in from the car and take a drive across town to have her phone connected—and the electricity as well. Then she could call Bess; maybe not tell her what was happening in her life at this point, about the dead thing and all. But just to speak to her, to hear her voice, maybe regain some of that inspiration Bess injected into her veins.

She rose then and went back outside to the car. Her suitcases were in the back seat—along with the dead thing! She could see him, only because he wanted her to. He was smiling at her, mocking her, the lower part of his face rotted back beyond the gums of his teeth. Kirsten couldn't get her suitcases. Not now. Not when this treacherous, deceitful bastard was in her car. And had been all along.

The noise she'd heard before, the car door slamming; it was a trick. He wanted her to think he'd left the back seat, that he was somewhere on the grounds, wandering around; in the woods perhaps. Then she'd feel safe because he wasn't near her, breathing down her neck, the same as he had during the long drive home from Colorado. The son-of-a-bitch!

Well, she had to use the car, and he still couldn't kill her; not while she was under the protection of the Lord. She started to climb inside, but then he was no longer in the back seat. Now he was in front, sitting close to the steering wheel, beckoning her to come to him. Kirsten quickly closed the door and started down the road on foot, completely ignoring the sound of the door when it opened and closed behind her.

She had to walk eighty feet to the main road to catch the bus, and her leg hurt something awful. The last thing she wanted to worry about at this point, was when he would catch up to her, and when he intended to kill her . . .

There were footsteps coming up the back steps. He heard them and tried not to think about it. What more could they do? They'd already taken his wife . . . *And his son* . . . He and Patricia were the only ones left.

Henry Wittaker got up and poured himself another cup of coffee, his eyes automatically drifting out of the window, coming to rest on the Corvette parked in the driveway, the FOR SALE sign still in place. Buddy's car. He quickly went back to sit at the kitchen table. Tears had begun to line his face, and that was the last thing he wanted to happen—to cry, to drop his guard and admit *they* were smarter than he'd given them credit for.

Demons did drive! Why didn't one of them drive a car through the wall of a restaurant and park it on top of his son? And didn't the bastard take off on foot before Henry had a chance to see what he looked like? And before the police came? And wasn't the car stolen?

That was pretty much the way it happened, he told himself. Now he had to forget it and move on. If he didn't, if he allowed the same anger to control him now as it did when they killed Bess, well, hell, they'd win again. Patricia would be easy prey. Therefore, he had to shelve all thoughts of revenge and keep his guard up. He had to stand over his daughter like a man and protect her until he was able to force her to leave.

He got up then and went to the den, leaving his coffee behind. He tried to cross the hall separating the den from the kitchen without incident, but the *rat* had come up the back steps and was standing by the door to the basement. Henry couldn't see him because the fucker didn't want old Henry to see him. But Henry was able to hear him; breathing and growling and laughing to himself like a real nut-job. A small bolt of shock resounded in Henry's brain; he was scared.

And the funniest thing about it was, the *rat* had been roaming the house for so long now, Henry shouldn't have been afraid of it. But the damn thing was so insistent upon getting Henry's attention that most of the time, it acted like a small, spoiled child; a dangerous one, but a child just the same. Banging and slamming things and growling at the top of its lungs whenever Henry ignored it.

Other times it would retaliate differently. That's when Henry really got scared. Like when the fucker stayed invisible, as it was now, and made no noise. You never knew where it was hiding; where it would pop up next, or when it would kill. Oh yeah, it did everything it could to scare him. He just couldn't ignore it. And now he realized there wasn't much left in the area of his sanity.

"Daddy? What's wrong? Why're you just standing there like you're in a trance?"

It was Patricia's voice, coming from behind him. But Henry didn't answer at first. He had to be sure it was her. These bastards were full of tricks. They could've been using her voice to get through to him. He turned slowly, half expecting to see some deformed horror standing there, smiling in his face. But it was Patricia, coming down the stairs, with the same quiet, graceful movements that reminded him of Bess, before she got sick.

"Why don't you answer me?" she wanted to know. "Is something wrong?" Her voice was gentle and soothing compared to the bastard standing behind him.

"Uh . . . I was headed for the den, but I have the strangest feeling I left something behind, in the kitchen. I'm standing here trying to remember what it was." Asshole, he said to himself, because he was embarrassed. Patricia didn't believe in *rats* and here she'd almost caught him conversing with one. Well, anyway, thank God the *rat* was silent now.

She touched his arm and studied his face with the same worried expression she used so much these days. "Daddy, are you going to the den to read those books? Will it be another day of searching for answers?"

Henry felt his temper rising. Just because she didn't believe in demons was no reason to question his sanity. Goddamn, he wasn't crazy. He knew what he was doing. But she was his child and she was concerned, so he tried to understand her point of view.

"Are you searching for answers? Because if you are," she continued, "WE'RE WATCHING YOU, DADDY."

He drew back in shock, his breath coming in short spurts. There were painful spasms racking his chest, around his heart. They'd tricked him again. He turned and ran towards the den, ignoring the sound of laughter echoing in his ears, and he never looked back. If he had, he was certain he would've seen this thing that had pretended to be Patricia in its natural form. And he couldn't take that. Not now.

For now he had to get back to his books. There was an answer to all of this, a way to get rid of these bastards forever. Only, finding it wasn't easy.

Henry was near the den when the front door opened and Patricia walked in. She smiled when she saw him, then frowned with concern because Henry's face had drained white and he seemed faint.

Carol Anderson was making breakfast when she spotted a moving truck in the driveway next door. A truck had also been there yesterday afternoon. And that confused her. She imagined they were moving in, and she wanted to stop them! But it was only a delivery truck; from the House of Water Beds on

Sunrise Highway.

They were moving in *today*. And she wanted to stop them!

"Mommy, when're we eatin'?"

"Yeah, Carol," Burt bellowed. "For Christ's sake, let's get this show on the road."

She already had a stack of pancakes piled high on a platter near her. She grabbed another platter and began to fork bacon onto it. But her movements were clumsy and hampered. Those people, those innocent fools were moving in . . . and she hadn't done a thing to warn them. Oh, Lord, the sin was on her soul.

"If ya paid better attention to your own, and less to what was goin' on next door, we wouldn't be havin' problems." Burt used his hands to grab the food from the serving platters when she laid them on the table. She felt her stomach wretch.

It was wrong, the things he did. She had five children, sitting there watching their father act like a pig, while all the time she was trying to teach them manners. Still, there was little she could do about his vulgarities. She'd let him continue on like this for so many years, that it was too late to correct him now. This was her cross to bear.

"Did ya hear me, Carol? Did ya hear what I said?" She nodded silently as usual. "Then say somethin'. Let me know your brain ain't dead."

The children began to giggle under their breath. They thought Burt was funny. Oh, yeah, she whispered inwardly, Burt's a real comedian; as long as someone else is at the brunt of the joke. But she ignored him and let it go because her mind was on more important matters. She hadn't warned those people next door. Now it was too late. Too late to correct Burt and too late to warn them.

Kayle was in the kitchen with Aaron Pace, drinking beer, when Erica came in. She'd finished unpacking their clothing and was about to make Kayle keep his promise to help with the pots and pans. But two things threw her off; Kayle's drinking, and Aaron Pace! Why was Kayle drinking beer? How did Kayle know Aaron Pace? She'd been so careful when it came to their relationship.

Did Aaron stop by to start trouble?

How could she sit across from him and pretend she'd just met him?

She stiffened and walked casually into the room. Kayle had hung her new curtains at the windows. She stopped to fluff them up and tie the sides back; to allow sunlight to wedge across the kitchen. But she was nervous and clumsy. One of the rods let go and fell on the counter. The clanging noise it made seemed louder than it should have. Aaron laughed. The bastard!

"Hey, Erica," Kayle said. "Come here and meet a swell guy. Works at the station. One of the best fuckin' mechanics we got. Not countin' me, of course."

It sounded as though the beer was speaking for him, considering the bad language. Usually he only cursed when he was angry. Then too, Kayle liked Aaron. That was strange. Kayle didn't like many people, especially if they happened to be in direct competition with him.

While Kayle's back was turned, Aaron Pace decided to make intimate gestures toward Erica. He slid his tongue over and across his lips to show what he had in mind. Erica was tempted to tell him to go to hell. But then she'd have to do a lot of explaining to Kayle; and he must never find out the truth, or she'd be dead—for sure!

"This here's Aaron Pace. My *best* friend," Kayle said in a drunken display of affection.

"Hello, Aaron," Erica said, forcing a smile. "I've never heard of you before. Been working with Kayle long?" That should've been a question that didn't need asking. But, like the elusive Kayle, Aaron had his secrets too, and seldom confided in her when it came to his personal life.

His personal life, she thought disgustedly. How could you sleep with a man for so many years and allow him to keep so much to himself? She'd been a fool, for *both* of these bastards!

"You mean Kayle's never even mentioned my name?" Aaron grinned in that old, arrogant manner she found so appealing. "Why . . . Say, buddy, I'm hurt." Then he directed his attention to Erica. "We been working together for some three years now."

Three years! She wanted to scream. No wonder Aaron knew so much of her business, things she never remembered telling him. Like when they were first thinking of buying a house; Aaron mentioned it over the phone and she hadn't told him about it yet. Then they found the house in Monroe, and he not only knew the exact location, but what it looked like.

Now, here he was, sitting across from her, wearing a know it all, shit-eatin' grin. She wanted to slap him, but held back. "Well," she began in an attempt to get even, "has Kayle ever mentioned our children? His and mine? You must meet them."

It was Aaron's turn to get angry. He knew more about those kids than good, old Kayle ever would.

"I'll get them." She left and went into the living room to call the kids from the bottom of the stairs. But first she laid her head back against the wall; her nerves were dancing under the skin. Aaron's presence, along with the knowledge that he'd been working with Kayle for so long, had given her quite a jolt. Then to find Kayle drinking—

"I love you, baby." It was Aaron. He'd come up from behind. He ran his arms around her waist and cupped her breasts, squeezing them gently to show her what she meant to him.

But Erica wasn't ready for this. She was too angry yet. She pulled away and spun to face him. "Who's idea was it to start drinking? You know he doesn't drink. Why did you do it?''

"He had the beer on him when he picked me up,''
Aaron answered quietly. "It was his idea to suck it
up.''

"He buys it for me. But he never touches it. You're
lying!''

She was raging mad at this point. Aaron was
sticking his nose into her personal life. And if he had
no intentions of sharing *his* secrets, then he had no
right to do this. And he certainly had no right turning
Kayle into one of the boys. "He's only drinking the
shit to impress you!''

Aaron stuck his hands into his pockets and raised
his chin defiantly. "*Ask* him if he didn't start on his
own." There was silence between them for a
moment, then Aaron's expression softened. He
usually gave in first when they argued. "Come on,
baby. Don't be mad at me.''

But Erica still wanted answers and right this
moment. "He picked you up, you said. Where?
Where do you live now, Aaron?'' He'd recently
moved and never told her where to. Yet, somehow
she already knew the answer.

"Right here in Monroe." The tone of his voice was
low and subdued as though he were waiting for
another explosion.

"Right here in Monroe," she repeated, her lips a
thin line of anger. "So you can keep an eye on me.
Right, Aaron?''

"No, I—''

"How long have you lived here?''

"Two months." Again his voice was barely audible.

"You're keeping tabs on me . . . Working with
Kayle . . . Now, moving here . . . What a fucking
nerve!'' Erica wanted to hit him for being such a
sneaky, low down jerk, but the smoke stopped her.

It appeared over Aaron's head as suddenly as it had
appeared over her own this morning, when she came
in the front door. It was white and sulphurous, like

cigarette smoke, only no one had been smoking at the time. That puzzled her. Where did it come from? Was it part of the mystery of this house?

Then again, she reasoned, it may have been caused by faulty wiring. Maybe the answer was that simple. Still, she didn't smell wires burning; it wasn't a chemical odor. It was different, more like cooked meat—slightly rotted, cooked meat.

"Look, baby," Aaron said nervously because she was angry with him. "I didn't mean to follow you here, but I had to. Especially since you tried to kiss me off that time over the phone."

Aaron wasn't conscious of the smoke; she wondered why not.

It was right over his head, slowly winding itself down and around his body. Erica was suddenly afraid for him, and for herself as well.

"I love you, Erica—I LOVE YOU, ERICA."

The same words were spoken twice, and yet, they sounded different the second time—harsher, more confident. Aaron's expression was different, too. He no longer had that pleading look in his eyes. Now he had the look of someone bold who knew what he wanted and was about to take it.

Erica backed away. This change in him was due to the smoke, she was sure of it. His eyes, she couldn't stop staring at them. She felt drawn to them; the allure was hypnotizing. Aaron normally had blue eyes, only now they were black; two amber pools of magnetic liquid, drawing her into their midst.

She stopped backing away and stared until a strange, yet familiar, warmth overtook her. She'd experienced this sensation before. Odd, but she couldn't remember when.

"YOU'RE NOT AFRAID OF ME, ARE YOU, ERICA?"

"No." Hell, she'd never been afraid of Aaron Pace.

"AND YOU'RE NOT AFRAID OF THIS HOUSE EITHER!"

"Yes . . . Uh . . . No." Why had she changed her mind? What was it about those eyes?

"OTHERS WILL TRY TO FORCE YOU TO MOVE. BUT YOU'LL STAY HERE, WON'T YOU?"

"Uh . . . Yes." She wanted to say no, but couldn't. Still, what if there were more incidents involving the children? What if they were really in danger? "Yes, I'll stay," she repeated, not knowing why.

"GOOD! I LOVE YOU, ERICA. AND IT COULD BE THE SAME WITH ME AS IT WAS WITH AARON."

The same as it was with Aaron? Wasn't she speaking to him now? He was standing in front of her. This was weird.

"YOU HAVE MANY QUESTIONS. THEY WILL BE ANSWERED IN TIME. TRUST ME, ERICA. AND REMEMBER, I'LL FUCK YOU WITH THE SAME TENDERNESS AS AARON PACE DOES."

Somehow that last remark broke the hold. Erica lashed out with her hand to slap his face, but her hand froze in midair before it connected.

"Erica! What's keepin' you?" Kayle's voice bellowed from the kitchen. "Come on back here, bitch!"

Who was he calling a bitch, she wondered angrily? Had Kayle let a few beers go to his head and undergone a personality change? He was nasty at times, true, but he never used profanity and her name all in the same breath. Erica suddenly felt she'd be a whole lot better off without either of these bastards—Kayle or Aaron Pace. One wanted to fuck her brains out, while the other was telling her what a bitch she was.

Well now, *fuck them*, she thought, and went upstairs to check on her children.

Mary Rogers had already made up her mind not to interfere when she had a sudden change of heart. At first, she'd decided not to tell Erica what happened to her that day in the house. How there were *heartbeats* in the wall by the staircase when she laid her hand against it. How she'd come to realize the house had a heart and a mind, but no soul!

Hell, Erica probably wouldn't have listened anyway. Erica wanted the house for the sake of the children. And Kayle wouldn't take any other—it was that house or nothing! So, Mary kept quiet.

However, now she'd changed her mind, and was sorry she'd waited so long. If only she'd opened her mouth before they put a deposit on the house, or before the final closing. Then again, what would she've said to convince Erica and Kayle not to buy the house? What would she say now? How could she tell them it had bad vibes emanating from its very pores?

Mary sat at the table in the kitchen sipping her morning coffee. But it wasn't very comforting. She'd hardly slept a bit. Nightmares! All night long! And every one of them was about Erica . . . and that thing! That four-headed beast with the reptilian body who had . . . a penis and an erection . . . just like a man . . . and he was after Erica.

If the dreams themselves hadn't terrified her half to death, the idea behind them would've driven her to fits of laughter. It was funny in a way. But still, it wasn't funny when he killed Erica! Oh no!

Mary shuddered and sipped her coffee for warmth, but it didn't help. Her mind kept going back to those nightmares. She was troubled by them, and she just had to say something to Erica. Maybe she wouldn't mention the four-headed beast. Maybe she'd just mention the others, because there was more than one threat in that house; more than one psychotic . . . One psychotic what?

Certainly not ghosts. Ghosts weren't much of a threat. No, it wasn't ghosts she sensed. She ran her fingers through her thick, white hair and almost cried. The words were in her mind and on her tongue; descriptive words that well-defined those monsters. And yet, she was afraid to even think about them . . .

Lord, Jesus, they were such horrors!

And the dog—he was ONE OF THEM! A large, black dog, she saw it, in Erica's house—*black and trim and mean*—but, Erica didn't have a dog. Never had and said she never would. It was just too dangerous to consider having a dog with the children around. Oh, Lord, was this real? Was it happening now or was it another look into the future? There were so many unknown mysteries concering Erica's house.

However, one thing was for certain. Erica's life was in danger; the children were in danger; Kayle was in danger. She smiled at that despite her anxiety. Kayle they could have. Why, if they twisted his balls around his neck and strangled him, it wouldn't brother her one bit. But then, the whole idea was idiotic! It wasn't Kayle they were after. No! It was Erica, and the children as well.

Mary was also aware of another important factor. Her own life would be on the line if she went to that house and spoke the truth in their presence. Hell, they'd have no choice but to try to kill her. One didn't fool with demented psychotics like them, or interfere in their schemes without suffering somehow.

But then, Erica was her child; her *only* child. And those kids of hers were the only grandchildren Mary would ever have. No one was about to rob her of that, no matter what the consequences! She rose with determination, rubbed her spine, and went to the phone to call a cab. She was going to Erica's, and she was going to pray for the best to happen.

And, she was going to warn Erica never to get a dog as well!

11

The Gate Keeper had the situation well under control —Erica was living in the house. He'd been out front this morning, disguised by the blessed darkness of invisibility, when Erica drove up with Kayle. She walked right past him and never knew it. He smiled, and wondered how she might've reacted had she seen him, in his natural state. But this was no time to dwell on nonsense; there was so much to be done. Especially since phase two of his plan was in motion—Kayle was drinking.

If all went according to plan, Kayle was about to become a memory. The man couldn't handle his liquor; he was getting nasty. Erica wasn't thrilled about having a mean drunk stuck up her ass. Therefore, Kayle had to be scared into drinking more; into really losing it. Physical violence was the next step in the master plan to get rid of Kayle.

The Gate Keeper stood at the top of the stairs, on the second landing of the house, and listened to the voices of the children. Dirty, sniveling, little wimps. Crying for "Mommy" at every sound, every strange movement. To think these were future disciples of his Lord. This was a challenge to end all challenges. The little bastards had to be toughened up, had to be taught to worship at the shrine of sin, had to have

hatred instilled in their libidos. He had his work cut
out, all right.

However, when and if he succeeded, they were *his*
—to dispose of. He smiled and watched Erica's body,
the slow, sensual movement of her hips when she
passed him on the stairs and went down the hall to
her bedroom. *Cunting bitch,* that one. In fact, the last
time they met, he came close to wanting her for
himself; close to making her his own personal bitch. It
was an idea that lingered, until this morning when
she committed the ultimate sin: she tried to slap his
face.

Next time her hand wouldn't freeze in midair. Next
time it would fly off at the wrist, leaving a sickening,
bloody stump in its place.

Bored with the vision of Erica's ass swaying down
the hall, he turned and slithered downstairs. Aaron
Pace was still standing near the kitchen, frozen in
time. This was too wonderful for words. Erica
imagined she'd been speaking to Aaron and he had used a profanity in reference to their love-making. "BUT
NO, ERICA, IT WAS I," he laughed to himself. Still,
she was mad at Aaron, never wanted to see him again.

He'd had a busy morning. He'd destroyed the image
of both of the men in Erica's life. She'd soon be rid of
them. Then she was *his;* to use and dispose of. He
released Aaron from his trance and headed for the
den.

The Gate Keeper was sure of an easy victory at this
point. Not like the hard time he'd had with those
spics, the ones who started this mess and then ran
like their asses were on fire. Those Puerto Rican
bastards who thought they had the world by the short
hairs, what with their altar and black candles and
Satanic Bible—everything done to honor the beast.

They held coven meetings every week, without fail,
and imagined they were in charge. Thirteen people
under their control; naked and beating each other
with black whips, lighting candles and shouting

incantations to bring forth the beasts of old.

Nothing they couldn't handle at first. But things began to go wrong when they brought up Zadarous, Lord of the Seventh Level of Acheron; a handsome devil if ever there was one, even in his natural state. Old Zadarous never had to disguise his appearance.

Black hair and black eyes beautifully topping off a trim, well-toned body, he made the ladies catch their breath, and do unnatural things. He made them throw off their robes, go down on their hands and knees for him, while he either gave it to them up the ass or demanded a header. Sometimes he made them lay prostrate on the floor while he banged each in turn.

They all thought they were hot shit, those bitches, because Zadarous paid attention to them. But it was a joke! Zadarous laughed at those poor, pathetic cunts behind their backs; he used them until he tired of their inane attempts at pleasing him. And still the spics imagined they controlled the high masses. And Zadarous let them, while using them as pawns in a complicated game of soul snatching.

The Gate Keeper went into the den, passing a myriad number of Old Ones wandering around, "PATIENCE," he told them. "YOU WILL HAVE MUCH TO DO WHEN ERICA WALSH BEGETS MORE VICTIMS." Then his mind drifted back, once again, to the past. He thought about how good it used to be when Zadarous was here and the spics lived in the house. Zadarous was a stud, fucking anything that moved.

All went well until one used-up bitch became pregnant. Oh, the master beast was angry. She wasn't a chosen one; worthy enough to stand under the sign of the horns, worthy enough to bear an unholy child. Thus, the black forces of Acheron were set in motion against her; to the point where she miscarried at a high mass. Then she was used instead of the goat, along with the deformed embryo she dropped—she was the sacrifice that night.

Her throat was cut; the blood pouring from her veins drunk to insure that her psychic powers would remain with the coven. Her body was slit down the middle, from gullet to crotch; her heart and other organs consumed to give the members strength.

It was a warning! Satan had been toying with them up until then. But now he was telling them to cool their incantations; to stop bothering his people. The minor devils wanted to be left in peace. They resented being called forth to put on demonstrations of power for fools.

But did the spics listen? No! They continued calling up wise and powerful devils to spice up their meetings. So, the master beast, who has a wonderfully, intelligent sense of the macabre, sent up a devil that no one controlled but him!

The Gate Keeper took charge!

He became the new leader!

The spics ran, back to Puerto Rico! Some of the lesser devils ran after them. But their return to this house was of small importance now since Erica was here. She was a prize, one that would beget others. The Gate Keeper was sure of victory this time.

He slithered down into the black hole in the den to allow the cooling dampness of the walls to soothe his tired body. He was an old warrior, one who had seen his share of battles. At the moment, he couldn't remember which had been the worst in terms of personal injuries suffered.

He recalled the first of these so-called battles.

Most of them had been fought for the usual reasons; power, greed, possession. This was no different. It took place between Satan and that old, brain rotted bastard who prided Himself in being called the God of the Christians.

To begin with; Satan, his prince and master beast, was older than time itself. Why, he even preceeded the fabled Garden of Eden in the Christian Bible, that farcical accounting of so-called true life stories. Yes,

Satan was old. He was given life by the God of the Christians; a nasty, evil, old bastard if ever there was one.

Satan was beautiful; a feast to the eyes, on the same type as Zadarous. To see him was to fall in love; to want to devote your life, your soul, your very being to this stunning man. He was not only handsome, but also brilliance personified. The God of the Christians coveted his beauty and intelligence and jealousy cast him from the Heavens with thousands of his followers.

The Gate Keeper was among those who were cast out. Such was his hatred of the God of the Christians, that he vowed eternal allegiance to Satan, and offered his protection as a warrior as well. Satan was gratified. He made the Gate Keeper one of his own personal aides.

The Gate Keeper had held this very important position ever since. He protected his master throughout all of his appearances here on Earth; throughout the famines that struck Egypt and other powerful nations at the time, throughout the religious wars— the Crusades, and throughout the pestilence and plagues that struck Europe centuries ago.

But now his mission was far more important than any he'd been assigned thus far. Now he was after the possession of a soul that was sure to beget others. Satan had to build his armies, to swell their numbers. After all, the Christians were spewing forth dangerous prophecies. The Gate Keeper, aware of the content of those prophecies, had warned his master in turn.

Those so-called Christians, those he'd been exposed to for the past hundred years or so, all spoke of the second coming of Christ. Christ being that misfitted, low life, son of a carpenter who suffered from delusions of grandeur, who imagined himself the Son of God. Well, this meek, pious loser was supposed to return and retreive His people, then destroy the Earth by fire.

The master beast had a good laugh over that one. The only thing the meek, followed by the meek, would ever inherit, was a good kick in the ass. The strong would survive. Those who forgot that ingrained shit about compassion and mercy, those who followed their basic instincts and enjoyed life to the fullest, those were the future survivors!

However, even knowing this, the master beast began to worry. What if that son of a goat did manage to return? What if he did carry out His threats? He'd take all the choice souls and leave the crap behind! Therefore, a campaign was waged by Satan, starting some thirty years before, to put in his bid for some of the good stock, before it all went to the dog upstairs.

Now, thanks to the hard work and diligence of the lesser devils, the world was turning in the direction of the master beast. Christian souls were disgusted with formal religions. They were forsaking their former God, and taking up the flag of victory in the name of Satan. It was too delirious for words. Satan had lived to taste the sweetness of revenge.

And, since one choice soul begat hundreds, Erica Walsh was destined to join the ranks. She would be the magnet used to attract others. The Gate Keeper would destroy any who opposed him this time, as he had in the past.

Mary Rogers, he knew, was on her way to warn Erica. But, Mary Rogers spoke like an old, demented fool. Always yaking and carrying on about bad vibes. Of course, he had to admit, the woman had a point. And now she knew about the dog too, about Blue Diabolus. But she rattled on so, nobody paid any attention. At least Erica didn't. He wasn't too concerned with this visit.

The Gate Keeper rubbed his calloused back against the cool, moist, slime covering the walls of the black hole, like an old dog trying to shed fleas, and gave the subject more thought. Who else was there? Who else could be considered a threat? Kayle? Fuck, no! Kayle wasn't a formidable opponent. He was a weak, driveling bully, who'd been properly pussified by his mother.

Aaron Pace? He laughed and the Old Ones laughed along with him. Aaron Pace had studied the *book* . . . Aaron knew the words, but couldn't enforce the powers behind them. Besides, Aaron had a multitude of fears buried deep within his sub-conscious mind. The Gate Keeper couldn't wait to start using those fears against him. Aaron Pace was also destined to become a memory in Erica's life!

When he analyzed it fully, there was no one who had the ability to oppose—But . . . Wait . . . *Kirsten Larsen!!* The cunting whore! While it was true she wasn't strong enough on her own, Kirsten always brought help. Well, he'd fix her good this time if she interferred. And yet, if this was done right, Erica would listen to no one. It wouldn't matter how much help Kirsten Larsen brought in.

Then, perhaps the dead thing, the Old One he'd set upon her, the one who followed Kirsten like a second skin, wouldn't be forced to kill her.

Erica sat on the window sill in her bedroom and stared at the yard below. Henry Wittaker had kept his word. Grass seed had been planted. Tiny buds of newgrown grass were already bursting through the ground. All that was needed now, to make it complete, was a few rose bushes scattered here and there, a few azalea bushes, and a red maple in the center of the lawn.

She never had these urges before: to want to plant and seed and weed. But then, she'd never owned a house before. Whatever would've been done in the past, would've benefited the landlord. Well, now it was for her.

A few cars passed by the front of the house, two of them traveling pretty fast. Erica made a mental note to speak to Kayle about the possibility of installing a fence out front. The kids might be less prone to wander out into the road without thinking if they had to open a gate first.

Erica's gaze wandered across the lawn to the house next door. She saw a woman, a pretty brunette a bit older than herself, climb into a station wagon and start to back out of her driveway, but not before looking at Erica's house and falling into a short trance. She seemed worried. Maybe she knew something Erica should've known.

After she drove off down the block and Erica lost sight of her car, she dismissed the incident from her mind. Maybe the woman was upset because there were four children living in the house. Maybe she didn't like kids. Maybe she was afraid the kids would run wild and destroy her property.

Maybe she knew something about the house.

The children were in their bedrooms unpacking and making up their beds. She heard their voices drifting down the hall to her room. They didn't seem to be fighting or arguing. She smiled and marveled at how they'd grown and matured. There was a time she feared asking them to do anything because they were lazy. If she told them to merely sit up straight in their chairs, they whined and pouted.

Now, here they were, taking on the responsibility of fixing up their bedrooms. They were unpacking, making beds, and doing so without even a tiny protest. There was a lesson here. Maybe the problem in the past had been her telling them to do certain things. Today she'd left them alone, hadn't said a word, but was getting results. Children sure were strange creatures. Handling them wasn't easy.

Then again, maybe the idea of owning a home was the key. The house was large and roomy and in damn good shape. They could be proud to bring their friends home. Maybe that was it. The kids might've been showing their appreciation.

Whatever their reasons, Erica wasn't about to question them.

She leaned back to rest her head against the frame of the window and thought about lunch. She was hungry. The kids probably were, too. Although, they were so busy, they may not have been thinking about food. But she was. Only, Kayle and Aaron Pace were down in the kitchen drinking. She didn't want to see either of them. She didn't trust herself not to go into a rage and kill them both! The bastards.

"Didi," she called, hoping Didi would hear. Didi would make her a sandwich if she asked her to. Erica heard a door close, followed by the sound of light footsteps, those of a child, coming down the hall towards her room. Then the door opened and Didi came in.

"You call me, Mommy?"

"Yes, baby . . . Uh . . ." She smiled but couldn't finish. Didi was staring at her with that incredible look again: the one that said "I love you, and will do anything you ask." Every family had one of these kids, the doer, the one who couldn't wait to please, and begged for the opportunity. Erica felt she was taking advantage.

"Yes, Mommy?" Didi's large, blue eyes were as wide as anything. Her white blonde hair hung in soft folds over her shoulders. She was a beautiful, older version of Katie.

"Oh, God. Please don't let anything ever spoil our relationship," Erica murmured without thinking.

Didi rushed into her arms and held on tightly. "What're you saying? I'll always love you, Mommy."

"I hope so." She gently brushed the child's hair back, away from her face, and stared hard at those soft, blue eyes of hers. "I hope we'll always be friends."

"Oh, Mommy. Don't be silly," Didi said, quickly adding, "but I don't know about Katie. Being friends, I mean. She's actin' so strange."

Erica heard this and felt her heartbeat quicken in her chest. Didi didn't usually exaggerate. Katie was acting strangely? In what way? And why? She swallowed and kept her voice even, but it wasn't easy. "Oh, honey. Maybe you only think she's acting funny. You know, Katie's younger than you. Do you remember how it was when you were that age?"

"Yeah . . . But she's talking to herself. She's sitting in the closet playing with her dolls and . . . talking to herself."

Erica felt relieved. Katie's behavior had nothing to do with the mysterious happenings in the house. Didi wasn't home when she'd spoken to Sam and Katie about imaginary playmates. No wonder Didi was alarmed. "Your sister's a lonely child. She's by herself most of the time. So, she's invented little friends to play with." Erica hoped they were invented. What if they were real?

"You mean she's not crazy? That it's okay?" Didi was relieved. "Then I'll play with her. I'll get in the closet with her and play dolls."

"That's good, honey. You keep your sister company."

She watched Didi leave while hunger pains rolled in her stomach. It was too bad she hadn't asked for the sandwich. But then, solving her childrens' problems, and knowing they were happy, was more important than eating. Perhaps by understanding what Katie was going through, Didi would be compassionate enough to shorten the gap in years between them.

There was shouting coming from downstairs. Erica heard Kayle yelling at someone. She smiled and hoped it was Aaron. Maybe they'd get into a fist fight and save her the trouble of killing them both. But the next voice she heard wasn't Aaron's. It was Mary's. Her mother and Kayle were having a go at it, something they'd avoided over the years, despite their obvious dislike for each other. And now, it was up to Erica to break it up. Oh shit! They might even try to force her to choose between them.

She saw Kayle and Mary standing near the front door, shouting in each other's faces. The children had stayed upstairs. She was grateful for that much.

"You drunken bastard," Mary was shouting. "I only came here to warn—"

"What ya really mean is ya came here to stick your fucking, old snoot in our busi—"

"Fuck you!"

"And fuck you back! Ya jealous, old—"

"Stop this!" Erica raged. "No more! You hear!" She couldn't stand the pain of them doing this to each other.

Aaron Pace watched them from the doorway of the kitchen. He wasn't sure this was really happening. Kayle and Mary had never been crazy about one another, but they'd kept it cool because of Erica. Now Erica was in the middle. It was up to her to patch the wound. Goddamn! He was glad it wasn't his job.

The Gate Keeper watched from the hidden shadows of invisibility and laughed. Phase two was moving along just fine.

Burt Anderson was out back when the fighting started. He walked over near his rose bushes so he could hear better, and wondered what Carol would've thought if she were here now. Carol had been so worried about those people next door and the rumors about the house. How would she've reacted if she were here listening to the language he was listening to? Some mess of shit over there, he thought, and waved a hand in disgust.

Carol always fretted over the wrong people. Well, he wasn't having any more of it. Her always watching that place, swearing there were demons and ghosts living there, just waiting to pounce on some innocent victim. Innocent, his ass! Just listen to the language those bastards were using.

Burt was still listening when the back door to
Erica's house, the one in the kitchen, opened
noiselessly and a handsome stranger emerged. He
was tall, and well-built, like someone who worked
out at a gym every day. His hair was short and curly;
raven black, the same as his eyes. Burt sensed
movement and looked up in time to see the man
crossing the lawn towards him.

He was taken by his beauty. The guy was so
damned good looking, he should've been a woman.
"HELLO," the man said. "MY NAME'S PAUL." Burt
smiled and started to extend his hand until his gaze
fell from Paul's face and drifted down to his legs. *Paul
had none.* His body looked unfinished—as though it
had been put together in a hurry. But he was walking.

Burt felt himself go limp. Carol had mentioned
these things, not in so many words, of course, because
she'd been fearful of his reaction. Still, she'd hinted . . .
And he'd always laughed. But he wasn't laughing
now. He forced himself to move, forced his legs to
carry him to the back door of his own house. And he
hoped old *no-legs* wasn't chasin' him. How fast could
you run with no legs, he wondered, his chest heaving
for air?

Oh, yeah, Burt ran, like someone who'd had acid
poured down his pants. And he kept running until he
was inside. And he never looked back. And he never
mentioned this to Carol.

12

"Hello," she said, "this is Kirsten . . . Kirsten Larsen." She barely recognized Henry Wittaker's voice on the other end of the line. He didn't sound the same, she detected sadness. This wasn't like Henry. He was almost never depressed. "How're you doing?" she asked, more out of curiosity than politeness.

"Fine," Henry answered, trying to keep his voice even. He hadn't expected Kirsten to ever return. Her life had been in such constant turmoil. "When did you get back?"

"Just today." She wanted to ask for Bess, but hesitated. Henry sounded like he needed someone to talk to. "I missed being in New York—"

"Even after what happened? With the phone calls and the mail?" Henry didn't know if she wanted to pursue this. "Are you going back into your old line of work? With the police, I mean?"

"It used to be a challenge," she said absently, her train of thought drifting. Her *friends* were in the house, doing everything possible to frighten her. "I loved the work, and it wasn't easy. You know, helping to find missing persons. But it was different." It was a job. It paid well. She was a psychic, and had been ever since the accident split her skull in half and released something inside of her.

"It may've paid well. And I guess you did the right thing. A lot of folks might still be looking for their loved ones if you hadn't intervened. But that last job you did . . . finding all those bodies. That's what brought out the nuts." Kirsten had stumbled on the burial grounds of a Satanic cult. There were about twenty bodies, the remains of human sacrifices. They'd been missing for a long time.

"You know," he continued, "if you work for the police again, I'd use a different name. And I'd make sure my address didn't hit the papers. That's how those nuts found you the first time."

That was true. The press had made it easy for them. She still remembered the tons of hate mail; harassing phone calls around the clock. She wanted to stop talking about this; she wanted to forget it ever happened. She wanted Bess. Right this moment. But there was something in Henry's voice . . .

Her psyche took over, as it usually did when she probed for answers. Did Henry have money problems? He was speaking to her, and she tried to listen while her mind searched his. He was definitely hiding something, way back in the farthest reaches of his mind. He was fighting her, holding onto his secret with everything in him. But no, she was stronger. It was only a matter of concentration . . .

When she finally broke through, she wished she hadn't. Oh, Lord, this was a nightmare. Kirsten was involuntarily transported back in time, back to that motel room in Colorado . . . The dream . . . The man who had been outside arguing with the Gate Keeper . . . Henry! Oh, God, no. But yes, it was Henry. She should've recognized him.

Then again, it was nighttime. Henry had been in the shadows; the darkness had covered his body like a shroud. She never got a good look at him.

"I have some bad news, Kirsten." Henry was saying, "Bess is dead." Bess was killed, he wanted to scream. But the *rat* was outside of the den, listening. "I'm sorry to have to break it to you like this. You just came back, there should be better news."

The man in her dreams was full of pain inside where no one could see it. But she did. It was Henry seeking revenge for Bess' death. Bess didn't just die. The Gate Keeper killed her! Oh, God! That awful house.

"Kirsten . . . Are you—" Henry stopped talking when the door opened and Patricia came into the den. At least it looked like Patricia . . .

"Henry, I have to go. I'll call you back." She didn't know what shocked her more; Bess' death or the knowledge that Henry knew where the house was. He could tell her. But no. She wasn't ready for this just yet. Would she ever be? It meant facing the Gate Keeper again. Still, it was her job!

"I understand," he said. "But please call back. Keep in touch."

I need your help, was what he wanted to say next. But Patricia was here now, and the *rat* had been outside for an awful long time. The words were stuck in his throat, stopping the flow of oxygen to his brain. He felt faint. He hung up the phone and studied his daughter. She had the same, long brown tresses, and the same worried look as usual. But then so had that demon bastard, the one who did such a perfect imitation in the hallway a while back.

"I'm worried about you," she said.

Oh, yes, Henry knew she worried. However, were those words spoken to throw him off, to make him think this was Patricia? Or was this really his daughter? Did she have a soul? "I'm fine," he managed to say.

"No, you're not. Locking yourself up in here like this. You don't eat, you don't sleep. Daddy, this has to stop."

It might've been a trick to make him admit he'd been searching through those books, looking for an answer. They already knew this, but they wanted to hear him say it so they could laugh. Henry was no threat!

"Remember those stories you told us? Buddy and me . . . after Mommy died. Do you think he died for the same reason?"

Tears misted her eyes. It *was* Patricia. Those bastards couldn't cry, they didn't know how. He was grateful for that much. But he couldn't answer her, couldn't tell her the truth. The *rat* was listening. And waiting. The fucker was waiting for Henry to enlighten his daughter. Then he'd take the breath from *her* body, just as he had . . . NO! Just as the Gate Keeper had done with Bess and Buddy. But Henry was smart this time. He'd get Patricia to leave this house for good, without telling her what really happened.

"Buddy's death was an accident." And keep on thinking that way, he shouted to himself. Force yourself to accept that as gospel. That son-of-a-bitch was outside, reading his mind. Well now, fuck you, he thought, *and* your lord and master. Read that, asshole.

The *rat* banged three times on the wall. It was a warning!

"What was that noise?" Patricia wanted to know.

"What noise?"

She heard it. For the first time she was able to hear his *rat*. Oh, this was wonderful! And it stunk at the same time. He couldn't tell her. If he did, Patricia's breath would go the same route as Bess' and Buddy's. Those bastards would take it!

"Didn't you hear it? It sounded like someone was knocking at the door."

"Maybe someone is. Knocking at the door, I mean."

"No, Daddy. I keep hearing those noises and I run to answer the door, but nobody's ever there."

Think, asshole. You wanted your kids to hear the same things you heard. And now one of them does. Only now he had to convince her it was all in her mind. "This's an old house. Old houses are always full of strange sounds. The walls settling . . . the floorboards creaking—"

"Daddy, I know what I'm hearing. Someone's knocking—"

"How about some dinner? Boy, I'm hungry. Why don't you go slap something together? And after we eat, we'll go for a drive. Or take in a movie."

Patricia studied him for a moment, then, "Now I know how you felt when you were telling us those stories. We didn't believe you either." He started to say something, but she stopped him. "It's okay. I'm going." She stood by the door and looked back. There was a lot of sadness in her eyes, too much for one so young. "I'll call you when dinner's ready."

After she left, it was Henry's turn to listen at the door. What if the *rat* tired of this? The deceitful game Henry was playing? What if he tired of it and went after Patricia? He opened the door a crack and was relieved to hear the sound of pots and pans rustling in the kitchen. She was safe . . . For now, at least.

An hour had gone by since Kirsten had spoken to Henry. Her hands, she noticed, were still trembling. Henry was involved with that house. And yet, she wasn't surprised. After all, hadn't she felt something when she'd been driving back from Colorado? Hadn't she sensed that the closer she got to New York, the closer she was getting to the house in her dreams? The closer she was getting to her mission? The Lord, she knew, always supplied the answers. He wanted her to fulfill her life's work. So He helped her find the trouble spots.

"Lord," she prayed, ignoring the laughter coming from somewhere in the house, "Please don't let it be like last time." She couldn't take that. Bodies, so many bodies. Tortured. The skin peeled from their flesh, the people at the police lab had told her. The blood was drained from their bodies, their vital organs were missing. Probably consumed. She felt her stomach wretch with nausea.

The coven found her, with the aid of the press. They wrote, called, left things on her doorstep. Body parts: legs with no flesh on them, human arms, headless cats. Once they left a hat box and she knew she shouldn't have opened it, never should've looked inside. Every instinct, every fibre of her being, all of her psychic powers screamed at her—don't open it! But she did. There was a wig inside . . . with a human head underneath.

Oh, God! She dug at her flesh. Her nerves were crawling. And they were laughing at her now, as they had in the past. She shouldn't have come home. She should've resisted the urge.

She stared at her boardless windows and wondered why it wasn't lighter in here. Was it the trees in the woods behind the house? Did the trees block the sun? But no, it was her *friends.* They kept it dark in here.

She rose from her chair by the phone to stare from her living room window. Everything was in bloom, spring was here. Birds were building nests in the branches of trees she used to love before her accident, before her life became a nightmare. She used to stare at them—the trees—and dream and reflect on the past; on her childhood in Norway. She had such a bounty of memories. And hell, she was only in her late thirties, but she'd lived a full life. More than most people. She'd traveled extensively, both in Europe and the United States. She once had it all. Until the accident—

The dead thing was standing at the foot of a tree in the woods, watching her. She could see him. Something in her snapped at that point. She thew open the window and shouted, ''Go away. Get out of my life you hideous bastard!'' He laughed. Most of her *friends* had a real sense of humor, and he was no exception.

While Kirsten watched, he disappeared as if he'd never been there. She panicked and slammed the window. She knew he was no longer standing under the tree. No. He was on the move. He was headed for the house. She'd yelled, and he'd laughed. But she'd insulted him. They didn't stand for that!

Footsteps. Coming from behind her. Was it him? Was he able to move that fast? Or was it another of them, seeking revenge for the insult? She couldn't bare to look. "In the name of the Lord, Jesus Christ, I command you to be gone," she screamed aloud, still staring from the window. The words had to be spoken three times in succession. Three times to nullify the powers of the devil.

Everything the master beast did, he did in threes. All instances of bad luck, all instances of sickness, of death, everything came in threes. Sometimes it came in sixes. But mostly it was threes.

Her Lord took three days to die on the cross, he died at three in the afternoon. The beast chose the number three in defiance of her Lord. The bastard even chose three in the morning, not midnight as most people believed, to do his most effective work: his hauntings, his tormentings. "In the name of the Lord, Jesus Christ, I command you to be gone," she repeated twice more, knowing it would work, for a while at least. But only for a while. If she wanted a permanent remedy, she'd have to find a stronger solution.

There was a couple she used to work with when she investigated haunted houses. They had strong solutions. They helped her a lot, except, some of the demons they exorcised went home with them. And with Kirsten, too. She smelled cigar smoke. Speak of the devil, to quote an old cliche, she thought. The old horror who once roamed a house on Bank Street, right here in town, he came home with Kirsten. It was odd. Although she'd investigated local homes, she'd never worked with the local police. She'd made it a point to stay out of this area when searching for bodies.

That alone should've saved her from the notoriety and needless harassment. However, it wasn't meant

to be. Being driven from her home was part of it, part
of the punishment she received from the master beast
for working against him. Now, if she were to locate
that house and bring the couple in to exorcise the
demons, God only knows what he'd do. Not in terms
of her death. He wasn't strong enough to defy her
Lord. But he'd find some other way to torment her.

Kirsten left the window to return to her chair. The
cigar smoking horror was in it. He'd been dead for a
long time, too. He was all smiles, something had
tickled his funny bone. Then she spotted the dead
thing from the corner of her eye; coming at her with a
chef's knife. "In the name of the Lord, Jesus Christ,"
she began as tears streamed down her face. The strain
was beginning to show.

"How dare you scream in my mother's face! How
dare you!" Erica had been in so many different rages
that day, she feared having a stroke. The brain could
take only so much pressure. "And the language you
use—"

"She used it first!" Kayle bellowed. "I was only
defending myself."

He had a terrible beer odor to his breath. It turned
her stomach. And hell, she drank the stuff, too. But
she didn't go around shouting in people's faces and
contaminating their air. "She's old. You should've
kept quiet out of respect. But then you have none,
right, Kayle! You don't respect anyone or anything.
Including me! You son-of-a-bitch!"

He lashed out and slapped her so fast she didn't
have time to duck. Tears stung her eyes. Kayle had
actually struck her. It was the first time in the ten
years they'd been together. Erica rubbed the side of
her face. She was stunned. When she recovered, she
ran upstairs to her bedroom and closed the door.
Kayle hit her!

Was it the beer? She hoped so. She prayed he'd
regret it and he would, if she had her way. But what if

he didn't regret it? What if hitting her became routine? She walked over to the water bed and began to undress. There was a clean nightgown already laid out. She grabbed for it, and caught her reflection in the mirror over her dresser. A huge, red welt marred her face. The lines around her mouth grew taut with anger. Erica had no intention of becoming a statistic, of joining the ranks of battered women. Hell, no. She'd stab the bastard first.

Then, to be realistic, she thought about it some more. Stabbing him wasn't the answer even if she could bring herself to do it, to take a life. Kayle would be dead and out of her hair, true, but she'd wind up in jail. The kids would have no one—except possibly her mother. And Mary was great at spoiling kids, great at stunting their emotional growth.

Kayle's life had to be spared for the time being. At least until he hit her again. Then what, she thought? She could leave him. She could very well take the children and leave. And go where? To her mother's? Never! Or to Aaron Pace's? That was stupid. She didn't even know where Aaron lived; what street, what house number. Besides, Aaron wasn't financially able to support her.

Aaron never mentioned money, and seemed to have damned little of it. Aaron wasn't the answer.

Erica climbed into bed. It was nice and warm since she'd turned up the thermostat. She laid in one spot and listened for Kayle. What if he came up here and slapped her again? He had her where he wanted her. She had to stay with him; she had no choice. And Kayle was the type to take advantage when he had you by the ass. She kept her attention glued on the door until she heard footsteps coming down the hall. That had to be Kayle.

However, for one fleeting instant, her mind went back to the first time she'd come here, to this house. She'd been in this very same room with Henry Wittaker, and had heard footsteps. She imagined that was Kayle also, and she ran out to the top of the steps to tell him about the bedroom. No! She wouldn't continue, wouldn't keep on thinking about what had happened that day. It had to stop. It was Kayle this time! He was coming to bed!

She rolled on her side and listened to him coming through the door. Odd though, his footsteps were steady and even. He wasn't stumbling like a drunk. "ERICA, YOU AWAKE?" Kayle asked. And she knew it was Kayle. That was his voice, although, it did sound a little strange.

"Yes. I'm awake." She couldn't bring herself to turn and look at him. Not after what he'd done.

"I'M SORRY I HIT YOU. AND TO SHOW YOU JUST HOW MUCH, I'LL LAY YOU AS SOON AS I GET UNDRESSED."

Erica's skin crawled. She tightened her fists and wanted to hit him. What the hell was going on here? First Aaron had spoken to her as if she were a slut, now Kayle. She turned to face him, to let him know she was disturbed by his vulgarity. But she couldn't speak. Kayle was standing in front of her, true, and yet she didn't know how. His eyes were closed and he was out . . . unconscious. His body was slumped forward as if someone or something was holding him around the waist, supporting his weight.

She screamed when he straighted up and opened his eyes to look at her because . . . *those eyes weren't his!*

Katie was in her closet playing with Angelica when Erica screamed. But Katie chose to ignore her mother. Mainly 'cause her imaginary playmate told her to. Mothers were forever finding reasons to scream. Either it was because they were mad at you, or because they couldn't get their own way, or simply because they felt like it. And since Angelica was very smart for her age, Katie listened to her.

Didi didn't listen though. Mainly 'cause she

couldn't hear Angelica. But she had her own reasons for not running to Erica's side. She had been lying in bed, trying to decide whether or not to keep her promise to Erica—to play with Katie—when Erica screamed. Surprisingly, she never made a move to get up. Didi was used to this. Erica was probably yelling at Daddy again. They were fighting. No one interferred when they fought. So, Didi stayed put, and gave some more thought to the matter of Katie.

Her sister was still in that damn closet. This was so unlike her. When the hell was she going to bed? And why the hell did Didi promise to play with her? Sitting on the floor in an old, stuffy closet didn't do a thing for her. She'd rather stay out here, although it was stuffy here too. But there was a difference. She wasn't crammed in a closet with the door closed.

Katie did have the light on though. Didi could see it under the door: a bright, white-hot light, glowing for all it was worth. If Katie ran up the electric bill, Erica was sure to be pissed—*at her.* She was two years older—six, going on twenty-five, as Erica often said, and she was responsible for Katie. Therefore, she should make Katie turn that damn light off.

But then she'd have to listen to her sister's mouth! Katie hated to be told what to do. Didi got up and got her pajamas from her bottom dresser drawer, and started to undress. Katie took that opportunity to leave her hiding place in the closet. Katie was tired. Didi was standing there, almost naked, when Katie came out of the closet.

And wouldn't you just know it, Didi thought angrily, she'd left the damn light on. "Don't you ever clean up after yourself?" was all she could think of at the moment. "You shoulda turned the light off."

"Can't," Katie said absently. She let her doll drop to the floor and climbed into bed. "Can't turn it off."

"Why not?" Didi wanted to know. "You turned it on, didn't you? How'd you do it?" Katie, she knew, was too short to reach the switch. "How'd you do it?"

she repeated. "Didn't you stand on something?"

"I didn't stand on nothin'. And I can't turn the light off. It's Angelica. She glows in the dark."

Didi smiled in spite of herself. That was a pretty good answer. Katie was developing a stronger imagination. She shrugged and went to take care of it herself, but the overhead light wasn't on. There was, however, a bright, glowing light emanating from the rear of the closet, way back in the corner near the floor. Didi closed the door and leaned against it. She wasn't the least bit curious. She couldn't afford to be. There had obviously been some truth to Katie's statement, and Didi was terrified.

Kayle woke up on the floor of his bedroom. It was pitch black, he couldn't see a thing, and he had a terrible headache. A dull pain pounded behind his eyes when he sat up. He groped in the dark for the edge of the bed, and got to his feet. He couldn't walk at first, his legs were shaking. He wasn't sure they'd support his weight. What the hell was he doing on the floor? Did he pass out? That was probably it, and Erica, he knew, couldn't lift him. Now, if he could just make it to a toilet.

Kayle had been up here earlier. The delivery man had put the bed opposite the bathroom. All he had to do was walk in a straight line. He stumbled in the dark until he found his way. There was an awful taste in his mouth. Erica kept some stuff in the medicine cabinet. He found the mouthwash and looked at himself in the mirror over the sink. Jesus! He must've really tied one on. His face was pale, there were red spots on his eyeballs.

Erica must be pissed, he surmised. Their first night in the new house and he spends it on the floor. But hell, this wasn't something he did every day. He wasn't a drinking man. She had to understand, didn't she? But understand what? That he'd gotten drunk because he was afraid of the house, afraid to live here? Erica would never fall for it. What else could he say? That he was so overjoyed about moving into the house, he bought a case of beer and drank it to celebrate? *If* he drank a case. He couldn't remember.

He'd been in the kitchen doing a good job on the beer. Beyond that, he drew a total blank. Jesus, if beer took your memory away, he didn't want anymore of that shit. Now he had to convince Erica. He had to tell her he was sorry, and wouldn't do it again. If they were still on speaking terms.

She should accept his apology though. She drank beer. Not to the point he did, that was true, but she drank it. He just went a little too far.

Kayle splashed water on his face and looked around. Erica had done some job on this bathroom. Everything she bought looked good except the stuff didn't match the walls. There was a light green rug on the floor, and something light green and fluffy covering the toilet. But the walls were blue.

Then he remembered she'd bought some kind of wallpaper for the bathroom. White with green print. She wanted to put hanging plants in here, and God forbid they should clash with everything else. Well, the rug and toilet cover were a start in the right direction. Tomorrow night when he came home from work, he'd help her wallpaper. How could she stay mad at him then? She couldn't. In fact, she probably wasn't mad at him now. Erica took a lot before she lost it.

He opened the bathroom door; the light behind him wedging across the floor to the bed. He wanted to look at her. She was so beautiful when she let her guard down and went to sleep. Those were the times when that youthful look of innocence took over; the look she had when Kayle first met her. She'd been a child, but she let Kayle awaken the woman in her, no thanks to her mother.

Her mother . . . Was Mary here last night or did he dream it?

The bed was empty. Where the hell was Erica? What did he do when he was drinking? Had he been nasty and abusive? Did she leave him? He panicked. His nerves were like razors under the skin. And it wasn't the house this time that affected him. He could live with fear—he couldn't live without Erica. If she left him and took the kids . . . He ran to their bedrooms and checked. They were fast asleep in their beds. Erica would never have left them behind.

He ran downstairs and spotted a light in the kitchen. Erica was drinking coffee. There was a glaze over her face, as if her mind was a thousand light years away. She didn't notice him when he walked in. Kayle looked up at the clock over the stove, four in the morning. What the hell was she doing down here drinking coffee at four in the morning. Then he smiled. He must've drank all the beer. Otherwise, Erica would be drinking it now. You're a bad boy, Kayle, he thought to himself. Looks like you're in for it.

"Hi, baby," he said quietly.

Erica looked up at him, and he saw shock, or something like it, written on her face. She seemed too stunned to answer.

"Are ya mad at me?"

She studied his face, gazed intently at his eyes. Then her body went limp. "Thank God it's you."

"What?"

"Nothing . . ." she said nervously. Then her expression changed. "I shouldn't even be speaking to you."

For the first time since he'd come into the kitchen, he noticed an ugly bruise on her face. Her head had been turned a bit to the side, so he didn't see it. But when she looked up at him, there was the bruise. Then he thought about what she'd just said. How did she get that ugly mark on her face? He certainly didn't do it. Did he? Something hot stung at the base of his skull.

"What'd I do?" He slumped into a chair next to her.

There were black rings under her eyes. She must've been sitting here all night.

"Don't you remember? *This* is what you did," she said, pointing to the bruise.

Kayle wanted to die. This went against everything he ever believed in. He never wanted to be like his old man. Well, now he was. "Oh, God, Erica." He grabbed her arm, but she pulled away. She wasn't finished with him yet.

"You fought with my mother—"

"Oh, Christ!" he moaned. She'd never forgive him now.

"You told her to go fuck herself. You said she was jealous—"

"You'll never forgive me, will ya?" Kayle usually had a defiant attitude whenever he fought with Erica. But it was gone. This time he'd been the fool, and he was wrong. "Baby, please . . ." He laid his hand on her arm again, this time she didn't move away. But her flesh was stiff and cold to the touch, as if she still had her guard up. "It was the beer. I never hit ya before. Jesus, Erica, I love ya."

"You have some helluva way of showing it."

That was true. He deserved it; every word. "What if I promise never to do it again? No more beer. And what if I promise to tell Mary I'm sorry?" He did feel bad about that. Mary was a bitch in her own way, but she was old. He'd been way out of line. "I'll do anything ya ask me to. Just say ya don't hate me."

The lines on her face began to soften. "I don't hate you. I just don't like the things you do at times—"

"Thank you, baby." He reached across the table and cupped her chin in his hand. Her lips were so soft, her body so appealing. Kayle felt himself becoming aroused. "Please, baby. Come upstairs. You've probably been sittin' here all night." She didn't move. "Please," he repeated.

It was at least a minute before she answered, but to Kayle, it seemed like forever. She spoke quietly, but there was still a hint of anger in her voice. "I'll put my cup in the sink."

"No. Leave it." He wanted to hurry before the mood was broken. What if one of the kids woke up? What if she changed her mind? After all, she must've known what he was looking for. "I'll rinse it out in the morning. I have to get up early for work anyway." Work! Aaron Pace had been here. Wasn't he? Bits of it were coming back to him, but he shoved it to the back of his mind. He didn't want to remember. He never wanted to remember. He'd hit Erica, and he'd fought with Mary. That was enough.

"Come on, baby."

She rose and took his arm. Together they walked upstairs. Kayle couldn't stop staring at her; the bruise on her face, the blackness under her eyes, the slump of her body. She was walking funny, almost like an old woman with a dowager's hump. She suddenly looked awful. He felt the mood slipping, and tried to hurry before it was gone.

13

"Come on and finish," Carol Anderson said, speaking to her three youngest children. They took forever to eat. This was nonsense. "Some bacon and a few eggs shouldn't take this long. You'll miss the damn school bus." Then she'd have to drive them. Burt would have a fit.

There was a cup of coffee on the table, but she didn't touch it. The coffee was probably ice cold by now; it had been there for a while. Carol had poured it for herself with the intention of drinking it. But she couldn't now, not when she was so upset after looking at the house next door. Burt said she was nosy, but she wasn't. She'd been standing by the window, pouring coffee; looking out was a natural thing.

Last night was the first for that couple—their first night in that house.

She wondered if they were all right. Then, in answer to her question, she saw the husband leaving. He was probably going to work. Well, they were behaving normally, carrying on with their lives like everyone else. Unless . . . Unless they knew something was wrong with the house, and they were putting up a front.

Kayle climbed into his car and pulled away. She kept her gaze focused on him until he reached the end of the street and turned the corner. Then something inside of the house caught her eye: she saw dirty curtains hanging at *her* windows.

It was a shock. The curtains were usually washed every few weeks, whether they were dirty or not. But, Christ, these were filthy! What the hell was she doing? Had she spent so much of her time wondering about that house, and those unfortunate people who'd bought it, that she'd let her own house go?

There were grease stains on the wall over the stove. The handles of her cabinets were surrounded by grubby, little, handprints. The carpet needed to be vacuumed. Burt came in and saw her looking around; a worried expression on her face.

"My!!! You found time to examine the dirt."

Carol wheeled to face him, but said nothing. The few times she'd rebuked him in the past had turned out really bad. Either he lost his temper and shoved her, or he went into his famous routine and made a fool of her in front of the kids.

"Ya worry so much about that place next door, standin' there, starin' out the window, you're neglecting us!"

Neglect? Now there was a new word in Burt's vocabulary. She smiled. He did have a way of exaggerating to the point where she wanted to scream. However, when she stopped to analyze his words, there was an awful lot of irony in them. He'd been playing head games with her; trying to put her down, making her feel inadequate, so she'd push herself harder to win his approval. Well, she could damn well live without his approval!

And she wasn't about to try harder. He wasn't putting her into an early grave, and neither was this house!

"Ya just gonna stand there and smile like an idiot?" Burt wanted to know. "Why don't ya say somethin'?"

"Byyeee! I'm taking the kids to the bus stop." She turned and straightened her dress and started to leave. But Burt was standing in the middle of the room with a shocked look on his face. She couldn't resist the urge to really shove it to him for a change. ''Close your mouth, Burt. You look ridiculous.''

It was another beautiful day. The sun was warm and penetrating. The trees on her property were heavy with birds. Carol felt good, about her surroundings *and* about herself. She was full of confidence, something she'd given up the day she married Burt. Well, that man was about to see another woman in her.

''Hurry along, kids,'' she said as they were passing the house next door. She turned her head away from the sight of it. If anything could whack the hell out of her new found confidence, that place was it!

''Hey, Mom. They got small kids . . . Our age . . . Their kids going to school?'' Jack asked.

Jack was her middle child, her third born, and her only son. ''I don't know, honey. I suppose—'' Carol glanced at the house without thinking and stopped talking when the front door opened and Erica came out with her children. Oh, shit! This meant she had to say hello. She couldn't very well ignore the woman.

But what if she were invited next door for coffee? New neighbors were generally anxious to make friends. Well, she thought, no problem. She would do the inviting first. And she'd keep on doing it so she wouldn't have to go over there.

Carol was undecided about whether to keep walking or wait for Erica. Then she decided to wait. She'd have to face it sooner or later. She stopped and watched Erica coming towards her with her kids. Odd. She never noticed before, but the woman had dark circles under her eyes, and she was slightly hunched over when she walked.

She thought back to the few times she'd seen her before; such as the times she'd come to look at the house and the one time she saw her in the supermarket. Twice she'd been accompanied by an older woman. She was almost walking like that older woman now.

Why?

What changed her? The change was slight, but it was there!

Was it that house?

There was an ugly bruise on the side of her face. Carol had something in common with Erica; she'd had her own share of ugly bruises over the years.

"Hello," she said, extending her hand. "My name's Carol Anderson."

Erica smiled and took her hand. "I'm Erica Walsh."

"Erica? What a pretty name. And what beautiful children you have. Look at that blonde hair, and those pale blue eyes. They all resemble you."

Erica smiled and followed Carol to the bus stop. She didn't have much to say. There was a lot on her mind.

Burt was watching from the window. When Carol spoke to Erica, he clutched the curtains with such force he almost tore them from their rods. Carol was actually making friends with those people next door. That stupid bitch! How many times had he told her not to get involved with the neighbors. Especially now, when the neighbors were so weird. And yet, the woman had legs. He could see that. Her body had been finished, completed.

"What the hell am I sayin'?"

He went back and sat at the kitchen table. What the hell was he saying? That incident in the back yard never happened. People didn't walk around with no legs.

But Paul did.

No! There was no Paul. Nobody came out of that house. Burt was hanging over the rose bushes listening to the fight next door, and that was all. Nobody walked across that yard with no legs. Nobody! And yet, it seemed so real at the time. He could've sworn . . .

He rubbed the palms of his hands against his work pants, and wondered if they'd be invited next door now that Carol made friends with the woman who lived there. Well, that was out of the question. He just wasn't going. They could come over here. No! That was an even worse idea. He didn't want any part of them. What if they brought Paul?

Then he smiled, but it was a strain. If they brought Paul, they'd have to supply him with legs first. Couldn't have him strolling the neighborhood with just the upper portion of his body showing.

"What's so funny?" Carol asked. She'd come back without him even noticing.

Burt tried to hide his alarm. She'd entered so suddenly; had made no noise. He sat up straight and sipped his coffee. His hands were trembling but he managed to compose himself. "I was just sittin' here, laughin' to myself about you." It was a lie. Still, it was better than saying nothing. "I was thinkin' about how ya go outta your way to ignore me."

"How I what?"

"How you ignore me. Like when I ask ya *not* to get friendly with the neighbors. It's not askin' much. After all, ya got a house and a husband and kids. You ain't got the time."

Although he managed to keep his voice low and even, Burt knew he was building for a fight. This bitch had caught him with his drawers down—sitting there laughing to himself like an idiot. And it was her fault that he'd met Paul the day before. Hell, if she'd been home, he wouldn't have been outside listening to those bastards fight!

Henry Wittaker was ready to throw his hands up in disgust. The situation was becoming critical. He couldn't find an answer. He'd tried, but there was no remedy in his books, no way to get rid of the demons in his life. He didn't dwell on it for long though, he couldn't. One of them was watching, and listening, and reading his mind, while walking the hall outside of his den.

He laid his book down and stared at the shaft of sunlight streaming across the floor. From all outward appearances, it was just another normal day. It was mid-morning, it was beautiful outside, birds were chirping, the flowers on his front lawn were supplying outrageous scents. It was another normal day—for everyone but him.

He rose and went to the window, but that was a mistake. Buddy's car could be seen from this part of the house, too. There was an open wound inside of Henry's chest, around his heart. He was valiantly trying to keep his heart beating in spite of it. Why had they taken his son? Buddy was no threat. Hell, Buddy didn't even believe that story Henry told about the demons. Buddy laughed.

And the bastards still took the breath from his body! They turned him into one of those white-faced, corpses; one of those lifeless, three-dimensional, cardboard figures. And when Henry saw Buddy lying in a coffin, with that phony nameplate, Henry couldn't believe it was, or rather, had been, his son. Buddy's face was so pale and distorted. Both of his eyes and his mouth had been sewn shut. God, he didn't want to believe it was Buddy, but it was.

Henry remembered how badly the wake and funeral had gone. They had no friends, so, other than Patricia and him, no one came. It was so embarrassing. The funeral director kept asking when the other guests would arrive. And no one came.

Wrong, he said to himself, someone came—

He waked the body for two days before it was buried. Another mistake. That meant two days of sitting in front of a coffin, staring at a white-faced horror, and knowing his death was your fault! If you had chosen to keep quiet, he thought to himself, especially after what happened to Bess, the boy would be alive today. Still, Henry's intentions were good. He only wanted to warn his children before something bad happened.

The only thing was, when something bad did happen, Henry was powerless to stop it. Oh, Lord, what did he do to Buddy? What did he do to his daughter? She grieved so.

Patricia took it extremely hard, she'd been real close to her brother. And it broke Henry's heart to see her just sitting in front of the coffin in a catatonic state, staring at the body. After the first day he couldn't take it anymore. So he devised small schemes to keep her out of the main room. He began sending her places, any excuse he could manufacture. He sent her to pay the electric bill, then the phone bill. She protested, but he insisted. Those bills had to be paid, he told her. And it worked, she always went wherever he asked her to, leaving Henry alone with the body.

Another mistake!

Henry couldn't take it either, but he was a man, so he was stronger. Once he even grew strong enough to walk over and kiss his son. The flesh was cold and unyielding, but he kissed him just the same. Then he noticed that the tiny threads used to sew up the eyes and the mouth were showing. Buddy was coming apart at the seams.

Not funny, he told himself.

Henry went to look for the funeral director, to complain, but he was gone. There was a sign on the door saying he'd be back in an hour. Henry felt strange about that sign. He realized he was all alone in the place—except for Buddy. This wasn't right. The funeral director and his secretary were out. Some nerve! They'd left Henry to fend for himself. And they'd left him with a horrible dead thing laid out in a coffin for company. No! They'd left him with his son!

The room was darker than he remembered when he casually strolled back and sat down. It was colder in there, too. Henry was uncomfortable, but he figured it was the last day, so, what the hell. He could live with the cold. He sat back to stare at his son and wait for

Patricia when he noticed there was something wrong. The satin pillow under Buddy's head was lopsided. Oh, hell, he couldn't have that.

He rose and approached the coffin, and was almost there when something else occurred to him. How did the pillow get lopsided? *Someone* had to move it, and he was the only one there. He sure as hell didn't touch it. All he did was kiss the boy. He never laid his hands on the coffin or its contents. Then another, uglier thought, occurred to him—maybe Buddy moved it. Naw! It just moved, that's all there was to it. But how?

Fuck this shit, he thought angrily. The damn thing just moved! It didn't matter how. All that mattered at this point was fixing it before Patricia came back. He started to walk towards the coffin, using determination as a driving force, when something else occurred to him. In order to fix that lopsided pillow, he had to lift the body. Oh God. Could he do it? Could he touch the thing without feeling scared? Still, it was . . . had been, his son.

The head was cold and heavy when he lifted it. The hair felt funny, too. Coarser than he remembered Buddy's hair being when the boy was alive. When he'd been alive! Don't think about this, he scolded himself. Just do it! Fix the pillow! But he was scared.

Buddy's death hadn't been a natural one. He thought back to the stories he'd told the kids about ghosts, and what made them haunt as they did. Mostly, those ghosts had once been living, breathing, beings who'd died unexpectedly; either from a sudden sickness or accident.

Buddy died from a sudden accident. He died when that car landed on top of him.

Henry's hands were shaking. He couldn't believe this. He'd done a right good job of scaring the balls off himself. But, he continued to hold the head and was straightening the pillow when it happened—

No! He wasn't going to think about that ever again. A sudden noise in the room extracted him from his momentary trance. He was back in the den, and grateful for that. But what was that noise? Was it the *rat*? Had the bastard actually come in here? Henry heard it again. It sounded like someone was slapping their open hand against the furniture. It had to be that *rat* bastard, he angrily surmised. There was no one else in the house. Patricia had gone to work.

"Gonna let me see you today? Huh? Gonna show yourself?" Henry moved to the side, sliding his body against the wall. If he moved over to the corner of the room, he could get a better look at his easy chair, which was where the noise seemed to be coming from. Then he wouldn't have to walk right up to it, wouldn't have to possibly endanger his life. He kept going until he was almost there; to the point where he could see something. He heard the noise again and this time he saw what it was.

There was a hand slapping against the arm of the chair—a hand with the sleeve of a suit attached to it.

A suit just like the one Buddy had worn. No! He couldn't take that again; he couldn't suffer through what happened when he'd been straightening the pillow.

He'd been holding Buddy's head close to his chest, when the head moved. He died inside and laid the head back down without looking at the face. And then he started to walk away. And Goddamnit, he should've kept going! But nooo! Henry was curious! He turned, and saw Buddy, hanging over the side of the coffin with his eyes open.

"DAD . . . GHOSTS?" was all the boy said, but it was enough. Henry couldn't face it again. So he was doing now what he'd done that day—he was running, as far and as fast as he legs would carry him.

And this time, he had no intention of looking back.

Erica thanked the Lord for having given her the good sense to register the kids in school before they moved into the new house. This was her second day in the house, and she was blessedly alone—except for Katie, of course. Katie didn't go to school. But her daughter was in her room upstairs playing dolls with Angelica. Katie had given her imaginary playmate a name, something Erica, herself, had never done as a child.

Erica had doubts about encouraging Katie in the area of make-believe. But experts in the field of child psychology had written articles, tons of them, expounding on the validity of sound development of the mind. In other words, they were saying it was okay for her child to dream, that it was healthy, that it would turn Katie into a well-rounded individual. Erica still wasn't sure.

Hadn't this whole thing with Angelica started because someone spoke to Katie in her room, and frightened her? And Erica, wanting to calm her down while searching for answers, had given Katie this ridiculous story about imaginary playmates. Katie accepted it. In fact, the child dove right in and named her playmate Angelica. Now Erica was stuck with it, until she could find a sensible way to stop it.

She was in the kitchen, unpacking the pots and pans. Kayle hadn't kept his promise to help. But then, what else was new? Kayle didn't always follow through on his plans. In fact, the only important promise he'd kept so far, was buying this house. And that was all she'd allow herself to think about when it came to Kayle. Last night had been a nightmare, thanks to him. Well, not a complete nightmare. He did apologize in an awfully nice way.

She tore open a box labeled *cast iron pots* and dragged it over to a cabinet next to the stove. It was a pleasure to unpack when running out of room wasn't her main worry. There was plenty of cabinet space. She heard water running overhead. Katie was back in business, she thought, and quickly hurried upstairs. Katie loved to play in the bathroom, with the faucets in the sink going full blast. But Katie wasn't careful.

Sometimes she left the plug in, and the water ran until the sink was full. Then it ran over the sides. Erica didn't need a flood. Not in a new house.

The sound of running water came to her when she was passing her own bedroom. That was odd. Erica could've sworn she'd turned off the faucets. Oh well, sorry, Katie, she thought, Mommy's misjudged you again. The faucets in the sink in the bathroom were going full blast. She turned them off and stopped by the side of her bed to straighten the spread when the toilet flushed behind her.

Water was swirling inside the rim of the bowl when she went back into the bathroom. She could've hit the handle, without noticing, when she turned off the faucets in the sink. It was the best excuse ever. It closed all outlets, meaning she didn't have to analyze this. She went to check on Katie.

The hall was hot and stuffy. Erica couldn't wait until the fans were installed. Kayle said he'd put one out here, too. Kayle. She'd been trying not to think about him, about his drinking and the way he slapped her. Then when he came to bed . . . That was the worst! He'd been unconscious, but still, he'd walked and talked, and he collapsed when . . . when someone let go of him.

Erica had screamed, probably scaring the kids half to death. Thank God they'd stayed in their rooms. She, however, couldn't stay in hers, not with Kayle, not the way he was acting. So, she ran downstairs, which made no sense, because then she couldn't shake the feeling that she was being followed, that someone or something was running with her.

Then, when she was in the kitchen alone, drinking coffee, there was a hand on her back, and a voice in her head whispering promises. It spoke of love and possession and tender sex. However, maybe the voice had been her soul, doing some wishful thinking, and not some mysterious force. Kayle was such a brute when it came to sex.

But he changed. Last night he changed. After he came down to the kitchen and got her, they made love. Real love. He was tender, concerned. He was almost as good as Aaron Pace, and that confused her. If Kayle stayed like this, she didn't need Aaron.

"Mom. Why ya standing there holding onto the door?" Katie wanted to know. There was movement in the hall behind her. Erica had seen something, but it happened so fast she didn't get a good look at it.

"Uh . . . No reason. Listen, do you wanna help Mommy unpack some pots." All of a sudden, she didn't like the idea of leaving Katie up here alone.

But Katie had other plans. "No. I wanna play with Angelica."

"Is that your little friend?" She still found the idea disturbing. Then again, Angelica was made up, wasn't she?

"That's my friend. And she's nice. Wanna meet her?"

Oh, God, Erica thought. I hope she's not real. If she is, I'd rather not meet her. Then she scolded herself for panicking when there was no reason to. Angelica could've been a true, imaginary playmate. She didn't necessarily have to be a part of the mystery behind this house.

"Wanna meet her?" Katie persisted.

"Sure, honey. Why not?"

Katie led the way. Holding Erica's hand, she led Erica into her room and over to the edge of her bed. Erica sat and looked around. The girls were keeping the place clean; their spreads were on neatly, there were no wet towels or pajamas draped across the furniture. Erica was pleased. Katie sat next to her after letting her doll drop to the floor.

"Don't do that." Erica said, stooping to pick up the doll. "Daddy paid a lot of money for this." She was holding it by one arm, and for some strange reason, had the feeling that someone was holding the other. The sensation she experienced was that she was being

helped. Ridiculous! "I still think you belong downstairs with Mommy, Katie."

"Can't do it. Angelica will be all alone."

Erica smiled. At least she was happy. "When do I
get to meet this Angelica?"

"Right now. She's here. She's sittin' next to me on
the bed."

"Hello, Angelica." Erica smiled into thin air.
"Pleased to make your—" Damn if there wasn't an
indentation on the bed, next to Katie. A small one, the
size of a child. *Someone* was sitting on the bed with
her and Katie, but it was *someone* she couldn't see.
Don't panic, she told herself.

Suddenly, the idea of make-believe playmates
didn't sit too well with her, even though her daughter
had been lonely. And Erica was taking the blame.
She'd been wrong to encourage Katie to develop her
imagination in this area, no matter what the experts
said. Especially in this house, when your mind didn't
need much of a push to begin with.

"Come on, Katie," she said forcefully. "We're
going downstairs. Just you and me. Now!"

As much as Kayle tried to prevent it from
happening, bits and pieces of the night before kept
coming back. He'd picked up Aaron Pace that
morning, and although there were a lot of questions
he wanted to ask Aaron, because Aaron had been
there, he drove to work in silence and let it go at that.
He just couldn't ask. The answers would've been too
painful to deal with. Hell, he had enough problems
dealing with what he could recall.

Then too, from what Erica had said, he'd made a
fool of himself. And her opinion was generally biased
because she loved him. So, if she thought he'd been
way out of line, what did Aaron think? Aaron was just
a friend. Kayle's self-opinion was at an all time low.
He didn't need anyone else reaffirming his opinion.

However, just before noon, Kayle had his head

stuck under the hood of a car when the most amazing thing happened. Aaron Pace mentioned the night before, but not in the sense Kayle had expected. Kayle was doing a tune-up, which was unusual. He worked in a gas station, as a mechanic, but transmissions and heavy-duty repairs were his specialty. Tune-ups were always left for the newer mechanics to tackle. But if one of them didn't show, and most of the time they didn't, Kayle had to do it.

He was putting in a set of AC spark plugs when he felt someone watching him. He looked up and saw Aaron standing next to the car. "Hey, Buddy," Aaron began, "you been real quiet today. And I think I know why. You're upset, and I wanna say I don't blame you. That old lady of Erica's and her stories . . ."

Kayle said nothing; he couldn't. Parts of Mary's conversation had already come back, and those parts reflected his own feelings about the house. And he could live without her opinion; he didn't need an old mealy-mouth bitch, who could pick up on bad vibes scaring him worse than he was. And now Aaron knew.

"Do you believe her?" Aaron wanted to know. There was a hint of something in his voice. Kayle couldn't quite put his finger on it, but it sounded like sarcasm.

"No," he lied. "And I don't wanna discuss it." That should've been enough. Aaron should've left him alone. But he didn't.

"You have to talk to someone. What I mean is, you had that fight with her and all. And okay . . . you were wrong for that. But she shoulda minded her own business. It's your house, man. If you're happy there, it don't matter about nothing else."

Yes, it does, he thought to himself, it certainly does. Kayle had only sensed that taint in the house. Mary knew where it was coming from.

"I know you're depressed, but you shouldn't be. All her bullshit about heartbeats in the wall. Yeah, sure.

Like the house was alive and breathin'."

It is! Oh, Jesus, Aaron, you don't know the half of it, he thought. And if it isn't, then there's something alive and breathing in the house, only we can't see it, which makes matters worse. Did she mention something about a dog, he wondered?

Aaron was wearing his old faded cowboy hat and his boots. Kayle had been tempted at times to tell him there were no cowboys on Long Island. Still, the way he dressed suited his personality. "And what was the rest of the shit? Something about a black hole in the den? I think that's what she said?"

"That's it," Kayle said abruptly. "She said it was a . . . a what?" He stopped and thought for a moment. Aaron knew the answer and cut in.

"An entrance to hell." His voice was solemn; too solemn. He was trying not to laugh. Oh yeah, Aaron was being sarcastic all right. "An entrance to hell," he repeated.

"I seen that in a movie once," Kayle said, trying to make Aaron believe it didn't bother him in the least. Aaron laughed, and that's where it ended. But Kayle was dying inside. There was more truth to Mary's statement than anyone knew. "Uh . . . would you show me where that store is? You know, the one where I bought the beer last night? I wanna pick up a case."

"Sure, buddy. But your old lady's gonna be pissed!"

"I work for it!" He needed the beer, badly, but just for a while, until he got used to whatever was in that house.

Aaron smiled broadly. "It's your funeral."

Kayle hoped not.

" . . . and Katie's acting so strange. But Mommy says it's okay," Didi told Sam. They'd just gotten off the school bus. She'd waited for Sam, to talk to him, while Todd ran ahead with Jack Anderson, the boy next door. "Do you think Mommy's right?"

Sam never hesitated when he answered. He knew Didi could be trusted not to repeat anything to Erica. "No. She's wrong. Mommy told me the same stuff. An' I know she's wrong."

Didi mulled this over for a moment, then, "Mommy said Katie made someone up in her head. . . To play with . . . 'Cause she's lonely. But, Sam . . ." She didn't know how to tell him the rest.

Sam, however, made it easy. "It wasn't made up. Someone was in my room, too. And I ain't crazy."

"And I'm not either," Didi said. "Katie's friend isn't make believe. I heard her, Sam. I heard her this morning, talking to Katie." Tiny goose bumps lumped her flesh. "And it was awful. It sounded like a little girl, 'round Katie's age, but it was an awful voice . . . But, Sam . . . I couldn't see her . . ." She stopped just outside of the front door. "I'm scared to go back in that room."

Sam became indignant. Didi was his favorite sister. Nothin' was goin' to scare her and get away with it, not while he was around. "If somethin' bad happens, you come and get me. I'll help ya."

Didi smiled, but said nothing more. Sam was a good kid, but that's all he was: a kid. The help she needed was more in the line of grown-up help. She needed Erica or Kayle to help her.

Katie was in her closet playing dolls with Angelica when she heard the front door close. Must be the other kids, she thought, coming home from school. She didn't move to go down to greet them as she usually did. They were only gonna have their snacks anyway. And Katie wasn't hungry.

She hoped they didn't wake Mommy up. Mommy was taking a nap, thanks to Angelica. Her playmate wanted to play dolls, but Mommy had dragged Katie downstairs. So, Angelica got mad and made Erica think she was tired. Then, as soon as Erica fell asleep on the couch, because Erica was afraid to come up here, Katie climbed the stairs to play with Angelica.

"I HEAR SAM AND DIDI. WHERE'S TODD?"

Katie was amazed. Angelica heard everything. She had real good ears. "Don't know. Maybe he's outside playin'."

"WHY DOES SAM FIGHT WITH YOU?"

Katie looked at her, into those magnetic black eyes and couldn't answer. Why did Sam fight with her? She never did anything bad to him. She had to think about it some more before the answer came to her. "He says I start all the fights."

Angelica smiled. But Katie felt a sudden chill because the smile wasn't a friendly one. Still, she had nothing to fear. Angelica liked her. "HE FIGHTS WITH YOU TOO MUCH. HE TORMENTS YOU." Angelica stopped smiling then. "HE NEVER WANTS TO PLAY WITH YOU, DOES HE?" Again Katie couldn't answer, because it was true. Sam never wanted to play with her. "MAYBE HE'LL PLAY WITH ME. I HAVE SOME GAMES I WANT TO TEACH HIM."

"Teach me first?" Katie pleaded. "Please, Angelica?"

"NO. THESE GAMES ARE SPECIAL. THEY'RE JUST FOR SAM. LATER, WHEN HE'S ALONE IN HIS ROOM, I'LL GO PAY HIM A VISIT. YOU STAY HERE."

"Okay. An' maybe Sam'll become your friend too."

Angelica doubted it.

14

Todd was next door playin' with Jack Anderson. God, Sam was bored. He laid across his bed, letting his head and feet dangle over the sides, and stared at the floor. He thought about doing his homework, but that could wait. Homework was boring, too.

Of course, he didn't have to stay in his room alone. Erica had connected the Atari set to the television in the living room. So, it wasn't as if there was nothin' to do. Still, Kayle had come home early and Kayle was playin' with it. And Kayle was drinkin' beer again. Geez.

Why, only this morning his father had said somethin' about drinking when they were havin' breakfast. He'd made a promise to his kids—not that he had to—fathers were always in charge. But Kayle said he wasn't drinkin' no more, 'cause when he drank, he got nasty. And here he was, drinkin' again. Sam figured he was better off stayin' in his room.

But there was nothin' to do here.

Then again, he could always go play with Katie. She was all alone in her room, talkin' to that *friend* of hers. Didi had gone down to the kitchen to do her homework. Said she could concentrate better down there. But Sam knew that wasn't the reason Didi had left. Didi was afraid to stay in her bedroom alone with Katie. And hell, Didi was smarter than him, so maybe she had a point, and Sam should stay outta there too.

He got up and twisted himself around until his head was on the pillow. Maybe he should just go to sleep for a while, take a nap. If he could. If Kayle didn't get nasty and fight with Erica and keep him awake. Sam closed his eyes. Geez it was God awful hot up there. Where were those fans? Kayle bought them this afternoon, then he put the damn things in the garage. Said he'd install them on Saturday. "I promise," Kayle had said. Sure!

Well, maybe he would and maybe he wouldn't. A lot depended on his drinkin'. Sam hoped he didn't buy beer first. Sam continued to lay there, with his eyes closed, and think about different things. This was how he usually went to sleep; he wore himself out. One of those things was the subject of the tree near the back of the house, and the fortress he was gonna build. Todd and Jack Anderson could help—if Jack wasn't afraid of heights.

What fun that would be. They could start a club. A boys' club; no girls allowed. And that especially applied to Katie! Sam heard a whooshing noise. He'd almost been asleep, but the noise was so loud it stirred him awake. 'Course he didn't open his eyes— not in this room. Not until he figured what it was.

He heard the whooshing noise again. It wasn't so far away this time. It seemed to be coming from above him. It seemed like somethin' was flying around because he felt a breeze every time it whooshed by. What the hell was it? A bird? It had to be an awfully big bird to make that much noise. And if so, how'd it get in? Did he leave the window open? But then, he was sweating heavily, his armpits were sopping wet. The window had to be closed!

WHOOSH!

He was still scared to open his eyes, and scared not to. What if it attacked him? He had to see it comin'.

Then he considered callin' for help. But help was so far away. Besides, Kayle was drinkin' so that left him

out. Erica couldn' run fast; not up the stairs anyway.
At that point he wished he was back in the old house.
It was smaller, and had only one floor. Help would've
been there in no time.

WHOOSH!

Curiosity got the better of him, he opened his eyes
and wished he hadn't. It wasn't a bird! Oh, but it
should've been. That he could live with, he imagined,
even if it was huge and ferocious. No, no bird! Sam
looked up and saw a creature. He didn't know what it
was, so he called it a creature, with long white hair
stuck out at crazy angles. It was wearing a robe, a
black one, with tapered sleeves that came to the
wrists.

WHOOSH!

It flew over his head again, and it smiled as though
it was enjoyin' this—scarin' the pee outta him. Sam
got a look at its face this time, and again he wished his
eyes were still closed. Jeez, it was awful. The features
were all twisted outta shape. It reminded him of his
Grandfather Fred, Erica's Daddy. Fred had a stroke
before he died, and his face was twisted.

WHOOSH!

Its mouth was almost to one side of its face, and it
was hangin' open. Black lines marred its face near the
nose. Somethin' wet and disgustin' dribbled on Sam's
neck. It was saliva, he realized, droolin' from the
damn thing.

The creature stopped and hovered above him, its
eyes glued to his own. Lord, he wanted to scream, but
couldn't. Those eyes were red, hot, rivets of steel, and
they hated him. And one of its eyes was stuck out so
far he could see the veins behind it. Sam tried to get
off the bed, but somethin' was holdin' him back. A
heavy weight was keepin' him there, keepin' his arms
glued to his sides. Sam was more scared than he'd
ever been in his life.

But wait! There was a voice inside his head, and it
was talkin' to him, tellin' him not to be afraid. He

wouldn't be harmed. The big creature was lonely and had no friends. It wanted Sam to play a game with him. Nothin' complicated. Sam felt oddly relaxed; he was only half-scared now.

"IF I ALLOW YOU TO SPEAK, WILL YOU SCREAM FOR HELP?"

'Course not. Nobody would get there in time anyway.

"IF I RELEASE MY HOLD, WILL YOU RUN?"

'Course not. Sam had given his word; he said he would play a game. Then he wondered why he was doin' this, goin' along with what the creature wanted? He should've been scared enough to wanna get the hell outta there, no matter what the creature said. It seemed as though somethin' had taken over his mind, somethin' was makin' him want to cooperate.

"WHERE'S YOUR NOTEBOOK FROM SCHOOL, SAM?"

Geez. It knew his name. But how? And it wanted his notebook. "I ain't doin' homework," he insisted. "So if that's what ya got in mind, forget it!"

"NO, SAM. NO HOMEWORK. I NEED PAPER FOR THE GAME."

Oh, well, that was different. Sam quickly got his notebook and stood on his bed to hand it over, but it was refused.

"YOU DO IT. YOU TEAR OUT THE PAPER—A LOT OF IT. THEN ROLL IT INTO TINY BALLS, AND LAY IT IN A CIRCLE AROUND YOUR BODY."

Sam did as he was told. But somehow this didn't set too well with him. It was an awfully strange game. "What's it called?" he wanted to know when he was finished and sitting inside a circle of rolled up paper.

The creature smiled and continued hovering overhead. "CURIOUS LITTLE BOY, AREN'T YOU? WELL, I'LL TELL YOU . . . IT'S CALLED THE CIRCLE OF THE DEVIL!"

The rest happened so fast, Sam didn't have time to

respond. The creature burst into fits of laughter, then pointed one of its long, sharply clawed fingers at Sam, and the paper burst into flames. Sam was surrounded by fire! And again, the forces took control of his body. He couldn't scream and he couldn't move. Oh, God! The creature had tricked him and Sam was about to die.

Erica was in the kitchen helping Didi with her homework when Kayle first walked in with the beer. She glanced at the clock and that nearly drove him crazy. So he knocked off a few hours early, so what? He'd make up the time. Then she spotted the case of beer and her face froze. Kayle slammed it on the table and waited for her to say something, anything! In fact, it was almost a dare. But Erica said nothing. Instead, she took Didi and went into the living room. Shit on her, he thought, as he pulled the tab back on can number one.

She had no right doing this, looking down on him because he needed a crutch to be able to live in a house he bought for her and her brat, bastard, kids. Then again, to be absolutely honest about it, she wasn't aware of the strangeness in this house, so he couldn't be too hard on her. And if she ever found out the truth, that was all the more reason for her to appreciate him. He was keeping it all to himself, protecting her in a way. He gulped down the beer and pulled the tab back on can number two.

Just a few, he was only gonna have a few. Then, when he felt relaxed, he'd put the rest away. He took two long swallows and pulled the tab on can number three. He was feeling kind of mellow at this point, mellow enough to want to check out Mary's story. The things she said still bothered him, especially the part about the heartbeats in the wall. He didn't know it was that bad. Hell, the only contact he'd had so far with anything in this house took place when he'd been pushed on the stairs.

And that could've been laid up to imagination. If Mary hadn't put her two cents in . . . He got up and held onto the table for a moment to steady himself. He'd swallowed those beers too fast; they'd gone right to his head. After things stopped swaying a bit, he stumbled out to the bottom of the staircase. Erica was sitting next to Didi on the sofa. When she saw Kayle, she purposely turned away. Good, he thought. He didn't want her watching him running his hands along the wall and wondering if he was nuts or something. Let her turn away.

He took hold of the railing and studied the wall next to the stairs for a moment. He didn't see anything, but then he hardly expected to. How could you see heartbeats? He started up the stairs and tried to remember Mary's exact words. Hadn't she said something like she was mostly towards the top of the stairs when it happened? Well, buddy, let's go, he thought, let's do it.

He was three-quarters of the way up when he stopped and looked back over his shoulder at Erica. She was still doing a pretty good job of ignoring him, which was okay with him. Then he turned and faced the wall and saw it moving—It was pulsating, throbbing—No! The beer was pulsating and throbbing in his head, right behind his eyes. That's what he was seeing. Walls didn't breath. He mopped the sweat from his face with the palm of one hand and realized he was close to being sober.

And the wall was still pulsating, beat after beat, thump after thump. Almost like a heartbeat. He turned away and let his gaze wander to the door of the den. It was right opposite the foot of the stairs. All he had to do was walk back down the stairs and cross in a straight line. It was easy. *If* he wanted to see the black hole.

Without looking, he reached out and let his hand touch the wall. He had to, was forced to. Mary wasn't always wrong. Oh, Jesus! The heartbeat matched his own, it rose and fell at a constant rate.

Another beer, he needed another beer. He tried to keep his movements casual as he stumbled down the stairs and back into the kitchen and popped the tab on beer number . . . ? There were three empties on the table. This was number four. And this was definitely his last. He had enough problems just living in this asylum of a house without Erica being mad at him. So, he reasoned, if he stopped there, didn't have anymore, she could hardly be angry.

Maybe they could even talk, have a quiet conversation after the kids went to bed. And just maybe he could tell her about the walls. He stumbled back into the living room. Erica was still doing homework. "Where's the other kids?" He wanted to know.

"Sam and Katie are upstairs. Todd's next door." Her voice was cold.

"Next door? What the hell's he doin' over there?"

"Playing with the Anderson boy." This time her tone was different, it was challenging. She was telling him that if he didn't like it, Todd's being next door, he could go to hell. But Kayle surprised her. He kept his cool.

"That's good. The kids should have friends. There were no kids their age where we used to live and I felt bad about it." He glanced around and noticed the Atari game. Erica had connected it to the T.V. Should he? Christ, he hadn't played with the damn thing in ages. Erica was still watching him. Didi kept her head lowered. She looked nervous. Why? Kayle wasn't about to start anything. Last night was last night.

"You two go ahead with the homework. I'm gonna try some games. See if I can win this time." He turned on the T.V. and snapped in a game cartridge. Then he grabbed a joy stick, and plopped in a chair next to Erica. His beer was on the coffee table in front of her. After a few unsuccessful tries at winning a game, he picked up his beer and noticed it was empty. Shit! The bitch must've helped herself, she drank his beer.

No problem, he thought. He'd just get another. He stumbled back into the kitchen and pulled the tab on beer number . . . ? Fuck it. He wasn't countin'. Not anymore. This was stupid. It was his beer, he'd bought it, why should he count? And if that bitch didn't stop guzzling his beer, he'd fix her!

There was another game cartridge flashing on the screen of the T.V. when he came back and sat down. Who changed it? This was bullshit! He was playing with the Goddamn thing. They had no right to touch it. Well, he wasn't saying anything. That's what they wanted, they wanted him to get mad and lose his temper—Erica and Didi. Sittin' there pretendin' to be doing homework, when all the time those sneaky bitches had their paws on his Atari set.

He picked up the joy stick but didn't play right away. Instead, he let his attention wander to the staircase, the wall. It was pulsating heavier now. How were they doin it? Erica and the kids, how could they get the wall to move without cracking the plaster? After all, they wanted him out of here, and they were playing these games to scare him off.

Well, he wouldn't let them. He concentrated on his game. But it was no good. They were fucking up his brain in that area, too. The little ball on the screen was moving without him moving it. It was jumpin' all over the place and doin' crazy things. He got up and removed the game. He didn't like that particular one anyway. He snapped in another cartridge and sat down.

But it happened again. The game was going on without him, everything moving around as though triggered by some invisible hand. No! Not an invisible hand! Nothing invisible. Nothing like the thing that pushed him on the staircase. He just had no control over this game, that's all. And Erica was doin' it. The bitch! She was doin' everything she could to drive him crazy, to drive him from this house. Fuckin' with the wall and the Atari set. Drinkin' his beer when he wasn't lookin'.

"Kayle. Are you all right?" she asked, and it struck him funny. Here she was, trying to make him think he was nuts, then, in the next breath, she was askin' if he was all right. Well, he'd show her just how all right he was. He rose and stood over her, a smile frozen on his lips. She leaned back away from him. But she wasn't quick enough. He lashed out and struck her with a closed fist this time. No more open-handed shots for you, kid, he thought.

Erica screamed and grabbed her face. He brought his fist down again and connected with the back of her hand. Then Didi screamed. Kayle raised his fist again and gave Didi one. These bitches were gonna learn that he was no one to fool with. He was gonna teach them both a lesson.

Three people were screaming in the house. Sam was competing with Erica and Didi. Shit! This wasn't fair no how. Whatever was happenin' to them couldn't be all that bad. He was dyin'. Flames were lickin' up around his face. But wait. He saw someone through the smoke. And it wasn't that devil creature. It was a kid, around his own age. Katie? She was carryin' a little pail in her hands; the one she played with in the sandbox.

Water! She was throwin' water on his body and she was yellin'. He could hear her. She was sayin' somethin' about Angelica . . . She wanted to fix that Angelica! Who the hell was Angelica? It just couldn't be her imaginary playmate. Things that were supposed to be in your head didn't fly around the room and set people on fire. So, who the hell was Angelica?

"You okay, Sam?" Katie wanted to know when the fire was out.

He didn't know. In fact, he didn't know if he'd ever be all right after what just happened. The only thing he was positive about at this point, was that Katie loved him.

The throbbing pain in her leg had finally reached the unbearable stage. She had to do something. So, in desperation, she took a pill and laid down, leaving herself vulnerable. The pill, she knew, would soon put her out and they loved it when she was unconscious and helpless. But her Lord would protect her; even while she slept. So Kirsten's fears were minor.

She was dreaming now, taking a stroll through somebody's house. But it's a troubled place, full of misery. Oh, Lord, it's that house again. She saw herself through a haze, opening the front door and walking in. That was fine . . . until she reached the living room. There was a man hitting two women. No, a woman and a child. "Oh, God, stop it!" she screamed, but he was too drunk to listen. Besides, this was a dream, he couldn't hear her.

He was . . . what? What did she sense? Fear? Yes. He was afraid of the house, and with good reason. He drank to be able to live there. But this abuse, this physical punishment he was handing out. It was so unlike him . . .

She couldn't stop him, so she kept walking. There was a door . . . opposite the staircase. No! Don't go in there, she told herself. But it was useless: this was a dream. She couldn't control her actions. She opened the door and went inside. *They* were there, hundreds of them, ancient creatures, dangerous foes, and they were hovering around the black hole. Should she look? But the Gate Keeper was in there, hiding, waiting . . . for her—

Screaming! Someone was upstairs, and they were in grave danger. She couldn't look into the hole now, she had to see who it was. Oh, Lord, if only she had some control. But wait, she was moving outside, out to where the screams were coming from.

She crossed over to the foot of the staircase and looked up. The stairs, themselves, were long and steep, reminding her of the great, scaly spines of a huge dinosaur at rest. She climbed them, but hesitated when the wall pulsated and caught her attention. The heartbeats were here, in the wall adjoining the stairs. But she had no time to investigate. Someone was still screaming, and it sounded like a child.

It was a child. A small boy. But he wasn't in danger now. Another child was helping. She was putting out the fire. Oh, Lord, he was in the Circle of The Devil. Who put him there? Who did this? And yet, the answer was obvious: *they* were here in force, torturing this family, tormenting them. But why? Another question with an obvious answer: possession. They thrived on possession.

She took a step back when the closet door opened. Those poor, little, children; they were so unaware. The door opened behind them and went unnoticed. Kirsten gazed into the closet and wanted to scream. Someone was hiding in the shadows of invisibility. A man. Oh, and what a handsome man he was; the sight of him almost took her breath away. But he was evil; his very being existed on hatred. His eyes were black, and his hair, and his aura. He was a walking, breathing, entity of revenge.

And there was a dog. Oh, God, the dog was ONE OF THEM!

The children . . . She had to warn them . . . And yet, something came to her. It wasn't the children he wanted. No! It was the woman downstairs. He wanted her. She would be the instrument he'd use to enforce his revenge! The door closed and she couldn't see him anymore. Where had he gone to? Oh, Lord, she tried to follow, she tried hard. But her legs pained . . . and she was waking up.

No! Don't wake up until you see the rest! But it was

no good. She had no control over her dreams or their duration. She sat up in bed and wiped the sweat from her face. She was more frightened now than ever before after the revelation in her dream. There was a terrible force present in that house.

"Lord," she prayed silently, "please help and guide me in the oncoming fight. Please stand by my side."

Then she rose from her bed, and paid no mind to the sound of laughter echoing throughout the house.

Erica had quieted her daughter. She'd put cold compresses on her face and had given her two Tylenol tablets. Didi was fast asleep when she finally left her side and went to her own room.

She was in shock. There was no thoughts of revenge and of killing Kayle like she'd had the night before. At this point, she couldn't focus in on what she felt. The man had gone absolutely insane; she was living with a crazy. And this was serious, he needed help. She'd have to call someone, a doctor perhaps. Oh, better yet, a psychiatrist.

Her face, she saw, was heavily marred with welts when she finally got up the courage to look at herself in the bathroom mirror. She dipped a wash cloth into some cold water and winced when she laid it against her flesh. Those bastards hurt. She'd had some painful bruises in her life, but these were the worst. This was the time to call for help, she thought, when the evidence was so overwhelming, when you could see the damage. No one could question what Kayle had done to her, and to her daughter as well.

The worst part of it was, Didi was doing well in school and now Erica had to keep her home. She couldn't let the kid walk around like that. Christ, her teachers might get the wrong impression. They might think the child was a victim of abuse. And that just wasn't so. This was so unlike Kayle.

She snapped off the light in the bathroom and went to sit on the edge of the bed. Kayle changed when they moved into this house. She wondered if the move had been worth it. The dump they used to live in was a horror, true, but they were happy in a way. Kayle didn't drink or hit them. She took a cigarette from the crumpled pack in her jeans and lit it, inhaling as though she really needed that cigarette, as though it were a tranquilizer.

The smoke was extra thick and heavy when she exhaled, but she ignored it. This was hardly the time to dwell on what happened yesterday when the smoke had been filled with voices. She had more important things on her mind; such as, what to do about Kayle? She couldn't go on like this. In fact, she refused to even try. Now, not only was he beating on her, he was beating on the kids too. She wasn't about to stand for that nonsense.

In the morning, she planned on getting help of some sort. Maybe she'd even go to Family Court, speak to someone about these beatings. If Kayle had to go before a judge and take a good, verbal lacing, that would cool his pits. He'd think twice before he hit her again. And if that didn't work, SHE'D KILL THE BASTARD! Her anger was reaching a pitch. And that amazed her. Especially since she'd already gone over this in her head the night before. Killing him wasn't the solution.

"THEN WHAT IS THE SOLUTION, ERICA?"

There was a voice, coming from the most handsome man she'd ever laid eyes on. And he'd just walked out of her closet. Somewhere inside of her, she knew this was cause for alarm. And yet, she was strangely relaxed. "I don't know what the solution is," she answered. "You tell me."

"PERSONALLY, I'D THROW HIM OUT."

"Yeah, well . . . I've considered that. But then who'd support me and the kids?" Lord, was she ever relaxed. And this guy, whoever he was, he could put his shoes under her bed anytime. What a hunk! "By the way. What's your name? I mean, you seem to know mine and all."

"PAUL."

"Paul what?"

"JUST PAUL."

This was silly. Just Paul? Everyone had a last name. Still, it wasn't that important. "What're you doing here? What do you want?"

"I'M HERE TO PROTECT YOU FROM KAYLE. TO STOP THE BEATINGS."

Erica thought about what he'd said. She couldn't answer him. She was dumbfounded. He was here to protect her from Kayle? Why? Who the hell was he to walk in here and take over? She didn't need protecting. She was about to handle Kayle her own way. This guy, handsome though he was, could just leave.

"I LOVE YOU, ERICA. AND BECAUSE OF THIS, I'LL PROTECT YOU FROM KAYLE. THEN, IF YOU WISH, I'LL HANDLE YOU WITH THE SAME LUSTY AFFECTION AS AARON PACE."

He smiled and something stirred inside of her; her heart rose with passion. This man, this beautiful hunk of a man loved her. And he wasn't lying. She could hear the emotion in his voice. Had her prayers been answered? Had she found someone to replace the two men in her life? Someone to erase the hurt they'd both caused?

"ANSWER ME, ERICA. TELL ME WHAT TO DO."

Something burst through the haze of her mind at that point, and she felt disturbed, puzzled. She'd heard this voice before. And those words, she'd heard them also. But where? Then again, it seemed to have happened in this very same room. But when?

"I'VE ALWAYS BEEN HERE, ERICA. WAITING FOR YOU. I'LL WAIT FOREVER IF I HAVE TO. TELL ME WHAT TO DO AND I'LL DO IT."

"Could you give me some time to think this over?" Oh, God. She couldn't believe that statement came from her. It sounded so stupid, so juvenile. And here she was obviously dealing with a man of the world. But he was pleasant enough. He wasn't offended by her request.

"TAKE ALL THE TIME YOU NEED. I KNOW I'LL WIN IN THE END."

He walked back into the closet and was gone. She jumped up to look for him, but he was nowhere to be seen. Then she wondered if she'd been dreaming. Perhaps she'd fallen asleep. Handsome princes didn't just walk out of a closet and offer you the world. This wasn't the movies; things like this just didn't happen in real life.

Take all the time you need, he told her. *I know I'll win in the end.* She let it roll around in her head a few times. It sure sounded nice when he'd spoken those words. And yet, she couldn't help but feel there was a hidden meaning behind them. She sensed it. And that disturbed her a whole lot.

Aaron Pace had his forefinger hooked through the handle of a cup. He stopped drinking and examined what he knew to be an all-important digit: the fore-finger, the pointer. Then he wondered how it'd feel to cut it off; to just slice through his finger like it belonged to someone else. Hell, he couldn't do it. But he'd seen it done so many times. Oh yeah, he'd watched, in morbid fascination, as those . . . what . . . fools cut their fingers off.

Then, while the flesh was still warm and had not yet begun to deteriorate, the fingers were peeled back and every tiny, little morsel of meat was picked off the bone. And devoured . . . by the coven. He put the cup down and folded his hands together to protect his fingers. The drugs. It had to be the drugs. No one could be that crazy. Shit. You just didn't cut off your finger and feed it to a crowd. He smiled then, because even though he knew it was true, the idea sounded absurd.

The chair he'd been sitting in squeaked hideously when he got up to look out the window. The same car was parked across the street. It was only a matter of time before they came for him. Why had he gotten involved? What the hell had he been thinking of? Had his brains boiled over from the sun in California that he let himself do the things he did?

And Lorraine . . . That was the worst nightmare of all. Lorraine, his wife.

Aaron had gone to California years before seeking the good life. Fun in the sun, and perhaps a job as a movie extra. He was handsome enough. Everyone said he was, didn't they? But, after some added thought on the subject, he remembered. His mother had said it. And his uncle. They were the ones who said he had that rugged kind of appeal women liked, and that he oughta be in pictures.

So, good, old Aaron allowed conceit to dominate his senses. He took Lorraine and went to California. Lorraine was his new bride and, as he now fondly recalled, she was tall, and blonde, and sexy. Aaron had a hard time taming that one. Oh, he had his hands full all right. In fact, he could hardly keep the rest of the boys away. Especially on the beaches, when she wore those string bikinis that were nothing more than a couple of band-aids with strings attached.

Lorraine . . . Tears stung his eyes because he loved her still. And she loved him just as much until they joined that church. And what happened after that was not his fault! No way!

Aaron didn't make it in the movies, so he got a job as a mechanic. Lorraine worked as a waitress. Between them, they made enough to be able to afford a condo on the beach. A condo full of weirdos. But they didn't know it at the time.

One of the tenants had been handing out pamphlets and stuck one in their mailbox. It was about some church. Aaron had never been much of a church going person, but he'd read it, out of boredom, and

lived to wish he hadn't. Lorraine was in the shower;
they'd just made love and she usually jumped into the
shower afterwards, ahead of him anyway. He could
see her now as she came out to the patio; her long,
blonde hair hanging in damp ringlets, the terry cloth
towel she wore hiding her gorgeous body.

She was almost too perfect, and it was that aspect
that destroyed her—her beauty. "What're you
reading?" she'd asked.

"Nothing important. A pamphlet from some
church."

"From a church? Aaron you amaze me. You don't
even know what the inside of a church looks like."

She was sarcastic, and she mocked him. Maybe that
was the reason he insisted on going. "Yeah, but my
family's pretty religious, and my old lady's always on
my back about it. Maybe we should look into this one.
It's different."

"And that's what we need? A church that's
different? You wanna drag me to a church that's
different." She was beautiful, and tan and appealing.
He knew she was naked under the towel, and he felt
himself becoming aroused again. And hell, she
wouldn't mind. She never got enough.

Why had he stood silently to one side and watched
her with those other men? Those priests of the
church? They took her one at a time and he watched
and said nothing. And Lorraine loved every minute of
it. They mixed semen together with urine and wine
and made the members drink it as an aphrodisiac, and
he went along with everything, like a wimp! But no,
that was skipping ahead. He had to start at the beginning if this self-induced punishment were to be effective.

He took Lorraine to the church a few nights later.
He was bored. There was nothing else to do, so he
convinced her to come to church with him. And what
a place it was; he was very impressed. The decor was
all black and silver. There was a huge black altar at

the very front of the room, behind which he spotted a large, black, onyx table edged with silver trim. He looked around and saw inverted crosses and Satanic bibles. He remembered that Lorraine had sarcastically remarked that this was different all right.

They should've run. At that point, he should've insisted they leave. But it was so very fascinating, with its carnival-like atmosphere and the obviously sophisticated, intelligent people they met. This wasn't your ordinary run-of-the-mill church. The elite worshiped here. Who was he to wonder if this was right? Of course it was.

By the time the grand master came out and lit two black candles in silver sconces, signaling the start of the meeting, he knew he was hooked, they were both hooked. This was thrilling, this was exhilarating. He never knew church could be so wonderful.

The grand master began that meeting as he did all others. He sprinkled a sticky fluid over the heads of the members and chanted. "Hosanna, Satana. Lord of the Earth." Again, it was a mixture of semen, urine, and wine that was used, as he later found out. "Hosanna, Satana," the grand master repeated, followed by, "We are your servants!"

Every word that was spoken that night went against the deeply ingrained beliefs he'd been raised on, but Aaron paid attention, because hell, those words made sense. The grand master spoke the truth: the Christian churches of the world all damned his lord and master. But, at the same time, if it weren't for Satan, there would be no need for those very same churches. Satan kept them in business. They made money on his name. Good money!

Oh, Aaron's spirits were uplifted. His guilt over not being a steady church goer vanished. If his mother had been there, he was sure she would've agreed. Everything made sense. Oh, yeah, she would've been proud. He'd found the way, the truth, and the light. Satan was his prince. He'd do anything to belong, including taking off his clothing when the rest did, and giving his wife to any man with an urge. That last part bothered him a bit. But it was for the glory of Satan. So, who was he to question their practices?

However, eventually he did. He began to doubt their methods around the time he witnessed the very first, of many instances, of self-mutilation. Around the time the fingers began coming off! And it didn't end there. The second time he went to church, there was a human sacrifice: a *volunteer* who was anxious to die, who wanted to join her father in Acheron. That shocked the hell out of him. This woman laid on the table behind the altar and without being strapped down, let the grand master and others mutilate her body with small, sharp daggers. And she never made a sound. *Shit*. That must've hurt.

The end of his romance with the Satanic church began when a few members volunteered their own children, the so-called fruit of their loins, as *sacrifices*. These parents were so overcome with the words of the grand master—that brainwashing bastard as he now saw it—that they would've done anything. They would've given up anything, including their own children, to be considered worthy to stand under the sign of the horns.

Aaron couldn't take this part of it, and he let people know. He spoke against the church, he tried to make the members see his point of view. There was a lot of sickness associated with that church, mental illness long out of control. Oh yes, he was ready to quit. *But not Lorraine.* She'd given herself to the master beast, to the lord of lies, to his infernal majesty, with everything that was in her.

And that was her downfall. But it wasn't his fault! The only wrong he committed was in convincing her to join the church. But hell, she had a mind of her own, she didn't have to listen, didn't have to *volunteer* to become a *sacrifice!*

He begged her not to do it. "You'll die," he'd told

her when they were home, away from the influences
of the coven. "Do you understand? You'll die." But
she didn't listen, she wanted to die, to end this
miserable existence called life. Then she could live
forever in peace and glory with her father, in
Acheron.

Well, Aaron wasn't about to let it happen, not
without a fight. He planned on stopping her. On the
night of the big event, he came home from work with
the intentions of tying her up, if need be, to stop her
from going to the church for the evening services.

But he was tricked, deceived! Some of the coven
members lived in his condo. They'd heard the
ongoing argument between Aaron and Lorraine, and
they knew the truth. Aaron wasn't in agreement. So,
they came and took Lorraine before he got home.

Aaron found a note, *smeared with blood;* it was a
loving farewell from Lorraine. He ran to the church,
but he was too late. By the time he got there—
breathless and excited—she was already lying on the
black table with the silver trim behind the altar. He
saw her and screamed, told her it was crazy to go on
with this. She didn't listen. And the other members,
after hearing what he'd said, hovered around him and
said terrible things.

He could still see it: her body, her beautiful body,
lying prostrate and submissive on that table. And he
could still see the grand master carving ridges into her
flesh. And he could still hear her screaming. She
wasn't as into this as she'd thought. She wasn't
completely mesmerized with glory, or hypnotized
with the need to be with her father, Satan. She felt it:
every cut, every slice, every stab wound!

Aaron stood for it as long as was humanly possible
before moving to stop the ceremony. He ran to the
stage and fought against the priests, tried to keep
them from Lorraine. But they cheated. They cheated
by chanting and calling up the master beast himself.
Oh, he didn't want to remember any more of it. But

he couldn't stop the memories from coming back.

A tall, beast of a man rose up before him, right out
of thin air. He was handsome as handsome could be.
But he was evil personified. The look of the dead, of a
thousand ages of tortured battle, laced his expression.
Aaron was terrified, and he ran, like a coward.

But Lorraine kept screaming. He had to go back, to
at least try. So he went back to the stage, and still it
was no use. The master beast blocked his way, while
a horde of ancient horrors stood guard around him. It
was hideous, it was a nightmare. The cries of the
damned echoed in his ears, and Lorraine's voice stood
out above the rest. Flames of blackness rose from the
ground and scorched his flesh, singed his hair, and
burnt his nostrils with their acrid fumes. The odor of
overly-cooked, rotted flesh knotted his guts.

He was losing. They were cheating, pulling every
scare tactic in the book, and he was losing. And again
he ran, and he kept on running until he was safe. He
ran back to New York, to familiar surroundings. But
they ran with him. One didn't quit the church. The
church quit you!

Then he met Erica, and spent the last eight years of
his life loving someone else's woman. Erica, he
realized, was a substitute for Lorraine, and a poor one
at that. He loved her and all. And yet, no one could
ever take Lorraine's place. No one!

He glanced from the window and saw that the car
was gone. But he didn't feel good about it. They'd
come back. They always did. It was only a matter of
time before they made their move, before they grew
bored with tormenting him with their presence,
before they came up here and got him. He sighed and
figured it was just as well. Then maybe he'd find out
what happened to Lorraine—if she were dead or
alive.

15

Paul was there to offer a wealth of advice when Erica hung wallpaper in the bathroom, and he was only too happy to oblige. After all, Kayle was drunk most of the time, and in no condition to do anything. And, Erica was, as he convinced her, a helpless female. She needed a man's touch around the house. She'd already accepted his presence and the tiny detail about his domain being in her closet. So, helping her was easy.

As far as Paul was concerned, their working relationship could've been formed in heaven. He laughed at that. Erica was clumsy and giddy and all-female. He saw through her, read her mind. She loved it when Paul accidentally stroked her hand, and she loved it when his body brushed close against hers. My, Erica, he'd thought at those times, what naughty ideas you have. She wanted to try him out in bed. Well, hell, no problem.

He'd given his word: he promised to fuck her with the same tenderness as that wimp, Aaron Pace. And fuck her he would—when he was damn good and ready. But, for now, he'd kind of hang out and impress her with his macho air. He'd show her an easy way to tackle the heavy jobs Kayle was too drunk to do.

Making Erica totally dependent upon him for advice was step one in this particular phase, although, he had no intention of doing any physical labor himself. He did plan, however, on letting her live with the illusion that he'd done more than he had.

Erica had soiled her body hanging the wallpaper, and was taking a shower. Paul watched, without her knowledge, as she stood under a flow of steaming hot water and washed herself. She was naked, and almost alluring, if you paid no mind to the black circles around her eyes, or the slump of her body.

Paul did that to her, changed her physical appearance. Erica couldn't be appealing to anyone; there could be no more men in her life. He wouldn't allow it.

It was hard enough getting rid of those other two fagots. What if someone else came along and fell in love with her and she with him. Then Paul would lose out, his purpose would be defeated. Therefore, she was no longer allowed to look good, as he'd often heard her say. Of course, she, herself, couldn't see the change. However, he'd let her see it in time, after she was already hooked and in his control. By then, he hoped, she'd be as evil as he, and the change would seem normal to her.

Paul heard voices coming from the bedroom next door and knew it was time to leave. Angelica wanted Katie to bring her in here to talk to Erica. She had a most important question to ask, and it promised to be good.

Angelica was ready to kill this child at once! Katie had raised her voice, had screamed at her. And why? Because Katie imagined she'd tried to kill Sam. Of course she had. So what? Sam was an unruly child, with an unruly mind. Sam would make a piss poor disciple. Killing him was nothing compared to what was at stake here. Possession was the name of this game. There were four children to be had; four who would beget others.

And, she repeated in her mind, Sam was unruly, and that made him dangerous.

Unruly children had a way about them; they almost always spoke with a glibness of tongue that was astounding. Why, she thought, Sam could talk a blind man out of his eyes; and a mute out of his ears. And now, Sam was convinced there was danger in the house. What if Sam were to convince the others of this, and make them want to leave? No, she couldn't allow that to happen. So, Sam was out—and Katie, too, if she didn't learn to keep her mouth shut.

"YOU AGREED THAT SAM TORMENTED YOU TOO MUCH. THAT HE NEVER WANTED TO PLAY WITH YOU."

"Yeah, but you said you were gonna teach him some new games to play. Then he'd be friends. But ya tried to kill him!"

"DID I?"

"Yeah!" Katie yelled, then backed down. There was something in Angelica's eyes that scared her, some weird expression. Like Angelica hated her or something. "He's my brother," she whined. "Ya can't kill him. Please, oh, please, Angelica. Don't hurt him. Don't kill him."

"I WASN'T TRYING TO," she lied. This was beautiful, quite brilliant in fact. Katie would believe anything she said, because Katie was so gullible. "SAM IS MY BROTHER ALSO. I'M FOND OF THE BOY. IT WAS JUST A GAME THAT GOT OUT OF HAND."

"Ya mean ya weren't tryna hurt him? It was an accident?" Katie sounded relieved. Angelica was very pleased.

"Will ya teach me a new game, Angelica. Please, oh, please."

The sound of her voice drove Angelica wild. The namby, pamby little bitch with her cunting, whining

shit! She was ready to cut her tongue out. "I'LL
TEACH YOU SOME GAMES," she promised. "BUT
FIRST, LET'S DO SOMETHING ABOUT YOUR
SPEECH. OPEN YOUR MOUTH."

"Open my mouth?" Katie sounded appalled, and
scared. "Why? What're you gonna do?"

"YOU'LL SEE. IT'LL BE AN IMPROVEMENT
—FOR BOTH OF US. THEN WE'LL GO SPEAK
TO ERICA. I HAVE SOMETHING TO ASK OF
HER."

"But . . . Ya never show yerself. Mommy's scared
of you."

Angelica was not about to justify her request. Erica
would see her this time, but the same as Katie saw
her—not in her natural state. She smiled. No, she
couldn't scare Erica. She'd go on with this little girl
pose for as long as possible. In fact, at this stage of the
game, it might even work to her advantage. Erica
liked children.

"What're ya gonna ask 'er?"

Angelica smiled. "I WAS THINKING. IF I
CONSIDER SAM TO BE MY BROTHER, WHY
CAN'T I BECOME A TRUE MEMBER OF THIS
FAMILY?" She could think of no better way to
establish herself with the rest, and to gain their trust
and confidence, than to become one of Erica's
children. Then, taking the souls of her four 'brothers
and sisters' would be a battleless fight. They'd have
faith in her by then and would surrender without
question.

This was her idea, and another of those strokes of
genius that often came out of nowhere, and always
worked. Her only hope was that the Gate Keeper
would approve.

"NOW, BEFORE WE SPEAK TO ERICA, OPEN
YOUR MOUTH, KATIE." She was about to fix this
bitch but good. No way was she going to continue
listening to her childish pratter.

* * *

Carol Anderson had been out back pruning her roses, and, for a change, minding her own business, when it happened—

Burt, she knew, had gone to town to pick up some parts for a car he was working on. Before he left, he'd given her a stern warning: stay away from those people next door. He didn't want any more of those kids in his house, etc. etc. etc. Burt was a pain in the ass. Jack finally found a boy his own age to hang out with, and Burt wanted to ruin everything.

Well, she intended to listen to the first of his warnings and disregard the rest. In other words, she'd ignore those people over there, just for today, and take care of some of her badly neglected chores.

It was nice and warm out back, a perfect day for gardening. She was down on her hands and knees, pulling out weeds, when she felt someone staring at her. She didn't look up right away, she was leery about doing it at all. One never knew who would pop up in one's yard, especially with that place next door being as it was. But the feeling wouldn't go away, and then a shadow fell across her, someone was standing by the fence, blocking the sun.

Carol gathered her courage and glanced up, half expecting to see Erica. But it wasn't Erica. It was a handsome, gorgeous man, and he was smiling at her. She'd never seen him before. If she had, she would've remembered.

"HELLO," he said.

She detected a strangeness in his voice and ignored it. She was nervous and probably overreacting. "Hello, yourself."

"MY NAME'S PAUL. I LIVE NEXT DOOR."

"Pleased to meet you, I'm Carol Anderson." He lived next door? This wasn't Erica's husband: she knew Kayle. Maybe it was her brother or a cousin. "How do you like the new house?" What a question, she thought. Unless they haven't noticed anything yet.

"IT'S NICE. BUT IT'S A BIT . . . SHALL WE SAY, STRANGE?"

She knew it. She just knew it. They've discovered the truth, and now it's too late. Erica's already bought the house. If they moved out or sold it, they'd lose a lot of money at this point. Why hadn't she said something before this happened?

"I WAS WONDERING IF YOU COULD EN-LIGHTEN ME. PERHAPS, TELL ME SOMETHING ABOUT THE HOUSE AND ITS FORMER OCCU-PANTS."

She glanced around as if she expected Burt to come running up and start yelling at her. She wanted to say something, in fact, she had to. She'd waited too long as it was. Still, she didn't want to give Burt another excuse to fight with her. Paul noticed her anxiety and spoke up.

"IS THIS A PROBLEM? I CAN COME BACK LATER."

Carol had at least an hour before Burt came back. Once he got himself into those auto parts stores, he never knew enough to leave. Burt had to look at everything in the whole Goddamn place, he had to examine every new tool they had, every new piece of equipment. "No. It's no problem. Come into the house. I'll fix us some coffee."

Paul climbed the fence and followed Carol inside. He knew why she kept looking at the clock. He'd already scanned her mind. Her fagot husband was due home soon, and she wanted Paul out before he showed up. Well, Paul would be long gone, but not before he'd found out what he came here for. He wanted the truth: how much did this woman know about the house next door, his house, and how much of it was she willing to blab to Erica?

He understood from the others in the house—his ancient disciples—that this woman had lived here for years. She spent a lot of time looking over that fence out back, and through her kitchen window as well.

She must've picked something up along the way. And
if Paul were to eliminate all obstacles in his quest for
the possession of Erica, he should perhaps start here.

Carol plugged in the Mr. Coffee machine and sat
down. The coffee was already measured and ready to
go. Burt insisted she fix it ahead of time. This way,
he'd always have fresh, whether she was home or not.
"To begin with," she said, "I know a lot about that
house. Things nobody else has ever noticed. Not even
my husband."

Paul wasn't too sure about the last part. Burt knew
enough. He sat back in his chair and smiled, giving
the bitch his complete attention, while she talked and
told him things that amazed him. She'd obviously
spent a lot of time watching that house, more than
he'd imagined. Well, now. Paul had no choice. It was
either kill her outright or frighten her into keeping
quiet.

That decision was something he'd have to think
about. Meanwhile, he had to be sure Erica never
came over here. Never!

Erica had the funny feeling she was being watched.
And yet, she was alone in here. Paul left long ago. She
saw him. He walked back into the closet and was
gone. Oh, Paul, she thought. If only you never had to
leave. If only Kayle would go and not come back, then
we could be together.

She thought back to the first time she'd met Paul. It
was only yesterday, but it seemed longer. Then she
thought about her silliness and the childish answer
she'd given him. Paul wanted her to spend the rest of
her life with him. Erica asked for time to think about
it. What a stupid thing to do! Paul was the answer to
her prayers: a man's man. He was the one person
capable of replacing both Kayle and Aaron Pace.

Thankfully he came back. He'd given her another
chance.

Was it love she felt, was that why she missed him?

Had she fallen this soon, this fast? It had to be, she
reasoned, and her heart quickened for at least the
tenth time that morning. Paul was everything she'd
ever hoped for in a man: he was kind and gentle like
Aaron, and he was hard-working and resourceful like
Kayle. Oh, Lord, he was just too perfect.

But . . . Was he real?

She quickly erased that question from her mind.
She didn't care if he were real or a figment of her
imagination. He was the one man she felt she could
willingly spend the rest of her life with. But, what if
Kayle found out? She was forever living in dread
because she was afraid he'd find out about Aaron
Pace. Now she had Paul.

Then she discovered something amazing: she didn't
care if Kayle found out. What could he do? Leave her?
Let him! What else? Would he beat her up perhaps?
Oh, no. Paul was there to protect her; why he'd said
so himself. She and Kayle were through as far as she
was concerned, finished, history.

She stepped out of the shower and draped a towel
around her body. There was a noise directly outside,
coming from her bedroom. Shit! She hoped it wasn't
Kayle. After beating her and Didi, he got so drunk last
night that he couldn't go to work today. This was
awful. Yesterday he'd taken off early, so he lost pay
there, and now he was losing the whole day. How the
hell were they going to pay the mortgage?

Then again, he wouldn't pay it if he found out about
Paul, and left her. Erica had to think of something and
fast. She had to come up with an idea for paying her
bills without using Kayle's money.

The bathroom door opened abruptly. Her heart
caught in her throat because she thought it was Kayle.
But it was Katie. She felt her body relax and she
smiled. "Hi, honey."

"Hello, Mother."

Erica stared at her with amusement. Hello, Mother?
Katie must've been going through a stage. She thought

that was awfully cute. "Where's Daddy?"

"He's in the kitchen, drinking beer. I saw him a moment ago."

Erica felt relieved again because he was downstairs, away from her. And yet, her insides knotted into a ball: he was drinking again. Oh, Christ. Now what? Would it start again, the beatings? Then she remembered Paul. He'd stop Kayle from hitting her. He promised he would. "Did you speak to him? Was he nasty?"

"Yes. He was. I asked him about the ceiling fans, when he planned on installing them. He said to tell you to do it. So, I'm relaying the message—you do it!"

That didn't sound like something Kayle would say. He was rotten when he wanted to be, but he always took care of heavy repairs around the house, with no argument. And Katie—this didn't sound like Katie, your average four-year-old. Not only was she speaking on an adult level, but she was damned nasty, too. What in the name of God was going on here?

Don't panic, she warned herself, keep it cool until you can figure this out. "I'll have to hire someone to install the fans. I can't do it."

Katie scrutinized the bathroom, examined the wallpaper. Then she focused her attention on Erica and Erica saw something different, an almost grown-up attitude in her expression. It meant that the changed pattern of her speech wasn't necessarily due to a stage she was going through. "Who put this up?" she wanted to know.

"I did. But I had help."

"Well, then ask that person to help you install the fans. Why hire someone when you obviously can't afford to?"

Erica was ready to scream. This was definitely not a stage that Katie was going through. And this was no child that she was speaking to. It was a woman, conversing with that same mental attitude Erica

loathed: that sophisticated know-it-all type of bullshit
she hated. Erica wanted to slap Katie in the worst
way, but she was suddenly frightened. She wished
Paul were there. He'd comfort her, tell her what to do
concerning all of these mysteries.

There was another noise outside of the bathroom
door. Paul! Had he come back? But Katie spoke up
then. It wasn't Paul.

"Angelica is outside. She wants to meet you, very
badly."

Erica felt her nerves dancing beneath her flesh.
Angelica had turned out to be an invisible indentation
on Katie's bed the last time Katie insisted she meet
her. Oh, God. She wasn't up to this.

"Come in here, Angelica," Katie said before Erica
had a chance to stop her.

Erica stiffened and prepared herself for the worst.
But then a real child came into the bathroom; a little
girl whom Erica was able to see. And what a pretty
thing she was. Erica was impressed. She had long,
black hair that hung in ringlets, and black eyes, and
she wore a frilly, white dress. Erica glanced at Katie
and smiled. "This is Angelica?"

"Yes."

"Hello, honey." Erica studied her some more
before noticing the resemblance between this child
and her newest love, Paul. They both had black hair
and amber-colored eyes. That was odd. Angelica
looked enough like Paul to be his child. Then again,
Paul was single, he'd told her so. Therefore, Angelica
could've been taken for his sister.

"WILL YOU BE MY MOTHER, TOO?"

The question was obviously directed at Erica. And
it threw her off. This child wanted Erica to be her
mother? What a thing to ask, especially when she
must've had parents of her own. She was so well
taken care of.

"YOU DIDN'T ANSWER. I SAID, WILL YOU BE
MY MOTHER, TOO?"

Erica smiled and looked at Katie for help. Katie should've said something. After all, Katie must've known Angelica's parents. "I'm sure your own mother would be very offended if I said yes," Erica quickly stated. Then she bent down to touch Angelica's arm in a comforting manner. But she straightened back up when the child brushed her off. "You see, honey—"

"IS THAT YES OR NO?"

While Erica watched and felt helpless, Angelica's expression hardened. Her eyes became two bitter orbs of hatred, her mouth tightened into a thin line. Erica was frightened by this and didn't know why. It was only a child, a small, frail child. Why was she so afraid?

"AM I TO BELIEVE THAT YOU'RE REFUSING?"

"Well, yes . . . But—"

"Mother, how could you! Angelica has no one!"

Katie was talking that way again. Erica was so confused by everything that was happening around her. But she kept her head. "Katie! I can't. She's someone else's child. That's obvious. Look at how well dr—"

Angelica disappeared in a puff of angry, black smoke and was gone. Erica fell back against the sink and could say nothing.

"Are you satisfied?" Katie wanted to know. "Now you drove her away. Are you happy?"

"What's all this shit? What the fuck's goin' on?" Kayle wanted to know. He'd opened the bathroom door without either of them noticing, and now he was leaning against the frame in an angry, drunken poise, waiting for them to answer. Erica's heart pumped faster when she noticed that his fists were balled up and ready to go.

Kayle had watched the three oldest children getting ready for school and said nothing. Shit. They didn't wanna speak to him anyway, he thought. They were scared of him. He was a drunk, wasn't he? And hell, here he had a couple of drinks a few nights in a row, to steady his nerves, and they were all but condemning him to death.

He stared at Didi, at the bruises on her face and felt his stomach turn. He'd never hit his children before. Never! Then again, the little bitch was her mother through and through. And Erica well deserved to be pounded around, so the kid must've too. "I thought you wasn't goin' to school?"

She lowered her head and stared at the table when she answered. "Mommy said it was okay."

"Mommy said it was okay," he repeated sarcastically. "And what if I don't like it. Mommy ain't the boss around here—I am!"

Sam spoke up and defended her, in the nicest way he knew how. He wasn't about to smart-mouth Kayle, not with him drinkin' all that beer and gettin' nasty. "Mommy said to tell them at school that she fell . . . If anyone asks."

Kayle smiled and felt his face stiffen. He realized he wasn't quite sober yet. "Mommy seems to have all the answers." The three kids waited, nervously scuffling their feet and keeping their heads bowed so as not to look at him. "Go on," he said. " Get outta here before ya miss the bus."

Mommy, he noticed, wasn't walkin' them to the bus stop this morning. Probably because Mommy's face had been kicked in the night before. And Mommy was embarrassed. Serves her right, he thought. That'll teach her not to drink his beer, and fuck with his brain when he's playin' with the Atari set. And she'll keep her hands off the wall, too. Then he wondered how Erica had done it; how she'd made the wall move and pulsate in time to the rhythm of a heartbeat. And what a beat it was.

That bitch could've put Xavier Cugat to shame!

His mouth was acrid and dry. He needed something to drink, but all he had was coffee. And who wanted shitten old coffee anyway? He wanted some beer, but hell, he'd really sucked it up the night before. Drank a whole case. He considered going to the store for more, but his head was pounding and he was in no shape to drive.

He heard the sound of water running—Erica was in the shower. That meant she'd finished putting up the wallpaper. And if Katie relayed his message, Erica would start installing the fans soon after. Not that she could, but she'd try just to spite him. Like she'd hung the wallpaper to spite him. Well, fuck her, he thought, she could go get some beer first!

Kayle staggered up the stairs, carefully keeping his attention focused straight ahead. He didn't want to look at the wall, and didn't care if it was moving or not.

There were voices coming from the bathroom, sounded like three women talking. That confused him. What was Erica doin', holdin' a fucking PTA meetin' in his bathroom? What were those broads doin' in there with her? Well, he wasn't standin' for this! This was an invasion of his privacy and he had damned little privacy as it was. He opened the door and burst inside in time to catch Katie screaming in her mother's face.

Erica, he saw, was layin' back against the sink. Her face was white and she looked shocked about somethin'. He listened for a moment before he realized that Katie was one of those women that he'd heard. Katie sounded different somehow. She was loud and nasty. Well, he wasn't standin' for that. Erica could take the shit if she wanted to. But she wasn't takin' it in front of him.

"What's all this shit? What the fuck's goin' on?" Kayle asked, then waited for an answer. But he got none from Erica. So he turned his attention to Katie. "What're ya doin' in here when your mother's takin' a shower? What're ya botherin' her for?"

Katie didn't seem frightened of Kayle and this

frightened Erica all the more. Katie stuck her chin out defiantly and answered him. "You told me to relay a message. And I did. You didn't tell me to wait until she was finished taking a shower!"

The words had barely been spoken when Kayle lashed out and brought his fist down across the side of Katie's face. Erica screamed and jumped at him. She was afraid of him, but this was another of her children—her baby as a matter of fact—taking a beating from this bastard. Kayle saw her coming and backhanded her with his left hand. Erica fell back against the sink and screamed again.

Kayle raised his fist to hit Katie one more time and found it odd that she wasn't crying. He'd really given her one the first time, but it hadn't seemed to effect her one bit. Well, now he'd try harder; do a better job. However, he was about to bring his fist down when something stopped him—Erica's towel had fallen off when he slapped her back against the sink. She was hunched over—her natural pose lately it seemed—and she was naked. He felt aroused.

He looked back down at Katie and grabbed her by the arm, leading her out and across the bedroom to the door. "You get lost. Go play with yer fuckin' dolls for a while." He slammed the door behind her and wondered if he was up to this; up to laying Erica. Christ, he was still half-drunk. But the urge was there.

He rubbed the scar on his face and started back across the room when the closet door swung open, slamming back against the wall when it did. That stopped him. And pissed him off at the same time. He'd have to remember to give that bastard Wittaker a call about these closets fuckin' opening an' closing anytime they felt like it: as if they were really human and had life of their own—

Something wandered into his mind then: the wall by the staircase, the den . . . Maybe they had life in them, too! And maybe, he thought angrily, this was

more of Erica's doing. After all, she was tryin' to drive
him away, tryin' to get him to leave. And just because
he was drinkin' to sort of steady his nerves. He
stormed over to the closet and slammed the door.
He'd fix her ass. Just wait 'till he got that bitch in bed.
He'd show her who was boss!

Kayle could see her from where he was standing,
naked and submissive. He felt aroused, felt an
erection starting. He wanted her and badly. "Get out
here, bitch," he commanded, then he ducked when
the closet door slammed open behind him again.
Kayle wheeled angrily, but froze when he saw *something* . . . Someone had been standing in the open
doorway . . . Someone who wasn't there now.

And Christ, Jesus, it looked like that *Nick:* his
mother's boyfriend, the one who'd broken his jaw. He
rubbed the scar on his cheek and knew he never
wanted to face that crazy bastard again. "Erica, come
here." This time it sounded more like a request. He
heard her coming behind him and didn't turn, he
couldn't. He had to keep watchin' that door—just in
case.

"Are you doin' this? Makin' the closets open and
close by themselves?"

"No . . . Kayle, I—" She sounded scared.

"Tell me the truth." His voice was low and quiet,
but there was an edge to it. "If you're doin' it, tell
me."

This time she didn't answer at all, and that angered
him. He saw a confession in her silence. If she wasn't
guilty, she'd be denyin' it over and over. He felt his
rage building again. This was too much to take,
especially after last night, especially after what she'd
done to him then. He wheeled to face her. She was
visibly frightened, but that was too bad. Now she was
gonna get just what she deserved.

He raised his fist to hit her . . . But he couldn't. It
wasn't Erica standing in front of him now. Hell no.
Now it was his mother, naked and defiant: as naked

as she'd been that night so long ago when Nick had broken his jaw. He remembered now. Funny, he'd never been able to before. His mother had been naked, and while he laid on the floor after Nick got through with him, she'd gotten dressed real quick like and left with her boyfriend.

"Mom . . . Why?" he sobbed as tears of indignation welled up inside of him. But she didn't care, the same way she didn't care before.

"Get him, Nick," was all she said. Then she smiled and turned away from him.

Kayle wheeled to face Nick, and saw him coming out of the closet, brass knuckles in place. This wasn't fair. Kayle wasn't big enough to handle Nick. Kayle was only a child, barely nine years old, wasn't he?

He screamed when Nick brought the brass knuckles down across his face with such fury he was knocked to the ground. And Nick hit him again and again. Kayle covered his head with his hands, but it was no use. Every blow connected. His face was on fire, his head throbbed. Then Nick cheated; he kicked Kayle in the balls, then in one of his kidneys. Kayle screamed over and over and rolled his body into a fetal position to protect himself.

The flesh of his jaw was laid open, and the jaw, itself, was hanging slack. It was broken again, he just knew it. Nick was doing a number on him this time: worse than before. He wondered how long he could bare it, and he wondered too if Nick would kill him this time.

Erica had run back to the safety of the bathroom when Kayle raised his fist to hit her again. She planned on locking herself in there to keep away from Kayle. But then, she stopped. Katie was next door. If Kayle couldn't get Erica, he might go crazy and attack Katie. Erica was helpless, and terrified as well. This time she knew she had to take positive action against Kayle. She had to call the police when Kayle was finished with her.

She turned, willing to take her beating to spare Katie, and was amazed to see Paul beating Kayle. Paul had come out of the closet in time to stop Kayle from really going to town on her. Paul probably heard her screaming in the bathroom before, when Kayle first hit her, and came running to help. Oh, well, she thought, Paul was keeping his promise. He was protecting her.

And yet, Kayle, she noticed was taking an awful beating. She hoped that Paul wouldn't hurt him too badly, even though Kayle did deserve it for acting like such a bully. Christ, beating her, and beating the kids.

Something was puzzling her thought. Kayle kept yelling "Nick, don't!" Who the hell was Nick? Was it someone from his past? And why was Kayle so afraid of him? More mysteries, she thought, and turned and walked back to the bathroom. Somehow, she could no longer bear to watch Paul beating Kayle as he was.

16

"Daddy, did you get the mail?" Patricia asked on her way out the door. "I put it on the table in the foyer."

"Thanks, doll." It was late morning and another beautiful day. Henry was in the den, but, surprisingly enough, he wasn't doing research. It was futile anyway. The people who wrote those books he'd been reading had probably written them on theory alone. None of them, it seemed, were well-versed in occult matters.

The mail, when he went to glance at it, consisted of the usual garbage: a few bills, some flyers from supermarkets. And yet, there was something that caught his attention. It was a card. He was able to tell from the shape of the envelope. Who the hell would be sending him a card, he wondered? It was nobody's birthday. Besides, they had no friends to speak of and few relatives and even those were distant ones.

When he opened it, Henry was amazed to find a mass card inside. He turned the envelope over and found it had been postmarked in Monroe. That puzzled him even more. He doubted that anyone local or otherwise, either knew or cared, that his son was dead. Unless . . . Oh, right, he thought. Erica Walsh lived in Monroe. It had to be from her.

She was that kind of a person; to send a mass card.

Oddly enough though, there was no return address on the outside.

At this point, Henry wasn't sure he wanted to read the card. Buddy had only been dead a few weeks, the pain was still prominent. And besides, Buddy wasn't really gone, he was forever roaming the house. The boy just refused to stay in his coffin, in the ground. He refused to accept his own death. So, he came home. Henry saw him a lot, and wondered if Patricia had, too.

If so, there'd been no mention of it.

The card had a really nice picture of the Crucifix on the front of it. However, when Henry took a closer look at the figure of Christ, he smiled. His mind was playing tricks on him: he was near the end, sanity was just around the corner. Nobody depicted Christ like that, *hanging upside down.*

Then he opened the damned thing and took a quick look at the signature. He had to know who sent it. But there was none; just a set of initials—G.K. Well, hell, it was awfully nice of the Gate Keeper to send a mass card.

"YEAH, DAD. SOMETIMES HE TRIES TO BE NICE."

Henry didn't turn to see who it was. He didn't have to. It was Buddy. His son had come up from behind, without Henry's knowledge, and had leaned over his shoulder to read the card. Henry had been so taken by that picture, by that unholy desecration of his Lord, that he never took notice until now, when Buddy spoke to him.

Without turning, Henry mustered up all of his courage and spoke back. "You're dead, you know." This was the perfect way to get them back to the grave, tell them they're dead!

"YEAH, I KNOW."

"Then why're you here? Why don't you go home?"

"THIS IS MY HOME."

Henry's heart was breaking. He wanted his son,

more than anything else in the world he wanted
Buddy to stay, and for things to be as they were. But
this was wrong. The boy was dead. "Buddy?"

"YEAH, DAD?"

"You have to go." He choked out the words and
held back the tears. "You don't belong here."

"WELL . . . YOU SEE, I CAN'T. *THEY* WON'T LET
ME. EVERYTIME I TRY, *THEY* STOP ME AND
SEND ME BACK HERE."

This was an outrage, and Henry didn't have to ask
who *they* were. He knew! He wheeled to face Buddy,
to comfort his son, to tell him he'd find a way. But he
couldn't talk. Buddy was decaying and Henry
realized it was due to a number of things. The length
of time he'd been dead; the change in the climate
outside—this was spring—making it warmer in here.
"Please go away," he said, his voice barely audible.
"Please try."

One of Buddy's eyes was hanging forward on his
cheek. The other was a black hole. He focused on
Henry and promised he would, he would try. Henry
ran to the den and slammed the door behind him. His
chest was heaving with shock. His heart had to give
out soon, it couldn't take much more.

And yet, there were no answers for him—no place
to go for help. He couldn't get rid of the demons, and
now he couldn't get rid of his son. Unless . . . But no,
he didn't want to involve her. Kirsten had enough of
her own problems. She ran away a year ago to escape
from a nightmare, and now she was back, hoping to
find peace. Henry couldn't dump this on her. Not yet
anyway.

He got a bottle from the liquor cabinet and poured
himself a shot to steady his nerves. Then he found
that one wasn't enough, so he poured another. There
was no noise coming from the hall outside. Maybe
Buddy had found a way. Christ! He hoped so. At least
before Patricia got home.

But that idea was absurd, as he soon realized.

Buddy had been hanging out for a few days now. She had to have seen him at least once in that time. Then he surmised that she probably had and was keeping it to herself. Patricia was like that; always protecting him, hiding the truth, the same as he'd done with Bess. Funny how things had changed and sort of reversed themselves.

In fact, lots of things had changed around here since Bess died.

Bess. Oh, God, he missed her. But he didn't want to; not anymore. He didn't want to feel that emptiness, that hollow feeling, like something inside him was gone. Because then the rage took over; he wanted revenge, and that was dangerous. Look what the Gate Keeper did to him the last time . . . But he fucked the Gate Keeper, that bastard. He got even.

But it was short lived. The Gate Keeper fucked him back and had the last laugh after all. There was a fungus growing on Henry's body, down in the area of his penis. He'd never seen anything like it. It was green, and had the consistency of moss around the perimeter. And there were white things, spores it seemed, shaped like tiny pimples, sprouting from the middle. He considered going to a doctor for help, then changed his mind. No doctor in the world could do anything for him now. This was not your ordinary fungus. Hell no, it was demon fungus, demon shit!

And it would probably kill him as it ate its way through his body, like it was doing now. Still, he felt no pain. But, that was part of their plan. Remove the pain and old Henry might not become alarmed. But Henry was alarmed. He was one step ahead of them in that department. He was alarmed enough to keep watching the shit grow, to be ready for the end when it came.

He poured himself another shot and relaxed in his easy chair. All three of those shots should've done their intended job. They should've kept him from thinking, should've kept his mind from wandering.

But there was too much to hide, too much that he was
trying not to remember. Like the night he took on the
Gate Keeper and had his trial by fire. He could recall
that particular incident as though it happened five
minutes ago.

Henry remembered standing by the gate, the one
that had opened by itself, the gate under the hideous
tree. He was standing there and he remembered
glancing in the window and seeing a myriad number
of ancient faces—all ugly and deformed. But he
wasn't afraid of them—they were powerless assholes,
shit heels in the echelon of hell. The only powers they
possessed had to be triggered by the big guy, the head
honcho, the Gate Keeper.

There was a light over the door around the front
that kept flickering. And that meant one thing:
someone was materializing, energizing their hateful,
glutted body so that Henry could see him. And see
him he did. That's when Henry first felt fear, when
he saw that hideous thing in front of him. It had a
huge, reptilian body like a lizard, and it had four
heads. Each head was different.

They all resembled something in the canine family
with their large, slanty eyes and pointed snouts. But
one had real long teeth, razor-sharp at the edges, for
chewing human bones, it said to scare him. Another
had eyes that shot fire from its pupils. Oh, shit, he
remembered thinking, and knew he'd taken on more
than he could possibly handle by himself.

But he had no intentions of backing down, or of
running like a coward in the face of its mocking
laughter. "You killed my wife, you bastard."

"FUCK YOU AND YOUR WIFE," it growled, then
added, "AS A MATTER OF FACT, I DID FUCK
YOUR WIFE. AND SHE WAS GOOOOD!"

Henry went out of control at that point and attacked
the hideous bastard. But he never made it, never
reached the body; something stopped him. There was
an object between him and the mighty Gate Keeper: a

revolving circular saw, a big one, and it was suspended in mid-air. Henry spotted it after he made his move, and he was moving with everything that was in him—the rage he felt over Bess' death, the indignation he felt because she's suffered so.

Oh yes, he was moving on top of the bastard. He was ready to do a number on him. But this thing got in the way. And Henry was moving too fast to stop himself and he ran right into it. It was hanging sideways at first, and it took his hands off, then his arms. Henry screamed in shock, he was crippled for life. He had no hands, no arms. And the thing didn't stop there. Hell no, it turned itself around and started on his body. Huge, painful, chunks of flesh were strewn about the yard, like lawn decorations. And blood, oh, Christ, he never knew he had so much blood inside of him.

He was dying, he had to be. No way could he ever survive this. What a fool he'd been. Trying to seek revenge against a force that was older than time itself, and stronger than anyone could imagine.

The blades were sharp. Sharp and precise. He was being dissected with such precise, surgical skill that it amazed even him and, at the same time, drove him half-crazy with pain. He wondered about his children, about who'd look after them now. Bess was gone, and he was almost gone.

His body had been stripped of most of its skin: his internal organs were exposed. His legs were gone. He spotted them lying near some bushes out front. His pant legs were still wrapped around them, but they didn't hide the two stumps that showed where those legs had once been attached to his body.

"HAVE YOU HAD ENOUGH?" The Gate Keeper wanted to know. "SEEK YE FURTHER REVENGE AND YE WILL SURELY DIE."

Henry was standing in front of him by this time, standing on those severed legs and he didn't know how. He glanced down and saw that his hands were still on the end of his wrists, the wrists were still attached to his arms and his arms were still attached to his shoulders. A trick! It had all been a hideous mind-snapping trick. But, he'd felt the pain—

"I SPARED YOU BECAUSE YOU ARE STILL OF VALUE TO ME."

He could hardly believe what he was hearing. This murdering bastard had hypnotized him: had played head games to force Henry to cooperate. Well, he just wouldn't! No way! He wasn't lifting a finger to help this son-of-a-bitch.

"I TOOK YOUR WIFE. AND I'LL TAKE YOUR BRAT, BASTARD, KIDS NEXT."

Henry hadn't said anything, hadn't refused out loud. How did it know? But the answer was so simple. It had read his mind. He had to be careful; he had to somehow keep his thoughts to himself. And he had to cooperate, for a while at least, until he found a way to defeat them. Otherwise, they were willing to take the breath from his kids next.

"DEFEATING US IS IMPOSSIBLE, HENRY. AND YOU'RE RIGHT. WE WILL TAKE THE BREATH FROM BUDDY AND PATRICIA—UNLESS YOU GIVE US ERICA WALSH."

Erica Walsh? He couldn't do that, be a party to what they had in mind. Besides, hadn't they killed Bess as a warning to him, to keep him from selling the house? Now they wanted Erica Walsh. He was very confused, as well as frightened.

"ERICA WALSH WILL MAKE A GOOD DISCIPLE. SHE WILL BEGET OTHERS. AND, SHE WILL BE AN EASY VICTORY, ONLY BECAUSE SHE LIKES HER LAY. BUT NOW, ERICA DOESN'T WANT KAYLE BECAUSE HE POUNDS HER TOO HARD. AARON DOES IT BETTER. SHE WANTS A MAN TO FUCK HER LIKE AARON. AND I'LL BE THAT MAN. ALL YOU HAVE TO DO IS CONVINCE HER TO BUY THE HOUSE."

"I can't," he moaned. "Her husband is against it."

''YOU'LL THINK OF A WAY I'M SURE . . . TO
SAVE YOUR CHILDREN.''

Yes, he'd think of a way, in fact, he had to find a
way, if only to save his kids. He was a salesman,
wasn't he? Sure. He'd sold insurance, and now real
estate. He'd turn on the charm and get Kayle to buy
that house.

''NOW, HENRY. I KNOW YOUR WIFE IS DEAD,
AND, UNLIKE ERICA, YOU'RE NOT GETTING
LAID MUCH LATELY. IN FACT, I KNOW YOU
HAVEN'T BEEN GETTING MUCH AT ALL THESE
PAST FEW YEARS. SO . . . I'LL SUPPLY THE LAY.
YOU JUST DO THE WORK. THIS WAY, WE CAN
BE FRIENDS.''

That's when Henry saw the change, saw the four
canine heads disappear and four, lustful, female
heads appeared in their place. And all four had that
look—they wanted him! And the fool, he took it. He
laid the Gate Keeper when the Gate Keeper took on
the guise of a female. And all this time Henry had
been wondering why the bastard had done it. Why
he'd allowed himself to be used for Henry's sexual
gratification.

In fact, Henry had been wondering about this for
months now. Then he stopped wondering when the
fungus appeared. Oh yeah, Henry was the one who'd
gotten fucked all right. The Gate Keeper didn't want
him dead, not right away at least, because he needed
Henry; had to use Henry to get Erica Walsh to buy
that house. However, once this was done, he wanted
to make sure that Henry didn't live to tell any tales.

So, he let Henry use his body just so Henry would
catch the fungus: the fungus was a slow killer. And
the fungus was killing him a day at a time—

''DAD. I TRIED, BUT I CAN'T LEAVE.''

Buddy had come in without him noticing. Henry
heard the voice and looked up at Buddy and started to
cry. But no, he couldn't do this. He couldn't give in
just yet, not while he was still breathing. He picked

up the phone, dialed a number and hesitated until someone picked up on the other end of the line.

"Hello, Kirsten," he said, "I was wondering if we could get together." The *rat* knocked three times on the wall of the den. The *rat* was in the hallway outside, issuing a warning. Henry ignored it and kept talking. "Yes. There's something I have to discuss with you. And it has to be soon. It's very important."

Is this gonna take much longer?

Kayle had scribbled an ugly message on a slip of paper and shoved it towards the nurse at the front desk. He'd spent a good part of the morning, and early afternoon, in the hospital, getting examined, having x-rays taken, and now he was waiting to have his jaw wired—it was definitely broken. Nick had done it again.

"Please be patient. Someone will be with you shortly."

Oh, sure, he thought, that's the same old line they used on everyone. He was lucky if he was out of there before the bars closed. Jesus! He needed a drink, and bad. A brew to steady his nerves. What a shellacking he'd taken. There wasn't a spot on his body that wasn't bruised or swollen in some shape, form or manner.

And it was that house—that fuckin' crazy house that did this to him.

But why? He was only straightening his wife out. He was just gonna slap her a few times to get her to stop her shit. And whammo! Something or someone attacked him, beat the hell out of him. Kayle went back and sat on the bench in the waiting room, looking back over his shoulder as he did. A tall, long-legged, blonde nurse had passed him in the hall and it was all he could do to keep his hands off her. She was some looker!

She could've worked on his body anytime. But, with his luck, he'd get some frumpy, old, double-breasted broad with fat thighs to assist when his jaw was wired. The blonde stopped at the front desk and began sorting through charts. Kayle tried to light a cigarette but couldn't hold it between his lips. He rubbed his hands against his pants and realized he was still shook up. And why not? He had to go back to that house and face God only knows what again.

He had no choice. And he might be looking at another beating if Erica had anything to do with it. After all, she was responsible for this, she had to be. He'd been on the verge of pounding her good when he'd been attacked.

But attacked by whom? Nick? It looked like Nick and the guy hit him like Nick would've hit him. He'd used the same brass knuckles. Only, Nick had to be in his sixties by now and the guy doing the imitation was young. It couldn't have been Nick.

The next question was, how did Erica find someone to impersonate Nick when she didn't even know who he was? The only ones who knew him had been Kayle and his mother. And his mother was dead. That was puzzling all right.

Kayle felt someone watching him and looked up in time to exchange glances with the blonde nurse with the long legs. Hell, she could wrap those legs around him anytime, he thought. She smiled at him, like she was really interested, and he tried to smile back, but it hurt too much. Jesus! She was something! A body that wouldn't quit and a million dollar face besides.

Kayle watched while she picked up a chart and headed in his direction. He felt his whole body go limp. She was takin' him inside: she was gonna help wire his jaw. His prayers had been answered. And if he had enough time alone with her, he was gonna ask for her phone number. He wasn't about to let someone like this slip from his grasp.

And screw Erica if she found out. He was gettin' tired of her anyway; her and her bullshit. Fuckin' with his brain, drinkin' his beer, and now havin' him beat up. Oh yeah, kids or no kids, it was gettin'

around time to move on. And if he could move on
with this blonde—

"KAYLE WALSH?" she asked and smiled.

"Yes." He was apprehensive. He rose from his
chair without giving it another thought.

"PLEASE COME WITH ME," she said. "I'M
YOUR NURSE AND MY NAME IS LORRAINE."

Carol Anderson heard the sound of Burt's car
coming up the driveway and quickly put on a fresh
pot of coffee. Paul, with her help, had drunk the other
pot, the one she'd prepared in case Burt wanted some.
Paul, she thought, and felt her heart skip a beat. What
a man! And to think she'd been weeding her garden
and minding her own business when he walked into
her life.

What a man, she repeated to herself.

He made her feel young and giddy and alive. He
was such a wonderful person, and a gentleman to
boot. Why, hadn't he told her she looked wonderful
when she'd apologized for the dungarees she'd been
wearing. Carol usually wore dresses, but she could
hardly have worn one to weed the garden. And he
understood. Funny, Burt never did.

She went to the kitchen window because Burt was
taking so long and found him standing next to the
fence speaking to Erica. And, oh, God, look at Erica,
she thought. Someone had done a *dipsy* on her face.
Probably her husband, she surmised.

Carol was rinsing out a coffee cup when Burt
slammed the front door so hard he almost took it off
the hinges. "Carol! You bitch! You've done it to me
now!"

Paul wouldn't have spoken to her like that, she
thought. But then, Paul wasn't an insignificant little
man with a Napoleonic complex. She sighed and
turned to face Burt. "What am I supposed to have
done now?"

"What have ya done? I'll tell ya what ya done. Ya

told that woman next door that I'm a handyman by trade. That I fix cars for people and do repairs around their houses."

"Well . . . You do. So what's the big deal?"

Burt noticed her sarcasm and slammed his open palm on the table in front of her. "What's the big deal?" His voice was low, his speech clipped. "She wants me to install some ceilin' fans later this afternoon."

Carol shrugged. "She's willing to pay you for it, right?"

"That don't matter," he bellowed, sending spasms of anger down her spine. "I still hafta go inside that place."

Carol smiled, and it felt so good. "If you don't believe there's any truth to the rumors about that house, then what's the big deal?"

She had him! Right by the balls! And Burt knew it! He couldn't answer her, *and* he couldn't refuse to install the fans. If he did, he'd have to explain how he felt, about how he'd seen no-legged Paul in the yard a few days ago. "I guess there is no big deal here," he said quietly, then he rubbed the back of his neck and turned away from her. "Besides. . . We can use the money. She wants me to put a fence in the front yard too . . . Ah, like ya said, she's willin' to pay."

Somehow, Burt just knew he was gonna regret this.

Erica was in the kitchen with Paul when the phone rang. She figured it was Kayle, letting her know the extent of his injuries. Kayle was like that, no matter what he did to you, his hurts and needs were more important. Well, she wasn't about to answer the phone, the hell with him, she thought. Not after the way he ran out of there an hour before, bleeding and moaning and looking for sympathy. And after slapping her just because she was trying to defend Katie. The son-of-a-bitch!

Then she half-smiled to herself because Kayle

hadn't said a word when he left. He couldn't, his jaw
was broken. Paul had seen to that. The phone was still
ringing and she was doing a good job of ignoring it until
Paul spoke up.

"AREN'T YOU GOING TO ANSWER IT?" Paul
wanted to know.

She shook her head and said nothing. Let it ring, she
thought.

"IT'S NOT KAYLE. IT'S AARON PACE."

"You're sure?" she asked and realized it wasn't
necessary. Paul had a strange way of knowing things.
"I don't care to speak to him either." Aaron showed
what he was a few days ago when he'd practically
called her a slut. "The hell with him, too." She didn't
need Kayle or Aaron: she had Paul now.

"ANSWER THE PHONE AND TELL HIM, ERICA.
TELL HIM YOU'RE THROUGH."

Wearily, she rose and picked up the receiver just as
Aaron was about to hang up. "Hello." Her own voice
sounded hostile to her. Well, it was more than he
deserved.

"Hi, babe," Aaron said quickly. "For a minute
there I didn't think you were home."

"Yeah, I'm here." Now she sounded bored.

"Can you talk? Uh . . . Kayle's home, isn't he?"

"No. He's not here, and I don't care to discuss
why."

"He's still drinking, right?" She didn't answer. He
took that as a yes and sighed before going on. "When
he didn't come into work today, I figured somethin'
was up. Are you okay?"

"I'm fine, Aaron. What'dya want?"

She heard dead silence, then, "Are we back to that
stage? I need an excuse to call? You know, Erica, I
told you somethin' once before, remember . . . I was
gonna have a talk with Kayle?"

"Go ahead. Tell Kayle anything you want to . . .
Kayle and I are finished anyway. It doesn't matter
now." She felt a raw wound opening somewhere

inside of her. She couldn't believe it was true, but it was—she and Kayle were finished, after ten long years of living together.

"You mean there's a chance for us? We can finally bring it out in the open?"

She looked at Paul and said nothing. She was finished with Aaron, too.

"Can I see you today?" Aaron wanted to know. And again she kept quiet. Besides having Paul there, she didn't want Aaron to see the bruises on her face. He'd kill Kayle for sure, and Kayle had taken enough of a beating from Paul.

"Erica . . . What's wrong? You're not saying anything."

"I'm kind of busy today. I really can't."

"Okay. But what about tomorrow. It's Todd's birthday. You're having' a party, right?"

Erica almost gasped out loud: with all the mess going on around her she'd forgotten. "Oh yes," she said quickly. "Yes, I'm throwing a party for him . . . Tomorrow night."

"I'll see ya then," he said, then added, "I love ya, babe."

Erica went back to sit next to Paul. She was still in a daze. There was so much to do. She had to get a cake, and party decorations. And the way her face looked, all bruised and swollen, Christ, she hated the idea of going out. People would stare at her and she'd feel like a fool. It had been bad enough when she'd been speaking to Burt over the fence a while back. But, it had to be done. Tomorrow was Todd's birthday.

"WHAT IS THIS THREAT?" Paul asked, interrupting her thoughts. "SOMETHING AARON WANTS TO TELL KAYLE." He already knew the answer. In fact, he knew more about Erica than she knew about herself. But forcing her to say it out loud would humiliate her, and he liked the idea of seeing her squirm.

She didn't answer at first. She got up and stood by

the window and looked out. She'd been kind of hoping he wouldn't ask. However, if they were going to have any kind of a life together, he had a right to know. "Aaron Pace is the father of my children."

"REALLY!" Paul feigned surprise.

"When I met Kayle ten years ago, I didn't know he was sterile. In fact, he didn't know it either. But he is. I mean, he's got a low sperm count, and it's the same as being sterile. You see, I couldn't get pregnant, no matter what. So, we were both checked by doctors because we wanted kids."

She turned to face him before going on. Paul was looking at her as though he understood. Well, at least he wasn't judging her too harshly, she thought. "Kayle could've been helped, his count could've been raised. But his so-called manhood was at stake. Then I met Aaron Pace. This was about two years after I started living with Kayle. And Kayle and I were having problems . . . And Aaron was . . . Well, he was there, that's all. He was a man and he could give me children."

"IN OTHER WORDS, YOU WEREN'T IN LOVE WITH HIM. NOT AT FIRST."

"No, I wasn't. I used him. And I guess in a way he used me, too. Then, after we started having kids, we sort of fell in love. But I didn't *mean* to deceive Kayle, even though I did. I really thought that having children would bind us together. We spent two years fighting each other, I wanted a good relationship."

The whole thing sounded absurd, as she suddenly realized. How could you have children by one man to cement your relationship with another? But, at the time it was happening, it made perfectly good sense.

"I met Aaron in a bar," she continued. "I was there with Kayle. We had a fight and he left. Aaron came over and offered to buy me a drink. I didn't refuse. I know I should've, but I didn't. And one drink led to another and then another, and before I knew it, I was in Aaron's apartment. In his bed."

The phone rang again. She ignored it for the second time in a row. "As drunk as I was, I knew that Aaron was special. He cared about me. He didn't just jump my bones. He took the time to make sure I enjoyed it when he made love to me that night. And I did enjoy it. And, when he said he wanted to see me again, I figured why not? He turned me on, made me feel sooo good—"

"AREN'T YOU GOING TO ANSWER THAT?" The phone was still ringing.

"No! And I don't wanna know who it is either! Let me finish this while I still have the courage. After seeing Aaron a few times, I came up with the idea of having children by him. I mean, I didn't think we were going to last this long—eight years. I figured he'd dump me and I'd wind up with just Kayle again. And if I had a kid or two, Kayle might change. He might take on responsibility—"

"BUT HE NEVER DID!"

"No, he didn't."

"SO IT WAS ALL FOR NOTHING."

"I still have the kids. And that's enough for me!"

"AND NOW AARON WANTS TO GIVE KAYLE A LESSON IN BIOLOGY, RIGHT?"

Erica was stunned by what he'd just said. How did he know? Aaron had used that expression weeks ago, but she'd never told anyone. How did Paul know the exact words Aaron had used? It was almost as if he'd read her mind and that bothered her. "I'm going up to change," she said. "I have to go to town and order a cake for the party."

And, she needed time alone, time to be able to think about what was happening with Paul. Maybe she could make some sense of this if he wasn't around.

"DO YOU WANT ME TO LET THAT BURT IN WHEN HE COMES TO INSTALL THE FANS?"

She nodded silently and ran upstairs. This was crazy. Paul knew about Burt and she hadn't told him about that either. She'd spoken to Burt just a while ago, but it was such a small, insignificant detail that it seemed hardly worth mentioning. And yet, Paul knew about that also. Something was wrong here.

Paul watched her go and smiled to himself. Erica, he knew, was alarmed by his knowledge of her affairs. And, he'd purposely done this to let her know he was no fool and that she'd better not pull any shit behind his back. She'd have to be careful around him; she'd have to be faithful and loyal to their new found relationship—or else. And that was how he planned on keeping her in line.

Burt didn't know that Erica wasn't home when he rang the doorbell. Otherwise he would've waited until later on to install the fans. Why take the chance of running into Paul? He laid his toolbox inside the front door and felt anxious when he heard someone coming. When Paul opened the door, Burt felt his insides crawl up to his throat.

"WHY, HELLO . . . UH . . . BURT, ISN'T IT?"

Burt said nothing at first. He wanted to run but there wasn't any sane or valid reason for running; not yet anyway. "Hi, Paul," he said, annoyed with himself for the nervous inflection in his voice. "Sorry I couldn't hang around the other day. I left somethin' on the stove. That's why I hadda take off like I did."

"I UNDERSTAND COMPLETELY. PLEASE, COME IN."

Burt reached down for his tools, and that gave him the perfect opportunity to see if Paul had legs. And of course he did, which puzzled Burt to no end. He figured he must've been seeing things the other day, or rather, *not* seeing them too clearly, as in the case of Paul's legs. Maybe the sun had been in his eyes. Or maybe Carol's stories about this house, and the strange goings on, made him hallucinate.

Whatever the case, he was happy to see that Paul finally got himself a pair of legs.

"Mrs. Walsh said she wanted four fans installed

upstairs. Three in the bedrooms and one in the hall. Is that correct?''

''I BELIEVE SO. THEY'RE IN THE GARAGE.'' He'd be damned if he was about to carry them inside. Let Burt do it.

Burt glanced around and looked towards the stairs. He realized he was no longer nervous. This house seemed the same as his; nothing strange or phenomenal about it. He was inside and nobody had killed him yet. He turned back to Paul. ''I'd like to look at the ceilings before I get the fans. If they hafta be reinforced, that's gotta be done first. No use draggin' the fans in here.''

Paul smiled and nodded as though he understood. Then Burt started thinking about what a nice guy he was. And he felt bad because he'd run from him the other day. But it wasn't his fault. It was Carol and her crazy stories. Now she had him imagining things. Well, he'd have to straighten her ass out—once and for all. She couldn't be doing this to him; making him seem foolish in front of people.

The upstairs bedrooms were real hot. Burt agreed that the fans were sorely needed. ''But, what about the attic fans,'' he asked Paul. The house had a pitched roof. That meant there either had to be a full attic or a small crawl-space above the second floor. ''Did her old man check to see if there was any fans up there?''

''I DON'T HEAR ANYTHING RUNNING OVER-HEAD. SURELY IF THERE WERE FANS, WE'D HEAR THEM.''

Paul was suddenly acting tense and this puzzled Burt, but he ignored it. It was probably all in his head again. ''Not necessarily,'' Burt said. ''Depends on how high up they are. If they're close to the roof, you won't hear them. Not with the insulation and all.''

''I DON'T REMEMBER ERICA MENTIONING ANYTHING ABOUT AN ATTIC OR FANS. BESIDES, IF THEY WERE UP THERE, WHO

WOULD TURN THEM ON?"

"There's an automatic switch, usually in one of the closets. Makes it easier to turn 'em on an' off. Ya don't even hafta go up there. Uh . . . let's see . . . Where's the master bedroom?"

Paul's mouth was a thin line. He looked upset about something, but Burt ignored it and followed him to Erica's bedroom. Burt knew, from experience, that if there was a switch down here, it would have to be somewhere in Erica's closet. The builder had done this in a lot of these homes. He guessed to keep folks from running up and down ladders to turn the fans on and off.

"We got a switch in our bedroom closet," Burt said and pushed the clothing on the rack to one side. There was a switch on the back wall just as he'd suspected. "See . . . here it is. This means there are fans upstairs. So, why ain't they workin'." He reached back for his toolbox and removed a circuit tester.

"WHAT ARE YOU DOING?"

Burt noticed a tightness in Paul's voice. "Oh, this ain't gonna cost any extra," he said. "I just wanna see how much juice's in this switch. I hafta take it apart to check it out." Burt removed the plate covering the switch and applied the circuit tester. Then he shook his head in disbelief.

"SOMETHING WRONG?"

"Yeah, the power's there, only . . . somethin's interferin' with it, drainin' it off before it connects with them fans upstairs."

"WHAT DO YOU THINK IT IS?"

Burt turned and faced him and wanted to ask him why he was so nervous over a lousy switch. But it was none of his business. "Can't tell ya 'till I check out the line. Maybe it's rotted up above this point. That'll cut off the juice. Meanwhile—" Burt turned and flipped off the switch. "Might as well not waste her electric. Right, Paul?"

Paul didn't answer.

Burt turned to face him again and found himself alone in the closet. Paul had suddenly vanished into thin air. Burt shook his head and figured Paul must've gone downstairs for somethin' and he just hadn't noticed him leavin'. And yet, Burt couldn't shake the feelin' that he wasn't entirely alone in that closet.

He could just about hear someone breathin' and it wasn't him. Hell, no. And whoever it was, they were breathin' hard, like they'd been runnin' real fast or . . . like they were annoyed for some reason or other. Burt stood quite still for a moment and listened. His stomach was knotted with apprehension. But this's crazy, he said to himself, 'cause he couldn't see no one.

And since he didn't believe in ghosts and no longer believed in people walking around with no legs, he figured he'd better go downstairs and look for Paul. He put his tools outside the door and was sliding the clothing on the racks back in place when he heard a clicking noise. The switch in back had gone on by itself—

"FINISHED SO SOON, BURT?"

Burt grabbed his chest and thought he was gonna faint. Paul had come up behind him and hadn't made a sound. "Uh . . . No . . . I was goin' downstairs to look for you." That nervous inflection was back, he noticed.

"WELL, NOW YOU FOUND ME."

"Yeah . . . Uh . . ."

"SINCE I DON'T KNOW WHAT ERICA HAS IN MIND CONCERNING THE FANS IN THE CRAWL SPACE UPSTAIRS, WHY DON'T YOU GO AHEAD AND INSTALL THE OTHERS?"

Burt smiled and just nodded. That was a good idea —and the sooner the better. He wanted to get the hell out of there. Paul made him nervous as hell, even if he did have legs at this point. After all, Paul didn't seem to know if there was an attic or a crawl space, or if there were fans up there, when Burt mentioned it before. Now, he was tellin' Burt somethin' and using a positive attitude.

Paul knew more than Burt imagined he did. And now the mystery was gettin' thicker as Burt suddenly realized that the switch in back had somethin' to do with Paul's being here, and not being here. And that was about as far as Burt would allow his mind to wander in search for an answer.

17

"The car came through the wall of the restaurant and killed my son," Henry Wittaker was telling Kirsten Larson. Henry had come to see her, looking for solutions to his problems. But deep inside, he was wishing he hadn't. Kirsten had a lot of *rats* roaming her house, and he was awfully nervous. Still, when he'd called earlier in the day and asked to see her about something important, she'd been nice enough to insist he come right over. So, in a way he was willing to overlook her *rats.*

"The driver took off before I could see who it was. And, of course, the car was stolen. So, the police couldn't trace the driver that way."

Kirsten put a pot of fresh coffee on her dining room table and sat down beside Henry. Although she'd been in the kitchen making coffee, she'd heard every word that was spoken—and then some—because her *friends* were making remarks.

"Henry," she began, "there are disciples of Satan who are nothing more than killing machines."

He was more than a little familiar with that expression. He'd used it when he'd spoken to Buddy and Patricia about the Gate Keeper. Henry had referred to him, and minor echelon devils like him, as killing machines.

"They roam the earth," she continued, "maiming and killing at his command. Their only purpose is the destruction of life as we know it. They are very good at what they do, and very good at not getting caught—"

She turned away from him then, mainly because she didn't want to see that look in his eyes, the one that said she was crazy, when she finished her line of thought.

"Go on," he prompted.

"Some of those disciples are dead and some are alive. And sometimes it's hard to tell them apart—the living from the dead."

"I know that," Henry said without hesitation, and made her feel at ease. "I mean . . . Bess is dead—really dead! But Buddy's not. They're keeping him alive to torment me—"

"Oh, God, Henry. You poor thing," she said. He hadn't mentioned that part of it until now. Oh, Lord, it was awful.

"OH, GOD, HENRY. YOU POOR THING."

The lights over the dining room table flickered as Kirsten's words were repeated; then the sound of laughter echoed in the air. Henry heard it and chose to ignore the sarcasm, for now anyway.

"Don't listen to them," she said. "They're trying to get to us, to scare us, so we'll stop."

"It's cool," he said and sipped his coffee before going on. "Besides Buddy, I'm here for another reason—"

"The house! You've come to tell me where it is. You need—they need—my help. The people who live there are in danger." She touched his hand because he'd drained white. "Henry, I've been dreaming about this house, and I knew when I spoke to you about Bess, that you were somehow involved with it. It's my next mission."

"Forgive me. I never know who's real anymore. You seemed to be reading my mind. I mean, you knew what I came for without me telling you. For a minute there I forgot you were such a damned good psychic. I thought maybe you were one of *them*." The feel of her hand was soft and warm. This was Kirsten all right.

"They must be doing some job on you! But I'm here now, you're not alone—" Kirsten gasped when the dead thing, the one who'd come into her life several weeks ago, appeared in the doorway behind Henry. He turned and saw it himself. His heart pounded heavily in his chest. "In the name of the Lord, Jesus Christ, I command you to be gone," she shouted three times in rapid succession.

As Henry watched, the demon turned and left. "It works!" he cried and turned back to look at her with hope written on his face. But there was something awful in Kirsten's voice when she responded, something resembling complete resignation.

"Only for a short while. If this were to be truly over and done with, it would take much more than I can offer. I need help."

Henry heard her and felt his heart stop. If anyone could've helped him, it surely would've been Kirsten. But now, if she said she was helpless—

"Let me explain. There are people I work with, demonologists, who've spent a lifetime studying these atrocities. You know what I'm talking about, don't you?"

He nodded silently and she continued. "What I usually do when faced with a situation I can't handle, is I feel something out, then report back to them. In this way, I'm telling the people I work with just what they're up against. And they do the rest."

Henry felt much better after she explained. It wasn't as hopeless as he'd imagined. "How do you set it up? And what can I do to help?"

"Well . . . First of all, I should feel my way around that house, touch everything to see what vibes I can pick up. But it really isn't necessary in this case. I've already been there several times in my sleep. So, I'll go to the next step, which is the utilization of biofeedback equipment. It's very sensitive and generally lets me know the extent of the powers I'm facing.''

"Do you use tapes?" he wanted to know.

"Very good, Henry! Then you understand about the tapes."

"Yes. I know that their voices are on the same decibel level as dog whistles. Animals can usually hear the beasts whereas we cannot. But tapes are different. Cassette tapes will pick up anything, including their voices.''

"YOU DON'T NEED TAPES TO HEAR US, HENRY."

The overhead lights flickered again. Kirsten rose and turned them off. It was semi-dark in there, so she opened the curtains on the windows to allow more light into the room. Henry wondered why she kept those curtains closed to begin with. He was now able to see the woods out back, and it was a lovely, soothing view. However, something dead and hideous was standing in the woods watching the house. In fact, it resembled the creature who'd been standing in the doorway a while ago. When he spotted it, he understood.

Kirsten excused herself and left the room for a moment, after which she returned with a recorder. She placed it between them and snapped in a cassette. "Now, I want you to repeat your story once again. I feel it's better if I have something on tape to present to those people I've spoken about. And frankly, I should've done this before. Then you wouldn't have to relive the pain.''

"It's all right, Kirsten. I'm fine."

Henry repeated his story and kept talking until Kirsten interrupted him at one point. "Okay. Now, what you're saying is they killed Bess to keep you from selling the house. Correct?"

"Yes. They wanted me to stop showing it, but then

they changed their minds *after* I brought Erica Walsh there. They wanted Erica to buy the house so they could possess her. You remember what the Gate Keeper said—what I told you before—one soul begets others. And he said he'd kill my kids next if Erica didn't buy the house.''

''So, you convinced her to buy the house.''

''No, she decided to buy it on her own without any pressure from me.''

''Then why did they kill Buddy?''

''They didn't want me telling my kids about them. And too, my daughter had just gotten through saying that I should've warned Erica about the house. Patricia thought I'd committed the cardinal sin by keeping the truth from Erica.''

''Patricia's in danger too, you know.''

''Yes,'' Henry said helplessly, ''but I can't get her to leave.''

''Maybe I can. And I'll work on Buddy too, on sending him back to his grave.'' Kirsten paused for a moment, as if she were deep in thought, then, ''I'm picking up on something,'' she said, ''but it's distorted . . . It's about Erica . . . I don't believe they want Erica's children, just her.''

''Oh, but they do. The only reason they're taking Erica first is because, as the Gate Keeper said, 'For with the mother comes the children.' ''

Kirsten's eyes glazed over again. She seemed to be analyzing his answer. ''Yes. . . I only just now realized you're right. They have someone working on the children . . . A small child . . .'' She came out of her trance and focused her attention on him. ''Henry, is there a small child?''

Henry thought back to the child who lived in the house with them, the one with the dark hair and the dark eyes; the cute one who nearly scared him into a heart attack the last time he saw her. ''I can tell you what she looks like.''

''I already know. And I know something else as

well. She's not really a child. Rather, she's one of
them—disguised as a child. And, Henry, she's
extremely dangerous."

"When will you call your friends?" he asked
quietly.

"After my visit. Will Erica be receptive?"

"I'll call her. I'll ask."

"Before you do, give me her address and phone
number." He saw something sad in her eyes when
she looked directly at him. "This is only as a
precaution . . . You know . . . In case—"

"I'm dying, Kirsten. As I've already told you, I'm
aware of it. It's only a matter of time. Give me something to write with and I'll give you the information.
It's a good idea for both of us to have it." He quickly
wrote it down while she continued.

"The first thing I have to do is find out how much
harm those Spanish people did, the ones who lived in
the house before Erica, for surely they were
responsible for triggering off the evil. And I must
warn Erica, there can be no more spells cast in that
house, no more chanting to destroy them."

Henry was puzzled. He couldn't understand what
she was trying to say. "No more chanting to destroy
them?" he repeated. "The Spanish people created
them by chanting to call them up. They didn't try to
destroy them."

"How do you know, Henry? How do you know what
they did? Using Satanism and witchcraft to get rid of
evil spirits is not entirely unheard of. Some demonologists use the evil to destroy the evil. But it must be
done right. . . Or, you can give the beasts added
strength."

"You think those people made them stronger that
way?"

"Yes. I do. And I must warn Erica. There is to be no
further use of spells of any kind before I call my
people in. Because if this is done, and the beasts grow
stronger than they are, I won't call my people in. I

won't endanger their lives to save fools. Because then it will be out of control and too dangerous for anyone to handle."

"I understand. And don't worry. As far as I know, Erica doesn't have any friends who were ever involved in Satanism or Witchcraft. So we're safe there." Henry rose to leave. "I'll say goodbye for now. I've taken up enough of your time as it is."

"Don't be silly, you're helping me complete my mission."

She walked him to the door. As Henry passed the window, the dead thing in the woods was gone, he noticed. Where to, he wondered? Then he erased it from his mind. He didn't really care where the demon bastard had gone.

"One more thing before you leave. There are three types of spirits, Henry, not two. You forgot the *spirit of the Lord.*"

It was just like Kirsten to remind him of the spirit of the Lord, he thought. And that was probably why she was still alive while two members of his family were dead and he was dying. Kirsten carried her Christianity in her heart, constantly, while he tended to use it like everyone else. In other words, Henry only turned to the Lord when he needed something. Besides times of stress, he forgot the Lord even existed.

Henry was driving back home, a distance of about thirty miles or so, give or take a few, and he was surprised because traffic was light. The roads were usually crowded with rush hour drivers at this time of day. However, since there weren't many cars on the road, he knew he'd make good time. Perhaps he'd even get home before Patricia did.

Damn! He hated the idea of her being alone in the house. Especially now that Kirsten had confirmed his fears. He wasn't crazy, the demons were really there, and they were dangerous. The situation was worse than he'd imagined. That really shocked him. Hell, thinking something was the way it was, and then finding out you were right put things into an entirely different perspective.

They were real! They were dangerous! They lived in his house! Oh, Lord, how did it get so bad?

Erica's house was badly haunted because of those Spanish people and their cursed chanting and spells. Nothing like that had ever gone on in his house. He was the original owner, so nobody knew it better than he. Then again, Kirsten told him that her house was spooked because some of them had followed her home—

Something brushed against his hand when he reached for the floor shift, something cold and stiff. And it felt like a hand!

Henry glanced out the corner of his eye and saw nothing; mainly because there was no one in the car with him. He smiled, but it was an effort. Hell, here he was, spooking himself as usual. And this was ridiculous; he was on a main road, in broad daylight, with a few cars around him. What could happen?

His thoughts drifted back to Kirsten, and what she'd told him about her house being spooked. He figured that must've been the way it happened to him. At least he knew it was true with the *rat;* that bastard had followed him home from Erica's, way before she bought the house. Why, the son-of-a-bitch had just jumped in Henry's car one—

He heard noises; someone whispering. And yet, that was impossible. He was alone in the car. The radio—it had to be the radio. But he checked and it wasn't turned on. Had something followed him from Kirsten's house?

No! He was alone! Nothing had followed him from Kirsten's. But the *rat* did follow him from Erica's, it jumped in his car and stayed invisible so Henry couldn't see him. "In the name of the Lord, Jesus Christ," he began and stopped when laughter assaulted his ears. One of *them* was in the car with him, riding next to him . . . well, not exactly next to him. The console separated them, and Henry was thankful for that much. But still, it was in the passenger seat.

What the hell was going on, he wondered? Was he going to drag one of these bastards home with him every time he went out? It had to stop! Henry was getting sick of it. He pulled his car onto the shoulder of the road and got out. Then he went around to the passenger side and opened the door. "Get out!" he commanded. Laughter assaulted him again. "Get out of my car, you bastard!"

The engine began to sputter as if the car were about to stall. Henry ran around and climbed in, gunning the motor to give it gas before it died out. But it was no good. There wasn't enough juice flowing from the battery; something was draining it off. Henry's heart pounded heavily in his chest when he realized what was happening.

It wanted to materialize! It was draining power from his car so it could show itself to Henry! But Henry didn't want to see it, and didn't care if he never *did.* He pumped the gas with everything that was in him and listened as the engine sputtered and died. Oh, God. There was a form sitting on the passenger side. He could see it from the corner of his eye. But he wouldn't turn and look.

"HENRY," it said. "I'M A GIFT FROM THE GATE KEEPER. THE FUNGUS IS WORKING TOO SLOW, AND YOUR MOUTH IS RUNNING TOO FAST!"

It was the dead thing from Kirsten's house, the thing with the holes in its face and rotted flesh on its body hanging in layers. He couldn't bear to look at it and turned away. And it laughed at him because it knew he was scared.

Henry's mind raced into high gear at that point. The word death came to him. Death! He was now about to die. And hell, he hadn't finished his business yet; hadn't convinced Patricia to move, to GET OUT! And

now, he never would, because they were about to
turn him into one of those pasty-faced corpses—one of
those three dimensional, cardboard figures that he
loathed so much.

Oh, Lord, it wasn't fair. Not fair at all! He wasn't a
bad person. He didn't lie or steal or purposely cheat
people. So, why was he being punished in this
manner? And what about Bess and Buddy? They were
good people, too. His crotch was burning, down
where the fungus was. It was on fire and the pain was
spreading, the burning sensation was spreading.
That's how they were going to kill him, he thought.
They'd speeded up the killing process of the fungus.

He clutched at his clothing and tried to unfasten his
pants. He had to see, had to know the rate of speed at
which it was moving. Then again, what for? So he'd
know if he had ten minutes left, or maybe an hour?
The flesh of his stomach burned something awful. He
tore the buttons off his shirt and spread it apart and
saw . . . white spores and green slime crawling up his
mid-section at an incredible rate, devouring his flesh,
eating through the many layers of his skin.

And now it was different. He'd never seen it like
this; he'd never noticed before. It had a head and
arms and it was alive. Something living had been
growing on his body and eating him and he'd never
noticed. He looked at the slime and it looked back at
him and grinned.

Henry couldn't take this. He wanted to die—now!
Fast! To get it over and done with. But he was helpless. *They* were controlling his destiny at this point.
And yet, the creature next to him was gone . . . Had
left . . . Henry couldn't see it. Had it released its hold
on his car?

He turned the key and cranked the engine, but it
didn't start. It wheezed and died out. The battery was
dead. Henry smiled. He couldn't use the car; he had
to do it on foot. Well, hell, no problem, he thought.
It'll hurt more that way, but only for a moment or

two, and then the pain would be gone. At least he wouldn't have to go on as he was: with something *living* and *breathing* and *laughing* chewing at his insides.

He opened the door and checked the on-coming traffic. It was heavy. Good, he thought. Then he waited for the right moment and stepped out into the road . . .

Patricia answered the phone on the first ring. Henry was late getting home from wherever he'd gone to, and she was worried. If anything happened to him, she'd be alone. Then again, it wasn't so bad when you considered that Buddy was still there.

"Hello," she said, "Yes, this is Patricia Wittaker."

Buddy was sitting in front of her at the kitchen table, watching her intently. His head was tilted back and he was focusing with his one good eye. Judging from the expression on her face, he knew something awful had happened to Henry. He tried to read her mind, but it was blank. She must've been in shock. He waited until she hung up and started to ask, but she volunteered the information, speaking as though it were just incredible.

"Daddy's dead. He was killed on the highway. He walked into traffic . . . and was run over by several cars before anyone could stop."

"THAT'S ABOUT ALL OF US NOW. WE'RE ALL DEAD."

Patricia's face was white; her eyes were glazed over. He wanted to ask the ultimate question, and wondered how she would respond.

"ARE YOU GONNA LEAVE NOW?" he wanted to know. He hated the idea of being here—in this house —alone. And since *they* wouldn't allow him to go to his grave, he had to stay where he was. "ARE YOU GONNA LEAVE?" he repeated because she hadn't answered.

"LEAVE? AND GO WHERE?" she asked, and was

startled by the sound of her own voice.

"YOU'RE TALKIN' LIKE ME NOW."

"YES," she said. "ONLY I HOPE I DON'T START TO DECAY LIKE YOU."

She couldn't stand the idea of not looking normal. And yet, it was a lot to ask since *she was dead*—as dead as Buddy was. In fact, she'd died at the same time. Only Henry hadn't noticed it. Probably because Henry had gone into deep shock over Buddy, seeing his son lying in front of him with a car parked on his body. And hell, it wasn't hardly fair that he hadn't noticed her; that she was lying under the car, too.

However, unlike Buddy, she'd been able to rise immediately and resume her role as Henry's daughter because *they* wanted him watched—closely. And who was in a better position than Patricia? Henry trusted her, told her everything.

"I GUESS NOW SINCE HE'S DEAD, THEY'RE NOT CONTROLLING MY VOICE ANYMORE. IT DOESN'T MATTER WHAT I SOUND LIKE. IT'S FUNNY, YOU KNOW, DADDY HAD A KNACK FOR TELLING THEM APART FROM OTHER PEOPLE. I ALWAYS THOUGHT YOU SOUNDED THE SAME, EVEN AFTER YOU WERE DEAD, BUT DADDY KNEW THE DIFFERENCE . . . POOR DADDY."

She couldn't cry. Not because she wasn't sad, rather, it was because she was dead. And since Henry was too, her captors must've felt it was time to remove those qualities that made her seem alive. They had controlled her emotions, and had given her the ability to display them. Now, there was no further need for her services, so they took her soul away.

"WHAT'S GONNA HAPPEN TO US?" Buddy wanted to know.

"BEATS THE HELL OUTTA ME," she said and got to her feet. "YOU WANNA SIT IN THE LIVING ROOM AND WAIT? MAYBE SOMEONE WILL COME AND TELL US WHAT TO DO."

18

Mary Rogers hadn't been to Erica's since the day she'd moved into that dreadful house where there were heartbeats in the wall by the staircase, and something frightening in the den. And now she had reservations about going there for the evening, especially after Kayle yelled at her the way he did, and said those awful things to her. Still, it was Todd's birthday; so she had no choice. Grandma just couldn't stay away.

When the taxi pulled up in front of Erica's, Mary almost told him to turn around and take her home. There was an evil hanging over that house; hovering like thick, black storm clouds, and it was waiting for her, to suffocate her, to choke the breath from her body. And those bad vibes were hitting her again.

But Todd had been standing out front and he got all excited because Grandma was there. The other kids were excited, too. They shouted and alerted their friends, the ones who'd come to the party. Everyone made a big deal out of Grandma. By the time she reached the living room, her three oldest grandchildren were holding her by the arms and around the waist, and were damn close to pulling her to the floor. Erica stopped them, then she gave Mary a kiss.

Mary almost went into shock at the sight of her: the

bruises on her face, the dark circles under her eyes, the way she was walking, slightly hunched over as though she had a dowager's hump. Erica saw the look on her mother's face and quickly turned away.

"I fell . . . on the stairs," she said and led Mary into the kitchen. "There's someone I want you to meet. His name's Paul."

Mary didn't believe what Erica had said about falling on the stairs. Erica's explanation only covered the bruises, and possibly the dark circles under her eyes, if you were willing to stretch it a bit. But it certainly didn't explain why she was just about walking like an old woman.

Paul, when she met him, was as handsome as handsome could be, with his dark curly hair, and his sparkling amber colored eyes. Mary was very impressed. "Hello, young man." This could've meant the end of Kayle, she thought and smiled. "Tell me, Erica, where did you meet him?"

Paul smiled back and said nothing. Erica busied herself making tea and remained silent. Aaron Pace was there too, Mary noticed, although she wasn't particularly happy to see him. He was another pain-in-the-ass leach, sucking her daughter's blood for everything he could get. She hoped he'd had the good sense to at least bring a gift for Todd, since Todd was his son.

"Where's Katie?" Mary wanted to know once she was settled with a hot cup of tea and a seat next to Paul.

The question seemed to throw Erica off, and for some reason or other, Mary felt she was awfully nervous. "Uh . . . She's upstairs. Playing with Angelica."

"Oh, that's nice. Who's Angelica? A little girl from the neighborhood?"

"Uh . . . Yes. As a matter of fact, she is from around here."

Erica offered her some finger sandwiches, but she

refused, even though she hadn't eaten dinner. She'd been too busy shopping for a present for Todd. There was something about this house that took your appetite away.

She thought about the day Erica first showed her the house and the discoveries she'd made: the heartbeats in the wall and that thing she sensed in the den. Then she shuddered and tried to push it behind her. This was no time to be hypering out, so to speak. But she couldn't relax, even taking into account the fact that she was here, in the kitchen, and away from those basic disturbances.

There was something around here that bothered her a lot, a strangeness. *Someone strange?* But no, she had to stop this or she'd wind up spoiling Todd's birthday. "Are you going to take a tape of the children singing?"

"Oh, sure," Erica said. "I've already got the recorder set up in the living room."

"TAPING THE CHILDREN'S VOICES?" Paul asked, then added, "I THINK IT'S A GOOD IDEA." But somehow, to Mary, he didn't sound overly enthusiastic despite what he'd said.

"Yes, it is a good idea. You see, Paul, my daughter keeps those tapes as a sort of diary of important events in the childrens' lives. She started this long ago, and thankfully, she's kept it up. You should ask her to play then sometime."

"They're really somethin'," Aaron said, trying to be pleasant. However, Mary noticed there was an edge to his voice, and he kept shooting looks at Paul. Aaron was jealous, that was obvious and Mary loved the idea. Perhaps if he felt threatened enough, he'd see to it that Erica left Kayle and married him. Not that he was any bargain, but the children bound them together.

"IF EVERYONE AGREES THEY'RE GOOD, THEN YOU'LL HAVE TO PLAY THEM FOR ME SOMEDAY, ERICA."

"She might not have the time," Aaron insisted.

"Where's Kayle?" Mary asked, more out of curiosity than any real sense of missing him. "Is he working?"

"Yeah," Aaron broke in. "He got stuck at the shop."

Mary doubted that, just from the way Erica was looking at Aaron alone. It was as though she hadn't been able to think fast enough, so Aaron was offering an explanation to cover for him. But they could've saved themselves the time and the effort. Mary, very frankly, didn't give a shit if he never came home.

"Those are some bruises, honey," she said and studied Erica's face again. "You'll have to be more careful on those stairs." Why was Erica lying to her, she wondered: about falling and about Kayle? This was something new.

"Yeah, howdya like that? Her falling and all? But she's always rushing around . . . never pays attention to what she's doing" Aaron said.

"Hello, Grandmother. I heard you were here. I came to see you." Katie had just walked into the kitchen with her doll under her arm.

"Grandmother?" Mary smiled at her. "Oh . . . We're speaking like an adult now?" She shot a quick look at Erica to see if Erica thought this was cute, too. But Erica had an odd expression on her face: her eyes were wide, she was biting her lower lip. Mary made a mental note to speak to her alone, after the party, and turned back to Katie.

"Where's Angelica, your little friend?"

"Upstairs. Playing with my dolls."

At that point she noticed something strange about Katie, too. Katie didn't seem to be entirely play acting with this grown-up role she'd assumed. "Why don't you bring her down to meet Grandma?"

"I will, after a while."

"Are you coming home with Grandma tonight to keep her company?" Mary often took Katie home for days at a time. Katie didn't go to school yet. So it gave the child something to do and Katie was good company for Mary.

"Uh . . . No, Mom. She can't go."

Erica, Mary noticed, had jumped up awfully quick with this refusal. And this wasn't like Erica.

"Why not?" Katie wanted to know, with a belligerent tone of voice.

"You heard your mother," Aaron said. "Don't ask questions."

"I'll be upstairs if you want me," Katie said and left.

"More tea, Mom?"

"Uh . . . Yes. Please." Mary could've used a few tranquilizers in her cup at this point. There was so much going on here: Erica's appearance, and Kayle wasn't home yet, and Katie was acting funny. She suddenly wished she'd stayed home.

Erica poured her tea and laid it down in front of her. There was silence in the kitchen now. Somehow none of them could think of anything to say. Mary heard the children playing in the living room; they sounded awfully loud. The silence around her seemed to amplify the noise. God, it was awful, she thought. She was getting too old for kids' parties. Erica put a large, white box on the table and Aaron jumped up to help her get the cake out.

"I think it's time," she said to Mary. "They're getting wild in there. This'll keep them quiet for a few minutes."

"Let me help," Mary offered, but Aaron was helping her, and in a way, Mary was happy about that. She was getting to the point where Erica's nervousness was rubbing off. She felt a slight throbbing in her temples, the start of a good headache. That, along with the arthritic pain in her legs and back, made her feel just awful.

Bad vibes were hitting her from every direction, too. And she couldn't imagine why. She purposely had stayed in the kitchen, away from what was out there in the rest of the house, and yet, it didn't help. The kitchen was tainted now also. Oh, God, she had to speak to Erica, to make her realize what was going on here.

"ARE YOU ALL RIGHT, MARY?"

Paul put his hand over hers in a gesture of warmth, but . . . it wasn't warm. His flesh was cold and rigid, reminding her of Fred, her late husband. When he'd died and had been lying in his coffin, Mary touched his hands a lot, hoping that somehow the life in her body would, through some miracle, flow into his, and he'd come back. But it didn't work. Still, she remembered the feel of him. Paul felt the same.

"I'm fine," she said and tried to slip her hand from beneath his, but he wouldn't let go. He held onto her as though he knew how this was affecting her, and he was enjoying it. Bad vibes were attacking her brain, filling her mind with images of burning flesh and death, and eternal banishment. *Hell is for lovers,* she thought and wondered why.

But it just popped into her head, like those other strange and frightening ideas that came to her whenever she set foot in this house. Oh, yes, hell *is* for lovers . . . and it's for you too, Mary, something screamed inside of her, because Fred's there and he's waiting for you and he's not quite dead—

She began to dream then, with her eyes wide open . . . And, oh, it must've been a dream, it had to be—or hallucinations. She could see inside of her body, could see her vessels pumping blood, and her heart, she could see her own heart. But wait—something was crawling towards it, something that didn't belong there: a horrible thing with black hair and a stubby tail. It was—

"Mom, are you okay?" Erica had her hand on Mary's shoulder. Well, at least it was soft and pliable, not cold and unyielding like Paul's was.

"I'm fine," she managed to say. "I'm just not

feeling well. Maybe I should take Katie and leave, after she has her cake . . . That is, if you'll change your mind and let me take Katie home.''

"Do you want to lie down?" Erica wanted to know. She looked worried. But she was also playing with her hair, which meant she was annoyed at Mary and trying to hold her temper. Mary was being insistent about taking Katie home and Erica was trying to be patient about it. "I'll take you upstairs to my bedroom.''

"No. I'll be okay. Just let me sit here.''

"All right. . . Umm . . . Do you think you could hold out until I do the taping? It won't take long.'' Erica glanced at Paul then as though he'd just *said* something. But Mary didn't hear him speak. "I guess it's okay if you take Katie.''

"Good,'' Mary said and was finally able to slide her hand from beneath Paul's. "Then I'll stay for the taping.'' But she didn't want to. She didn't want to stay in that house any longer than she had to, because now the truth was self-evident. She'd waited too long —too long to warn Erica about the house. And now the house had a strong foothold in her daughter's life, and so did Paul, that evil bastard!

Paul was one of *them*!

He smiled at her as if he'd read her mind. Then he got up and walked towards the back door. "IT'S WARM IN HERE," he said to Erica. "I'LL BE OUTSIDE IF YOU NEED ME.''

Paul had two good reasons for leaving. First, he had to sneak over to Burt's house and *see* what he could *hear*. He imagined Burt was upset because his children were at Todd's party. People like Burt were unstable "mouth-wise" when they got upset. They talked a lot, and usually about things that were better left hidden.

For instance: he might talk about what happened in the closet yesterday with the light switch—how Paul had disappeared when he turned it off, and then suddenly reappeared when he turned it back on again. Paul didn't care if he told Carol, but if they had company and Burt was blabbing it to them . . .

Secondly, he wanted to wait for Aaron Pace. Aaron had been giving him those looks all evening, the ones that said *Erica's my girl and you better keep your paws off.* Well, hell. Paul had to set the boy straight on that issue. Aaron was the one who had to watch his step. Aaron was the intruder in Erica's life at this point.

Burt was seated in the living room with his shoes off and a beer in one hand by the time Paul positioned himself at the window. Burt sounded angry; he was yelling at Carol, telling her she shouldn't have sent those kids next door. "That Paul's there. And that son-of-a-bitch's weird."

"No, he's not!" Carol said and jumped to her feet in outrage. "He's a very nice person."

"You don't even know him." Burt shot back.

"Yes, I do—" Carol gasped after that. She realized she'd slipped and told Burt something she never should've. She sat back down and waited for the explosion to come.

"Oh, yeah!" Burt got to his feet and hovered over her menacingly. "You know him, huh? Tell me, Carol, when did you meet him? What goes on here when I'm not home? Whatdya do, Carol? Let good looking guys into the house so's ya can lay 'em?"

Paul smiled at the compliment. And although he hadn't layed Carol as yet, he knew he'd get around to it eventually.

The day he'd gone to see her, to find out what she knew about the house, he'd gone with the intentions of killing her, if need be, to keep her from telling Erica the truth. However, he found her to be extremely gullible and cooperative. And, since he sensed her inner passion for him, he felt she'd make a good disciple also, one that could be easily manipulated.

The sound of a slap, of a hand striking flesh drew him back to the scene in the living room. Carol was crying. Burt had just slapped her. And he wasn't finished by any means. Paul's eyes flashed with anger. Carol was an ally now. She'd promised to keep everything she'd told him about that house next door to herself. Plus, she wouldn't tell a soul about Paul's visit that day, and Paul believed her.

Of course, at this point, she'd made the mistake of letting something slip to Burt. But Paul felt it was a forgiveable mistake, one that had been committed while defending him. Therefore, Paul was willing to overlook it. She'd improve with time. And since she was also one that would beget others—which was an unexpected bonus of sorts—it was up to him to protect her.

He wanted to kill Burt, but not in front of her. Carol was an extremely sensitive person. And Paul imagined the act of murder, especially what he had in mind, would turn her off to his cause. Therefore, he had to exercise caution in the area of revenge, until she changed and became one of *them*. So, for now, physical punishment would have to be enough.

Burt raised his hand to hit her again, while Carol covered her face and cried. Paul smiled and narrowed his gaze on Burt.

There wasn't too much to recall after that, not in Burt's mind anyway. At least he didn't remember how it happened, although he did take the pasting of his life—administered by his own hand. He literally beat the shit out of himself. And he couldn't stop, not even when he realized what he was doing. Why, it was as though his hand belonged to someone else.

And Carol—that bitch. She just sat where she was and enjoyed the whole thing, like she was watching some comedy movie on T.V. But Burt planned on having the last laugh. He planned on fixing her ass but good, just as soon as he was able to move around a bit better.

Paul read his thoughts and laughed out loud. Burt was as good as dead and was too stupid to realize it. Then Paul rose to his feet and walked back to the fence separating Burt's house from Erica's. He'd stand there and wait for Aaron Pace. Aaron was another boy who needed straightening out.

After fifteen minutes or so, he saw a cab pull up in front of Erica's, then he saw Mary Rogers come out of the house with Katie, climb into the cab and leave. Somehow he knew Erica would change her mind and let Katie go home with Mary, especially after he implanted the suggestion in her mind. Erica was another one who was easily manipulated, she'd do anything he wanted. Then he laughed again as he paused to wonder how Mary would react when she discovered that Angelica was with them. She just couldn't *see* Angelica—not yet, at least.

Mary Rogers was another one who needed straightening out. He'd discovered that much just by holding her hand. He wanted to know exactly how strong her powers were; could she sense who he was by the feel of his hand alone? The answer, unfortunately for Mary, had been *yes*. Evidentaly her powers of sensation were stronger than Paul had given her credit for, and now, something had to be done. Mary was a dangerous obstacle in his quest for the possession of Erica.

Aaron Pace figured he had it made: Kayle wasn't home, the party guests had left and Erica's kids—*his* kids—were in bed. The timing was perfect. Now if he could talk Erica into bed, that would make a nice evening even better. However, one tiny detail had him bothered to hell and back. It was Paul!

Who was he? How did Erica meet him? He'd left a while back, but as he'd said, only to get some fresh air. That meant he planned on returning. And with Aaron's luck, he and Erica would just be getting it on, and that bastard would come knocking at the door, and spoiling everything.

Aaron was upstairs with Erica. He'd kissed the kids and said good-night, and was now seated next to her on the water bed. Erica, he noticed, was depressed and she looked like shit. Not counting the bruises on her face, she also had dark circles under her eyes and her body looked funny, all bent out of shape. However, in view of the eight years they'd spent together, he was willing to overlook her current appearance. In fact, he had to if he wanted to get laid.

"Wanna talk about what's wrong?" he asked. It was hard to have a decent conversation, he thought, when you were turned on and ready, and had to listen for someone at the door at the same time. But he was so desperate for Erica's body, that he would've done anything at this point, including, listening to her talk about how much she missed Kayle, if that was the problem.

"Erica. Talk to me," he insisted.

"Those fans aren't doing much good, are they?" she mumbled.

"What fans? What're you talkin' about?" He followed her gaze up to the ceiling and realized she'd had her fans installed. And yet, she was absolutely right, they weren't doing much good. It was hot as hell up there. "Is this what's depressing you?"

"No. Don't be silly," she said and got up and walked to the window. She was looking for someone it seemed.

"Is it Kayle? Is it 'cause he's not home?"

"No. I'm not depressed over Kayle."

That was a lie, and he knew it. They'd been together for ten years, and this was the first time he'd ever missed one of the kid's parties. No matter how much they fought and argued, Erica had to be feeling something. Unless . . . Unless she was telling the truth, and there was someone else—

"Okay! All right! I want it up front. Tell me, Erica, are you upset because Paul left and didn't come back?''

Her shoulders heaved with a sigh before she turned to face him. ''Maybe you'd better leave. It's getting late.''

''Bullshit! I want the truth. Are you and that new guy getting it on?'' Aaron was outraged. He was not about to be replaced by Paul, especially not when Erica and Kayle were practically through with each other. And especially not when he'd spent eight years waiting for her to leave Kayle. He needed her: she helped erase the memory of Lorraine. ''Answer me!''

''Aaron, go home. I'll call you tomorrow.''

''Oh, no. I—''

''*Now,* Aaron. Just leave. Just get out.''

''Okay, bitch!'' he screamed. ''Ya don't hafta tell *me* twice. I'll leave. But let me tell you something before I go. Ya better take a good look at yourself in the mirror and thank God I even wanted ya.''

After he left, Erica looked in a mirror just for the hell of it. Other than some bruises on her face, which she'd mostly covered with makeup, she was the same as always. She'd never been considered beautiful, but she was pretty. What, she wondered, had Aaron been referring to? She was beginning to worry about him!

His behavior was erratic to say the least. Telling her she was lucky to have him! The egotistical, presumptuous bastard! Who the hell did he think he was talking to? His wife? She probably got sick of his shit too and left him.

Then her mind wandered back to the rumors that had once been circulating in the town where she used to live. It was said that Aaron killed his wife: that he took her to California and got rid of her before coming back to New York.

Those were just rumors, weren't they? She'd always imagined they were. However, she wasn't so sure at this point. She'd seen the violent side of his nature once too often these past few weeks to suit her.

Maybe it was time, as Paul had suggested, to dump

them both—Aaron and Kayle—and start a new life with him. After all, she'd already agreed to this. And yet, saying she'd do something, then actually doing it, were too different things. She was scared. How would she live without either of them around? Would she miss them a lot? And would Paul treat her decently once they were gone? Only time would tell . . .

Lorraine was having a hard time lugging the food into the house and Kayle wanted to help, but she wouldn't allow it. She told him to just sit on the couch and relax. And hell, he thought, there were at least six bags of groceries. Lorraine wasn't built for this heavy lifting. Lorraine was tall, and yet, there was something fragile and delicate about her and the way she carried herself.

She sure wasn't like Erica. Erica was a workhorse—good at heavy lugging and a natural born breeder. Look at how easily she'd knocked out four kids, like it was nothing. But then Erica was built for having babies and Lorraine wasn't. Kayle had to be careful not to get Lorraine pregnant if their friendship advanced that far.

"YOU'RE DEEP IN THOUGHT. DO YOU MISS ERICA?"

Kayle had practically told her the story of his life with Erica on the way home; the whole, entire, sorry mess. So, she knew about Erica. "No. And I'll never miss her again, not as long as I have you." Oh, how corny, he thought. That sounded like the words to a song. And yet, he meant it, every word. Lorraine smiled and went on into the kitchen.

Although Kayle was having difficulty speaking, since his jaw had been wired and all, Lorraine seemed to be having *no* difficulty understanding him. Which was great. Erica wouldn't have made that much of an effort. And now, he had to stop comparing the two. His life, as he knew it with Erica, was just another chapter in the past—it was over. He was at Lorraine's, in her home, and she'd invited him to stay forever.

Of course he didn't know if this thing with Lorraine would last that long. After all, most relationships started out that way, they were *supposed* to last forever. Then what went wrong with him and Erica? He came out of his little trance in time to see Lorraine coming towards him, carrying a glass of beer with a straw stuck in the top. This, he knew, was the start of his liquid diet and he tried not to think back to the last time, how bad it was when his jaw had been broken before.

"ARE YOU HUNGRY?" She wanted to know.

"Only for you," was his answer.

"THEN LET'S GET TO BED. LET'S NOT WAIT." Lorraine smiled and took his hand, pulling him from his seat on the couch with little or no effort. Kayle was amazed; she was a lot stronger than he'd imagined she was. He put his arm around her tiny waist and followed her lead to the bedroom.

She had a real nice house. Everything was ultra-modern, done in black and white, and the funishings looked expensive. Then he wondered why she'd picked him, when, at one point in her life, she'd obviously done better. He didn't know what nurses earned, but a woman alone, supporting herself, could never have afforded this kind of a lifestyle. She must've had a rich boyfriend.

When they reached the door of the bedroom, she paused for a moment. Kayle figured she'd changed her mind, but she hadn't.

"YOU STAY HERE. I'LL TELL YOU WHEN TO COME IN," she said and went inside, closing the door behind her. Kayle waited for what seemed like forever, and was about to go and retrieve his beer when the door opened and Lorraine stood there and took his breath away.

She was wearing a black negligee, the kind you could see through and she had nothing on under-neath. He looked at the creamy flesh of her body, barely hidden by the loose fitting, black fabric and felt instant arousal. His hand shot up involuntarily to rub at the scar on his face, but he came in contact with a bandage. The scar was going to be bigger this time, he thought, and he might even look hideous.

"I LOVE A MAN WITH A SCAR ON HIS FACE," she said as if she'd read his mind. "IT MAKES HIM LOOK SO RUGGED."

She walked towards him, never taking her eyes from his. He could smell the sweet, perfumed essence of her body and thought he was about to go insane. He'd never met a woman like this before, one who was willing to give herself to him in complete submission. At least that was the impression he was getting, the vibes she was throwing off.

Her body was up against his and swaying by now. She was grinding her lower torso in small circles and giving him short, hot kisses on the neck. "TAKE ME, KAYLE," she said. "TAKE ME AND MAKE IT ROUGH. DON'T PAMPER ME."

Kayle heard her and felt he must surely be dead. The impressionist who'd been imitating Nick had killed him and he'd gone to heaven. No way in hell could this be real. He picked her up and carried her inside. He was going to make it rough all right and he thanked God that he'd finally met a woman who appreciated his style.

Aaron Pace was still upset by the time he reached the front yard. Then, when he saw Paul coming across the lawn from the house next door, something inside him snapped. "Hey, bastard," he yelled. "She's still mine. You keep your paws off."

Paul smiled at his arrogance. "DID YOU GET LAID?" he wanted to know.

"What the fuck is it your business?" Aaron asked and squeezed his fists until his knuckles turned white. He was ready. One more word and Paul's ass was his!

"IT REALLY ISN'T ANY OF MY BUSINESS," Paul said and smiled. "I JUST WANTED TO KNOW IF ERICA DITCHED YOU YET."

Aaron growled and made a grab for Paul, but Paul stepped to one side and tripped him, sending Aaron flying to the ground. Aaron hit with full force, striking his chin on the concrete walk, scraping his flesh so hard that it bled. Aaron sat up when he was able to and stared at the blood dripping onto his shirt. This was too much, he thought.

First he'd been rejected by Erica, and she was nothing to look at anymore, and now he was being made a fool of by no one less than her new boyfriend. This was bullshit! He rose to his feet and lunged at Paul again. Although he'd already decided that Erica wasn't worth fighting over, his pride was involved here.

Paul didn't move aside this time. Rather he stood his ground and let Aaron hit him. Aaron struck him in the face and quickly withdrew his hand after it connected with Paul's jaw. Christ, his hand hurt. It was like punching cement. And yet, Paul didn't seem bothered in the least. He was still standing there, smiling with that maddening grin of his as though nothing had happened.

"ARE YOU FINISHED YET?" Paul wanted to know.

"Not on your life," Aaron said and raised his fist to strike again. And yet, something was wrong here. His fist felt funny, like something was missing. He glanced down at it and realized that one of his fingers was missing, up to the second knuckle.

That threw him into shock. The cut was clean, there was no blood. And his finger was gone—

"JUST LIKE OLD TIMES," Paul said. "DOES IT REMIND YOU OF ANYTHING? THOSE COVEN MEETINGS PERHAPS?"

"I never gave them my finger," Aaron insisted. "I never fed it to a crowd. Whadya think I am, crazy or somethin'?'' But it puzzled him just the same. The cut was old. The finger had been gone for a long time now. And it was the one thing that disgusted him most, and scared him badly, too. The idea that someday he'd get involved in a coven again, and this time he would mutilate himself. ''Maybe you took it,'' he told Paul. ''Because I never gave it up.''

''WELL, IF YOU NEVER SACRIFICED YOUR FINGER, THEN PERHAPS IT'S LYING AROUND HERE SOMEPLACE. MAYBE IT'S ON THE GROUND WHERE YOU FELL. I'D LOOK FOR IT IF I WERE YOU, AARON.''

''Uh . . . Yeah . . . I'll look . . . Nobody just loses a finger.''

Paul knew he'd won. For now. He'd used one of Aaron's worst fears against him and had defeated him without lifting a finger . . . A finger? He laughed at that, and knew that next time, Aaron wouldn't be so lucky. Paul would take his finger; in fact, he planned on taking several of them, *and* his toes too.

Then again, maybe Aaron would smarten up. Maybe he'd realize that Paul had the power to read into his fears and to play on them, and to use them against him. Maybe Aaron would behave himself, and stay away from Erica. Then Paul wouldn't have to take his body apart, piece by piece, until he was dead.

After all, Paul wasn't entirely a killing machine. He hated the idea of killing someone who was almost as evil as he. Like Burt Anderson, for instance. Burt was an evil, black hearted bastard and Paul hated the thought of doing him in. But Burt was stupid and had a big mouth. Burt was about to blab his ass off to anyone who would listen. Paul had no choice other than to kill him.

Aaron, however, was smart. Aaron might learn his lesson and stay away and keep his mouth shut too. Then Paul would gladly let him live. After all, Paul never knew when a bastard like Aaron, who had no conscience whatsoever, would come in handy.

19

Mary Rogers rose earlier than usual. Katie was staying with her, and Katie almost always woke up starving. Sometimes though, Mary suspected it was an act, because, according to Erica, Katie barely touched her breakfast at home. She was finicky and fussy and ate little.

Then again, Mary went out of her way and made homemade blueberry muffins and bacon and eggs. Maybe that was the problem at home; maybe Katie got tired of dry cereal. But with four kids to feed and so little time before the school bus came, Mary could sympathize with Erica. Hell, she raised only one child herself and had a hard time doing that.

"Need any help, Grandmother?"

Katie had come up behind her without making a sound. Mary was startled but she managed to smile and asked for a kiss. But Katie didn't kiss her, she made a face instead. "Are we getting too old to show our love for Grandma?" Mary asked, pretending to be hurt.

"No. But you wear falsh teeth and your breath is terrible in the morning."

Mary couldn't speak. Perhaps the child had a point. And yet, for a four-year-old, the phrasing had been so intelligently worded. It sure was puzzling. "Sorry," she said. "Sit down. I'll get you some hot cocoa."

"I'd rather have coffee!"

"Now look, Katie! I don't know what's come over you, but enough is enough." She softened her tone then. "You want Grandma to be angry with you?"

Katie sighed and said nothing at first, then, "I'll take the cocoa. As a matter of fact, make it two. Angelica will be out soon."

"Angelica?" Mary wasn't sure she'd heard right. "Did you say Angelica?"

"Yes. She stayed here last night."

Mary placed the cocoa on the table and walked back to the stove. She thought she was losing her mind. Other than Katie, she didn't remember bringing anyone home last night. She fixed a plate for the child and placed it beside her. Katie was doodling on a napkin, Mary noticed. She'd drawn a long, rectangular-shaped box, like a coffin, and had written the word *Assgar* next to it. Then, while Mary looked on, she wrote *Zadarous* and *Mindalius*.

This puzzled Mary. The child couldn't write her own name, and here she was writing complicated names. And they couldn't have been made up: the vowels were all in the right places, making them names she could pronounce. Most children her age placed letters side by side, without any thought to vowels and uniformity.

She wanted to ask Katie who'd taught her to do this, but there were other, more important questions, that demanded preference. Where was Angelica, and when did she get here? For some reason, she was apprehensive about asking, scared almost.

"Katie?"

"Yes, Grandmother?" Katie answered without looking up.

"Let's get this straight. What about this friend of yours? I don't remember her coming here last—"

"Angelica's an imaginary playmate. You can't see her." Katie's tone was bland, as if she were telling

Mary that the subject was closed.

But it wasn't. At least not as far as Mary was concerned. "Does your mother know about this?"

"Yes. And according to experts in the field of child
psychology, an imaginary playmate should give me a
broader imagination and make me a happier adult—
when I grow up."

"Really!" Erica had lied to her again, and this time
about Katie and her friend, Angelica. When Mary
asked if Angelica came from their neighborhood,
Erica had said yes. But then, to be asolutely fair about
it, Erica had a house full of company at the time.
Maybe she was embarrassed about this imaginary
playmate thing.

"Assgar, Zadarous, Mindalius. Who are these
people?"

"Oh . . . just friends of mine. Would you like to
meet them sometime?"

"Are they imaginary, too?" She was not feeling well
at this point. Her nerves were almost in a state of
shock.

"Yes, they're imaginary." Katie looked at her then,
and smiled. But there was something wrong with that
smile.

Mary had to sit down, she felt faint. And awfully
scared by now, but not for herself, for Katie. "And
what is that object you're drawing? It looks like a
coffin."

"Oh, but it's not. It's a music box. In fact, it's
Angelica's music box. And it sits in my room, along
the wall near the door. *Only, nobody can see it but me.*"

"What does Didi think of all this?" Her other grand-
daughter must've been scared to death. Hell, Mary
was more than a little upset and she was an adult. She
couldn't even begin to imagine Didi's fear.

"Didi's a pain. She thinks she's hot stuff. She
refuses to accept my friends and she keeps to
herself."

Mary couldn't blame her there. "Why does

Angelica need such a large music box. I mean . . . it looks awfully big. Why must it be so large?"

"She sleeps in it. That's why it has to be large."

Just like a vampire, Mary was tempted to add, but didn't. "Eat your breakfast, honey, before it gets cold."

This was too awful for words. The house was tainted, and Erica was tainted because of her relationship with Paul, and now to find that the taint had spread to her grandchildren . . . Or to Katie, at least. She wasn't sure about the others. Why had she waited so long to tell Erica about the house? If she'd foreseen the bad vibes and the heartbeats in the wall, and that thing in the den, then why hadn't she been able to foresee the rest of it—the possessions?

For surely they had to be possessed. There was no other explanation for what was happening. She looked at Katie and wanted to die. A four-year-old child writing names that had a demonic sound to them and drawing coffin music boxes for an imaginary playmate. Good Christ, she wanted to die!

"YOU JUST MIGHT GET YOUR WISH!"

Mary heard those words and felt a cold sensation at the base of her neck. She looked straight at Katie, but the child had a mouthful of food, it couldn't have been her, not unless she'd been reading Mary's mind. Mary hadn't spoken aloud. And the voice she'd heard; there had been a cold, vileness associated with the sound of it.

She sighed and wondered when it would all stop, all of the strange and horrible things that were happening. It was just too awful, she couldn't take much more.

"YOU MIGHT NOT HAVE TO IF YOUR WISH COMES TRUE. YOU WANT TO DIE, DON'T YOU?"

The voice came from behind her. She heard it clearer this time, and was puzzled because there was no reaction from Katie. Either the child was ignoring it, or . . . it was all in Mary's head! She turned, even though she didn't want to, and looked over her shoulder and saw nothing! Absolutely nothing! And yet, someone was breathing back there, near her bedroom door. The sound was faint, but it was real.

She knew then that the taint had spread to her own house, and she wanted to run instead of facing it head-on. Mainly because the evil she sensed was a powerful force, consisting of more than one creature. Oh, yes, she thought. There were many, too numerous to count. "Katie. Finish eating. Grandma's going inside to get dressed. Then we're going for a walk."

"Why?"

Again her voice was bland, as though she was bored and wanted to stay right where she was. But Mary ignored her tone. She was in charge here; she didn't care what Katie wanted. "Because it's a beautiful day and we should be outside enjoying the sunshine. Not cramped up in the house."

Mary rose without another word and went to get dressed. She was close to her bedroom door when the sensation first hit her, she felt as though she'd just passed someone by. Then she felt someone had turned and was following her, someone she couldn't see.

When she walked into her bedroom without closing the door, only to hear it slam behind her, that confirmed her suspicions. There was someone here, someone who'd come uninvited. She had to get ahold of Erica, to plead with Erica to get help. They both needed help—someone professional to remove the taint. And it had to be done now—today; hopefully in time to stop the possessions.

"And she made me feel like I was outta this world, on another planet . . . I never knew one man could be so lucky."

Aaron Pace had been listening to Kayle describing

his new girlfriend—and it incensed him. Kayle had, for all intents and purposes, deserted Erica and the kids. He wasn't going back home, not ever, he'd told Aaron, after which Aaron had been tempted to ask if it was okay if he moved in with Erica. But he held off and listened. Kayle was supplying him with ammunition to throw in his face later on.

"Are you havin' a hard time understandin' me?" Kayle wanted to know.

"Not in the least. You've been telling me about some new girl of yours. But that still doesn't explain how your jaw got broken."

Kayle turned away from him and stuck his head back under the hood of a car. "It was an accident," he mumbled.

"Really! Uh . . . Listen, I'm running to the store for some coffee and danish. You want something while I'm there?" Aaron was looking for an excuse to get to a phone. He had to call Erica and tell her about Kayle, and how it was definitely over between them.

"You can get me somethin' cold to drink," Kayle said pulling out his wallet.

"Oh, hey, buddy." Aaron waved him away. "It's on me."

"Thanks, Aaron . . . And don't forget a straw . . . Please!"

Erica didn't answer until the third ring. He was afraid for a moment that she might be out somewhere. Then he'd have to use another excuse to leave the station to call her. "Hi, babe," he said when she finally picked up.

"Hello, Aaron." Her voice didn't sound the same. It sounded hollow and bland. She was probably depressed over Kayle, he surmised. Or, she could still be angry at him for the nasty things he'd said last night. Then he heard Paul in the background telling her to say "hi," for him.

For some unknown reason, Aaron glanced down at

his fingers when he heard Paul speaking. He seemed to recall something . . . A dream he had last night, and it involved losing one of his fingers.

"Aaron, are you still there?"

"Uh . . . yes, I'm here . . . How're things going?"

"You mean do I miss Kayle, don't you? And the answer is no. I'm glad to be rid of him."

"AREN'T YOU GOING TO TELL HIM THE WHOLE STORY, ERICA?"

He heard Paul in the background again and became annoyed. "Tell me what? What is that bastard try'na say?"

"Nothing important. It's just . . . Well, there's something I have to say, but I'd rather say it to your face."

"Oh yeah!" Aaron was angry now, and was sorry he'd called. "You ain't the only one who's got somethin' to say. I called to tell you that Kayle didn't come home 'cause he's got another woman . . . and he's living at her place." He had intended to sort of work up to this, but 'she gave him no choice. She and that Paul, having a good time behind his back. Well, telling her like he did was his revenge.

Erica sighed heavily, and again he heard that dullness in her voice when she spoke. "I figured as much. And to tell you the truth, I don't really care—"

"I'll bet!"

"Did you call to fight with me? Because if you did, you can just damn well hang up. That's all you do lately—fight with me. Like those nasty things you said last night. . . how I was lucky you even wanted me . . ."

You are, he thought. Her looks were slipping and fast! Then again, he needed Erica. She made him forget the past. "I'm sorry, babe. Please forgive me. I'm just kinda up in the air. I mean, now that you and Kayle are through, it's a chance for us. But now you got that Paul hanging around . . ."

She didn't say anything this time and Aaron got real

fidgety and shuffled his feet. Even if she'd denied having a relationship with Paul, or the relationship Aaron imagined they had together, he would've felt better. But she remained silent, and that made him feel uncomfortable. "Listen, babe. I gotta go. I'll call ya later, okay?"

After he hung up he realized it was time to take some serious action on his own behalf. If he wanted Erica, really wanted her, he had to start eliminating the competition. And that meant starting with Kayle—if Kayle gave a damn now that he had someone new. Anyway, Aaron planned on giving him that lesson in biology he'd often mentioned to Erica. Then, once Kayle was out of the way, Aaron intended to take on Paul.

He picked up his bag of groceries and headed for his car. But then, for some strange reason, he had to stop and examine his fingers again. Odd, he thought, every time Paul's name cropped up in his mind, he felt he had to look at his fingers and make sure they were all there. Damn! It was the craziest thing.

Erica laid down the receiver and turned to face Paul. She was upset over his constant interference in her personal life. Although she was aware that he was sticking his nose in for her own benefit, it still bothered her. She'd been with Aaron for eight years now. And, out of respect for the time they'd spent together, she felt Aaron deserved more than a hateful goodbye, even if he was a pain-in-the-ass lately.

"THE MAN'S BEEN A PAIN-IN-THE-ASS LATELY. YOU JUST SAID IT TO YOURSELF. AND REMEMBER THIS, YOU WERE TRYING TO KISS HIM OFF BEFORE YOU MET ME . . . YOU WEREN'T NICE ABOUT IT EITHER."

She stared at him in the oddest way. Paul had given her an answer without her saying a word; something he'd been doing a lot of lately. "Are you—"

"READING YOUR MIND? YES. DO YOU

OBJECT?''

"I certainly do. And I wish you'd stop it!''

"I WILL . . . WHEN I FEEL I CAN TRUST YOU. NOW, THOSE FANS UPSTAIRS AREN'T WORKING RIGHT. DO YOU WANT ME TO CALL THAT BURT, AND HAVE HIM COME OVER HERE WHILE YOU'RE GONE?''

"Oh, God," she said and sat down next to him at the table. She'd planned on doing some shopping, but she hadn't told Paul. This was getting to her, this mind-reading act. "You can do anything you want to. I'm going out." She rose abruptly and started to leave the room, but Paul stopped her.

"BETTER NOT LEAVE YET. MARY IS ABOUT TO CALL, AND SHE'S VERY UPSET.''

Erica shot him a look and continued to walk out of the kitchen. Paul got up and went after her. She was angry with him. This wouldn't do. Erica might start making plans to dump him next. Then he'd have to kill her, and his mission would be a failure. Of course, if she were a disciple of his *now,* as Lorraine had been when they killed her, then Erica would be his even in death. But she wasn't a disciple yet, and that made the difference.

Erica was near the bottom of the stairs when he grabbed her and forced her back against the wall. Then he pushed his body up close to hers, so she could feel his manhood, his passion for her, his desire.

"IT'LL WORK OUT BETWEEN US. YOU'LL SEE," he husked in her ear.

Erica put her arms around his neck in a loving display of emotion. That surprised him. Her anger seemed to have left her quite suddenly. She was more of a pushover than he'd imagined.

"I know it will work, Paul. Just . . . Please be patient with me. I've known those two men for a long time now. And this separation from both of them came . . . too fast."

He leaned into her body and held on until he felt her lower torso move up against him. "I KNOW IT'S DIFFICULT, LOSING BOTH OF THEM AT THE SAME TIME. BUT IT'S BETTER THIS WAY. ONE BIG HURT AND IT'S OVER."

"That's true," she whispered. "And it's good I have you to fall back on." She raised her lips to his, to kiss him, but the phone rang and she knew it was her mother. Paul had said that Mary was upset, and Paul didn't lie.

Erica answered the phone and stayed on for several minutes. Paul came back into the kitchen and listened, and managed to pick up most of the ensuing conversation before Erica hung up. Mary knew about Angelica. But not everything. Mary felt that Katie was suffering from a delusion. Katie had referred to Angelica as an imaginary playmate and Mary knew that Angelica was real.

She was terribly bothered by this—among other things. She wanted to warn Erica about the house, and its occupants, and about the dangers they were all being subjected to by staying there. Paul smiled. The old bitch had done well. She'd figured most of it out in just the few short hours the girls had spent with her.

"Did you know that Katie was writing names and they sound demonic?" he heard her ask Erica. Well, hell, they were friends of Katie's now, he thought. What was the problem? "And Katie's been drawing a so-called music box that Angelica sleeps in. Only, it looks like a coffin . . ."

Paul knew then that he'd have to work fast. Mary had to be eliminated at once! And he wondered why he'd waited so long; except that this was Erica's mother, and he was afraid that her death might depress Erica to the point where she'd start acting strange. He might lose control of her. And yet, because of what Mary had just said, he'd have to spend a great deal of time convincing Erica that she was wrong; that there was nothing evil about the house. And hell, if he'd killed her a month ago as he'd planned to, he wouldn't be going through this now.

Burt stood at the front door and rang the bell. Somehow he just knew he was gonna regret this. Paul had called a while back to tell him that the upstairs fans he'd installed weren't working properly. And so Burt was here because he stood behind his work— guaranteed it, in fact. And yet, maybe the reason those fans weren't running properly had something to do with Paul—with his being there and *not* being there.

If the incident in the upstairs bedroom closet yesterday had been for real, and not a hallucination, then it was Paul's fault. He didn't know how, he just knew it was. He rang the bell again, and prayed that Erica was home. Hell, what if Paul came to the door? Then, as if to say his prayers had been for nothing, Paul came to the door.

"OH, BURT . . . DO COME IN."

Paul was looking at him strangely, like he had two heads. And Burt was puzzled at first. Then it came to him: he had bruises on his face from that beating he'd taken last night, the one he'd given himself. "I fell down the back stairs," he quickly explained.

"MY, BURT! YOU MUST LEARN TO BE MORE CAREFUL," Paul said and smiled.

Burt was a bit annoyed because he found himself wondering if Paul was laughing at him or just being pleasant. But he said nothing and followed Paul up the stairs. As they were approaching the top landing, Burt got a taste of the heat Erica had been complaining about and it was awful. Jesus, he thought, it all but took your breath away.

He went on up and stood under the fan in the hall and looked up to examine it. The damned thing was running on high gear, but it was only helping to circulate the heat. And Jesus was it hot! He'd been up there barely a full minute and already his clothes were stuck to his body with sweat.

"NEED A LADDER, BURT?" Paul wanted to know. Burt nodded and Paul went into Erica's bedroom and got one.

Paul was being very efficient today, Burt thought. Here he had the ladder all ready and waiting, as though he feared Burt might use the lack of one as an excuse to leave. That made him mad. Just who the hell did they think they were dealing with, he wanted to know? He was a man with a good reputation, and a lot of clients, and he stood behind his work. And what's more, he didn't need this. He'd made money before Erica hired him, and he was sure to keep right on making it without any help from her!

Burt started to climb the ladder when he remembered the switch for the fan. He'd forgotten to shut it off. No way was he going up there with the damn thing running. Paul was standing nearby and turned off the switch as if he'd read Burt's mind. Weird, Burt thought, this house was weird, along with everyone in it. He was tempted to leave, to offer Erica her money back. Let someone else do this and put up with this weird stuff. Then again, his reputation was at stake here. He had to fix the damn fans or at least find out *why* they weren't working.

The hall fan, from all outward appearances, seemed to have been functioning properly. Hell, it had been spinning okay. But then where was the cool air, he wondered. He reached into his back pocket and brought out a screw driver. The fan would have to be taken apart and the motor checked. Otherwise, it was hard to tell what was wrong here.

"WHAT'RE YOU DOING?" Paul wanted to know. "WHY DON'T YOU JUST TRY EXAMINING THE FAN FROM THE OUTSIDE . . . WHY TAKE IT APART?"

Burt hated this. And it was always the same. Here was some asshole, who didn't know the up end of a hammer, telling him what to do. Hell, he'd already looked at the outside of it. But then, Paul was in charge here—he was the boss. Burt had to do as he was told before doing it his way, which was the right way! He took another fast look at the screws on the blades, at the blades themselves—

There was someone inside the fan, right in the middle of it, near the light fixture, and that someone was staring down at him. He shook his head to clear his eyes, and looked up again to find that he'd been right the first time. Then he figured it had to be a mirage—like when people on the desert were dying of thirst and saw water holes and such. And hell, it was hot enough up there to make him think he was on a desert. So, he was seeing a mirage.

But was it, he wondered? There was a little man, with red, blistered-looking skin and a bald head. And he had tiny pointed ears; and the most hateful expression ever written on his face. Burt felt cold chills dancing down his spine; especially when he saw that the little man had thin, red arms, and the biggest, fucking claws he ever saw, where there should've been hands.

He was frozen to that ladder with fear. And yet, something deep inside was telling him to get down off the ladder, to run. Some inner instinct was yelling, *Move, you fool, and you'll be safe.* Burt decided to pay heed to those warnings, and started to climb down when he spotted Paul near the switch, turning it on.

"Don't!" he screamed, ducking his head when the fans began to whir around the top of his skull. Paul was trying to kill him, he surmised. He had to be, this was no accident, he'd deliberately turned the fan on. Not that those blades circling overhead could kill him, but they could hurt him real bad. They were spinning faster than anything he'd ever seen before, reminding him of the rotors of a helicopter.

He started to climb down the ladder again, but found that he couldn't. The blades were spinning with such force they were creating a suction and it was drawing him up and into them. The inside of his skull was cold with fear. Something was dancing on his scalp; it felt like bugs, but he knew differently— it was his nerves. If he was sucked up into those blades, at the rate of speed they were going—He knew what the rotors of an airplane could do to your body.

And okay, these blades were wood, not metal, so maybe it wouldn't be quite as bad. But he wasn't willing to wait around and find out. He had to take some action, he just couldn't stand there and wait to die, or get badly hurt. Still, the suction was so powerful, it was literally pulling him to his death. And, to make matters worse, Paul was laughing at him.

As a matter of fact, lots of people were laughing at him. He could hear their voices. The little man overhead was laughing at him, too; laughing and waiting. If the blades didn't get him, the claws on that little bastard would. And that scared Burt enough to make him mad!

"What're ya tryna do?" he shouted down to Paul. "Are ya tryna kill me?" He felt it was so, but he wanted to hear Paul admit it to his face.

"WELL, BURT," Paul said and threw his hands up in helpless defeat. "YOU'RE JUST TOO SMART FOR ME. I CAN'T PUT ANYTHING OVER ON YOU, NOW CAN I?"

Burt held onto the ladder, and tried not to get sucked up into the blades, and shuddered because he'd been right. But why, he wondered, why did Paul want him dead?

"BECAUSE YOU KNOW TOO MUCH AND BECAUSE YOU TALK TOO MUCH," Paul answered, as if he'd read his mind. "IS THERE ANYTHING ELSE YOU CARE TO KNOW?"

Burt's head reeled and he felt sick. Paul was trying to kill him because he knew too much. Shit! He didn't really know a helluva lot about Paul, other than the fact that he once had no legs, and the electrical switch

in Erica's closet controlled him. Was that too much to
know? Why?

And now Paul wanted him dead, and it seemed to
him there wasn't enough of a reason. Shit again! Well,
Burt wasn't into begging, and never had been. But in
a few minutes he was gonna be dead. This put things
into an entirely different light. "Please," he begged,
"Let me go . . . An' I promise, I won't say anythin'
about you or this house."

Paul cupped his chin with one hand, as though he
were giving the subject his full attention, then he
smiled up at Burt. "I'LL TELL YOU WHAT. IF YOU
MANAGE TO CLIMB DOWN THAT LADDER,
WITHOUT EITHER THE BLADES, OR MY LITTLE
FRIEND UP THERE, KILLING YOU . . . I'LL LET
YOU GO."

Burt didn't believe him. There was something in his
voice, as well as the expression on his face, that said
he was lying. But Burt had no choice. The force of the
wind from those blades was growing stronger; he was
being sucked up into the open arms of the little horror
inside the fan. "Ya promise?" he asked. "Do ya swear
to God you'll let me go?"

"YES," Paul said and his smile grew even broader.

Burt took a deep breath and reached down, with
everything in him, to grab the rung below. Once he
had hold of the rung, he exerted himself and pulled
until he was one step down. But it wasn't easy. His
body was still sore from the beating he'd taken.
However, despite this, he managed to repeat the
process—step by step, painful rung by rung. And he
was doing it, man, he was really cruising down that
ladder.

The last step proved to be the hardest, probably
because he was so tired from struggling against the
forces overhead, and against his own fears as well.
But he did it; he kept going until he was able to stand
beside Paul, which was a victory in itself. "Thought
ya had me . . . Right, Paul?" he yelled. "Thought ya

were gonna kill—''

Burt stopped cold, his mouth wide with shock, when he saw two thin, red arms, with claws on the ends, dangling in front of his face. My, you little bastard, what long arms you have, he thought dully, and screamed when the claws stuck into the sides of his neck. The tiny mirage with the hateful expression was about to kill him. ''Paul,'' he yelled, hating that tone of desperation in his own voice. ''Ya promised. Ya swore to God!''

''I SWORE TO YOUR GOD, NOT MINE . . . BESIDES, I LIED. IF YOU DON'T LIKE IT, DO SOMETHING ABOUT IT.''

Although it was a strain, Burt smiled over the irony of the situation as his legs left the ground. When Paul lied and said he'd let him go, Burt forced himself to believe him. He had no choice, he didn't want to die. So, he'd beaten the fan, he'd defeated the blades, and Paul had let him. Somehow Paul had given him the strength to climb down the ladder, because Burt never could've fought the force of that wind on his own.

Paul was a sadistic creep, he had to be. He wanted Burt to feel elated with victory, even if it was short-lived. This way, Burt would feel that he'd won, only to find out that he hadn't. Paul must've gotten his jollies that way. And hell, if Burt knew he was still gonna die, he would've stood his ground and died with some dignity. Now, thanks to Paul, he'd been reduced to the level of a wimp; a sniveling, begging, fool!

Paul stood below the fan and listened to Burt scream when the little demon pulled his body through the revolving blades and into the heart of the fan. Then he stepped aside when large drops of blood dripped from the interior of the fan itself. Burt, he knew, or what was left of him after going through those blades, was literally being shredded to pieces. And that was more than he deserved for being such an idiot and having such a big mouth.

Then Paul made a mental note to have some of the ancient ones come up here and clean the mess before Erica got home. Erica was sure to be horrified if she discovered what he'd done to Burt. She wasn't a disciple yet, and therein laid the problem.

However, Paul was certain that once she was his, once he owned her heart and soul, that she'd take over. Erica was going to be one bitch! He just knew it! In fact, she'd probably wind up doing things that would shock the ass off him!

Carol Anderson waited all afternoon, and the better part of the evening, for Burt to come home. Burt, she knew, had gone next door to fix the ceiling fans he'd installed the day before yesterday. They weren't working properly. And that puzzled her. Burt might've been a lot of things, but he wasn't sloppy about his work. He was a craftsman, who took pride in everything he did.

The problem with those fans had to lie within the electrical wiring, she surmised. Burt was probably rewiring the upstairs bedrooms to accommodate the extra load. Then she found herself wondering if she really wanted him home after what happened last night, after he'd slapped her the way he did.

Then again, he'd paid for it, and boy had he ever! He gave himself a far worse beating than any he'd ever given her. Of course, she didn't fully understand why—what motivated him to attack himself? And she didn't really care. At this point, all she knew was that it was the funniest thing she'd seen in a long time.

Someone was coming over the fence near the back of the house. It was a man; she could tell that much, although she couldn't see him too clearly. It was dark outside. She watched for a moment to see if it was Burt, before realizing it couldn't be. The man was tall and thin, Burt was short and chunky. Now who the hell—Paul!

Her heart stopped in her throat, and she felt butterflies fluttering about in her stomach. She ran her hands back through her hair to smooth it out and straightened her dress. Then she quickly plugged in the coffee pot and sat down to steady her nerves. Paul certainly couldn't see her like this—all aglow over him.

First of all, she was married. And secondly, it wasn't proper to let a man know how you felt until you were sure of his feelings.

She heard him knocking at the back door and ran to open it before one of the children did. "Paul? What a surprise," she said when she opened the door. Then she was angry with herself because her nervousness had spread to her voice. She wondered if he'd noticed.

"CAROL, HOW LOVELY YOU LOOK," he said and focused his eyes on her face, her body. Then he came on in without being invited, as though he was that sure of himself.

But she didn't mind, not in the least; especially when he got up real close to her and she gazed into those amber-colored eyes of his and saw them dancing with passion. Without moving an inch, she reached behind him and closed the door, hoping that Burt would stay away a little longer.

20

Erica was feeling kind of down. Kayle had left her for another woman, and where she should've been expressing gratitude, she was depressed. Ten years was a long time. So was eight; the length of time she'd spent with Aaron Pace. And now that was over as well.

She snapped off the T.V. because there was nothing on, and went into the kitchen for a can of beer. Didi was in there with Sam; doing homework. When Erica walked in on them, Didi flashed a smile, and gave her that incredible look again—the one that said, *you name it and I'll do it*. Erica wrapped her arms around the child's neck and winced at the bruises on her face.

Was this what she missed Kayle for, she wondered? Did she want him back so he'd have another chance to pound on her kids again? Maybe kill them next time? Kayle had been acting pretty irrational towards the end, just before he'd taken his broken jaw and left.

"How's it going?" Erica wanted to know.

Both kids smiled and shook their heads as if to say it was homework, how could it go? Rotten at best.

"Need any help?"

Again they smiled and silently shook their heads. Did this mean they were growing independent, she wondered? Suddenly her knowledge wasn't needed as far as homework went? She sighed and realized how useless and lonely she felt, how much she missed Paul. He'd gone out about an hour before. At least when he was there, she never felt lonely. She'd asked him not to go wherever he was going, but Paul told her he had something important to take care of.

For a man who lived in a closet, he sure had a lot of outside business to handle. That puzzled her at times. Only she tried not to dwell on the mystery because everything to do with Paul was a mystery.

She walked to the window and glanced out. Night had settled a couple of hours ago; there was a full moon shining through the trees next door. This was a night made for lovers, she thought, and that depressed her even more. She'd spent a lot of moonlit nights alone during these past few weeks, waiting for Kayle to tire of his latest fling and come home. Only now it was different, because he was never coming home again.

Erica turned away, to free herself from the entrancing hold of the full moon and the night, and heard the children whispering behind her back. That was strange, she thought. They usually spoke right up; at least in front of her, if not in front of Kayle.

"Mommy, is Daddy ever comin' home again?"

Sam had asked the question, but he didn't sound too unhappy, she noticed. "No. He's not."

"Yippee!" The two yelled in unison.

Erica was silently perturbed. She could understand Didi's not wanting Kayle to come back, but Sam never said anything one way or the other. She felt a little bad for Kayle's sake. But before she could allow herself to think on it for any length of time, Sam asked another question, one that disturbed the hell out of her.

"How come ya look so bad, Mommy? Like yer sick?"

Sam was the second person in less than twenty-four

hours to mention how terrible she looked. She honestly couldn't see it. She shrugged and wondered what they were seeing that she wasn't. "I don't know, honey. Maybe I'm just tired."

She watched them pack their books into a neat pile and get up. They were going in to watch T.V., as they usually did after their homework was finished. Then she realized that once they left, she'd be alone in the kitchen. She took a sip of beer and wished Paul would come home.

"Can Sam sleep in my room? In Katie's bed?" Didi wanted to know.

The mere mention of Katie's name sent Erica's brain reeling. She started to recall Mary's conversation today, then shook herself free. The child was waiting for an answer. "I don't see anything wrong with that. I'm sure Todd won't mind spending the night alone."

Sam smiled at Didi. "Ya see. Mom's okay when Daddy's not home."

"What's that supposed to mean?" Erica wanted to know, although she didn't have to ask. Kayle was a miserable bastard who never wanted the kids to do anything different. And he often forced his opinion on Erica, who in turn, went along with his wishes to keep peace in the house. "Daddy's a beast and I'm the pushover. Is that it?"

"I don't know." Sam shrugged his tiny shoulders and continued to stand at attention, as though he expected an awful reaction from Erica.

She wanted to smile because he looked so serious, and hell, she wasn't really angry. "Get yourself a Coke and watch some T.V. while you can. Bedtime's eight o'clock."

After they'd gone, Cokes in hand, Erica sat at the table and laid her beer down next to their books. She was bored, and lonely. This was absolutely the worst night of her life. And, because she was alone, her mind began to dwell on everything that had happened since they'd bought this house: the tragedy of her separations from Kayle and Aaron, Katie's strangeness . . .

And Paul lived in a closet!

What was she supposed to do when they got together, she wondered, go into the closet and lay on the floor with him? She smiled at that and figured the beer must've been affecting her. But the smile didn't last for long because something else came to her, a memory from her recent past . . . She recalled the incident on the staircase the very first time she'd come to this house, and she tried to forget it before the memory grew and loomed in front of her like a tiny vignette.

But the memory was stronger than her resistance. She was on the landing upstairs, looking down, as those horrible footsteps climbed up to greet her. And she couldn't see anyone, not a soul. And then, when the individual force got close and surrounded her body, it whispered to her, said it loved her and would protect her—*after* it threatened her life to show its powers.

That incident had been in the back of her mind for days now—the voice she'd heard had been identical to Paul's! And, at one point, she'd heard several voices, but there was only one set of footsteps, as though the body of the entity was composed of more than one individual, as though its soul was inhabited by many.

"Hey, Mom!" Sam shouted, shattering the stillness around her. It was like the howl of a wolf on a dark night.

Erica steadied herself and looked up. He was standing in the doorway with her recorder in his arms. She wanted to scream but held back. It wasn't Sam's fault that he'd scared her so badly. "What is it, Sam?"

"I wanna bring this in here, 'fore it gets broken and we get blamed."

"Good thinking," she said and rose to retrieve the recorder. She'd left in on an end table, near the couch, after using it for Todd's party. This was great, she thought, she could while away some of those lonely hours ahead of her by playing the tape from last night. And just maybe it would take her mind off those horrible thoughts—the ones she'd been having before Sam came in and scared her half to death.

"Mom?"

"What?" Now she was losing it. This kid had a million questions, and he'd saved them all for tonight it seemed.

"Paul said ya should wait 'till he's here ta play the tape from the party."

"Why?" This was bullshit. Paul was out and having a good time for himself and he wanted her to wait. Well, piss on him, she thought.

"I don't know why," Sam said, shrugging his tiny shoulders. "But that's what he told me ta tell ya."

"Thanks." She watched Sam disappear into the next room, and waited ten minutes to make sure he was gone, and wouldn't come back, before rewinding the tape. While the recorder was doing its thing, she went to get another beer and a fresh pack of cigarettes. Along with the children singing *Happy Birthday* to Todd they'd each taken turns leaving a small message and Erica couldn't wait to hear them—

"Mom?"

She looked up to see Sam standing in the doorway again. She was ready to kill by now. "What, Sam?"

"Me and Didi're goin' upstairs. There ain't nothin' good on T.V., so we're gonna play with our toys."

Erica nodded silently and felt a bit strange about this. Todd was next door with Jack Anderson. If Sam and Didi went upstairs, she'd be all alone down here.

There would be nobody on the lower level of the house but her . . . .

Then again . . . she *hoped* she'd be alone . . .

Unless someone came by to visit . . .

Someone she was able to *see*, of course, as well as *hear*.

"Are ya gonna be okay down here alone?"

"Yes, Sam. I'll be fine." If nothing strange or exciting happened, that was.

Sam continued to stand in the doorway as though he had one final question, but was too afraid to ask it. Erica couldn't take the suspense. "What is it, honey?"

"I wanted ta ask ya . . . is Paul movin' in here to take Daddy's place? He hangs around a lot . . ."

"Maybe, honey. Paul and I are discussing it now. I'll let you know."

After Sam left the room, Erica was alone again, and again her mind began to wander. . . Paul lived in a closet, and Paul's voice was similar to that horror in the hall upstairs. What had she done by committing herself to a man she barely knew? A man she barely knew anything about? And to be perfectly honest, he scared her sometimes, like when he read her mind. How did he do it? Did he use mirrors or the art of illusion?

The recorder had stopped rewinding. Erica pressed the play button and lifted her beer to her lips. The children were singing off-key and that made her smile. She listened to *Happy Birthday* and *how old you you now?* and a few other songs before she realized something was wrong.

She rewound the tape and listened carefully this time, and heard it again. There were strange voices in the background on the tape, adult voices . . . only they weren't singing. They seemed to be discussing something. She rewound the tape again and tried to figure out who those voices belonged to. Aaron Pace had been in the living room with Erica and her mother, Mary, but they weren't talking when the tape was running. Paul had left before they even cut the cake. It surely was a mystery.

Again she rewound the tape and turned up the volume so she could hear what was being said in the

background. Only it was useless—the children's
voices were mostly drowning out their conversation.
Then, out of desperation, she placed her ear against
one of the speakers and barely made out the phrase,
"KILLED HENRY WITTAKER." Chills stung the
base of her neck and she quickly hit the stop button
on the recorder.

Henry Wittaker *was* dead; she'd read it in the paper
only this morning.

And he wasn't *killed!*

His death had been an accident.

Poor man . . .

Evidently his car had broken down on a highway
just above Nassau County. Henry stepped out into
traffic by mistake, and was run over as he was going
for help. So, it was an accident. She rewound just that
part of the tape and listened up close to the speaker
and again she heard the phrase, "KILLED HENRY
WITTAKER." This time, however, she wasn't so
quick to turn it off. This time she let it run and heard
those same voices laughing as though there was something humorous about Henry Wittaker's death.

Then she caught another phrase that sounded like,
"KILLED OLD BESS AND BUDDY, TOO." There
was more singing by the children, then, "PATRICIA
WAS CUT LOOSE."

Killed old Bess and Buddy, too? As Erica now
recalled, Henry Wittaker's wife was named Bess.
She'd read it in the papers when his wife died. And,
oh, God! His son was named Buddy—Erica had read
that too . . . In fact, besides Henry, the only other
survivor of the accident that killed his son had been
his daughter Patricia! Now these people were
claiming to have cut Patricia loose. What was going
on here, she wondered?

"FUCKING BRATS WITH THEIR FUCKING
SINGING!"

That phrase had been mostly buried under the
children's songs, but she heard it and felt her body go

limp; her nerves were dancing under the skin.

"AND HE'LL LAY ERICA, PAUL WILL. AND THEN SHE'LL BE HIS . . ." That particular phrase was followed by loud, boisterous laughter.

This was impossible! She couldn't be hearing this, not the things they were saying. She rewound the tape and listened and heard those horrible voices again. Impossible, she repeated. She'd been doing the recording herself. If anything like this drivel had been spoken aloud, by God only knows who, Erica would've heard it.

Someone must've fooled with the tape and recorded those hideous phrases after the party. Someone had gone to the trouble of taping over the tape, and had spoiled the whole thing.

Goddamn! If this was supposed to be a joke, it wasn't funny, not in the least. This was important to her, a cherished memory to be added to the rest. And now, some ignorant bastard with a warped sense of humor had gone ahead and ruined her tape.

She was mad enough to kill when she rewound the tape to the beginning and played it through without stopping. "Happy birthday to Todd," the children were singing, while a voice in the background whispered, "FUCK HIM!" Erica was incensed. And it didn't end there, it grew worse as the tape progressed. The children were constantly being made fun of, in a cruel and vicious way.

Those people on the tape were repeating things the children had said, and, either they laughed afterwards or else they uttered obscenities. Threats were made against *all* of their lives. Erica heard a small girl speaking towards the end of the tape and realized, as her heart pounded heavily in her chest, that it was Angelica. "THEY WILL ALL DIE," Angelica said and laughed.

Erica sat there for what seemed like hours and did nothing but replay that tape until it was indelibly etched into her soul. Hatred seared the base of her skull. Who did this, she wondered? Who could've been so vicious? Not even Kayle, with his arrogance, and his "the world owes me" attitude would have been capable of anything this rotten.

And the worst part of all was that besides Angelica, she'd recognized some of the other voices. They sounded like they belonged to the entity in the hall upstairs. One set of footsteps and several voices, she'd thought at the time, and it had been a mystery to her then as now. But at least she knew she wasn't crazy, for here they were again, the same voices.

And Paul's name was mentioned on the tape!

Lately he seemed to be at the core of everything.

She made up her mind then to get rid of Paul. There was an evil associated with him, and although she was unable to reason it out, the taint was there, on his soul. Erica was positive of this.

But Paul was there to protect her from Kayle, a small, inner voice whispered to her.

And yet, who was there to protect her from Paul?

But the answer was obvious—Aaron Pace! Aaron loved her enough to see that no one ever hurt her again.

In the morning, she'd call Aaron and tell him that it was all right to move in. Then she'd tell Paul to take his ass and move out!

She smiled and drank the last of her beer. She was almost at ease now that she'd been able to come to grips with her problem. Aaron would replace Kayle, not Paul as she'd originally planned. She heard the door slam out in the living room followed by Todd's voice saying he was going to bed. Then she heard him running up the stairs outside the kitchen.

"Okay, honey," she called to him. "I'll be up in a minute."

Erica was suddenly tired, which wasn't odd since she hadn't been able to sleep at all these past few nights. But there was a lot on her mind keeping her awake. And now, things were different. Oh, yeah.

She'd mostly resolved her problems. She took the tape out of the recorder and threw it across the room. Paul and his friends could go right to hell! Then she rose and turned to go upstairs.

"HELLO, ERICA."

It was Paul! How long had he been standing behind her, she wondered, as her body trembled with fear? And how much of her mind had he read before she'd stopped thinking?

"AREN'T YOU FEELING WELL? WHY, YOUR FACE IS GHASTLY WHITE."

Angelica followed the old bitch and the brat around until she swore her legs would fall off and she'd be reduced to walking on stumps. GREAT SATAN'S BALLS, that old woman could shop! And there was Katie, trailing along behind, putting on an act as usual. "Of course I don't mind if you look around, Grandmother. No problem," Katie had said.

But Angelica minded—a whole lot. The only thing that made it bearable was her wonderful veil of invisibility. Oh, hell, what fun. When someone got too close to her, she kicked them in the shins, or, as was the case with one gimpy-legged stud, she grabbed him between his legs and wouldn't let go. Then she laughed when everyone in the store thought he was a nut for jumping and screaming and holding himself the way he did.

However, that novelty soon wore thin, along with everything else. She was bored—wasting her talents. Angelica was a killing machine, programmed for destruction. To her, nothing could compare with the thrill of killing, of snuffing out a life, of choking the breath from a victim. Nothing!

Night was falling by the time Mary and Katie decided to head home. Mary seemed troubled, and made it overly obvious by continously looking back over her shoulder. She suspected that someone was following them. Even when she reached the front

door of her apartment, she paused to check again
before pushing Katie inside, then rushing in behind
her. However, a closed door never stopped Angelica,
not once!

"Who were you speaking to when you made that
call before?" Katie asked, once they were settled in
the kitchen. "And how come you didn't wait until
you got home?" Katie's gaze drifted to the black
phone on the counter near the stove.

Angelica was pleased: Katie was voicing her
suspicions. She'd taught the child well.

Mary didn't answer right away. She was making
dinner, and kept her back turned and her head down
to avoid looking at Katie. "I wasn't calling anyone in
particular."

"Well, then, why bother? I mean, we were out to
enjoy ourselves. Isn't that true, Grandmother? If the
call wasn't important, then why take time away from
me to place it? You could've waited until we got—"

"Forget about it," Mary said. "If I wanted you to
know all my business, I'd tell you!"

Katie stared back at her for a long time without
saying anything. Angelica watched tiny lines forming
around her mouth. "Did you call my mother? Is that
it? Is that what you're hiding?"

Mary wheeled to face her. Angelica had never seen
such an incredulous look of indignation on anyone's
face before. "Who the hell do you think you're
talking to? I can't imagine what you're trying to prove
with this grown-up thing, but it had better stop!"

Katie scowled and got up and left the room. Mary
watched her go, then she sat at the table and put her
hands to her head. Her face was pale with anger, and
her heart was pumping very fast, perhaps too fast for
someone her age. She sat there for a moment and
acted as though she were having trouble breathing.
Angelica was nervous. What if the old bitch died on
her own and spoiled everything?

Then, in an attempt to salvage some of this for

herself, Angelica walked up behind Mary and placed her hands on the older woman's shoulders. Mary must've felt something, because at that point she glanced around as if she knew someone was in the kitchen with her, someone she couldn't see. Well, Angelica thought, maybe Mary couldn't see her, but she'd damned well be able to see what Angelica had in store for her.

Her own LIVING DEATH, as ordered by the Gate Keeper!

"RELAX, MARY. AND CLOSE YOUR EYES."

Angelica's voice was but a whisper on the wind. It was there, but not really. And it was entrancing enough to make Mary close her eyes.

"DREAM OF SOMETHING WONDERFUL. DREAM OF FRED."

Mary didn't know why, but her thoughts suddenly turned to Fred and happier times in her life. She dreamed of Fred and his reaction when she announced her pregnancy; how he'd held her close in the night and whispered things that were so sweet. Her heart was slowing down, she noticed. That was good. It really had her worried there for a few minutes. But now that she'd concentrated on something as wonderful as Fred—

"HELL IS FOR LOVERS, MARY. FRED'S THERE AND HE'S WAITING FOR YOU."

Her heart gave a sudden lurch and started to pound out of control again. Those were the same exact words Paul had put into her head, and now they were coming back to haunt her. Fred was coming back to haunt her . . . She could see him . . . Oh, God, he'd been dead for so long . . . There were holes in his face . . . His bones were almost devoid of flesh . . .

She tried to open her eyes because she didn't want to see anymore. And if she opened her eyes, this horrible vision would surely be gone, she thought. But Fred was waving to her, telling her he needed companionship. You see, Fred, she wanted to say, I'm

not deceased yet, and you are. So, it's impossible. He
was touching her, rubbing something up against her
body, something with black hair and a stubby tail . . .
It was a dog! The one she'd feared—

She looked behind Fred and saw her own heart. It
was as large as her body . . . And the dog was no
longer being held by Fred, it was walking over to her
heart . . . It seemed to want to devour the flesh. She
watched it crawl up and over the sides, its long,
jagged teeth sinking in. There were pains in her chest;
horrible, white, hot pains, and it felt as though
someone, holding a branding iron, was sitting on top
of her, stabbing her with all their might.

Mary screamed and the sound of her own voice
echoed in her ears. She opened her eyes and fought
for a breath of air. Nausea gripped her insides. It was
dark in here, wherever she was.

She knew she wasn't still in her kitchen; there was
no light and her body felt cramped. She was in a
small, confined place, like a coffin. Was she dead, she
wondered? Had she died and now had awakened to
find herself buried under tons of earth with a sealed
lid over her face? But no . . . She ran her hand around
and felt no silk, or anything like the fabric used to line
a coffin. She did feel something though . . . Plaster
board.

A light went on somewhere? It seemed to be outside
of the place she was in. That was odd, she thought.
She was looking through a wall of some kind . . . next
to a flight of stairs . . . in Erica's house! Oh, God. She
was in the wall, and there were heartbeats all around
her, some slow, some as fast as her own. She pounded
her fists against the wall and cried out. But no one
came.

Couldn't they hear her? Erica and the children?

Her breathing was heavy, and that was no good.
There wasn't much air inside the wall. She had to stop
this, conserve what she could. But what if she died before anyone realized where she was?

Oh, God, there was . . . something in here!

She felt it touch her arm.

She wasn't alone in the wall.

She wanted to turn and look, but she was afraid.

It was so dark in there.

Something was breathing on her, and drooling. A dog! With a big head. No! There were several heads, all breathing on her and laughing and whispering. This was the creature she'd sensed; the one she feared the most. And the truth became self-evident . . .

She, alone, had felt the bad vibes in this house. And, instead of letting it go, she'd allowed those bad vibes to nurture themselves until they grew. She was able to see what was happening here, and what she had seen frightened her enough so that she should've STAYED AWAY! But she hadn't! She had taken it upon herself to warn Erica!

But, Erica was her child! She had no choice!

And now, there were no choices left. Her curiosity was doing her in. Mary had too many questions concerning the wall and its heartbeats, and now, she was part of it, PART OF THE WALL! This was to be her coffin, her tomb. She would spend an eternity here, her heartbeat blending along with the others.

Erica! She saw Erica coming down the stairs, and she screamed. But it was useless. Erica walked on by and opened the front door. Katie was there. And the child lies! I didn't ask her to leave! Oh, Erica, Katie's a fraud. She left on her own, AFTER she and Angelica did this to me.

At that point, Mary gave up and abandoned all hope. There was a child standing next to Katie . . . and she could see that so-called child now where she'd never been able to before. An evil, hideous, twisted, little demon—Angelica! And hell, that was strange. Erica was acting as though Angelica weren't even there. And that made things worse, made the truth more glaring.

Mary could see Angelica now because she was ONE

OF THEM!

Thump after thump, beat after beat, her heart came in tune with the rhythm of the wall . . . And her voice rose and became part of the terrible cacophony of agony she'd heard when she first came to see the HOUSE . . .

Aaron and Kayle were having a beer the following morning when the subject of women came up—mostly it was Kayle's new woman they were discussing. Aaron was trying to be polite, and listened for a while before anger got the better of him.

"Hey, buddy, does this mean you and your old lady are finished?" he asked, although the answer was obvious.

"You ain't kiddin'! I shoulda left the bitch long ago and I would've if it weren't for the kids." Kayle had trouble speaking through the bands of his teeth, but somehow he managed to make himself understood. "And now I got Lorraine . . ."

Kayle continued talking, but Aaron stopped listening when he heard the name Lorraine. Jesus, he thought, what irony! Here, Aaron had taken over Kayle's woman because Erica helped him forget about his own Lorraine and the past as well. Now Kayle had himself a woman named Lorraine, and for a moment it made Aaron wonder? Kayle did say she was a voluptuous blonde . . . Then again, it couldn't have been the same one. His Lorraine was dead, had died in California, strapped to a coven's table, tortured—

"Hey, Aaron. Somethin' wrong?"

"Uh . . . No. Not really. It's just . . . There's something I have to tell you. And I know you ain't gonna like it!"

Kayle narrowed his eyes. "Is it anything to do with Lorraine. 'Cause if it is—"

"Hell, no, budddy. It has to do with Erica." Aaron was elated because he was finally getting the chance to shove it to this egotistical bastard. And, at the same time, he was nervous. Lately, Kayle had been prone to extreme violence. Not that he was afraid of him, he just didn't know what to expect.

"If it's about Erica, I don't really give a shit about hearin' it. To me, she's as good as dead!" Kayle picked up his beer and started to leave, but Aaron stopped him.

It was time: Aaron had to tell all. "How much do you know about biology?" Aaron wanted to know.

"Biology? What the hell's biology got to do with Erica?"

"Well, buddy, you see . . . it's like this. Erica is platinum blonde with blue eyes. You're dark with dark eyes. According to what I learned in school, three of your kids should be dark like you. Dark hair and eyes are what they called domi—"

"What're ya tryna say? Ya tryna tell me those kids aren't mine?" Kayle sounded outraged. But Aaron continued anyway.

"All I'm tryna say is this, seventy-five percent of your kids should take after you 'cause you're dark. Dark genes are dominant . . . that's three out of four. Now . . . You have four kids with platinum blonde hair and blue eyes. You figure it out."

"What're ya really tryna say? That my kids are freaks 'cause they don't run accordin' to what should be? Is that it?" Kayle was still angry, only now he sounded more curious than anything.

"I'm not calling your kids freaks."

"Then you're sayin' I ain't their father! Then who is if I ain't?" Kayle sounded calmer this time. Aaron was the curious one now.

"I am," Aaron said and stood his ground. "See, Kayle, I got the same coloring as Erica . . . and they're my kids." He expected to be attacked at any minute. But Kayle surprised him by just sitting where he was and staring at him as though he couldn't believe what he was hearing. Then Kayle smiled, and that struck him as being very odd. A man tells you your kids aren't yours, he thought, and that he fathered all four while you were paying the bills . . . Aaron would want to kill under the circumstances.

"Well, now. That makes it nice for me. I was worried about bein' able to support two women. Erica, 'cause of those kids. And Lorraine, 'cause I love her. You just solved most of my worries. If those kids are yours, as you say they are, then you support them." Kayle took his beer and started to leave, but then he turned and smiled. "I ain't even gonna ask for any details. I don't care when it happened, when ya fucked her! *She's yours, buddy!*"

Aaron was struck dumb. He never expected this. He wanted Erica, true, and he wanted vengeance for her sake, but Kayle's words had just turned it around and made it backfire. Now Aaron was the fool. He had to support those kids whether he wanted to or not. Something he never had to worry about before.

And, to make matters worse, it was up to him to eliminate Paul. Kayle was out of it now; therefore, Kayle could hardly go home and play the role of jealous lover. So, Aaron had to do it, and truthfully, he was more than a little leery of Paul. Hell, just the mention of his name alone and Aaron had to check his fingers to see if they were all there. It was the damndest thing—

Aaron had gotten up to go back to work when he'd made the mistake of allowing his gaze to wander. And wander it did: right across the street to the car sitting at the curb; the one with the black glass covering the windows so he couldn't look inside and see who was after him. He knew most of the members of that coven back in California . . . But, somehow, he'd never been able to see who had been following him all these years.

Not that he really cared. He just wanted to know the name of his killer, or killers—whichever was the case—before the coven made its move.

21

The bedroom walls were sweating again when Erica finally woke up. It confused her for a moment: she forgot she was living in a house with no radiators and no valves. Valveless radiators, simmering with heat, were one of the major causes of sweating walls, she knew. But this house had baseboard heating.

She got up and went to the bathroom, choosing to ignore the droplets of water staining the walls that had driven her crazy with confusion the time she came to show the house to Mary. Once in the bathroom, she splashed water on her face and turned her thoughts to Katie, and what Katie had said last night. Mary, her very own mother, had thrown Katie out! That was incredible.

The throwing out part was so unlike Mary, and was bad enough by itself. But then Mary had made a bad situation even worse: she'd given a four-year-old the responsibility of finding her own way home—late at night. Something was wrong. Maybe her mother was growing senile. She was past sixty, if that was the age for senility to set in. Erica wasn't sure. At any rate, she had to call Mary and straighten this out.

Katie could've been lying.

Perhaps she left on her own. But then Mary would've called Erica when she discovered that Katie was missing. And since Mary didn't call, Erica felt there might be some truth to Katie's story.

And why, she wondered for the hundredth time, didn't she take the initative herself? Why didn't she pick up the phone and call Mary last night? Why did she let it go? It almost seemed as if there had been a reason not to call, as though something had held her back . . .

The clock on her end table said 8:30 when Erica came out of the bathroom and she panicked. The children missed the school bus! Damn! She'd overslept. Why? Then she remembered the drink Paul had given her to quiet her nerves. Right after she'd played those tapes. Those Goddamn tapes! Oh yes. She was angry at Paul because his name was mentioned, and she'd been ready to throw him out.

However, Paul had come into the kitchen unnoticed, had read her mind, and wouldn't leave. She was overwrought, he'd said. She needed a good night's sleep. Then he fixed her a drink. And it must've been good and stiff, she surmised, because she passed out cold when her head touched her pillow.

"Didi, Todd, Sam . . . Come on, get up. You're late for school." She was standing outside of her door, calling the children, and for some reason or other, her voice echoed and resounded in her ears. The house sounded hollow inside, like a tunnel, or a cave. It was strange, and cold, and seemed empty.

"Didi, Todd, Sam!" She called again, then decided to shake them out of bed because they weren't responding.

There was movement in the hall . . .

Someone walking . . .

In front of her!

Someone who had seemingly cropped up out of thin air!

It was a woman, she could tell that much. But Erica couldn't see her face. "Miss . . . Hello!" The woman continued on, approaching the stairs as though Erica had said nothing. "Who are you?" Erica asked, and noticed a stitch in her voice. "Answer me, damnit!"

Forgetting the children and school, she ran and clutched at the woman's shoulders, but her hands passed right through her as though she'd grabbed nothing but air. Erica tried again, and again it was the same. She was puzzled and frightened. Was this a ghost? A specter? She'd heard that some houses were haunted, but she never considered the possibility that this one was.

Bullshit! She had to admit the truth, the facts as she'd known them all along: *there was something wrong with this house.* And hell, they had ghosts, that's all. Here she'd suspected the trouble had been much worse, that the house had been inhabited by something dangerous and frightening—

The woman turned and what Erica saw almost caused her to faint: she was looking at herself! But that was impossible! No! Incredible! Then she realized that although this person was looking directly at her, she seemed not to notice Erica. She had a puzzled expression on her face, as though she'd forgotten something and was trying to remember before going downstairs.

Erica reached out and tried to touch her again, to touch herself again, because that was what she had been looking at. Her twin, her exact double, wearing her clothes. And God, it was unnerving. The woman brushed past her and returned to the bedroom. Erica followed, not wanting to, but feeling compelled to at the same time.

It was all so weird. Was this really happening? Or was she hallucinating again? Were those gases in the house mixing together and making her see things? It seemed—No! Yes! Yes, that was the answer. It seemed as though she was either envisualizing an ESP experience, or, and most probably of all, she was seeing herself through a time-warp of some kind.

As she watched, "Erica" came from the bedroom and went downstairs and out through the front door. She followed and tried to convince herself that she was awake and this wasn't some horrible dream. Paul was down in the kitchen. He came out and witnessed the whole thing. She turned to him and silently asked what was happening? Paul smiled. If he knew the answer, she'd have to wait until he was good and ready to reveal it.

There was one thing bothering her though: one thing she couldn't wait for the answer to. The woman was her, but then again, she wasn't. She was haggard looking. There were dark circles under her eyes, and her body sloped forward, making her look older than she was. Paul said nothing, although Erica was sure he knew what was on her mind. Hell, he always seemed to know.

Was she seeing herself in the future, she wanted to know? Was it taking place ten years from now, or ten days from now?

Paul took her by the arm and led her upstairs to the mirror hanging over the dresser, and for the first time Erica was able to see the truth. There were no illusions as there had been these past few weeks. Paul stripped the veil of naivete from her eyes and the truth became self-evident: she looked exactly like that woman!

She had the same dark circles, the same slouch to her body. And all this time, others had seen it, but she had not. And when everyone had asked that question, "Erica, are you sick or what?" it was only because they had been able to see what she couldn't.

"You, bastard!" She turned and faced Paul, knowing this was his fault. Somehow, he alone had been responsible for everything strange and incredible and tragic that had happened to her these past weeks. "You, bastard!"

"I LOVE YOU, ERICA. YOU'RE BEAUTIFUL TO ME."

"You're warped, you son-of-a-bitch! Warped!" She was beyond anger. Her nerves seared her flesh, her brain burned with indignation. She grabbed a bottle of perfume off the dresser and hurled it through the mirror. As it smashed and shards of glass fell, she headed for the one in the bathroom. She had no intentions of stopping until every mirror in the house was nothing more than a memory.

Paul, she knew, was a very sick person. He had to be to have done this to her. And she was damned if she'd beg him to undo the damage. Why he'd probably just laugh and tell her he'd take care of it in time; especially since she'd had thoughts of dumping him. And especially since Paul had read her mind last night and knew exactly how she felt.

No. She'd have to wait until he was ready to restore her to her normal self. In the meanwhile, she'd be damned if she'd allow a mirror in this house now that she could see herself as she was!

Paul watched her vent her fury and was glad. Erica had spirit. She could react. There was hope for the bitch yet. He left the room and went downstairs to wait until she was finished. The children were in school. Katie had awakened them after Angelica had put a silent suggestion into her head. And, after they left, Katie went back to her room to talk to Angelica.

Erica practically had the house to herself and could smash to her heart's content.

As he was passing the wall running parallel to the stairs he heard many cries of anguish; the many pleas for mercy, uttered by the victims trapped inside. Those victims, he knew, were a part of the network of hatred upon which he thrived. They were trapped in there, along with a myriad number of his disciples; trapped for all time to come, or until he decided to end their misery with eternal death.

And, strangely enough, the loudest voice he heard belonged to Mary Rogers. For an old woman, she had some lungs, he thought. Then he laughed and went on down to wait for Erica.

Henry Wittaker's death was no accident. She had forseen it days ago, as she had foreseen so many other painful incidents in the past. She clutched a slip of paper in her hand: Henry had given her Erica's name and address. Should she call, she wondered? Would Erica be receptive? Was it too late?

Had the Gate Keeper won?

The only way to be sure at this point was to actually place the call. But then she couldn't. Henry's death indicated one fine point: he'd been so right about his feelings and the stakes involved. Otherwise, Henry would still be alive. He was killed to silence him, to keep the truth hidden. She had to wonder about the extent of the powers she was facing. Was it the Gate Keeper alone, or were there others on the same level as he?

She also had to wonder if she wanted to become involved again.

Of course, they couldn't kill her; she had the protection of the Lord. But they could drive her from her home again. Their disciples could put on the old pressure if she interferred. Then the nightmare would replay itself, like an old movie on late night T.V. Kirsten recalled the hate mail; the harassing phone calls that never seemed to stop; the packages they left on her doorstep. The body parts . . . The severed heads . . .

Who was this Erica that she should put herself on the line for her, and leave herself open and vulnerable? Why, oh, Lord, she wanted to know? But the answer was obvious: this was her mission in life. And if Kirsten stood aside and did nothing, Erica and her children were sure to follow in Henry's steps. For demonic possession, to her, was on an equal level with death.

"THAT'S YOUR OPINION, BITCH!"

"Shut up, all of you!" Kirsten rose and turned off

the lights that were flickering overhead, adding strength to the disciples of the beast. Then she opened the curtains and ignored the dead thing standing in the woods. She picked up the phone and started to dial, but the phone went dead. "In the name of the Lord, Jesus Christ, I command you to be gone," she repeated three times in rapid succession.

She tried the phone again and this time the call went through. But there was a lot of static on the line: they still had partial control over the call. "Hello," she said when it was picked up on the other end. "May I please speak to Erica Walsh?"

"THIS IS ERICA. WHO ARE YOU?"

The voice was strange. It sounded like a woman's, but there was something about the tone that bothered Kirsten. "You don't know me, but I'm a friend of Henry Wittaker's—"

"AND WHAT HAS THAT TO DO WITH ME?"

She sensed an abruptness now, a nastiness. "Henry asked me to call . . . You're having problems with your home?"

"I THOUGHT I WAS RID OF THAT SCREWBALL WHEN HE GOT KILLED. NOW I HAVE TO LISTEN TO YOU AND THE SAME OLD BULLSHIT? I'M NOT PUTTING UP WITH THIS . . . DON'T EVER CALL HERE—"

"But you need me, need my help. If it's as bad as Henry said it was . . ." There was a pleading quality to Kirsten's voice that disturbed her. Why plead when she was doing this woman a favor? Then again, was she really speaking to Erica? "I'd like to come—"

"HEY LADY, FUCK OFF!"

The phone was violently disconnected on the other end. Erica, or the person imitating Erica, had hung up. Kirsten heard a dial tone but held the receiver to her ear as she wondered again if it was too late. Or should she place another call and keep on calling until she was sure she was speaking to Erica?

"HEY, BITCH. HANG UP."

She heard another voice coming through the receiver, speaking over the endless hum of the dial tone. This was followed by hissing and growling. For all intents and purposes, this was an impossibility. No one should've been able to get through. Her phone was off the hook, she was holding the receiver. Erica's line had been disconnected when the phone was hung up.

Nobody should've gotten through!

"WE'RE NOT JUST *ANYBODY*, BITCH!"

Kirsten slammed down the receiver when she realized the thing on the other end had been reading into her thoughts. The situation was more dangerous than she'd imagined. Erica was being protected. Those bastards were guarding her, eliminating all who opposed them, such as Henry Wittaker, and probably others that she knew nothing about. They also had control of her phone . . .

The big question now was, did they have control of Erica? If not, then maybe it still wasn't too late.

She picked up the receiver again with the intention of calling Erica's home and really giving it to those bastards, but she never got the chance to finish dialing. The phone rang while she was holding the receiver in her hand. She stared at it and was only partially surprised. They'd done the same thing moments before: used a dead line to get through.

"Hello," she said. This time there was an angry attitude reflected in her tone. "There's something you want to tell me?"

"STAY AWAY!!!"

The voice was a strong one, and had been surrounded by others. It was a cacophony of madness: hissing, growling, and a great deal of wind. She smiled. The old Gate Keeper was showing off. But it didn't scare her. She'd taken him on years ago and would many times again. She placed the receiver on its hook and made up her mind never to call again. Next time she'd actually go to Erica's house and face them on their own territory.

First, however, she'd spend some time in prayer, building herself up both emotionally and spiritually. Those things were tricky. They played on your thoughts, your fears and used them against you. She had to strengthen her psyche in order not to leave herself open and vulnerable to their taunts. Because, if she weakened and lost her temper and fought them in careless anger, her own possession was next.

Paul hung up the receiver and smiled to himself. Kirsten had done well, thanks to Henry Wittaker. The bitch had actually managed to find the house. Which meant they would again become locked in battle. However this time one thing would change: Paul had every intention of winning!

"Were you speaking to someone on the phone?" Erica wanted to know. She'd become so exhausted from her previous rage, smashing every mirror in the house, that she'd been forced to lie down and sleep for a while.

"YES, DEAR. SOMEONE CALLED . . . BUT IT WAS A WRONG NUMBER."

She rose from the couch and rubbed her eyes. She was dazed and still slightly in shock from having seen herself as she was: ugly and deformed. "Paul? Why did you do this to me?"

"ARE YOU SO SURE IT WAS I?"

"Yes. You can do a lot of things other people can't . . . I mean, look at how you read my mind and all."

He smiled at her and forced a gentleness into his voice. At this point, Erica would've responded to nothing less. "I'M PROTECTING MY INTEREST. YOU SEE, I LOVE YOU, ERICA. AND I WANT NO OTHER MAN TO DESIRE YOU."

It was her turn to smile, but not with warmth. She was angry and astounded. "How could you want me like this? What kind of bullshit is that?"

"TO EACH HIS OWN. I SEE BEYOND OUT-

WARD APPEARANCES. I LOVE YOU FOR WHAT
YOU ARE . . . INSIDE."

She seemed pensive now, as though she had to
think about his answer.

"I'M TAKING YOU FOR WHAT YOU ARE.
PLEASE ACCEPT IT." He opened his arms and saw
her hesitate. But then she walked into his embrace
and laid her head against his chest. "POOR THING.
YOU SEE, YOU NEED ME AS MUCH AS I NEED
YOU." There was silence between them for a
moment. Then, "IF I RESTORE YOU BACK TO
WHAT YOU WERE BEFORE, I HAVE TO SET
CERTAIN GUIDELINES."

"All right, Paul. I'll do whatever you say." Her
voice was timid, almost meek, heavily veiling the hint
of passion he detected.

"I'M A JEALOUS LOVER, ERICA. AND I DON'T
ENJOY SEEING OTHER MEN STARING AT YOU.
CONSIDERING THIS, I MUST INSIST THAT YOU
WEAR NO MAKE-UP OR DO ANYTHING WITH
YOUR HAIR THAT WOULD MAKE YOU SEEM
ATTRACTIVE TO OTHERS."

"Anything you say, Paul. You're in charge now."

Paul smiled and wondered what Kirsten would
think if she were here now. She was really wasting
her time and didn't know it.

Three out of four should be dark like me.

Kayle let the phrase roll around in his head a few
dozen times that day. Then he went to a bar and had a
few beers, sipped them through a straw, and tried to
imagine how he *really* felt about the kids not being
his. About them being Aaron's.

Of course, he'd been purely *tickled* first time he
heard it: figuring he wouldn't have to support Erica
and her bastards. Him and Lorraine could live real
good on what he made—not even counting his second
job; the one Erica didn't approve of. Bitch! Always
tellin' him what to do and how to do it. And all the

time, here she was, layin' his best friend . . .

Well, to be honest about it, Aaron had only just become his best friend this past year. Erica, however, had been best friends with Aaron for at least eight years! Maybe nine.

How could she do this to him? Making love with him and then runnin' off to meet Aaron someplace; layin' in his arms and probably tellin' him what a good lover he was too. Playing both of her men like an old fiddle. Then, when Kayle thought it over, Erica had never said anything good after he was finished with her. Maybe Aaron was better in bed. Otherwise, she would've had him once and stopped.

Bitch! How many others did she have, he wondered? Did she pass herself through every hand in town? And all the while she was living with him and actin' like his wife, without a formal ceremony of course, and takin' his money every payday just to feed someone else's kids! Man, that pissed him off!

How could she do such a thing? And when, if ever, did she intend to tell him? Makin' him feel like those kids were his. It was always "Daddy this," and "Daddy that," like he was some kind of fool. And he was, or at least had been.

Four out of your five kids should have dark hair. Or was that three out of four?

He was so angry and confused, he couldn't recall how it went. And the beer wasn't helping any. Erica was sticking it to him but good. Look how she'd managed to very nicely extract him from his own house, probably so she could have Aaron move in! First she'd fucked with the wall—made it move so it scared him. Then she fucked with his Atari set—made it move so it angered him. Then she fucked with his brain and conjured up that Nick, and made him move so he'd whip Kayle's ass.

And to think he'd really loved her. Had his heart set on spendin' the rest of his life with her. And what's more, he loved those kids, too. Why, even now, knowin' they weren't his, it hardly made a difference. He still loved them . . .

And six of them should've had red hair!

He glanced down at the bar and realized he must've drank an awful lot. He'd laid a fiver down when he first came in and all he had left now was a bill and some change. At fifty cents a glass, that was *mucho* beer. He laughed at that.

"Hit me again," he told the barkeep. "And please, a clean straw."

Two of his kids should've been bald!

Kayle sat there for a few hours longer, allowing his seeds of anger to nurture themselves and take firmer root in his muddled brain. The nerve of that Aaron Pace! To just, nice as can be, walk up, and casually lay somethin' like that on him: your kids are mine! He wondered what kind of a reaction Aaron had expected. Then he smiled because it had been too perfect for words. He'd given it to Aaron, thrown the ball in his court. He told Aaron to support his own children. Kayle was finished handin' out the food stamps.

But then, it wasn't really Aaron that he had the quarrel with: it was Erica. Hell, any man will take a lay when it's offered. He did himself at times. Layed 'em all, big and small. No, it wasn't Aaron's fault. It was that sassy bitch who wrapped herself in foil to preserve the good so's she could hand it out to any man with a jigger between his legs. Oh yeah! It was Erica's fault! And Erica wasn't gettin' away with it— no how!

Kayle didn't remember much of the trip over. All he could remember was that he'd gotten into his car, started it up, and the little demons in his brain took over: drove him straight to Erica's. And to tell the truth, he wished he did remember more, 'cause then he'd know why he was layin' outside of his own house, with bloodstains on his clothes.

Then he wondered if the blood was his, but it must've been. His body hurt like hell, all over. He got to the feet and staggered to the car. Once inside, he just sat and stared at the house, trying to figure out what happened.

He had a knife . . . Yeah, he did. It was that filetin' knife he used for fishin'. He usually kept it in the car 'cause it was awful sharp and he didn't want the kids —*Aaron's kids*—playin' with it when he wasn't home. He went after Erica with that knife—

And the kids. They tried to stop him. And he was afraid of hurtin' them at first, 'till he remembered they weren't his kids anymore. He had Erica on the stairs, he'd pushed her down and was layin' on her, tryin' to stab her and tryin' not to think about how excited she was gettin' him at the same time. He wanted to get in a few good shots with his knife and wound up stabbin' the wall.

Someone howled when he did that: like the wall was alive and not made of plaster board. Kayle shuddered and forced it out of his mind as though it never happened. Walls don't howl!

What mainly upset him though, was how the kids had interferred. Like he was a stranger now that he and Erica were through. And that's how they made him feel—like someone who didn't belong and perhaps never did.

Todd came runnin' down the stairs and jumped over him, he recalled, when he'd been layin' on top of Erica. And Todd pulled his hair to make him stop. Then he seemed to recall chasin' Todd while Erica pounded on his back to his attention away from the boy. Real tricky bastards they were. Everyone was tryin' to get him away from someone else, and hittin' him to do it. They all took turns, her and them kids.

Then Kayle recalled chasing behind Erica, with the knife still in his hands, when she ran upstairs to her bedroom. And all the while she kept yellin' somethin' . . . Somethin' about *Paul* bein' in her closet, and *Paul* would save her. Shit! Now she was hidin' them in her closet. And he wasn't positive at this point, if it had been this Paul or someone else, but he sure took a pastin'. Some guy beat the shit out of him good and proper.

He looked at the house again and wondered why he'd gotten so drunk. If he'd been sober when he came here, he would've stood a better chance. Next time, he'd be sober! Kayle started the car and peeled out when he left the curb.

Erica was still crying when the phone rang. Paul was upstairs, so the decision to ignore the phone was hers—totally! It could've been Kayle for all she knew. That maniac! Then again, what if it was Mary? She'd been trying, without success, to reach her mother all day.

"Hello," she said and realized she had the sniffles. Whoever this was, they had to know she was crying.

"Hi, babe . . . It's Aaron. . . Something wrong? You sound like you're upset."

She didn't really want him to know about Kayle. Paul had beaten Kayle enough as it was. But if she lied, and said she was crying because she was lonely, instead of shaken up, Aaron would come running over. And Paul wouldn't like that!

"Erica! Answer me. What's wrong?"

She had no choice but to tell the truth. "Kayle was just here . . ."

Aaron said nothing at first. But she could hear labored breathing on the other end. He was angry. "What'd he do?" His words were tight and clipped: he must've had his teeth clenched. Then she found it odd that his breathing was so intense and so loud that she could've been listening to two people instead of just one.

"He tried to kill me. . . And the kids—"

"He's dead! Wait'll I get 'im!"

"No . . . Aaron, please. There's been enough . . .

Paul was here. He took care of—"

"Oh, I see. You got Paul now, so you don't need me."

That's not true, she wanted to say. But Paul was upstairs. Maybe he was listening, although not necessarily reading her mind because he was so far away. "Oh . . . I wouldn't say that." Again she heard that same labored breathing. But if Aaron understood her —the meaning behind her message—he shouldn't have been angry.

He was silent again, then. "What you mean is . . . You can't talk. At least not over the phone."

"Exactly."

"I get it . . . Listen, babe. Hang in there. Things'll be different in a few days 'cause I'm moving in . . . Soon as I get a coupla matters taken care of. Then Paul can take a walk for himself. By the way, you ain't afraid of Paul, are you?"

"No. Not really," she lied and prayed it sounded like the truth. Aaron must've been more relaxed; she heard him laughing under his breath. "I'm not afraid of Paul."

"Fine. Just so long as we got that straight . . . Now, I have another idea. How would you like a dog?"

"A dog?" She wasn't sure she'd heard right the first time. Suddenly, there was an awful lot of static on the line. "Did you say a dog?"

"Yes. A dog . . ." His voice sounded peculiar, as though he was surprised by his own suggestion. "Funny I just now thought of it. . . Anyway, at this point, there's only one that comes to mind. You see, after I get rid of Paul, suppose I'm at work and Kayle shows up again . . . He's been acting like a psycho lately . . . Who're you gonna have to protect you then? So, I was just now thinkin' . . . If I buy you a doberman, Kayle's gonna have his ass chewed to pieces if he comes around and starts anything . . ." His words trailed off making Erica think he was still amazed at his own idea.

She'd never given much thought to owning a dog, not with small children around, and especially not a *Doberman*. It was just too dangerous to consider. But Aaron was right. What if she were alone and Kayle showed up? This time he'd had a knife. Next time he might get to use it.

"You don't have to say yes or no just now," Aaron said. "Let me bring one over tomorrow and see how it works out. Okay? Meanwhile, I'll start putting my things together and get ready to move in. If that's what you want."

"Yes. Please do." She heard his laughter again, just before the line went dead.

After he'd hung up, Erica held the receiver to her ear and wished it were him she was holding instead. She wanted Aaron's arms around her; she wanted to hear him whispering in the night—

"ERICA? ARE YOU STILL THERE?"

The receiver was like a hot potato in her hand; she almost dropped it. Paul's voice had come over the other end of the line and she didn't know how. There was no extension upstairs!

"I HEARD THE ENTIRE CONVERSATION. EVERYTHING THAT WAS SAID BETWEEN YOU AND THAT AARON PACE . . . AND I'M COMING DOWN TO DISCUSS IT—"

Her heart jumped in her throat. All this time she'd been worried about Paul reading her mind, or somehow overhearing her conversation with Aaron. So she'd given Aaron little hints about what was going on, and Aaron understood and openly responded. But it was all for nothing because Paul had been listening to them firsthand, directly over the phone. And she didn't know how . . .

She hung up the receiver and sat down at the kitchen table to wait for Paul. In her heart she kept wishing the doberman were here with her now.

22

Aaron Pace woke up early the next morning and remembered something awful: he'd promised to buy Erica a doberman! God! What had possessed him to even think of buying such a dangerous dog? They were nervous and skittish and had always scared him a bit.

Why, only the month before hadn't he read an article in the paper about dobermans? Some woman bred them—had a load of showdogs—and she kept two of them in her bedroom. Good for her, he'd thought at the time. But the dogs turned. One night they got mean, and nobody will ever know why because the old woman was found dead, in front of her door, like she was trying to escape with her life. At least that was the given impression.

The two dogs were standing over her, guarding their kill. After they were shot with tranquilizer guns and carted off to the pound, the police finally got a look at the body. And shit! There were gouge marks all over where the dogs must've taken turns biting her and bruises, especially around the throat area.

He shuddered and wondered again why he'd suggested a doberman. It was like his mind wasn't his own when the words came through his lips. And not only that, but he'd suddenly had a vision of a particular dog. The old man who owned the gas station where he worked bred dobermans. And he had this real nasty one. "A good watchdog," the old man had said, singing the praises of that beast to high heaven.

But it shouldn't have been to high heaven. The use of that phrase and thinking about the dog at the same time was totally absurd! And yet somehow Aaron knew he was the one to buy for Erica. In fact, the compulsion was so strong—and unexplainable—he could hardly wait to get his hands on Blue Diabolus, the dog's legal name.

Aaron had some helluva job getting the dog inside of Erica's kitchen. The damn thing seemed to have a mind of its own, and a strong one at that. It kept heading for the den. And hell, he thought, there wasn't a thing in there yet, no furniture, nothing. Just an empty room. Erica was still trying to decide if it should be a sewing room or a spare bedroom.

It sure was puzzling that the dog was so attracted by an empty room. Erica was puzzling also. Her looks had changed again. The dark circles had gone and the dowager's hump. She looked pretty good.

"Hello, there," Erica said when she saw the dog. "You're a beauty. What shiny black hair you have." She was trying to make friends, but there was a strain in her voice, one that told him she was afraid of Blue.

"He'll settle down in a minute or so," Aaron said looking around. "Where's Paul? It's funny not seein' him here . . . Hanging onto you as usual." He saw tiny lines form around her mouth and knew she was angry and was holding back. Then he looked down at his fingers, although he tried hard not to.

"Paul's gone," she said dryly. "He was upset because I told him you were moving in."

"Oh, ain't that too bad. You hurt his feelings and he left." Aaron was still struggling with the dog, trying to hold him still. In exasperation, he dropped the leash and watched as the dog ran for the den and plopped down outside the door, as though he were standing guard. "I think he likes that room. Must be somethin' about it that catches his fancy."

Then Aaron turned his attention to Erica. "I don't wanna discuss Paul now. He's gone and that's it! I gave my landlady the word, told her I was movin' in a few days. I got some things to settle . . . and I'm coming here . . . for good."

With that, he pulled out his wallet and extracted a few, crisp, one-hundred dollar bills and handed them to Erica. Her eyes grew wide with amazement. Aaron had never offered her money in the past. But then, she'd always had Kayle to support her. "Take it," he said. "There'll be more."

"Where did you get it? I don't want to take everything."

"I got some savings," he said and diverted his gaze as though he were embarrassed by her display of what he took to be gratitude. "I gotta go now. I gotta get to work. Uh . . . There's a bag of food for Blue Diabolus—"

"Blue Diabolus? What an odd name for a dog."

"Well, you can change it, you know. Dog'll get accustomed after a while. Anyway, I put the bag in the back yard. Figured you'd want to feed 'em out there."

He kissed her quickly and left. No need to overdo the affection at this point. She was his now, totally and forever. There was plenty of time for extended embraces, and not on the sneak either. He climbed into his car and started to pull away from the curb when he felt eyes watching him.

He looked up and swore he saw someone standing in the window on the second floor, in Erica's bedroom. And damned if it didn't look like Paul. He fought the urge to examine his fingers and stared at the window and wondered if he was crazy or what. He was staring at a darkened shadow, an illusion almost, something lightweight and airy: ethereal.

Then he shook his head and figured it must've been
the way the sun was hitting the window. It had to be.
There wasn't really anyone there, at least not anyone
he could point to and call by name. Christ, it sure was
odd. That house was odd, and sometimes it gave him
the willies. But, since he'd be spending the rest of his
life there with Erica, he had to shake that feeling of
. . . what . . . being scared? And fast!

Sam loved the dog to pieces. A big, full-chested dog,
whose body narrowed down when it got close to its
stubby tail, it reminded him of a horse. 'Course,
horses didn't have short ears that stood at attention,
or stubby tails and horses usually had kind eyes. But
Aaron said the dog was just actin' skittish, and to
ignore anything he read in its eyes.

The dog was black, and somehow, Sam couldn't
remember what kind it was; except that the word
started like *Dober* or something of that order. He took
the dog out into the back yard and ran it until its wide,
muscled chest heaved for air. This was a dog he could
be proud of. When Mommy said they were gettin' a
dog, he was afraid for a minute there she had one of
them small, fluffy things in mind. A poodle.

But Blackie was different. Blackie was tough and
bold. And Blackie seemed to like him best of all the
kids, besides Katie that was. "Here Blackie, here
boy." Sam grabbed a stick off the ground and hurled
it into the air, then watched as Blackie jumped up to
catch it. Hell, that dog had wings, he thought. Lookit
how high he could jump.

"Sam." Erica called through the screen door. Sam
smiled and knew why she wasn't opening it. Erica
was afraid of the dog. "Will you feed Di—Uh . . .
Blackie for me? Please, honey?"

"Sure, Mom."

And Paul can help, he thought to himself. Paul was
standing by the side of the house where Erica couldn't

see him, and acting kind of sneaky. Probably since Mommy didn't want him hanging around anymore, and Paul had promised to leave because Mommy was real mad. But he broke his promise. Mainly because, as he'd told Sam, he "LOVED ERICA."

Geez his voice was deep.

Sam was in the process of feeding Blackie when Katie came out back. But Katie wasn't alone. She was talking to that imaginary playmate friend of hers, the one Sam couldn't see. And that made Sam nervous. It embarrassed him in front of Paul, too. He didn't want anyone thinkin' his sister was *nuts*.

"NOW THAT WE'RE ALL HERE," Paul said quietly, "IT'S TIME TO MAKE PLANS. AARON PACE IS MOVING IN SOON."

Katie smiled at her playmate, smiled at thin air, and that confused Sam. In fact, everything going on around him confused him. "What plans?" he wanted to know.

Paul smiled, and seemed amused, but Sam got nervous. Paul was weird at times, like when he smiled and somehow didn't mean it. Sam detected a coldness about Paul. "I LOVE YOUR MOTHER. AND I WILL HAVE HER. BUT IT MUST BE DONE IN SUCH A WAY THAT SHE REJECTS AARON PACE. I DON'T WANT TO TURN HER AGAINST ME. THERE'S TOO MUCH AT STAKE HERE."

"Then, why don'cha just go in and tell her," Sam said. "Why're ya pullin' all this?" He still didn't understand. But Paul smiled again and focused his gaze on Sam. And there was somethin' about his eyes that held Sam's attention. He couldn't stop starin' at them eyes. Sam was a bit shook when he heard voices in his head tellin' him things, but before he knew it, it was over and done.

"Do you understand now?" Katie asked.

Sam nodded his head and smiled. He smiled at Paul, then Katie, and finally Angelica. It was odd to think he could see Angelica now when he'd never

been able to before. Angelica was real nice. She was
pretty, too. Sam liked having all these new friends:
Paul and Angelica and Blackie. And Katie could
probably be considered a friend now too—if he was
willing to stretch it a bit.

Erica was alone and had time to think.

The scene with Paul had gone differently than she'd
expected it to. She remembered sitting in the kitchen
and dreading the idea of facing Paul, especially since
he'd overheard her conversation with Aaron. He
knew he was about to be replaced. At the time, she'd
also given thought to how Paul had been reading her
mind and stealing what little privacy she had.

Anger began to well up in her. She felt indignant!
Here was a man she barely knew, one who lived in
her closet, taking over her life. What was she—nuts—
that she was allowing this to happen?

"EXPLAIN YOURSELF, ERICA," Paul said, once
they were face to face in the kitchen.

"The hell I will! I don't have to explain anything to
you, pal. And as far as our relationship goes, friggin'
forget it! I took enough shit off Kayle for ten years. I
don't have to take it from you."

"LOOK AT ME, ERICA. LOOK INTO MY FACE
AND TELL ME YOU DON'T CARE."

"No! Everytime I look at you something funny
happens inside. You're not twisting me around
anymore, Paul. I want you to leave."

"I THOUGHT YOU LOVED ME."

"So did I. But since you've become such a bossy,
beligerent bastard who wants to run my life, I've
changed my mind. And, changing my mind is a
woman's perrogative."

"ERICA, I—"

"Don't say anything," she ordered. "Between you
and Kayle . . . You both seem to come from the same
mold. And I don't need it. Not anymore. Aaron is the
only decent thing that's happened to me in my whole

entire life. And Aaron's the man I choose! Not you!''
She turned to look at him and found it odd that he was
smiling. He wasn't crushed by her rejection.

''AND WHAT IF AARON DOESN'T WORK
OUT?''

''He will,'' she assured him. Aaron was different.
He didn't make demands on her life.

''YOU'RE SUCH A STRONG WILLED BITCH! UH
. . . THAT WAS MEANT AS A COMPLIMENT. AND
NOW, I'LL ASK AGAIN. IF AARON DOESN'T
WORK OUT, WILL YOU BE MINE—HEART AND
SOUL?''

There was something in the way he'd said ''heart
and soul,'' that disturbed her. But she let it go and
shook her head yes. Poor Paul, she thought. He'd be
waiting a long time to collect. She and Aaron were a
match made in heaven. And it was going to work this
time—come hell or high water!

Kayle didn't go to work that day. He was still hung
over from drinking and sore from getting beat up.
And he was mad as hell over those kids: how Erica
had lied to him. But, as he soon realized, Lorraine had
the day off, he shoved his anger to the back of his
mind, for the time being anyway. No use taking it out
on Lorraine.

They were having coffee in the kitchen. Lorraine
was at the stove, filling a plate with danish. He stared
at her in that filmy thing she was wearing and started
thinking how lucky he was when he had a sudden
inspiration. This was the woman he wanted to spend
an eternity with. She obviously loved him and the
way he took her in bed: rough and ready. And she
was not the kind to shack-up with a man on a long-
term basis.

So, if he wanted her, really wanted her, he had to do
something and fast.

Then he thought back to his mother and decided not
to make a hasty decision. After all, it was what she

did to his father, and his father having to marry her
and all that, turned Kayle against marriage in the first
place. Then he figured it was a good thing he hadn't
married Erica. Those kids weren't his and he wasn't
stuck supportin' them anymore. But, if Erica had a
ring on her finger—

"WHAT'RE YOU THINKING ABOUT, LOVE?"
she wanted to know.

"About how good you are for me and how I'm
startin' to really fall for you." He stopped and looked
into those crystal blue eyes and knew he was sunk.
This was a decent woman, one he couldn't afford to
risk losing. "Lorraine. Will you marry me?"

She said nothing at first. Insted, she turned her back
and asked, "WHAT ABOUT ERICA?"

"Well, you know we were livin' common law. And
after what I found out, I'll never . . . " His voice
cracked with the hurt.

"POOR, DARLING." She turned and ran to him.

He found a certain comfort in her arms. He buried
his head in the crook of her neck and cried as he'd
never cried before. When it was over, he kissed her
and felt it was time to bear all. He told her about his
mother and father, and about Nick. She rose at one
point and poured two fresh cups of coffee.

Kayle continued, telling her things he'd never told
anyone, Erica especially. Erica usually had somethin'
to say, somethin' negative. But Lorraine was
different: she could sympathize.

However, when he was nearing the end, he realized
he'd purposely omitted one thing: the truth about his
part-time job, the one Erica didn't approve of. He
wondered if Lorraine would feel the same.

Well, he thought, only one way to find out. He'd go
ahead and tell her. "Lorraine," he began, "I got me
this part-time job. Pays real well. Fact is, with this
extra income, you don't even have to work!" She
smiled and he was encouraged to continue. "The old
man who owns the station has me come back at night,

after it's closed. To strip down cars. New ones. I don't know where they come from and I don't ask no questions. All I do know is, the parts are worth a fortune, so I make a lot of money." He looked at her and begged for understanding.

"IS THAT IT?"

"Yeah . . ."

"AND YOU WERE AFRAID TO TELL ME? OH, KAYLE. IT DOESN'T MATTER WHAT YOU DO. I STILL LOVE YOU."

He rose and pulled her into his arms and made up his mind then and there: if he let her get away without marrying her, he was crazy.

Aaron figured there was no time like the present to begin his life with Erica: and tomorrow wasn't promised to us, and tomorrow he might be dead. So he quickly packed and was able to move in that very night, although it was late when he pulled up in front of Erica's. The lights in the house were off. They had to be in bed.

No problem, he told himself. He'd just leave his bags downstairs and go on up to Erica's room—which was his room now. He was in the process of taking his suitcases and dumping them on the sidewalk when he again felt eyes watching him. It was that same feeling he'd had earlier when he'd dropped the dog off. And for some reason, he could smell Paul. Yes, smell him like he was practically standing there beside him.

He fought the urge to look at his fingers and instead glanced up at the window on the second floor and saw nothing. The ethereal projection he'd imagined seeing this afternoon was no longer there. He smiled because the sun hitting the window had caused what he had seen. He'd known it all along, but he had to be sure.

The front door was unlocked, as though Erica had read his mind and knew he planned on moving in tonight. He started inside, but hesitated and looked back over his shoulder before closing the door. There were no cars at the curb. Whoever they had following him tonight sure was a slow-ass driver. But then, it took all kinds to make a coven.

Aaron stumbled in the dark, searching for a light—the wall switch near the front door wasn't working, something he'd have to fix—and was startled to see a pair of bright, shiny eyes focused on him. They were over near the door to the den. He blinked and saw they were still there. Then he glanced around to see if perhaps those eyes were really eyes or a reflection of light from somewhere outside hitting an object in the room.

It wasn't until he heard a low-throated growl, the kind only a dog can make, that he began to relax and smile. Nothing spooky here. Maybe those stories Mary told Kayle about the house, the ones she'd recounted when she'd been real excited and unable to stop herself, had been nothing more than Mary's imagination. Aaron stuck his hand out to pet the dog—

And realized it had been a mistake!

A horrible one!

"Blue Diabolus! Don't!" he screamed and pulled his hand back. But his movements were too slow, he'd taken too long, and the dog had taken off one of his fingers, right up to the second knuckle. Just like old times, he thought, and stared at the blood as though it would stop bleeding by itself. He felt he was back in the coven and had mutilated himself, cut off his finger to feed it to a crowd.

But no, he'd fed it to a dog!

The fucking dog was chomping and munching on his finger!

The greedy son-of-a-bitch had no intentions of sharing it with anyone.

He was startled when the overhead light went on with the suddenness of a shot from a loaded revolver.

Erica was there, at the top of the stairs, and like him, she was screaming.

Paul was there too, back in the shadows. No. Paul was *part* of the shadows. Aaron could barely see him. But he saw enough to notice that Paul was smiling, and the smile had a message to it: it said, "I TOLD YOU SO!"

"You should've stayed at the hospital," Erica said once they were home again. It was close to three in the morning and from the looks of things, it would be a while before she got to bed. "They wanted to keep you."

"Yeah, well . . . I decided I'd be better off here. Although I can't imagine why." He sat down and stared at his heavily bandaged finger while Erica just watched him. That last remark wasn't called for.

"What makes you uncomfortable about living here? You were so anxious to move in, hell, you couldn't wait until—"

"Where's the dog?"

"Probably in with the kids." She felt herself soften then. Aaron had been through a lot, he only said what he did because he was still stunned, she imagined. "Why don't you go to bed?"

"After a while . . . Look, I wanna talk. I made a mistake bringin' the dog here. And thank God, he attacked me and not one of the kids."

He went into the kitchen and came back with two beers. Erica felt herself stiffen. This was like old times, except Aaron wasn't usually nasty when he was drinking. And right now, she could use something in the line of a drink herself. Then she remembered the pain killers in her purse. "Before you touch the beer, they gave me some pills at the hospital."

"Forget it. I never take drugs. I'll use the beer instead." He quickly drank from his and continued. "Now, like I was sayin', tomorrow I think I should get rid of that dog—''

"Oh, Aaron, you can't. The kids are so attached—''

"Do you see what he's done?" he asked, pointing his bandaged finger at her. His voice had suddenly risen. Was he in shock or angry, she wondered? "Isn't this enough? You wanna wait until—'' There was a movement upstairs! He saw the dog and stopped talking. Erica followed his gaze and jumped to her feet.

"Sam! Get up! Sam! Come and take Blue into your room,'' she said and noticed the panic in her voice. She was afraid of the dog too, but wouldn't get rid of it. If Kayle showed up now and she was alone . . .

"Blue?" Aaron wanted to know. "What happened to Blackie?''

There was something about the look on his face—suspicion—that's what she saw. But why? "I told Sam the dog's real name. And he and the other kids liked it better. That's all. Aaron, what's wrong?''

Aaron saw another movement and realized it was Sam. He looked up and smiled, then cringed inside when Sam smiled back. "Fucking weird,'' he mumbled. "Paul and Sam . . . And Katie. Fucking weird people.'' He watched Sam take the dog and go back into the room. Then he heard the door close and felt safe.

"Did you say something, Aaron?''

"Uh . . . No. I was just thinkin' out loud.'' He was still in a daze from having lost his finger. He looked down at it and stared as if it were just incredible that it was gone. "Paul had something to do with this.''

"Paul seems to be taking the blame for everything lately.'' That wasn't fair, and she knew it. A low blow, struck when the man was down. And frankly, there were times when she'd felt like Aaron: that Paul was responsible for a lot. Aaron was sitting now, quietly drinking his beer. She decided that enough had been said for one night and left matters alone. "Finish your beer, and come to bed.''

"You go on without me. I got some pain killers to drink."

She started upstairs, but something Aaron said after that stopped her. "Say hello to Paul if he's hidin' in your bedroom. And tell him I ain't afraid of him. That's why I came back." It wasn't the beer talking; he hadn't drunk that much yet. No, there was another reason for this.

"What's on your mind?" she wanted to know and turned to face him.

"Oh, nothing." Then he lowered his head as if he couldn't look at her. "Don't listen to me . . . I'm still upset . . . There're things I never told you, things connected with losing a finger. It just shook me real bad, worse than it would most people. Please go to bed, baby. I'll be up in a while."

Erica said nothing and went on upstairs. Aaron was asking for understanding. He was hiding his past— boy was that an old familiar story—and expecting her to act as if she knew what was going around inside of his head. Jesus! Just like Kayle! She felt anger welling. She seemed to have a knack for picking the same type of man over and over again. This was getting monotonous.

Kayle had hidden things from her, as had Paul. Now Aaron said he was doing the same thing. She sighed and quickly undressed. What was it about her that made them hide the truth concerning the past? Did she appear insensitive or stupid, that she was unable to comprehend? And now, Aaron was dumping on her, insulting her, because of his own hidden personal problems.

Erica was damned if she was going to stand for this hiding things bit and be a dumping post for everyone at the same time.

Then something else came to her and she felt her anger peak. Aaron was attacked by a dog he'd bought to protect her from Kayle! Sort of poetic justice. Why didn't *he* protect her from Kayle? Why didn't *he* beat the shit out of Kayle and tell him to keep his distance? Paul did. What was Aaron, some kind of a wimp that he couldn't settle this like a man? And then to criticize Paul—

"I TRIED TO WARN YOU ABOUT AARON. BUT YOU WOULDN'T LISTEN."

She felt her heart pounding heavily in her chest. Paul had come out of nowhere. And after he'd promised to stay away, too. She rose to confront him, then realized her heart wasn't pounding because she was angry. It was more in the line of passion. She walked to him and put her arms around his waist, hoping he'd get the message. But he pushed her angrily away.

"YOU THROW ME OUT FOR THAT FAG DOWN-STAIRS . . . AND NOW, BECAUSE HE CAN'T PERFORM, YOU WANT ME TO? GET LOST, ERICA!"

She was shocked! She'd imagined Paul would love her no matter what. After all, wasn't that what love was all about: tolerance and understanding? "Paul, please . . . Don't be angry."

"I DON'T WANT TO HEAR IT."

She stood and was silent for a moment, then, "Didn't you say you'd be waiting if it didn't work out between Aaron and me? Weren't you the one who promised to love me forever?" The words echoed in her brain. He'd vowed to love her with the same lusty affection as Aaron Pace. Well now, she thought, here's his chance and he's backing down. Paul was just like the rest. *Another asshole she didn't need.*

Paul's hand lashed out and connected with her jaw. She was knocked to the ground. And yet, somehow she wasn't a bit surprised by his actions. They'd all hurt her one way or another. She laid there and tried not to cry. This bastard wasn't getting the best of her.

Erica didn't recall too much after that, except Paul attacked her with a ferocity she'd never experienced in her life. There were open-handed blows and fists coming at her from all directions, as if more than one person was involved here. The bites were the worst. After he was finished and had gone, she examined her body and saw the teeth marks. They looked like they'd been administered by an animal of some sort: a dog—several dogs.

She laid across her bed and tried not to think. There had been three men in her life thus far, and all of them had the same intentions: they wanted to hurt, to dole out pain, be it physical or mental. She closed her eyes and felt herself drifting off to a troubled sleep. And it was the oddest thing. The bruises on her body, the bite marks, suddenly stopped hurting as if they weren't there.

Someone climbed in next to her—

She felt the water bed heaving with their weight—

Was it Aaron?

"HAVE YOU LEARNED YOUR LESSON? DO YOU KNOW NOW WHAT I CAN DO IF YOU CROSS ME?"

She opened her eyes and saw Paul. His face was different though, not twisted with anger and rage. It was soft, sort of mellow.

"IT DIDN'T HAPPEN, ERICA. IT WAS AN ILLUSION," he said and covered her lips with his.

Paul waited until she was asleep to slip out of bed. There were two people he had to take care of. Aaron was the first. Aaron was bolder than Paul had given him credit for. A suggestion had to be implanted while Aaron was drunk. One that he would remember, but not quite. Like the finger suggestion. Aaron would be afraid and not really know why. Then he'd leave and Paul wouldn't have to kill him. Hell, Aaron was just too much of a bastard to enjoy doing away with.

The second person Paul had to see was Carol Anderson next door. Only, that visit wasn't business, that was strictly for pleasure. Carol had surprised him the first time he'd taken her to bed. She'd struck Paul as being so meek. Well, he thought, one should never judge by outward appearances alone, and that made him smile.

23

Erica was mowing the lawn when the children came home from school. The grass had gotten so high in the few short weeks she'd been in the house; it was starting to look shabby. At one point, she heard someone calling and stopped to wave at Carol Anderson next door. Carol was smiling, but the smile was real, not the automatic masklike gesture it usually was. There was something different about her; she was glowing, happy. Her old man must've taken a powder too, Erica surmised, and laughed in spite of herself.

Then she wondered if Carol was as happy as she, and quickly decided it was impossible. Erica had Paul! And Paul was the fulfillment of her dreams. She was thinking about last night and how he'd made love to her and how wonderful it had been, when the kids came down the block and brought her back to the present.

"We're expecting company. So put your books—"

"Who is it, Mom?" Sam wanted to know.

"A friend of Paul's. Her name's Kirsten Larsen, or something like that. She called today and Paul said to let her come over. We have to be nice to her, you hear me. No matter what she does or what questions she asks, we have to be nice."

She watched them run into the house and realized she was just about talking to herself. Well, they'd better be listening, she thought angrily. She'd gone to the trouble of emphasizing the *nice* part because four children together, in the same house, sometimes was a nasty combination. Either they fought or they picked the right time to show their stuff—like when you had company—and it was embarrassing.

Paul came out then and took the mower from her hands. He told her to go freshen up while he put it away. As he was walking to the back of the house, Erica saw him wave at Carol. There was a silent exchange between them and something not right about the way they stared at each other. Erica decided she'd have to speak to Paul.

"Mom," Todd began as soon as she got upstairs. "Tell Sam to leave Aaron's suitcases alone. He wants to put them in the closet."

"Aaron will be here tonight to pick them up. So leave them alone, okay? Or better yet, let's put them in my room."

Aaron had changed his mind and decided not to move in. He'd support her and the kids, he'd said, but left without saying another word—except that he'd be back to pick up his things. At this point, though, excuses and explanations weren't necessary. It was because of the dog.

"Where's Blue?" she asked Todd. He was helping her carry Aaron's suitcases to her room.

"Chained up out back."

"Make sure he stays there. Okay?"

Kirsten Larsen showed up an hour later and the effect was stunning. Erica was mesmerized. She had long, thick, auburn hair, and crystal blue eyes, and long lashes and even longer finger nails painted fire engine red. And yet, it wasn't her outward appearance that was so attracting. It had more to do with her mannerisms and the way she carried herself.

Erica sensed that Kirsten was special.

"Henry Wittaker asked me to drop by," Kirsten said, once they were settled.

"Henry Wittaker? You mean before he died?" But Paul told Erica he invited her over. She tried to remember Paul's exact words.

"Yes. Henry made the request before he died. He was a dear friend," Kirsten said, her eyes glossing over. "Actually we met through his wife."

Erica was only half listening. She was still trying to figure this out. Then Kisten's next statement brought her to.

"Bess spent close to a year in the hospital with me."

Bess and Henry again, she thought. Why were they somehow connected with her . . . and Paul. "Uh. . . I'm sorry to hear you were in the hospital for so long. Were you very ill? I know she was."

"It was . . . Uh . . . I had an automobile accident. But I'm okay now."

That was odd, Erica thought. She didn't really sound convincing. "May I ask you why you're here today?" She wanted to mention Paul, but didn't.

"I came to see you because . . . I don't know where to begin. It all seems so incredible. But please bear with me. I'll start at the beginning, at the point where I came into this."

She listened as Kirsten continued and tried to remain calm, even when the subject of the house arose. Henry had gone to see her before she died, and had told her about the strange goings on here. And while she didn't say it outright, Kirsten hinted that Henry's death had something to do with the house, as did Bess' and Buddy's deaths.

Erica listened intently, but found her mind drifting back to the tape from Todd's birthday and the statements made about Henry and how *they* killed him and Bess and Buddy, too. Patricia, she gathered, was the only lucky one of the bunch: she was merely cut loose, whatever that meant.

While Kirsten talked, she showed Erica one of the
many pieces of equipment she'd brought with her.
"This is a biofeedback machine. The cuff attached to
it goes around my arm and feeds impulses—my
impulses—back to the machine. In other words,
anything I feel that upsets the natural balance of my
system. You know, anything strange. The dial on the
machine records those impulses for me to analyze
later. Uh . . . I wanted to bring a tape deck to see if I
picked up—"

"A tape deck?" Erica felt herself drain white.

"Yes. If there are any entities present, the tape will
pick them up. You can't always hear them with the
naked ear. But a cassette tape is ultrasensitive, so
you'll catch them on there. However, it was either the
bio equipment or the recorder. I can't carry too much
at once. So, I'll have to come back if you have no
objections."

Erica nodded silently and thought about her own
recorder, but never offered the use of it to Kirsten.
She couldn't. Not now. Not when there might be
some truth to what Kirsten had said about the house.
She remembered the voices on her tape; how they'd
gotten there had been a mystery until Kirsten
explained it. And again, she felt Paul was somehow
involved with the house and the strange goings on
Kirsten wanted to expose. But . . . It was at Paul's
suggestion that she'd allowed this woman to come
here. What the hell was going on, she wondered?

"First of all, I'd like to speak to the children. Then,
when it gets darker in here, I'd like to take some
pictures—"

"Pictures?" This was all very puzzling to Erica.

"Yes. In the dark, without a flash. If they're here,
they'll show up on film."

Erica rose numbly and called the kids from the foot
of the stairs. She'd been right about this house, only
now it seemed the problem was far worse than she'd
originally imagined. And, continuing to ignore what

was happening wouldn't make it stop. There was
something else she had to face as well. Paul was the
core of the evil here. Paul! Her lover, the man she'd
waited a lifetime for.

The children were very cooperative, as Paul had
ordered them to be. Katie got right into it, telling
Kirsten about Angelica, then drawing pictures of
Angelica's music box, and writing names of her friends
—Assgar and Mindalius—on paper. Erica only then
realized that Katie was more involved with this house
than she should've been.

Erica had previously sensed that Katie's playmate,
Angelica, was a prodigy of the house. Especially after
she disappeared in a huff one day in the bathroom
when she'd been angered by Erica's refusal to be her
mother. Erica, however, had later dismissed the
incident from her mind, along with all the other
strange incidents. Erica had been so taken up with the
chore of juggling the men in her life, she wasn't able
to give proper attention to the horrors around her.
And now she was ashamed.

"Okay, children. Line up," Kirsten said. Erica came
to and noticed she had a camera in her hands. "I
promised to take their pictures first," she explained,
then added, "you don't have any objections, do you?"

"No," Erica said quietly and watched Kirsten
posing the childing, fiddling with her camera. After
all, Paul had said to cooperate, didn't he? And Paul
had been making eyes at the woman next door a
while ago, wasn't he? The bastard!

After taking pictures of the children, Kirsten asked
Erica to switch off the lights. "They'll show up better
if the films are taken in the dark with no flash." She
snapped five shots in rapid succession. "I'll take the
rest outside. I want some pictures of the front of the
house."

Erica looked out and realized that night had fallen.
This was spring, it got dark early. She turned to see
what Kirsten was up to, the lights were back on by

this time, and mutely watched Kirsten strapping on a cuff from the bio machine. Kirsten was working fast, too fast. She'd originally told Erica she hadn't wanted to take up too much of her time. However, as Erica now realized, Kirsten was nervous, her hands were trembling. It seemed as if she wanted to get the hell out of there as soon as possible because she was scared. Erica was numb with the shock of it.

"Before I forget," Kirsten began, "There's something important I have to say. Don't let anyone chant here."

"Chant?" What the hell was she talking about?

"I don't want to go into detail now. It's lengthy and there's no time to waste. However, I will say this. Chanting created the beasts, and chanting will make them stronger. So, if you know anyone who's involved in Witchcraft or Satanism—"

"Oh, no. I don't." Erica was horrified by her suggestion.

"Fine then."

Kirsten walked through the lower part of the house, as far as she could with the limits imposed by the cuff of the machine, and ran her hands along the walls. She seemed to be feeling for something, although Erica didn't know what. Her eyes were closed and she was mumbling as though in a trance, and then the strangest, most violent thing happened. She was in front of the door of the den, had her hands on it in fact, when the cuff began smoking, burning her arm. Kirsten went into shock. Erica shuddered when the dog howled out back. She ran and tore off the cuff and saw—

The numbers 3 and 6 were branded into Kirsten's flesh. "It means three sixes," Kirsten moaned, "The mark of the master beast himself." She ran then, packed up her belongings and headed for the door, fear written on her face. But then she stopped and looked around, and reached for Erica.

Erica could feel her body trembling violently when

she held her in her arms and whispered. "Don't be afraid. I'll be back." Then she left.

The children were in bed, Erica made sure of it before she allowed the shock to lift and be replaced by anger. Paul had fucked her—twice. Both last night and now, when she'd discovered the truth. Paul was a user. Well, she'd be damned if he was about to use her any longer.

She was sitting in the living room with the recorder in front of her when Aaron knocked on the door. She'd been trying to work up the courage to walk into that den: whatever was in this house, the den was its roost. After all, nothing had happened to Kirsten Larsen until she'd been standing outside of that room. Erica wanted to run a tape in there and see what showed up.

"I came for my suitcases," he said when she let him in and kept his head down. He couldn't look at her. "I can't stay here, and I hope you understand why."

"I do. And now if you'll excuse me, I have something to take care of." It was all very formal between them, and Erica liked that just fine. She picked up the recorder, anxious to begin now since Aaron was there. If anything happened, he could help. Or could he, she wondered?

"What're you doin'? What's going on?"

Erica was annoyed with him. Here he was leaving—but she hadn't cared when he'd told her because she had Paul—and yet he still wanted to stick his nose in her business. However, at the moment, Aaron was the only safe factor in her life. She faced him squarely and explained about Kirsten Larsen's visit, and what had been discovered. Her fears had become reality, and she told him what happened to Kirsten as well.

When she finished, Aaron wasn't doubtful or frightened: the mixed reactions she'd expected. Hell no. Aaron was angry! "Why didn't you level with me

before I came here? Why didn't you tell me what was
goin' on? You just let me walk in as though nothin'
was wrong?''

What a nerve, she thought! He was more worried
about himself and his own feelings than he was about
her and the kids. ''I wasn't sure! Or maybe I was and
wouldn't accept it. Whatever. Anyway, it's
happening and it's for real.''

''That woman. That bitch! You actually called in a
stranger . . .''

Erica started to say something in her own defense
but he raised his hand to stop her. ''Excuse me. Poor
choice of words. Paul called her in. Is that how it
went?''

Erica shrugged helplessly. She really didn't know
how the story went. ''All I know is, she's a friend of
Henry Wittaker's—''

''The real estate agent? Well, now I'm here. So I'll
handle it.''

''Handle what? How?''

Aaron turned and looked at the den. ''I spent a few
years in California. Me and my wife. We belonged to
this church . . . Anyway, I know how to get rid of 'em
better than that bitch does. I know the proper words
to use.''

''You mean chanting?''

''If you wanna call it that. Yes, it's chanting.''

Erica couldn't believe what she was hearing. When
Kirsten Larsen had asked her if she knew anyone
who'd been involved in Witchcraft or Satanism, she'd
gotten angry and said no. She didn't know any
weirdos. And now apparently she was wrong.
''Kirsten said they were brought here through the use
of chanting. And more of that will only give them
strength—''

''Bullshit! That's how much she knows. I've taken
on Satan twice in the past and defeated him.''

He sounded like he was lying, but Erica didn't
question him. He was angrier than she'd ever seen

him before. "Aaron, please . . . What're you going to do?"

"I'm going in there." He pointed to the den. Then she saw his body stiffen and he walked to the door and laid his hand on the knob.

"Please don't—"

"Erica! I know what I'm doing!" Then he smiled and his face softened. "Give me the recorder. I'll lay it right outside the door."

Her hands were shaking, she noticed, when she gave him the recorder. Poor Aaron, she thought. Bandaged hand, or no bandaged hand, he was going in there. "You sit down and just relax," he told her. "And no matter what happens, no matter what you hear . . . Don't come into the den. I'll be comin' out. Don't worry about that!"

Erica walked back and sat on the couch and saw him open the door and walk into the den. Once he was out of sight, her heart thumped in her chest. She could hear him, although she couldn't hear everything. She caught words that sounded like "Satanus," and "Diabolus." Christ, Diabolus was part of the dog's name, the doberman he'd bought her: *Blue Diabolus.*

Aaron screamed—

And that scream was hideous—

Like nothing she'd ever heard before—

Except when the dog got him and he'd lost his finger!

She rose and wanted to run to him. But he'd said not to. He'd told her to wait. And wait she did, and found it odd that the children didn't come running. Were they so deeply asleep that they couldn't hear, she wondered? Her nerves were slicing through her skin with Aaron wailing those pitiful cries.

Then it stopped, as suddenly as it had begun. And someone approached the door: someone was coming out of the den, someone she couldn't see at first. Oh, God, let it be Aaron, she prayed, and it was. Only—

He was holding his hand, the bandaged one. Blood was dripping. And then she saw what it was: somehow, he'd lost another finger.

Sam and Katie were in Sam's bedroom with Angelica when they heard Aaron screaming and decided to ignore him. Why should they run just because he was in trouble. They had no reason to worry about Aaron.

Todd and Didi were in the bedroom next door, sleeping, if you wanted to call it that. Paul had suggested they lie down, and soon after, both drifted into a trancelike state. Sam got up at one point and glanced from the window—before Aaron screamed—to check and see if Paul was still next door. Paul had gone over to see Carol Anderson right after he'd put the lawn mower away. Carol had been out in her yard and had waved at Paul and over he went.

While Sam looked on, Paul hopped the fence and came back home and then Aaron started yelling his head off. It sure was puzzling what was going on with these grown-ups. Also puzzling was the whispering going on between Katie and Angelica. They kept saying things to each other, things he couldn't hear, and then they giggled. Jeez. Girls were a pain!

"Sam," Katie said and looked sideways at Angelica. "We have a new game to show you. One you're sure to enjoy."

I'll bet, he thought. If it was anything like the Circle of the Devil, he wanted no part of it.

"THIS ONE'S DIFFERENT," Angelica said as though she'd read his mind. "COME ON, SAM. DON'T BE THAT WAY. WHAT HAPPENED BEFORE WAS AN ACCIDENT." She rose and went into his toy box where she extracted a rope. "THIS ONE'S CALLED HANGMAN. IT'S A WORD GAME."

"Then why do you need a rope?" he wanted to know.

"The loser has to swing from it," Katie said and

quickly added, "but you won't get hurt. We promise—"

She stopped speaking when the door opened and Paul walked in. Paul sure had a hateful expression on his face, Sam thought, like he wanted to kill the two girls—Katie and Angelica.

"WHATEVER YOU HAVE IN MIND, FORGET IT!"

"YES . . . UH . . . WE'RE SORRY IF WE OFFENDED YOU." Angelica's voice was shaky. That puzzled the hell out of Sam. Katie, though, was a different story. She didn't seem to be afraid of Paul and spoke right up, hands on her hips, like the little bitch she was.

"We were doing this for you."

"REALLY? KILLING SAM IN MY NAME WHEN I DIDN'T ORDER HIS DEATH. IT WAS FOR ME, YOU SAY?"

"My death? They was gonna kill me? Shit! Oh, man!" He turned on Katie while anger welled inside of him. "Why were ya gonna do it, Katie? She's a stranger," he said and pointed to Angelica. "But you . . . You're my sister. Why?"

Katie was sassy and nasty when she answered. "Because if you keep going the way you are, you'll be stronger than me. You'll have more power. After all, you control the dog, and that took some doing."

"SO NOW," Paul began, "WE'RE ABOUT TO FIGHT OVER WHO'S THE STRONGEST, WHO'S IN CHARGE. THIS IS LIKE BEING HOME IN ACHERON AND LISTENING TO THE LESSER DEVILS ARGUING OVER POWER." He turned to Katie and melted her defiance with a glance. Sam saw her change before his eyes: she became nice and mellow. "HATE AND ENVY ARE ADMIRABLE TRAITS. YOU'VE LEARNED WELL. HOWEVER, SAM IS ONE OF US NOW, AND YOU NEVER TURN ON YOUR OWN. NEVER!"

"Then what about Todd and Didi," Katie wanted to

know. "Can I kill them? They're different. They're not one of us."

Paul smiled. "BLOODTHIRSTY LITTLE BITCH SINCE YOU HELPED KILL YOUR GRAND-MOTHER, AREN'T YOU?"

"You helped kill Grandma? She's dead—"

"YES, SAM. SHE DID. INDIRECTLY, BUT SHE HAD A HAND IN IT. NOW, KATIE, IN ANSWER TO YOUR QUESTION. LEAVE THEM ALONE, TOO. TODD AND DIDI WILL SOON BE COMING AROUND. THE ONLY ONE I HAVE TO WORK ON—REALLY WORK ON—IS ERICA. SOMEHOW OR OTHER I'M LOSING HER. I CAN FEEL IT."

"SHE STARTED ACTING FUNNY AFTER KIRSTEN LEFT," Angelica volunteered. "MAYBE YOUR PLAN BACKFIRED."

Paul knew Kirsten was coming here, and that nothing could stop her once she'd decided to take on a mission. So he'd used reverse psychology by telling Erica to welcome her and cooperate. He had hoped that once Kirsten was here, in the house, she'd appear ridiculous, with all her talk about demons and the house being infested with them, and her bio equipment. But Erica had listened and Erica changed. "I THOUGHT AFTER LAST NIGHT, AND WHAT TRANSPIRED BETWEEN US, THAT ERICA WAS MINE. NOW I SEE THERE'S STILL MUCH TO DO. ERICA IS ONE STUBBORN BITCH! I'LL SAY THAT MUCH FOR HER."

"Why was Aaron screaming?" Katie asked more out of curiosity than out of any real concern.

"AARON FANCIED HIMSELF A DEMON KILLER, WITH THE ABILITY TO DRIVE US OUT." Paul smiled at that. "I HAD TO TEACH HIM ANOTHER LESSON. NOW HE'S OUT OF ERICA'S LIFE FOR GOOD. PERHAPS THIS WILL MAKE MY JOB EASIER FROM HERE ON IN."

"Tell me, Paul," Sam began and smiled at Katie. But there was something wrong with his smile,

something awful about it. "If they try anything
again—Katie and Angelica—will you stop them? And
can I help?"

"OF COURSE, I'LL STOP THEM. YOU'RE
UNDER MY PROTECTION NOW. AS A MATTER
OF FACT, I'LL DESTROY THEM BOTH, AND, AS
YOU'VE REQUESTED, YOU CAN HELP." Paul
approached Sam and patted his head fondly. Sam, he
thought, was going to be on the same level as Erica,
when and if he gained control of her, that was. Oh
yes, Sam was going to be one of his best. He was sure
of it! "COME, SON. LET'S GO NEXT DOOR. WE
HAVE MUCH TO DISCUSS.

"FIRST OF ALL, YOUR GRANDMOTHER'S NOT
REALLY DEAD, IN THAT SENSE OF THE WORD.
RATHER, SHE'S BEEN SENTENCED TO A LIVING
DEATH, WHICH IS DIFFERENT."

Sam smiled and was obviously pleased.

Lorraine waited until Kayle got off the phone with
Erica to allow her emotions to show. "MRS. KAYLE
WALSH! I CAN HARDLY BELIEVE IT MYSELF."

Neither could Kayle. To think he'd actually put a
ring on some woman's finger. Then again, Lorraine
wasn't just any old woman. Lorraine was special. So,
he'd married her. And yet, there was something about
the ceremony he couldn't quite get over. "Who was
that guy who performed the ceremony? Boy, was he
ever weird."

"HE WAS A FRIEND OF MINE." She sounded
offended. "I THINK IT WENT VERY WELL."

Kayle wasn't about to argue the point and make her
mad at him, except, there was a difference in what
had been done and what he'd expected. "How come
we didn't need blood tests and a license? I thought it
was a law?" Lorraine had taken him to some little
church on the outskirts of town. Everything was so
weird: the interior of the place, the minister . . . even
the minister's voice.

"DO YOU HAVE A PROBLEM WITH THE LEGALITY OF OUR MARRIAGE?"

"No." But he was lying. Something was wrong here.

"YOU SEE, KAYLE," she began and almost laughed. "I COULDN'T ACTUALLY GO THROUGH WITH A CONVENTIONAL MARRIAGE. A BLOOD TEST AND A LICENSE WERE OUT OF THE QUESTION."

He got himself a beer and a straw. He silently offered Lorraine a drink, but she refused. "Why were those things out of the question?" And please stop smiling that way, he wanted to ask. She was making him nervous. She'd never acted like this before.

"BECAUSE MY BIRTH CERTIFICATE IS INVALID."

"Really? Why is that?" Somehow he didn't want an answer.

"BECAUSE I'M DEAD. AND HAVE BEEN FOR A LONG TIME."

Shock hit Kayle's brain with the force of a thunder clap. She was lying. No one could be dead and look as good as she did. So, why was she lying? That was his next question. However, before he could ask, something incredible happened. Lorraine changed— Kayle's blood iced in his veins when he saw the hollow sockets where there should've been eyes, the missing nose, the exposed teeth. He sat down and held onto the table to keep himself from fainting.

"DO YOU STILL LOVE ME, KAYLE? I HOPE SO, BECAUSE YOU'RE STUCK WITH ME. YOU'RE MINE—FOR ALWAYS AND FOREVER."

"Who are you?" he asked, turning away. He couldn't stand to look at her.

"THE FORMER LORRAINE PACE—"

"Pace!" He heard the name and died inside. This was Aaron's missing wife: the one he was alleged to have killed. While he sat there and tried to hold onto his sanity, Lorraine told him a story encompassing her life these past nine years or so. She'd been killed during a coven cememony, but had been resurrected to serve her master. And serve him she did. She was the devil's disciple, calling herself, "SATAN'S SISTER."

She was also the one who had been responsible for killing Henry Wittaker's two children, Buddy and Patricia. She'd been driving the car that went through the wall of the pizza joint where they'd been eating and discussing her friends. When she was finished, Kayle looked up at her, telling himself he wouldn't cringe, and discovered she was the old Lorraine again, the voluptuous beauty he'd fallen in love with.

Then he wondered if he'd fallen asleep and had been dreaming. But Lorraine let him know it was real; it had happened.

"YOU WERE MY NEXT ASSIGNMENT. I HAD TO GET YOU AWAY FROM ERICA . . . AND KEEP YOU AWAY!"

"Why?" This was a nightmare.

"BECAUSE THE GATE KEEPER WANTS HER FOR HIS OWN. AND YOU WERE AN OBSTACLE . . . AS WAS AARON. BUT HE'S BEEN TAKEN CARE OF NOW ALSO. HE'LL STAY AWAY."

He wondered if she'd kill him now that he knew the truth?

"NO, DARLING. I'LL LET YOU LIVE. BUT ONLY FOR AS LONG AS YOU CONTINUE TO SATISFY MY URGES. AARON NEVER COULD MAKE LOVE THE WAY I LIKED IT. BUT YOU . . . YOU'RE DIFFERENT. YOU LIKE IT ROUGH THE WAY I DO."

"And this marriage ceremony bound us together? Is that why you waited 'till now to tell me the truth?"

"IT WAS MORE THAN JUST A MARRIAGE CEREMONY. BUT YOU WERE TOO DUMB TO REALIZE IT AT THE TIME. YOUR SOUL WAS BLENDED TO MINE, BRANDED WITH MY NAME. YOU BELONG TO ME NOW, KAYLE—YOUR LIFE

AND EVERYTHING YOU STAND FOR.''

Kayle smiled at the irony: he'd always sworn in the past that no woman would ever get the best of him. Well, now it was done, it happened. And this one owned him—heart and soul. He smiled at that and felt his brain go soft. He was losing it!

"COME, DARLING,'' she said and reached for him. "IT'S TIME FOR BED. THIS IS OUR HONEY-MOON, REMEMBER?''

Erica didn't go to the hospital with Aaron this time. She couldn't not after the truth had been revealed. After all, someone had to stay with the children, to protect them from those beasts or whatever the hell it was they called themselves. So, she did the next best thing: she called an ambulance and had him carted away, hoping he'd understand.

After he'd gone, she knew she couldn't go to bed and fall asleep: she'd be leaving herself vulnerable to whatever evil they had in mind. She sat for a long time and stared at a noisy T.V. without really watching or listening to it. Her head was spinning, running wild with the things Kirsten had told her. And it was all true: Aaron had proved that—the hard way.

Aaron had sacrificed two fingers so far.

The dog had taken the first. The dog was one of *them!*

Everything came in threes. Everything bad, that was.

The recorder lay on the table in front of her. Should she? Did she have the courage to listen again? Aaron had laid it outside of the door to the den before going in there, so it had to be full of their voices and their hateful expressions. She was purely dying to play the tape. What's more, Paul wasn't there—he had some business to handle as usual and had gone out right after Aaron was taken away.

"ERICA," he'd said in his sexiest voice, meant to

entice her. "I'LL JOIN YOU IN BED WHEN I COME BACK."

Well, she thought, he needn't rush on her account. She didn't care if that bastard never came back! She snapped off the T.V., rose and went into the kitchen for a beer. Old Diabolus was watching her through the screen door leading out back. There was something about the lights—the red ones flickering in his eyes—that disturbed her. She closed the door and locked it, then wondered if this would really keep him out if he had an overwhelming urge to get in!

The recorder made a horribly loud noise when she rewound the tape. God! It was enough to wake the dead, she thought, then smiled and hoped not. Aaron's voice was the first she heard when she switched it on. "Glory, Oh, Satanus. I, your servant am here to employ the Keys of your Calling to beg for your mercy. I will employ the fifth and the tenth and use them to reverse themselves."

The Keys of your Calling? What the hell was he talking about? From there on, she was lost. Aaron began to speak in a foreign language, one that wasn't even familiar to her ears. It wasn't French, or German, or Russian. And, while he spoke, there were many background noises: the angry howling of beasts, the scorned laughter of many. Sounds were assaulting her ears, a cacophony of madness, unearthly sounds, rhythmic and hideous.

She stopped the recorder at one point because she feared going insane. This was awful. It was worse than the haunting that Kristen Larsen had described. It was like falling into a lair of beasts and being subjected to their tortorous ways. She drank her beer and went for another—*Diabolus was now tied to the kitchen table*, she noticed—then she returned to her seat and hit the "play" button. She didn't want to think about the dog, or how he'd gotten inside.

Paul's voice came through this time. And it was awful . . . scared her badly . . . turned her stomach . . .

Paul was having the time of his life with Carol
Anderson next door. Erica heard this and didn't
experience the same jealousy as she had this
afternoon. In fact, as far as she was concerned, Carol
could have him. Then Paul got around to her.

He wanted to control her, to possess her soul,
because by doing so, he felt he could possess others:
her children, for instance. And Paul was willing to
employ whatever methods possible to accomplish this
control. Paul had molded himself after someone
named "Zadarous, Lord of the Seventh Level of
Acheron." He'd copied his form, his hair, the color of
his eyes, and had then used them to beguile "those
female pigs; Erica and Carol."

Laughter rang in her ears and she felt used. How
could she have been so stupid as to let herself go crazy
over a man who lived in her closet. What was she, a
complete fool? An idiot?

But no, her weakness was more in the line of
loneliness. She merely wanted someone to take
Kayle's place.

Kayle! He'd called a while ago, when she'd been
waiting for the ambulance to take Aaron to the
hospital. He wanted to tell her that he'd gotten
married. It was like a knife in her heart: he'd never
considered marrying her, but had taken the vows
with someone he'd only just met.

He wanted Erica to sell the house. They owned it
jointly and he needed money. "Let Aaron buy you
one," he'd said in his usual sarcastic way. Well, she'd
been angry at the time. And frightened, too. Where
would she go with four small children? However,
when she thought about it now, Kayle's suggestion
was brilliant! She'd sell the house, and, using the old
proverbial expression, kill two birds with one stone.

She'd get away from the demon beasts, those who
really owned this house, and she'd be getting rid of
Kayle for once and for all. Once he had his money,
there would be no need to call.

Aaron's screams brought her back to the present. That was the part where they'd taken his finger. Then she heard growling and was amazed because it didn't seem to be coming from the recorder. It seemed closer, like in the same room with her . . .

Blue Diabolus was now tied to the leg of the table that was closest to the recorder. She could feel his breath—hot and foul—on her face. She stared at his teeth, at the way the overhead light glinted and reflected off of them, the slobber on his jowls. Then she looked into his eyes and saw DEATH! Slowly she rose from her seat and slid the length of the table, away from him.

She wondered how tightly the leash was fastened. Then she wondered if the dog would get her before she was safely in her room with the door closed. She took it one step at a time, one foot up, one down, and was suddenly on the stairs, climbing for all she was worth. She was almost there, almost in her room when the dog made its move, when lightning struck in the form of a broken leash and a hundred pounds of gnashing teeth—

She felt something warm trickling down her neck and knew it was blood, her blood. The dog's head was nestled beneath her chin and he planned on eating her throat—

"Blue!" Sam commanded, "cut it out!"

Erica laid back on the steps and watched the dog jump over her and fall beside Sam. That was odd, she thought, and smiled. At least she felt she'd smiled, but her mouth barely moved. There was a man in her life after all, one who'd been there the whole time, only she'd been too busy to know it. Sam was her protector now. Sam controlled the dog.

But . . . Sam was only five years old; hardly the age to really be considered a man . . .

24

There was a bounce in her step now, she noticed, when she strolled down Main Street to the camera shop. Her leg wasn't on fire with pain. Kirsten had taken on a new mission, and for no sound reason, it always made a difference. She became a new person, whole, with no time to dwell on her own disabilities.

She'd wanted to call Erica this morning, but had to see the pictures first. This way, she'd have something to report and Erica wouldn't feel as though Kirsten had wasted her time. There was another reason she didn't call. She didn't want to go another round with the monster on the phone. It surely wasn't Erica she'd been speaking to the first time she called. There was a distinct difference in voice and attitude between the real Erica and the phony who'd posed as her.

She never bothered to tell Erica about the phone call . . .

Maybe she should've . . .

But then, there were a lot of things she'd kept hidden: like those visits she'd made to the house in her dreams. And too, she never mentioned her own hauntings; how they were trying to keep her from revealing the truth, and exposing them.

Maybe she should've been more open . . .

After all, she'd gone to see Erica with intentions of

telling the story from the beginning: leaving nothing out. Then she skipped over parts and carefully edited her own words. But it wasn't done on purpose. Kirsten usually tried to feel out the family she was dealing with. And mostly, she'd found, the average person wasn't mentally equipped to handle more than a few revelations at a time. Like Erica: the poor woman was scared to death.

Surprisingly though, the children were doing well. They actually appeared to be happy and well-adjusted, which wasn't a bit unusual. In situations such as this, where there's a haunting and intended possession, the young family members somehow manage to escape unscathed. The entities were generally known to go after the adult members first and then tackle the children. Maybe there was still time; maybe it wasn't too late as she'd previously thought.

The camera shop wasn't crowded, she noticed, but there were several people ahead of her. And she had to wait for what seemed like forever before her turn came. Kirsten saw a note on the packet her pictures were in and stopped to read it while she waited for her change.

"Not possible to print on standard paper. High Baryta content paper was needed and used. Photos appear to have been processed in exhausted chemicals. Varied streaks of light and dark areas are typical of this type of processing mistake. However, we checked with the lab, and the error lies either with your camera, or, the negatives were exposed to light before processing."

Kirsten should've been used to this. But it was always a shock when she received notes with her pictures: something unusual was on that film! "Varied streaks of light and dark areas," she read again and felt herself tremble.

"I'd like you to look at those before you leave," the man behind the counter told her. "This way we can straighten out your mistake so it doesn't happen again." He started to wait on someone else, then hesitated. "What happened to your arm?"

Kirsten had put some burn cream and bandages over the numbers branded into her flesh. She hadn't intended for it to attract anyone's attention. "Uh . . . Grease splattered when I was cooking." Kirsten wished he'd just leave and not make a big thing of this. She wanted to examine the photos.

"You gotta be more careful," he said and walked away.

The pictures were shocking. In the first five, those she'd taken in the dark with no flash, there was a huge entity resembling a tremendous bulk of static electricity hovering in a doorway. The photos had been taken at one second intervals, and in each photo the entity grew and advanced farther into the room.

Outside of the door itself, two things disturbed her: a smaller, white, hot entity—probably that Angelica, the four-year-old had told her about—and Angelica's music box. Katie hadn't been dreaming or making it up when she'd drawn it on a slip of paper for Kirsten. And although the music box wasn't in the house, was no where to be seen, it showed up on film. It looked like a white, almost ethereal coffin.

The darker splotches, on closer examination, were ancient beasts of various shapes and sizes. But they all had one thing in common; each was more hideous and frightening looking than the next, if possible. There was a face! A human one! It was a light shade of gray and cloudy in appearance . . . But it was there, behind the other entities in the last picture, as though they were trying to protect whoever it was. This was a vision of someone that the entities had gone to the trouble of conjuring up, someone who wasn't present at the time.

The face was the size of the entire room.

The face had been handsome at one time. But when Kirsten took the picture, it was obviously starting to

distort. Was it the Gate Keeper in disguise, she
wondered? She shoved the five photos back into the
packet and reached for those she'd taken of the
children—

Oh, good, God! The two youngest . . . They
belonged, were one of *them*. Their faces were
hideously evil, almost demonic in appearance. And
the glow in their eyes, bright red, as if the fires of hell
were reflected in them. The other two, Todd and
Didi, had veils covering their faces. It wouldn't be
long now before they were part of the group, too.

The pictures she'd taken of the outside of the house
were no better. She didn't see the Gate Keeper—he
must've been too busy to show himself—but there
was someone standing in front of the window on the
second floor. Someone tall and broad, and, from the
looks of him, he was a horror. His face wasn't like anything she'd seen before—

"Do you know how it happened?"

Kirsten almost fainted when she looked up and saw
the owner of the camera shop standing in front of her.
Those pictures had really shaken her up. "No . . . I . . .
Uh . . . Never mind. It's all right."

He looked at her strangely and suggested she bring
her camera so he could examine it. "There might be
something wrong with the lens. Or maybe it doesn't
latch tightly enough when you insert the film. That
would account for over exposure."

She quickly shoved the packet of photos into her
handbag. She couldn't explain this: he'd never believe
her. Then again, it would be worse if he did. People
might find out that she'd come back: the wrong kind
of people. "I'll do that," she said, "I'll bring my
camera in. Thank you."

Once she was outside in the air and was able to take
a deep breath to calm herself, the message on the
outside of the packet came back to her. The one about
the varied streaks of light and dark areas. People were
such fools; like the people in the lab where the photos

were developed. Couldn't they see the truth, she wondered?

But then, they were just that: people, and average ones, too. They knew nothing about entities, demonic hauntings. However, if Kirsten ever met one of those darkroom technicians face to face, she'd tell them! If the light and dark areas had been caused due to some unknown mistake, either with the camera or the way the photos were taken, then how come the light and dark splotches were uniform? They were in the same exact location on each film. It would make more sense if they hadn't shown up as they did.

In other words, a splotch here, a splotch there. But no, her splotches were uniform. In all five photos, taken at one second intervals, the splotches never changed locale, and that scared the hell out of her because she'd been *right*.

Kirsten couldn't wait to call Erica. But it had to be done in such a way so as not to frighten her too badly. Still, she had to make it clear, somehow, that Erica's house was infested, and not with your average house pests. No. This was far worse.

Kirsten drove home, her heart skipping its usual beat: her own fears were causing this, she knew. And yet, she should've been used to this by now. This wasn't the first time she'd investigated a house, and it wouldn't be the last.

So . . . Why do you panic each time, she asked herself? But then the answer was obvious; she was only human. And somehow she'd never been able to harden her psyche to the point where she could calmly accept the sight of those beasts.

She drove up into the driveway of her home and saw the mailman shoving a small package into her box. She panicked again. Had they found her: those covens she'd been harrassed by years before? They always sent her small packages . . . But no, she thought, wait a minute. They left packages on her doorstep—never sent them through the mail.

The return address of this new package had Erica's name on it. She should've been able to relax when she saw it, but what if Erica hadn't actually sent this package herself? Those entities had imitated her voice over the phone. Perhaps they could imitate her handwriting as well.

She opened the front door and ran to the phone and quickly dialed Erica's number, praying with everything in her that Erica, herself, would answer.

"Hello." It was Erica. Thank God. But she sounded strange, rushed.

"Hi. This is Kirsten. How're you feeling today?"

"Fine . . . And I don't mean to be rude, but I can't talk long . . . I'm moving."

"Moving?"

"Yes. This morning I put the house up for sale . . . And the real estate office found me a rental I can live in until it's sold."

Kirsten couldn't speak. Erica was selling the house! Erica must've realized Kirsten had been telling the truth. But running wasn't the answer. And now Kirsten couldn't tell her about the pictures, not when the woman was frightened so badly she was leaving her home before it was even sold. There was no telling what the mention of those photos would do to her.

"Are you still there?" Erica wanted to know.

"Yes . . . Look, running won't make much of a dif-ference—"

"I'm not running! I'm moving!"

"Yes . . . Well . . . Don't take the furniture. Throw it away."

"What? Are you insane? It's all new."

"Please do as I ask . . . And, Erica . . . Pray to the Lord, Jesus Christ, for strength and He'll help you. Put your life in His hands." It was all she could suggest since Erica wasn't giving her the chance to call in help: the demonologists who could exorcise those beasts.

"I've never been very religious . . . But I'll try."

"Please do," Kirsten said, and held onto the receiver even after Erica had hung up. It was truly Erica that she'd been speaking to this time. Oh, Lord, please help her, she prayed inwardly.

"FUCKING HANG UP THE PHONE, BITCH!"

Kirsten slammed it down angrily without saying a word. Then she realized she'd forgotten to ask Erica about the package. She'd forgotten to ask if Erica was really the one who'd sent it.

Kayle hadn't gone to work for days now. Lorraine wouldn't let him. Every time he tried to leave the house, she'd grab him and drag him back to bed. He was exhausted, totalled out, just like an old wreck of a car. He tried to get away by asking her what they were going to live on if he didn't work. But Lorraine fixed him! She had lots of money in the bank: more than they could possibly spend over a lifetime. Her Master had taken good care of her.

He sat in the kitchen and sipped a beer. Jesus, he thought, lately he was getting to be one helluv an alky. Beer for breakfast, beer for lunch. But it helped dim the memories, helped erase the nightmares. And it seemed he had much to forget. His whole life had been one angry, terrible mess, starting with his mother, then Erica, and finally ending with Lorraine.

However, when he stopped to analyze the situation, his life with Erica hadn't been all that bad. Maybe she'd slept with Aaron and the kids weren't his, but Erica was good to him. She took care of him. He always had clean clothes, and a clean house and good meals. And she slept with him whenever he wanted her to, and she put up with his brutality in bed.

So . . . Why couldn't he see this before the party was over, before it was too late? Why didn't he use his head and dwell on the good things that happened between them? Why always the bad?

"BECAUSE YOU'RE A FOOL!" Lorraine called from somewhere in the house.

Kayle felt trapped. She heard everything, knew everything, even read into his thoughts. This was awful.

He wanted to die.

Erica had suddenly changed her mind about the rental after speaking to Kirsten. She called the real estate agent back and requested a furnished house this time. They found one, across town, on the other side of Monroe. At first she'd wanted to move her furniture. It was new. Suppose someone broke into her house before it was sold and either stole her belongings, or vandalized them?

Then she'd spoken to Kirsten—Shit!

Actually, the truth of the matter was she was in a hurry and had to take the risk of losing everything. She had no choice. There wasn't enough time to GET OUT fast and take her furniture. The water bed, for instance, had to be drained of two thousand gallons of water before it could be taken apart.

This had nothing to do with her conversation with Kirsten, when she'd been warned not to take the furniture, she told herself, nothing at all.

Besides, the real estate people said they'd watch her stuff. And hell, if someone liked her home the way it was, they just might buy the furnishings as well. With this in mind, she took what clothing she could and loaded her car with suitcases, the kids, the dog . . .

She wanted to get rid of him, take the son-of-a-bitch to the pound, but the kids were heartbroken by her suggestion. And too, Sam could control him. So, she took Blue Diabolus along.

The new place was smaller than she'd expected. There were only two bedrooms. But there was a studio couch in the living room. The boys were annoyed, figuring they'd wind up sleeping on it as they had before they'd bought the house on Longacre

Drive. Erica, however, volunteered to sleep on the couch. There were no men in her life at this point, so she didn't have to worry where she slept.

"Tie the dog in the yard," she told Sam. "Then you kids can help bring in the suitcases."

"Hey, Mom," Todd yelled, "this kitchen's a mess. It's dirty."

"All right. I'll clean it. Don't panic." She looked around and saw there was a lot of cleaning to be done. Well, she'd take it one step at a time. And, since everything was on one floor, she might even enjoy not climbing stairs for a change.

"Mom?" Didi asked, interrupting her thoughts.

But Erica wasn't angry. Didi was her big girl, no job was too tough for this kid to tackle. She'd been a tremendous help to Erica the whole time she'd been packing to move. "What, dear?" she asked and drew the child into her arms.

"What makes walls sweat? The walls in the bedroom are dripping with water."

Carol Anderson saw Erica leaving and wondered if she was going away for good. She felt awful; they were only just starting to become friends and now Carol was losing her. And probably losing Paul as well . . . She felt crushed.

"I'LL NEVER LEAVE YOU," Paul had said the last time they were together. And she'd believed him. She'd laid in his arms, her body pressed up against his, and believed him—

"I MEANT IT. EVERY WORD."

Carol spun around and saw Paul standing there, his black eyes bright and shiny with emotion. Carol was so happy to see him she never stopped to question how he'd gotten into the house, or, more importantly, how he'd been able to read into her thoughts. All she did know was that Paul was here!

"But Erica left . . ." she mumbled and felt silly. Erica had nothing to do with him, as he'd already ex-

plained so many times these past few weeks. Erica
was a blood relative, a distant cousin, who'd gracious-
ly allowed him to live there.

"ERICA WILL BE BACK. I'M JUST WATCHING
THE HOUSE IN HER ABSENCE." He smiled and
extended his arms. Carol rushed to him, wanting the
safety and comfort she found in his embrace.
"DON'T WORRY, LOVE. AS I'VE ALREADY SAID,
I'LL NEVER LEAVE YOU!"

Aaron Pace had agreed to be hospitalized this time,
mainly because of the therapy he needed. He was
about to be taught to function without two of his
fingers. Funny, he thought. This type of mutilation
had always twisted his guts into knots, and he was
barely able to accept it, even considering that he was
the victim this time.

One good thing came of it though: the coven
members from California had stopped following him.
Somehow they knew he'd lost those fingers, and hell,
if he'd known they only wanted a pound of his flesh
for appeasement, he would've given them the
Goddamn fingers long ago!

"Hello!" he barked into the phone when it rang.
Then he felt ashamed when he heard Erica on the
other end of the line. "I'm sorry, babe. Just an off day,
I guess." But then, all of his days were bound to be off
from now on, and he knew it.

"That's okay. I understand . . . After what you've
been through . . . Uh . . . I called to tell you I moved."

"Really!" It happened so suddenly he could hardly
believe he was hearing correctly.

"Yes. I have the house up for sale . . . I'm renting a
place across town. I called to give you my new
address."

"I can't write it down . . . My hand's bandaged."
They had to take the fingers of his right hand, the
bastards!

"Well . . . I'll give it to you when I come to visit . . .

We shouldn't really lose contact—"

"No, we shouldn't. Considering the kids . . ."

"How do you feel?"

How do you expect me to feel, he wanted to ask, but didn't. He'd bought the dog himself, and lost one finger. Then he'd gone into the den, after she'd begged him not to, and lost another. It really wasn't her fault. He started to answer and heard a clanging noise on the line. She was calling from a pay phone.

"Just a minute," she said, "I'm digging for change."

"Listen, babe. Don't bother. I'm kind of tired. Give me a call when your phone goes in . . . You are getting a phone?"

"Yes. And you're the first one I'll call. I promise."

After he hung up he realized there'd been something depressing in her voice. And hell, Erica should've sounded different. After all, she'd moved, left that awful house . . . the one with the den. She should've been alive with excitement. Unless . . . Maybe she was still in shock . . .

His fingers pained him real bad. He wanted a pain killer, but he hated the idea of taking drugs. That's what that coven in California thrived on: drugs. He rolled on his side and closed his eyes. He needed sleep. And yet, it happened again. Everytime he tried to sleep it was the same story: he was back in that den . . . Where the walls were covered with a mossy slime, and it was alive and breathing . . .

Creatures too awful to imagine, even in your wildest dreams, surrounded him. Some were carica-tures of humans, deformed humans, with body parts of animals: tails, fins, hooves . . . Some were hunch-backs with twisted faces and evil, slobbering lips . . . and huge, fucking teeth. Others were downright hideous . . . One in particular had only one eye: a large hairy mole covered the spot where the other one should've been . . .

And Aaron had foolishly taken them on, had foolishly invoked the Keys of the Calling—*their own code*—and had tried to use it against them. Still, he'd been doing fine, so long as he'd used Key Number Five. It was the Tenth that led to his downfall. That was the most dangerous of all, especially since he hadn't really known how to safeguard himself; how to insure his own immunity against repercussions from the demons.

Aaron was sure he remembered the way it should've been done when he faced them. He was sure he knew how to use the words. But obviously he'd been wrong and using the Tenth Key was all it took to—

Oh, Lord. As he'd been thinking, dwelling on that terrible experience in the den, it came back to him. He was able to see the truth this time! They didn't take his finger. Hell, no. He'd done it himself. *He* was the one who'd cut it off! Oh, man. He saw it now, *exactly the way it happened.* He'd been chanting and had gotten so drunk with glory and power that he'd imagined himself back in that awful church . . . Someone handed him a dagger . . . And he sliced his own finger off—right up to the second knuckle—then threw it to the crowd.

He buried his face in the folds of his pillow and cried. Those bastards had made him do the one thing he feared most, the one thing that repulsed him the most. They'd gotten inside of him, read his fears, and used them against him. And yet, it was his own fault! His own . . .

He never should've lied about having defeated Satan twice, as he had when he'd bragged to Erica. He never should've allowed his stupid conceit to dominate his senses and turn him into a phony macho man. He never should've gone into that den . . . "I know what I'm doing," he'd told Erica. Sure he did! In fact, he was positive at the time. Only, it took the loss of another finger to show him just how idiotic and insignificant he really was.

25

Kirsten Larsen hadn't wanted to play the tape, not really. But she was a woman first, ahead of everything else, and because of this, her feminine curiosity took over. She got the tape deck from the bedroom, but not without having to invoke her Christian chant to get rid of a few beasts in there, and settled herself at the dining room table.

She snapped in the cassette and felt she wasn't entirely alone. She had that stared at feeling, glanced up and saw the dead thing sitting opposite her, smiling, with what little was left of his face. "Well," she said and promised herself she'd remain calm, "I don't know how you got in this time—"

"DOORS DON'T STOP US!"

Oh yeah! She'd forgotten . . . "Anyway, since you intend to remain here for a long time to come, and you'll probably wind up hearing this tape . . . it's all right if you stay." She was losing it, she thought, inviting a beast to join her. But then, she was under the protection of the Lord. "It's okay," she repeated and heard the dullness of her own voice.

"THANKS."

The cassette was from Erica. She'd even gone to the trouble of inserting a small message, at the very beginning, explaining why she'd sent it to Kirsten.

And how she hadn't known about Aaron's ability to chant or his connection with an out of state church. Kirsten felt herself stiffen with cold, felt her body go rigid with shock and felt she must've been dead when Aaron spoke on the tape and said he was going into the den.

The den was the very core of the evil in that house! The worst place he could've gone.

She listened to him invoking the Keys of the Calling. Oh yes, she was more than a bit familiar with the Code of the Devil. Oh, Lord, but Aaron was a fool . . . He should've stopped with the Fifth. But he didn't. He went on, to a higher level, one reserved for High Priests of the Church of Satan. They had the protection of the master beast. None of his followers would ever think of turning on them.

And too, those High Priests weren't trying to use the words of the powers of darkness to stop Satan!

"THE MAN'S A FOOL."

"Yes. And he paid for it." She heard him screaming and stopped the tape. She didn't, couldn't, listen to the rest. "I have a phone call to make," she told the dead thing.

"YES, I KNOW."

But he made no move to leave, to give her back her privacy. Then again, why should he? They had a way of finding out things: they had control of Erica's phone in the old house, and probably in the new one as well. She picked up the receiver and called information for Erica's new number.

"IT'S A MISTAKE TO CALL HER. SHE'S NO LONGER RECEPTIVE."

Kirsten felt anger welling. "Will you let me do what I have to without sticking your nose in?"

He got up and left the room. And she thought about his statement. They were generally right. However, she had to find out for herself. She dialed the number and waited.

"Hello." It was Erica.

"Hi . . . This is Kirsten. Are you enjoying your new home?"

"What do you want, Kirsten? I'm kind of busy."

What happened, she wondered. Erica had been so friendly in the past. Unless . . . Maybe they got to her . . . "I received your tape—"

"So!"

"May I drop by so that we can discuss it?"

She heard heavy breathing, Erica didn't answer at first, then, "What you mean is, can you drop by so that you can hug me again. Isn't that the real reason—"

"What! What the hell are you talking about?" Kirsten couldn't handle this. If Erica was speaking on her own, she had to straighten her out. However, if Erica was one of *them* now, it didn't matter what Kirsten said.

"You put your arms around me, and you whispered in my ear."

"To comfort you." Kirsten felt sick.

"You're not married, are you?"

"What're you implying?" Kirsten was outraged by this time.

"Lesbian bitch! Coming over here and trying to fuck me—"

Kirsten slammed down the reciever before any more was said. The dead thing had been right.

"OF COURSE. WE ALWAYS ARE."

He was back, sitting opposite her again. Oh, Lord, this was awful. She'd gotten to Erica too late to do anything to stop it. Erica, for what she knew of her, was a sweet, outgoing, sensitive person. But that wasn't Erica on the phone. Oh, it was her voice and all, but her mind wasn't her own. Kirsten's efforts had been for nothing . . .

"IT'S TIME TO LEAVE."

"You're driving me out again?"

He nodded. "YES. YOUR MISSION IS OVER . . . AND YOU LOST!"

Kirsten was ready to give up her life's work, this time for good. She'd lost again, and as a result, her punishment was the same as before. She'd have to wander aimlessly again, searching for a place to hide. She could stay and fight them. But there were so many, and she was so tired. At least when she was on the road, she had some sort of peace of mind. Oh, they bothered her—they followed her everywhere, you couldn't outrun them—but not as much. However, she had the awful feeling that this time things would be different . . .

For the first time in her life, she was about to inherit a close companion, one that would stick to her like a second skin.

"YOU'RE RIGHT ABOUT THAT. I'LL NEVER LEAVE YOU. WE'LL ALWAYS BE TOGETHER."

Erica hung up the phone and turned to Paul. "Are you satisfied?" she wanted to know.

"YES. THANK YOU."

He got up and tried to put his arms around her, but Erica wasn't having any of this. Not after she'd heard Aaron's tape and discovered Paul was screwing Carol Anderson, her former next door neighbor, behind her back. "I have to come first! I have to be number one!" Hell, she could've stayed with Kayle and had the same thing happen. Right this moment she could be sitting here wondering who Kayle was sleeping with this week.

Her mind drifted back then, for no apparent reason, to last night, her first night in this house. She'd been able to put up with the sweating walls, and the dog. But somehow, she couldn't stand the feeling that she wasn't alone, even after the kids had gone to bed.

She remembered tossing and turning on the couch for what seemed like hours. Then she must've dozed off . . . But something, no, someone, woke her up. A hand. She felt a hand across her rump. It felt like Kayle's . . . Her back was turned, she couldn't see, but she just knew in her heart that it was Kayle. He'd come back to her, had discovered she'd moved, and had followed . . .

At first she tried playing hard to get, then found herself wondering if she wanted him to touch her at all. Hell, after Aaron and Paul, Kayle seemed more of a madman in her mind than he had before. He was brutal in bed, and had slapped her around as well. And yet, she needed someone. She was lonely, and Kayle was better than nothing . . .

"Kayle—" she said and turned . . . And screamed—

"DO YOU STILL REMEMBER WHAT HE LOOKED LIKE?" Paul asked, bringing her back to the present.

She covered her ears and tried not to listen to him. And yet, she had to, he had a way of getting into her thoughts. "Yes! I remember!" But she didn't want to, didn't want to go back and see that face—if you could call it a face—again. There was one eye, and a huge, hairy, mole where the other should've been.

"There's only one thing I don't understand. How you came to show up when you did?"

When Paul had appeared, the monster left.

"I TOLD YOU . . . THAT'S WHAT I'M HERE FOR . . . TO PROTECT YOU." He paused and smiled at her. "REMEMBER THE PROBLEMS YOU HAD IN THE OTHER HOUSE?" She nodded silently. "WELL, YOU CAN GO BACK THERE AND FEEL SAFE. NO ONE WILL EVER HARM YOU AS LONG AS I'M AROUND. AS A MATTER OF FACT, WE'LL BOTH BE IN CHARGE."

"And what about Kirsten? Can't she give me the same protection as you?" She felt bad about the ugly scene on the phone with Kirsten. But Paul had been looking at her with those eyes of his, and the words had come out of her mouth before she could stop them. *He* did it! So, she'd asked him if he was satisfied because that's what he obviously wanted. "Kirsten has powers—"

"NOT AGAINST ME. NOT NOW AT LEAST. IT'S TOO LATE, ERICA." Aaron's chanting had helped *them:* gave them strength and practically guaranteed their success. "THE DEMON YOU SAW LAST NIGHT WAS ONLY THE BEGINNING. MORE WILL COME. YOU DO NEED MY PROTECTION. CAN'T YOU ACCEPT THAT?"

She turned away. This was too much to face all at once. She needed time. She cringed when she felt Paul's hands touching her, then she started to melt when he kissed her neck where the dog had bitten her. However, one thing still bothered her. "What about Carol? I heard that tape. And I won't be second best." There had been other things said on the tape as well, things she should've remembered, but somehow couldn't. Damn! Why had she sent it to Kirsten. She could've listened to it again.

"IF YOU COME BACK, YOU'LL BE NUMBER ONE, ERICA. I'LL LOVE NO OTHER. AND I'LL HANDLE YOUR BODY WITH THE SAME LUSTY AFFECTION AS I DID BEFORE." He hoped she would believe him, because he'd lied. Carol and he were lovers now. Erica could be his lover, too. But he had no intentions of limiting his affections to one woman. The possessions had to be maintained, at any cost.

"I'LL TAKE CARE OF YOU IN OTHER WAYS ALSO. I'LL GIVE YOU MONEY TO LIVE ON, LOTS OF MONEY . . . PLEASE, ERICA. SAY YOU LOVE ME?"

She turned and said the words. Paul felt she was his—heart and soul. And yet, there was one more test, one more challenge. Aaron Pace was coming to see her. He wondered if she'd change her mind and decide she loved Aaron again.

Carol Anderson waited for what seemed like forever. The children were in school, her chores were finished, and the house was spotless—and now, Paul was coming over. Or was he? Paul was more than an hour late. Had he changed his mind about loving her? She hoped not.

"I'M HERE, DARLING, JUST AS I PROMISED I WOULD BE."

He'd been standing behind her. She turned and rushed into his arms, her passion about to explode. "I LOVE YOU, PAUL," she said and kissed him.

Sam sure did love that dog to pieces. It was the best dog a kid could have. Not wimpish, Blue didn't run and hide when people came past the house. And he didn't pee all over when he got caught doing something bad. Sam threw the ball and watched Blue dash after it. Then he felt that someone was watching him. He looked up and saw Katie standing in her bedroom window with Angelica at her side. They were both waving at him. He was happy about that: they were acting like friends now. And he was happy as well to be back in the old house again.

Jeez, Mommy sure did confusin' things at times. Like tellin' them they had to move, then moving them to a furnished house where they spent exactly one night, then coming back here. What the hell was she thinkin' of, he wondered? Draggin' them all over town.

His attention was called to the dog then. The dog was speakin' to him, only not in words he could actually hear. Rather the dog was somehow inside his head, tellin' him that Katie and Angelica were comin' down to play with them, and not to trust them two sneaky bitches. "I KNOW, BOY," he said. "THEY GOTTA BE WATCHED. BUT I'M NOT SCARED OF 'EM. PAUL'S ON MY SIDE. HE GAVE ME YOU TO TAKE CARE OF ME."

Oh, yeah. Paul was his friend all right. And Paul was a good person. And like Paul said, "I'LL NEVER LEAVE YOU, SAM." So, the boy was secure in the knowledge that he didn't have to worry ever again:

not about Katie, not about Angelica, not about anyone! No one would dare hurt him with Paul and Blue Diabolus around!

Aaron Pace didn't know what to expect. He'd gotten out of the hospital in two days—after promising to go back for his therapy—to find that Erica had returned to the house on Longacre Drive. Shit! Didn't that woman ever learn her lesson? Did someone have to get themselves killed before she GOT OUT and stayed out?

And hell, it wasn't only her life she was endangering by going back; she was endangering the kids as well. Aaron had a good mind to go over there and take them away from her. That would teach her a lesson. She just couldn't go around playing games with evil houses that had evil dens in them.

He parked the car in front of the house and sat and stared for a long time. His fingers throbbed something wicked; the two stumps that was. He considered leaving and coming back when he was rested, or when he had more courage, whatever. But he couldn't even force himself to leave, not so long as he knew that Erica and the kids were in there, in with that nest of murderous demons.

Erica had so many things going on inside of her head, she feared her brain would burst. Her life was a shambles, a mess; a hideously radical change had occured and it didn't even barely resemble the life she'd had only weeks before.

Kayle was married and out of her life! Aaron was too frightened of what was happening around her to ever come back and resume their friendship. Paul wasn't what he seemed to be: he was a liar and a fraud, but he lusted after her with an undying passion, And why, she wondered? Why did a man like Paul chase her when she'd continuously done nothing but reject him?

Was it because he knew he'd eventually win? Well,
so far he had. She needed help in the form of
protection from the demon beasts she now realized
were a part of her life, and always would be. When
she ran, they ran after her. Paul stopped them.

She also needed protection in case Kayle flipped out
again. Paul had stopped him in the past . . . And too,
she needed protection from that dog, because Blue
Diabolus was one of *them!* Sam had stopped the dog
from killing her a few days ago. But how much longer
could a five-year-old continue to control a killing
machine, a roaring, howling mass of murderous rage?
Paul would have to be there to stop the dog.

And too, Kayle had stopped giving her money.
Aaron had given her some. But now, after what
happened with his second finger, why should he
support her when he was afraid to live with her? Paul
promised her money . . . Lots of it . . ."

Paul, that lying, fraudulent bastard was to be her
savior in white: her knight in shining armor. She had
to laugh at that, but it was a strain—

"DARLING, AARON IS HERE TO SEE YOU."

She couldn't, she just couldn't face Aaron now. She
was too upset over having no choice but to come back
here, back to this house and surrender her soul to
Paul.

"LOOK AT ME DEAREST. I'LL TELL YOU WHAT
TO SAY."

"Oh, Sure. Just like you did with Kirsten—"

"WHAT'S THE ALTERNATIVE? DO YOU HAVE
ONE?"

No. She didn't. That much was true.

"LOOK AT ME, ERICA. ONE MORE TEST,
THAT'S ALL. IF YOU PASS, THEN IT'S OVER.
YOU'LL BE HAPPY. AND YOU'LL LIVE WITH ME
FOR ALL TIME TO COME."

Aaron rang the bell and wanted to run. He knew
they were waiting for him; possibly waiting for

another finger. After all, Erica had said it best. "Everything bad comes in threes, Aaron." She said it every chance she got. Had been saying it for years now—

"Hello, Aaron."

He couldn't believe his eyes when she opened the door. She was more beautiful, more voluptuous than he'd ever remembered seeing her before. But, was it a trick? Were those bastards playing games with his eyes? Well, he'd wait and see! "Hi, babe. How's everything?"

"Come in and I'll tell you."

There was something funny about the way she'd spoken. Somehow the old . . . what . . . gaiety was gone? She was smiling, but he had the feeling that it was forced. "Where's the kids," he wanted to know once he'd gotten inside. He really wanted to inquire about Paul, but lacked the nerve. Then he had to look at his fingers again. It was the damndest thing . . .

"The kids are outside playing with Blue. Do you want a beer?" She sat down and studied him.

The dog was still there, he wanted to run again. "Uh . . . No thanks. I'm off beer for a while." There was silence between them while she continued to study him and he squirmed under her gaze.

Jesus, she looked beautiful, and it didn't seem to be a trick: he was really seeeing her as she was. And he tried to ignore her, to ignore her beauty. And he tried to tell himself that it was over between them so long as she lived in this house. But he felt desire building. Then he noticed a bandage on her neck. "What happened to you?" he asked and fingered his own neck in the same area.

"The dog scratched me . . . by accident."

There was more silence between them. Aaron couldn't stand the tension. It was driving him crazy. He wanted her so badly, enough to refuse to give her up without a fight. "Erica . . . I still love you." He paused and waited, but she said nothing. Then he

tried again. "I can't stay here. I'm afraid of this
house." There, he thought. He'd said it; he'd dropped
his macho routine and admitted the truth. Again she
made no comment. "Will you come away with me.
We could take the kids and get out of town. Go somewhere nice—"

"I like it here just fine."

This was bullshit. She was out of her mind, had to
be. Anyone with any sense at all knew this house was
just too dangerous to live in. Well, she could stay, but
not his kids., He started to ask her to call them: he'd
take them and GET OUT. However, the kids were
already there, lined up before him. And hell, he
hadn't even heard them come in.

Two of them were already lost to him; the two
youngest ones, he could see it in their eyes, the way
they were smiling and watching him, like they
wanted him dead. Todd and Didi weren't far behind.
But there was still hope and so long as he had hope,
those two were leaving with him.

"You kids go outside and play. I want to speak to
Aaron alone."

There was something about her voice then, something that reminded him of the old Erica. She turned
and looked at him, and parted her lips in a sexy way.
She wanted him, everything about her said she was
ready. He felt aroused and forgot about the kids
momentarily. "Come here," he said and watched her
come. The sway of her hips almost drove him insane.

She took his hand, his right one and kissed the
surviving fingers, sticking each one between her lips
until he could feel an erection starting. This was so
unlike her, he thought. She'd never acted so sexy
before. And whatever had caused it, Aaron didn't
mind a bit. "Oh, Baby," he said and started to wrap
his arms around her—

She had bitten down on a finger—hard! Jesus, that
hurt! "Enough, Erica. I get the point." But she
wouldn't let go . . . She was biting harder now,

twisting with her teeth. Oh, Christ! He never knew she had such strong teeth. "Erica! Stop it! What're you, nuts?" He didn't want to hit her, but she gave him no choice. It was either that or lose another finger. He balled up his fist, but couldn't raise it beyond his hips. Something was holding it down, pining it to his sides—

Aaron didn't remember too much after that, except for the normal scene these past few days: a bleeding stump, another finger missing, up to the second knuckle. "Everything comes in threes," she'd said, "Everything bad." So now, to prove it, she took his fucking finger! "Erica! Why!" he screamed, when he could talk, when the usual lump of shock left his throat.

"YOU THINK I'M STUPID. YOU CAME HERE TO TAKE MY CHILDREN. NOBODY TAKES MY CHILDREN. ESPECIALLY NOT YOU!"

Aaron wanted to die. He heard her voice, looked at her face, the blood on her chin—his blood—and knew she was one of *them*. And he didn't even have to ask how she'd read into his thoughts concerning the children. Mind-reading was a big part of their talent. "Don't bother to call an ambulance," he mumbled. "I'll drive myself. I know the way."

Paul saw him leave and rushed to her. Erica had passed the last test—she was his now. "DARLING, YOU'VE MORE THAN PROVEN YOURSELF . . . AND TO THINK I WAS RIGHT ALL ALONG. I KNEW THAT ONCE YOU WERE A PART OF THE GROUP, YOU'D TURN OUT TO BE ONE BITCH!"

"ERICA, WE SALUTE YOU." She stood next to Paul and watched the old ones gather around. Funny, she could see them now where she never could before.

"WE LOVE YOU, ERICA. WE'LL NEVER LEAVE YOU. NEVER!"

Make the Most of Your Leisure Time
with
LEISURE BOOKS

Please send me the following titles:

Quantity	Book Number	Price
————	————————	————
————	————————	————
————	————————	————
————	————————	————

If out of stock on any of the above titles, please send me the alternate title(s) listed below:

———	————————	————
———	————————	————
———	————————	————

Postage & Handling ————

Total Enclosed $ ————

☐ Please send me a free catalog.

NAME ————————————————————
(please print)

ADDRESS ————————————————————

CITY ———————— STATE ———— ZIP ————

Please include $1.00 shipping and handling for the first book ordered and 25¢ for each book thereafter in the same order. All orders are shipped within approximately 4 weeks via postal service book rate. PAYMENT MUST ACCOMPANY ALL ORDERS.*

*Canadian orders must be paid in US dollars payable through a New York banking facility.

Mail coupon to: **Dorchester Publishing Co., Inc.**
6 East 39 Street, Suite 900
New York, NY 10016
Att: ORDER DEPT.